Ghostwright

Ghostwright

Michael Cadnum

Carroll & Graf Publishers, Inc.
New York

For Sherina,
with special thanks to my parents,
Naomi and Robert Cadnum

This is the successor of the invisible . . .

—Wallace Stevens,
"Credences of Summer"

A figure so distant I see him only
when I look away.

—Hamilton Speke,
preface to *Buried Sun*

BEFORE

· 1 ·

There was dark, and there was light, and the light was losing. Shadows expanded, filling the space between
branches. The air was cold enough to hurt, and the remaining snow glowed blue in the twilight.

She would be home soon.

He took in a long, slow breath and held it. Moments like this
were life. Everything else, every other experience, was sleep.

Sometimes people cured by surgery of an arterial block wake in
old age to their still-human lives. These people grieve, stripped of
ignorance, realizing the years they will never see. And sometimes
it gives them such a shock they develop yet another form of de-
mentia, a madness caused by knowing that they have wasted their
lives.

As long as he could do this, sweeping in secret across the twilight, he was still alive.

His feet chose the places where the snow had melted, pressing
into the black earth so evenly and lightly each step left no print at
all. He was just outside the house now, his ear against the chimney
as he paused. The bricks were warm.

As warm as she would be when he touched her.

He stiffened. He crouched, panting so hard it hurt. A car
passed on the highway, the winter tires rumbling and hissing
through the wet. He did not breathe, and it was like playing dead
Caesar. Here I am, ladies and gentlemen: nothing at all. I am
gone, here and, at the same time, nowhere.

The car slowed, a vessel of light, pushing the darkness ahead of
it. It wasn't possible, was it, that I am out of practice? Surely they
see me.

The car on the road wasn't moving. It was stuck, frozen, locked
into a pot hole. Or worse: they were watching.

The magic is gone, he told himself. You can't play this part as
well as you used to. You've lost your touch.

Doubt: an actor's enemy. He knew his mind was not his friend.
Don't think, he commanded himself. Be empty. Even *Hamlet* is

mostly space, blank white around the wedding bed and the chalice of poison. Be blank, he commanded his soul. Dive deep into the earth.

The car still did not move, a square vehicle, a Jeep, he realized, stopped on the crown of the road.

They see me, he breathed.

The engine was grinding. The distant Jeep made the sort of growl that sounded both painful and crocodilian, and yet it went nowhere.

Go, he breathed. Leave me here alone to do what I have come to do.

Brake lights surged, faded, surged again. The rattle of the engine began to recede. The mutter of the Jeep faded, and there was only the hush of the countryside, the sound of skeleton trees taking their long, deep breaths.

He smiled to himself, his teeth cold for an instant. He was trembling, as in those dreams in which he could not remember his lines and the audience stared, lips parting to jeer. His breath was uneven, and he was amused at himself. You should do this more often, he mocked himself, and then you would not find it so novel.

He had promised his sister—never again.

But don't I have the right to love? Everyone else does, loving in their puny, limited ways.

The woman who lived here was, he surmised, recently divorced. Or perhaps she was a woman who had decided never to marry. He knew the pattern: boyfriends, but no one steady. She was an isolated, confused creature. But she did not admit this to herself. She thought of herself as independent, a woman with a career.

It was time.

For weeks he had walked miles across the hills to watch her from the bare trees, to listen at her window to the murmur of her phone calls, the blather of her television, the hush of her solitude. He had watched her with men friends over the weeks, walking arm in arm to the Porsche or the Alfa Romeo parked in the driveway. He had watched her standing with her arms folded, surveying what would be, in its season, a garden.

He knew the extra burden a beautiful woman carries is cruel, wearisome to the soul. And sex—what was it so often but a bartering, pleasing men so the men might feel some power, for even a few spasms of pleasure? Men wanted to possess. But he knew better.

He knew the best act of love, the perfect act that gave what people wanted most without ever fully realizing it.

Almost home, the voice whispered. She is almost home. He left the house, picking his way through the decaying snow. He found a hiding place that fit his body exactly.

The evergreens clawed at his clothing, and then the boughs were still. The snow was rotten, holes eaten through the glaze where water had sweated from the branches. It was not so cold after all, and he let himself grow still.

He knew how to be invisible. He waited in the evergreens, the black spruce beside the driveway, drawn within himself, standing upright like one of the trees. He loved trees, and felt a deep trust among the greatest of their kinds, the masters of sunlight and air, these deep-rooted sentinels which saw nothing, heard nothing, and yet knew how to heal, sap and bark, and give future to their kind.

Carefully, so slowly that it made no sound at all, only the faintest pulse in the air, he eased down the zipper of his pants. He loosened his belt one notch. Something steel in him shivered. He was a master at this artful waiting. He needed no yoga to guide him into the melting point between appetite and the cold air.

Headlights flared up the long driveway. The slush burned white for an instant. The automatic garage door shrugged upward with a sound like a gasp, one corner of the door, as always, heaving skyward first.

He slipped inside, and sank behind a plastic bag of humus.

The fat plastic hummock gave off heat. The sound of the car was loud, shaking the air. And then the engine fell silent. The garage door sank, hesitated, thumped shut with the softest of shudders. The car door opened, and the air was rich with the stink of auto exhaust, the stale air from the interior of the car— and her. The ersatz floral breath of cosmetics caught him, and the under-scents, too, the real smells, the presence of her body just steps away from where he waited.

She carried a package, and she left the kitchen door open so she could return to the car, the car door open, too, so the temporary, unbuttoned feel of things was what encouraged him to stand and drift like a span of smoke, a creature made of all-but-nothing, off to one side, avoiding the light like a man standing clear of an abyss.

From inside, in the kitchen, came the weighty clink of bottles. He had seen the empties in the recycling she had dragged out once a week to the edge of the road—imported vodkas and no mixers. He felt a glow of compassion, such sudden sympathy that it was physical pain in his bones. She was suffering.

He knew what her life was like. It was a routine, a day after day of hope, a reel of postage stamps, each one the picture of a future —a home, a pathway, an illusion. He knew: mortal pleasure passed. It kindled a moment, an hour, but then the soul lived on faith that joy would come again.

The refrigerator shut, a soft sound, like something taking place far away. Her step squeaked on the waxed floor, and a cupboard door shut, a sharp wooden *tock*. She nearly returned to the garage, but he could sense her indecision, that familiar near-pain of the bladder that caused her to hurry off through the house, her steps receding into silence.

One touch, and she would have no more disillusion, no more attempts to recover what was already lost, the simple faith of childhood.

His hand searched, lightly discovering and dismissing one object after another. He always used what happened to be there, the adept at work, the actor ad libbing lines more telling than the script.

His hand declined the gardening shears, the rusty scissors, the pruning shears, the Phillips screwdriver and the adjustable wrench in its wraparound tool bag. He had been right, it seemed, about the divorce. This was a man's half-ordered clutter, and the workbench was dusted over with the grit that accumulates in a garage over a span of many months.

His hand closed over a handle. He felt his face fold into a smile. Yes, this was something he could use.

It was not perfect, and would require a certain artfulness. He liked that: a challenge. There was the distant *chunk* of a toilet's flush, and her step was through the house again, a quick stride across the kitchen.

She was in the garage, stopping, tugging a package across the seat of the car. Tin cans clacked together. Paper rustled, plastic crackled and then she was turning, ascending toward the light of the house, remembering only at the last moment to return briefly to kick the car door shut.

He fell upon her silently, as from a great height, a man who was not there, a shadow, something flung carelessly across the half-dark.

She screamed, but his fist was in her mouth, her tongue a squirming thing. He embraced her, a lover come to ease her load, feeling for a heartbeat.

No, he breathed into her, it's all right. I have come for you.

The screwdriver buried into her skull, right where so long ago in infancy the fontanelle had knitted, there at the intersection of the parietal bones. There was an instant when the bone fought the core of steel. His fist lifted into the half-light, and slammed down onto the pommel of the tool.

Three times his fist hammered the screwdriver. Blonde hair went dark, glistening. One leg thrust out and up, into the door jamb so hard wood splintered. One arm spun, wheeling, and the other went so rigid it was stone and seemed to drag the shoulders, pulling the entire body downward.

He held her, soothing her, stroking her, easing her passage to the floor.

"It's all over," he breathed into her ears, because he knew she could still hear, that the dying lingered for minutes as their bodies became that other place, the world they had abandoned.

He knew the pleasure she was experiencing, her life sucked through the aperture in her skull upward into the eternal and more perfect void as he, with the tenderness to make her moment perfect, undressed her, whispering to her how beautiful she was in her finest moment, how beloved she was.

And even then there was no haste. This was not the compassionless lust of the man who wished to master the beautiful, seduce it, and employ it to his ends. The love he made was perfect, willing himself to follow her, his knees oblivious to the cold concrete until he ebbed into her entirely, as far as he could go into the passage beyond which he could only call to her, wishing her the good voyage.

He set fire to the rubber gloves and the prophylactic that, wet with seed, did not burn at all but only writhed, curling, wasting away.

It was a long but lovely walk home, under a sky that was

charred with cloud. His feet selected stones on which to step, picking through the decaying snow, leaving no trace.

The apartment, when he reached it, was too warm. The rooms
were too small. She glanced at him, and then stood unmoving.
"What," she whispered, "have you done?"

His sister could tell. It took her only a moment. She knew: he
had done it yet again. She put her hand to her throat, her lips
parted, and he wanted to say: don't worry.

He had lived his life, it seemed, in apartments like these, this
upstate New York cage just like the cages in a dozen other small
cities. He stroked her hair, kissed her cheeks, her tears. His sister
wept, and he sat beside her as she cried even into her sleep, into
her dreams, shrinking away from him, knowing what he'd done
and yet trying to lie to herself.

At last she was asleep.

He stepped into the living room, and snapped on the television.
He sank into the sofa, a man subsiding into ordinary existence
once again. The images shifted over him, the alternating print of
the images falling over him as he gazed without really seeing.

He sat for a long time, well into the night. He had used to
imagine that one day his own image would grace the television
screen, his own body-miked voice resounding, his life made multi-
ple, his mortal existence transformed into a Life. He knew how to
move so the mike didn't pick up anything but the sound of his
voice. He could act. But that was all long ago. It is I, he thought,
the Artist, springing up out of the dark to sit down and watch—
what? What am I looking at?

What am I looking at, sitting here enjoying the remnants of
pleasure? He stirred himself. My friend, he thought. It's my
friend speaking without making a sound.

The Artist found the remote. He turned up the volume, and the
famous voice made the lamp beside him tremble metallically, a
tiny, locustlike rattle. It's Hamilton Speke, he thought, plying yet
another talk show.

Speke was always showing up on television, accompanying hosts
grateful to give their ratings a healthy pulse. Speke's face was
always beaming from a magazine beside the candy at the checkout
counter. The Artist had always seethed, resenting his old friend's
championship role as healthy, successful figure full of life. But the
Artist had made no move to escape from the darkness where he

belonged and meet his friend again. Some creatures belonged under the rotting log, fat with the joy to be found under the stone slab. The Artist knew himself to be such a creature, and so the moving lips of the image of Hamilton Speke did not stir him to any more than the slightest dash of envy, a touch of salsa to the afterglow that still calmed him.

But then the Artist caught his breath.

He leaned forward.

He stood, rigid, unable to make another move, frozen with disbelief.

No—Speke couldn't do that.

Speke was talking about a play in progress, a play nearly finished, a play that was, the smooth-voiced host said, going to be the "long awaited masterpiece." Speke was agreeing, making that famous modest shrug and nod: "It's still a long way from being finished. Maybe a year or two away. But when I'm done, I think it'll be my most important play. At least, I hope so." Said with that easy confidence, that unassuming air that was both modest and untouched by doubt.

Speke began describing the play, and the Artist felt himself turning, cell by cell, to a thing of stone.

He can't do that, thought-screamed the Artist, the soundless howl deafening him to every word Speke uttered. Speke can't use that story. That story belongs to me. That's mine—the most important days of my life. Those were the days that began to change me from an ordinary man into the creature I am now.

Mine. My life.

He hurled himself out into the cold.

At last he was able to breathe. Buildings so often seemed like a trap to him. His shadow flowed ahead of him on the streetlight-glazed asphalt.

Of course he can use that story. He can do anything. He's Hamilton Speke, admired and even loved. And deserving the love of strangers, a man of color and heat.

The Artist felt himself laugh. Of course I can't write the play myself. No, it's not that. I tried, and the pages were always blank. That's my kind of perfection, the empty kind. To write the play I would have to be like Speke, sure of myself, comfortable under the lead blanket of the television lights.

The Artist let himself fall to the frozen muck. The tree above him made a breathy whisper, stirring like a rooted thing struggling to leap upward. Oh what a nimble self-deceiver I have been, thought the Artist.

Speke is taking what is mine. And I know how to stop him.

The Artist had lived like a man in a coma, a twilight human. Like a man who was so much air, a puff of exhaust—nothing. Hearing Speke, and seeing his beaming face, the sort of countenance people admired and trusted, handsome, bright with health, had changed everything. This was the anger that riffled the surface of seas, and heaved mountains toward the stars. The Artist's anger was like gravity, like the sun and moon.

You can't do this, Hamilton.

I know exactly how to take my old friend apart, piece by piece. I know the kind of women he craves, I know the kind of solace he needs, and I know the things that wake him at night.

I won't let you.

It will take months, but I have waited so long a little more time doesn't bother me at all. He smiled, looking upward into the now starless night. I'm on my way back, he promised the sky.

The darkness was coming. This time it would take what it owned.

And leave nothing.

I

KINGDOM OF DAYLIGHT

· 2 ·

There was a fire.

He couldn't see it, standing in the full, almost blinding light of summer, but he could smell it.

Hamilton Speke stood still, blinking in the bright sun, thinking *no*.

No, anything but a fire.

The land around him was carved out of sunlight—golden outcroppings, oat weeds upright and glittering in the heat. The heat was dry, each breath the taking in of curing radiance, the arid triumph of the California summer that Speke had always treasured.

The scent of smoke endured, but he tried to deny it to himself. Surely not, he breathed. There had not been a fire on this side of the lake for several years. There had been a fire here once—a bad fire. But surely luck would hold.

He was hiking a deer path at the edge of the estate, as he did nearly daily to get away from the telephone and the fax machine and the burgeoning business of being a man with a big name. He loved it here among the hills. He had bought Live Oak several years ago because he had never felt so at home anywhere, and because he loved the land and its animals the way he loved his own life.

And now there was the pepper of smoke in the heat. It could not be mistaken. It was the scent of trouble, a wavering, unsure poison in the slack wind. It stopped him, just as the sound of a voice would have stopped him, a voice from the sky calling his name.

Then the smell was gone. He did not move. A faraway quail sang, a lilting laugh, and hawks or, more likely, vultures circled the golden hills of the horizon. The hills appeared bruised, on the seaward slopes and the declevities of canyons, by the live oaks and the madrone. He breathed deep, and held the air in his lungs, searching the sky.

There, he told himself, you see. He struggled to convince himself. Everything's fine. There isn't a fire after all.

He broke into a sweat. There could be no mistake. There was smoke, invisible but real. The wind huffed, died, and rose again.

Can't be, he said as he began to run in the direction of the scent, his hands balled into fists.

The blaze spilled upward along the bank, and the smoke obscured whatever happened behind it, the figures of men vanishing, dissolving, and reappearing as the flames flagged and recovered.

The green county truck was angled up the slope, and behind the smoke figures strode, white wedges of dust flung into the smoke from behind the wrinkling mirage. In this drought, the rye weeds and the thistle all so much kindling, such a fire was death.

He tried to reassure himself. He was thankful—the presence of the county firefighters meant that everything was under control. Speke knew that every crisis could be met and won, and he hurried forward to help, glad to be there, eager to join the fight.

And then he fully understood what was happening.

He had to move quickly.

A black map of instant char spread beneath the truck, and a tire burst, a low bang and the long hiss of air. The flames had the truck, fire danced within the cab, the underhood streaming white and then, just as quickly, foul black.

Speke leaped into the bed of the truck and found a spade. He sprang from the truck, and plunged into the flames. He had always been quick to anger. He slashed at the fire as he strode through it, killing it, and he had the strangest feeling of battle joy, of challenge met.

And fear at the same time, searing fear. The soles of his feet felt hot as he stomped flames. He called to the men, their figures obscured by smoke that was everywhere, scalding each breath. Then the smoke was gone, lifted clean, the sunlight bright, blown clear by a sudden wind.

He turned back when a new hot breath ruffled the clothing around his body. The explosion blossomed downward, the truck lifted sideways by the blast, and then the fireball broke, a wriggling pond of gasoline spreading, carrying the flames.

Speke had broken a path through the ring of fire, but no one moved to escape. He called to them, but the fire was too loud. The firefighters were dazed, tight-jawed but still fighting. They were surrounded by flames, shoveling without panic but sweating heavily beneath their yellow hardhats. The fire was closing in.

Sparks had drifted behind the fighters, and the strengthening breeze had folded the flames back. The men were trapped in an oblong that tightened, men backing into each other. He called to them again. There were only four men, and they were young, their shocked eyes finding him.

They looked to him, without thinking, for leadership. He lifted his spade. "Come on," he cried.

He waved them to the smoldering break he had beaten in the flames. Smoke-tears wet his cheeks, and he could not draw a breath. The heat was so great he felt lifted into the air by the thermal, bouyant and sky-bound.

It was like running in a dream—a bad dream, when the psyche remembers what it is like to be powerless. Speke and the men around him could make no progress through the heat. Feet churned dust and ash, and seemed to go nowhere. The men ran, and time was meaningless, their bodies powerless.

And then they were free, the truck a box of golden heat, the doors flung open, the green paint peeling, replaced by iridescent blue steel.

They were outside the noose of fire. The men did what they were trained to do, cutting an even wider circle around it, working hard, but loose-limbed, now, the tightness gone, the battle only work, now, and not a fight for life.

One of the firefighters leaned against a tree, pant leg peeled back. His calf was blistered, and he grimaced as disinfectant was sprayed on the burn. Another firefighter was on the ground, eyes blinking as he inhaled oxygen through a mask.

A truck rocked up the fire road, its orange emergency light spinning. A yellow hose was unspooled, and water tore at the dry ground, battering the fire.

"Mr. Speke saved our lives," said one of the young firefighters, tossing it out to his companions lightly, as something delightful and even funny. It was uttered as a kind of joke because it was true. They passed around an aluminum canteen of Gatorade, and shook his hand, one by one.

Fire had killed before, on this land, not ten years ago, before

Speke had purchased Live Oak. A rancher had vanished, driving up to a ridge to overlook the smoke beyond, and when they found him days later he was a "charred grinning puppet." This was the description of Mr. Brothers', Speke's gardener, and a man not given to exaggeration.

"You got to sign my hardhat, Mr. Speke," said one, and Speke was handed a black marker and a helmet, and for a moment nearly signed the dirty white plastic strap or the underside of the bill before the encouraging voice said, "Sign it on top. Sign it all over."

He signed, his name deformed by the ridges radiating from the peak of the plastic helmet, his name awkward and bold, the handwriting, a graphologist had told him, after he had signed a cocktail napkin once years ago, of a man both optimistic and happy, a man who believed in life and was never afraid.

And Speke had laughed, flattered and at the same time amused. Because while he was optimistic, and while he believed in life, he was also very much afraid of certain things.

Perhaps it didn't show up in his scrawl, especially as it made its way across one after another of the plastic helmets, the big black name like the name of a saint, the name that would defend the wearer against any blow, no matter how savage it might be.

He was gratified at their insistence, and touched, but he did not find their request ridiculous. He knew the power of a name. "Sign my lunch bag, Mr. Speke," said one, and then the man added, in a way that touched him, "Sign it 'To Ellen.' "

Speke wrote the words, standing on the charred, brittle grass which still fumed, white feathers of smoke drifting upward in the heat. He was used to the deferential smiles of strangers. He was a big man, and had, he knew, the looks and carriage of someone who was uncommon. And with his smile on the cover of magazines nearly every month he knew that he looked like life itself to these men—these brave men.

Waking that night he found Maria beside him, and let his hand lie upon her hip. She stirred, slightly, easing back into him, halfwaking, inquiring after lovemaking or simply reassuring him, knowing that he had nightmares. She knew him well, he felt, and yet to him she remained part stranger, a woman he loved without yet knowing her past, even after months of marriage. This was good in a way, though. There was that promise of further discovery. He would travel gradually into her life, a man learning a new dialect.

But the memory of the fire kept him awake. He had wanted a perfect world, a world he could protect against the erosion of civilization. Perhaps, he chided himself, he had wanted to build a world that could not die.

"Celebrity playwright Hamilton Speke single-handedly saved the lives of a fire crew today in what proved to be—" He had heard that much on the evening news before he could snap off the television.

And now the heroic Speke was lying awake, amused at his own anxiety. Some hero he was, he thought, lying here thinking: how awful it would be if I lost all this.

If I lost this place, if I lost Maria—I don't think I could bear it.

But it's all right, he reminded himself. The fire is out.

Isn't it?

· 3 ·

I t was the morning after the fire.

He left Maria in bed. He kissed the faintest down on the lobe of her ear. She stirred, and smiled without waking. She liked to sleep more than anyone he had ever known. He had thought that sleeping too much was a sign of depression, classic melancholy. But Maria did not seem depressed as much as withdrawn from the dailiness around her. He found her all the more alluring because of this delicious mystery, this feline capacity for slumber.

He knew that she had nightmares, just as he did, although he did not know their nature. Sometimes he soothed her in the early hours, telling her that everything was fine. She struggled in her sleep, running as people do in their dreams, in quick starts. She spoke in her sleep, as well, warnings, anxious questions, from the tone. He could never quite make out what she was saying, and he felt guilty for trying to piece together the terrors and philippics of her dream life.

Sarah stood in the doorway of her cottage, drying her hair with a white towel. He waved to her, and she returned his greeting, the sunlight bright in her smile.

The early air was still brisk, and the morning overcast was just beginning to thin. He walked the deer path until he reached the acrid, burned-toast tang in the air, the scent of fresh burn gone dead.

There were the tracks of the county trucks, and the footsteps of the firefighters. And here, where the charred grass was matted silver, was the place where he had stood, autographing the helmets.

There, he told himself—the fire is out. What had made him uneasy, tossing on his clothes in such haste? True, sometimes a brushfire came to life again after a few hours. But this was so much perfect carbon, black skeletons which had been milkweed and thistle, madrone and chinquapin.

On the way back he paused at the mouse hole, slipped a saltine from his shirt pocket and knelt, breaking the cracker in his fist. Tomorrow, he knew, the cracker would be gone, and while Brothers, the gardener, would have laughed at him, he walked way from the mouse refuge feeling that he had done something infinitesimally minor and at the same time good, even necessary.

He felt serene sitting at his desk. He stared at the blank screen of his computer, and the serenity began to crumble.

How long would he continue to be unable to write this play? It had been eight months or more since he had sat under the hot television lights, gazing out at the cavernous television studio, mouthing the good news about his work-in-progress. "It's about Mexico, and the jungle, and discovering something no one is supposed to know about. It's about discovering a secret." He had gathered optimism about him, and continued, ignoring the hard red light on the camera, "and it's about two young men who fight over what to do with their discovery."

"What's the name of this play?" said the host, his smile a Chiclet-gleam, the very lips that had used the word "masterpiece."

"The Black Cat of La Guadaña." Speke had grinned back, not mentioning the truth: that the play stood exactly where it was now —nowhere.

He had even furthered the lie, the perfume of his own deodorant rising about him. "Maybe a year or two away," he had heard himself say, with the happy, bright tone of a schoolchild.

A year or two, he now groaned silently to himself. He had not written even a single stage direction. To be fair to himself, yesterday he had written the same line over and over again, erasing it each time. This was a typical day's work on this play.

There was a letter from a producer at his elbow, butter yellow rag paper and elegant letterhead made all the more potent by the cab driver prose of the executive. "Send us something. An act or two. Anything. Foreplay can't go on for years. We can start casting yesterday." Here was another letter, from his L.A. agent, paper so exquisite it didn't even crackle: they were already rejecting offers by actors to dub the Japanese version.

There was a story in him, and it was a story he couldn't begin to tell. The dialogue was dead in him, the characters gone but ever present. He ran his hands through his hair. He closed his eyes and would have prayed if that power, too, had not long ago evaporated.

He turned gladly at Sarah's step and was delighted at the armload she carried, the CD reissue of *Stripsearch,* the play cut down in length and in the cutting improved, he had to admit, although the cast could not be improved. The best male voice, the one with all the most energetic counterarguments, had died just weeks before of what the family would not admit was AIDS. The other voices, too, had gone on to other triumphs, other losses. Speke had agreed to sign dozens of these for an auction to benefit a local hospice.

There was a postage stamp size picture of himself beside the sizzling red gorilla type of his name—or at least it seemed so big, this grand shout of HAMILTON SPEKE beside a tiny, more youthful likeness of his face. A good picture, though, he said nearly aloud, and he looked up to see if Sarah knew what he was thinking.

She was the best personal manager in the business, a woman born to command battalions or run an industry. Steady Sarah. Ever calm. He could not manage a single day without her. And this morning she was, as always, professional to the point of anticipating what he needed, handing him the black indelible marker, cap off, the ink spilling a strange grim odor into the air.

"You look the same," she said. She had a remarkable voice, low and calming, and yet it was also the voice of command.

"How can you tell, looking at a teeny microchip-size picture like this?"

"I know the face," she said.

"Do you think I should put a message on it when I sign? Some sort of greeting?"

"You always say you like the plays to do the talking."

He caught himself nearly confessing, telling her abruptly "I can't do it."

I can't even think of what to write above my signature. I've signed thousands of autographs, in restaurants, airports, on the Appian Way and at the top of the Eiffel Tower, cramped, freezing and nearly suffocating against a rail. I have never hesitated for an instant, but now every word is an embarrassment.

"I can't possibly greet people I'll never know," he heard himself say, hoping she would agree.

But Sarah was happy to disagree, when he was wrong. "You're

good at that. You do it all the time. I couldn't begin to do it, but then, I couldn't write a play, either."

"Are you sure ink like this will write on this plastic?"

"It's the kind we always use."

"Once or twice it hasn't worked, and the ink just sort of beads. It looks like you tried to write in squid ink."

"It'll work." She turned back at the door. "Try it."

He began to write, and found himself printing, surprisingly neatly, the phrase of one of the characters in the play, the one who threw the bottle. It was a phrase he had picked up from a biography of Hemingway, something the boy Papa had said to impress his elders or himself. "Afraid of nothing."

That looked good, he thought. The printing was strangely like his father's draftsmanlike hand. He had considered this before— as I grow older I will become more and more like him. He glanced up at Sarah, but she couldn't possibly tell what he had written, not from the door.

"The Hemingway line?" she asked.

He smiled.

He signed his name.

He was just finishing the last of his signatures when Sarah's voice spoke from the intercom. "I've got the strangest phone call," she said.

He started to say, offhandedly, his usual, "Take a message."

But Sarah would never mention a "strange" phone call. He found himself gazing into the tiny intercom speaker, caught by something in her tone. "Who is it?"

She seemed to have anticipated his hesitation and said, her voice ascending in the tone of a question, "He says he's an old friend."

When she said his name he fell back, unable to make a sound. It couldn't be true. It was impossible. He thought: surely I misunderstood her. Surely she got the name wrong.

His hand crept to the telephone and stayed there. He could not command it to lift the receiver. He could only stare at it, his own hand, the intercom speaker, and the letters on the desk, as though he could not remember where he was.

Sarah was asking him what to do, and he could not move his tongue to respond.

Surely not.

He gazed at his hand like a man waking and unable to piece together what he saw. What he felt was beyond any emotion, but if there was any feeling at all through the shock and doubt it was joy.

But at once his disbelief took over. It's a hoax, he thought—it's a bitter joke.

Someone can't come back from the dead.

· 4 ·

Even when he heard the familiar voice on the phone, sound-ing exactly right, precisely the way Asquith *would* sound, Speke thought: it can't be him.

He felt that tug of disbelief he felt so often when someone showed him a photograph of a UFO, or Bigfoot, or the Loch Ness monster. He felt convinced, and yet he felt that there was some-thing wrong, something he could not name.

It must be a trick. But in that case, he wondered, who would be the trickster, the magician? The voice was dry, ironic. This was how the dead might indeed sound if they decided to call people on the telephone and extend greetings from that other country. This is how the living Asquith, the man himself, would sound. "Of course I'm alive," said the voice in response to Speke's amaze-ment.

"You vanished," said Speke, his voice breaking, strained, unable to carry the weight of his disbelief and the beginnings of his de-light.

"I've been busy."

It certainly must be Asquith. Nobody else could sound like that. "Busy," echoed Speke in wonderment, trying to divine the mean-ing in such a simple, everyday word. Whatever Asquith had been doing with his time, he did not imagine that "busy" would be the most apt description. "I tried to find you." Laughing, he added, "Of course, I know you're a genius at vanishing."

"You're right," said Asquith. "I'm hard to find."

There was a silence around Asquith's words, like the pale gleam of dish around a cut of veal. It was a matter of careful articulation, that theatrical precision, each word the plunge and parry of a fencer. But it was something else, too, a sense that the words sprang from a psyche unlike that of a normal human being. As-quith's words had to be translated out of another sort of mind into drab, common human speech. Asquith used words with a certain arrogance, even contempt: this is the way I must sound to be understood.

"I won't bother asking you where you were," joked Speke. By now he was convinced. Asquith was back.

He had, several years ago, hired two different detective agencies to find Asquith. These were not storefront operations. These were the kind banks hire, and movie companies curious about the habits of their stars. They had tracked him into four different emergency rooms, but Asquith had always just checked out, just hours before. One detective, a woman who worked for the most expensive—and greedy—attorneys in San Francisco, had told Speke bluntly, "He's either dead or dying, and even if you found him he'd be brain damaged. He was so drunk in Philadelphia at one point he stopped breathing. People like this aren't built to last."

Why wasn't Asquith talking? But of course, thought Speke, warming, Asquith had always worn silence, like an extra layer of clothing, an aura woven of deliberateness, of his own will. He was silent as a violinist might be, poised to play. He was reading Speke's temperament, his mood, his mental health.

Speke stood, nearly dropping the phone in a surge of enthusiasm. With every passing moment he was more amazed. "Where have you been? Jesus—all this time. I paid people incredible amounts of money to find you. You completely disappeared years ago."

He found himself carrying the conversation, and delighted to be able to talk to someone he had known so well. "Do you remember that woman I was seeing in Atherton? Her husband hired a detective who trailed us all over and ended up with nothing but a blurred telephoto picture of her with her arm around some male figure on Ocean Avenue in Carmel." He stopped himself. He was gushing, chattering—Asquith had always brought that out in him, and made him overeager to both impress Asquith and join with him in laughter against the world. He steadied himself, and said, with feeling, "It's wonderful to hear from you."

"Is it?" That reedy, superior voice caused just the slightest shadow to fall over Speke's soul.

"Of course it is," he responded, laughing perhaps just a bit too loudly.

"You sound," said Asquith thoughtfully, "happy."

Of course I'm happy, Speke nearly said. Why shouldn't I be happy? People are meant to be happy.

But there was something chilly about the way Asquith said this that silenced him for a moment. Asquith sounded healthy enough. They were both only thirty-nine, but Asquith had been the one to drink at dawn after a night of tequila in that bar in Cozumel, watching the tropical sun bloat over the horizon. Well, they had both tipped a few, but Asquith had lived on the stuff, swilling mezcal and chewing up the little worm. Asquith had been the one to discover how little sleep the human body required with a little help from amphetamines, and how blue the sky was if you ate peyote like Corn Nuts. And accident prone—three cars totaled in one year, unloaded guns blasting, one of them blowing off the back of the dresser one drunken pre-dawn.

Speke had been the good-looking one, the one who took in mauled cats and gave cash to impoverished strangers. Asquith was the one who was good at hiding, keeping to himself, drifting away from the party. His great skill had been in falling silent and communicating in his silence what he thought of all the gabbling, guffawing people around him. Asquith had never been likable in any traditional way. He had been keen, quick, and full of ideas, and that was all that mattered to Speke.

"I thought," said Asquith, his voice cutting the silence, "that I would come and see you."

There was a thrill in Speke's limbs. The framed manuscripts on the wall seemed to gleam. He had begun to believe that the past was vanished, the old faces bleached to nothing by time. He should have trusted life, fate, or whatever tides shaped life. To see Asquith again would be more than the reawakening of a friendship. It would be to rejoin a part of himself, a part he had mislaid and thought beyond recovery.

"I thought I would pay you a visit and discuss a little business," said Asquith.

And then, in the midst of his pleasure, Speke began to feel the smallest touch of doubt, as subtle as the trace of blood on the yolk of an egg. There was the telephone, here was the sound of Asquith's breath, his actual breath, in Speke's ear. What, he wondered, could possibly be wrong?

"Tomorrow," said Asquith.

Speke felt painfully apologetic. "Tomorrow is a mess. It's a disaster area. Any day but tomorrow."

What had made him call after all this time? Surely Asquith

never read *People* magazine, and certainly he hadn't run across the spread in *GQ*. One of the talk shows, perhaps, or the Oscar nomination, but that had been months ago. There had been so much media coverage lately that it was impossible to pin down what might have jogged the attention of this voice from the past. Surely, Speke told himself, he simply wants to congratulate me on *Stripsearch*—first the Tony award-winner and now the movie. Or maybe on *Flash*, still breaking records after two years simultaneously in New York and London.

"Tomorrow will be fine," repeated Asquith, and Speke could imagine his smile.

Tomorrow was a crowded day, the appointment book a mess of scribbled names and times. But he could make room for Asquith. The dry voice was deliberate and cunning. Speke knew the ways of his old friend. Asquith wanted him to feel anxiety. He was doing this on purpose.

But Speke's faith in himself, in good fortune, in life itself, was, for the moment, unshakable. It would be delightful to see Asquith. Tomorrow, though, was going to be a problem. Tomorrow was the day the biographer was coming, the man who could cap his already astounding career. You couldn't buy the sort of publicity Bell could give, and the man had decided on his own, without any prompting from anyone, to make Speke the subject of his next book. Not even forty, and he would be immortalized!

He had promised Dr. Murchison, the head of the film department at Stanford, that he would do Christopher Bell a favor. What a delightful favor—to let a well-known biographer pen your life. But Bell was in trouble, Speke had been told, suffering from what Murchison had hinted was both a penchant for gambling away his mortgage and buying cocaine off the street. Speke had to help Bell—he admired the man, and couldn't disappoint him. The truth was, Speke needed very little encouragement to let the biographer begin his research.

What was Asquith like these days? There was the usual sort of qualm: how do I look? How will he look? What if his taste in everything has changed and we have nothing to talk about?

Speke prided himself on being open-minded, flexible. He was not the hotheaded Speke of years past. He was calmer, now, successful. A man of good bearing, fine taste in all things. There was no doubt: he was famous, and wealthy. He had worked hard to reach this pinnacle. He had been the most impetuous, anxious man in the world, notorious for his nerves and alcoholic black-outs. But no more. He still relished life, but now he was strong as well as energetic. He was a new man.

His plays moved people. It brought them to their feet, ap-plauding. He got letters saying that his songs had stirred people from depression, from angst—had made people want to live. He was Hamilton Speke, a man who had helped give life to the world, and he was happy to hear from his old friend, his old partner.

"I know how to find you," said Asquith.

"Early, then," Speke heard himself say, with a voice that sounded steady enough, although Asquith would detect that rasp, that tremor, and even now he was chuckling again.

Speke was surprised to feel a chill. He was surprised to feel an ugly thought: what an irritating little laugh that was. I thought you would have wrapped your motorcycle around a tree, he nearly said. I thought you would have blown out your aorta on diet pills.

Speke himself had not always been as healthy as he was now. Once he'd awakened on Kauai completely naked but for one brand new hiking boot. He had huddled in the warm rain waiting for the night to come again, nursing aching thirst, shuddering with hangover, surrounded by feral chickens.

And then there were the nightmares, the terrible dreams that had plagued his nights as a young man.

He was pleased at the prospect of seeing Asquith, but he was also cautious. He could sense something stirring, something cold and heavy, something from the past. He tried to deny this uneasi-ness, but it was there.

Asquith waited, letting the silence grow.

But I am being polite, Speke reassured himself. Didn't he sound polite? He should be recording this conversation, so he could replay it and be reassured that he sounded polite. It was important that he not sound like the heavy-handed prick he used to be, before therapy and a little travel had made a wiser man out of him. Before Maria.

Twice he had paid five-figure dental bills to men who had irri-tated him at parties. After a little bourbon, it could be admitted, and each time over politics. Speke believed in Saving the Whales, and if a tree was spiked now and then, that was fine with him. In his view, any person who did anything to harm a wild animal should be punished. Severely. But he kept his temper these days. The new Speke was in top physical condition, had contacts and capped teeth, and was in love with a more peaceful version of life.

Still, Asquith was the only man in the world who really understood him, knew what he loved, and what he feared. Asquith knew his taste in women, in wine, in music. Asquith knew him as no one else in the world could.

"I know the way," said Asquith. There was a spin to his voice when he added, "I saw your house on television."

And then he was gone. There was only the electronic silence of the telephone, and the other, inner silence that resulted from a turmoil of feeling.

Speke made a fist, and stared at it.

Asquith wasn't coming here to see an old friend. He wasn't coming to have a beer or two and talk over old times.

Asquith wanted something.

· 5 ·

He was awake and it was still dark.
He had just had the nightmare, the old dream he had hoped was buried forever.

This is just perfect, he thought. The one night he really needed to have a good sleep. It was almost enough to make him wish for the old Seconal and tequila nightcaps he used to gulp. Today was going to be impossible. Asquith was coming. Bell was coming. And Scamp was coming—he had nearly forgotten that. They were coming to shoot footage for a television special.

He sat up, sweating.

Maria was beside him in the darkness, still asleep, but she, too, stirred. She whispered without waking, and he could not hear what she was saying. She tossed, and spoke again. She was warning someone, or begging him. He made out a single word: no.

Then he could hear a phrase, a sub-vocalized prayer. "Don't hurt me."

Christ—who would want to hurt such a lovely woman? He knew so little about this bride of a few months. Who had caused her to suffer in the past? Whoever it was, he would like to kill him. He himself needed Maria as he needed oxygen.

His own boyhood had been so ordinary. So sunlit and logical, the newspaper route and the howling, spitting mating of cats under the bedroom window. A loving but distant father, a smart and secretive brother: a childhood. But hadn't people been kind, really? The neighbors had always said good morning, out spraying dog dirt and leathered toad skins down their concrete driveways. His childhood had been safe and full of common mysteries, the run-over cat, the Kentucky Blue Wonders lifting the white, bare bean husk into the sun at the head of each sprout, a helmet, a trophy.

One very frightening thing had happened: a man had died on the front lawn. He had been watering his lawn when he turned blue, impossible, perfect blue, and collapsed. Hamilton, five years old and on his way from the bus stop, had watched as the Cadillac ambulance sirened its way up the street. The sheets of the stretcher had been so white in the sunlight, so crisp and neat. Even as a grown man Speke had suffered nightmares of this blue man turning his head to look right at him, and then slowly, jerkily, trying to get up to walk toward where he stood.

The effort was what always ended the nightmare. The blue man never actually climbed to his feet. It seemed that Speke's sense of what was real and what was impossible counseled even his dream life, an invisible editor. One of his therapists had been charmed by the phrase "reality principle," and had praised him for knowing exactly what was real. "That's rare," the therapist had beamed, "in imaginative people like yourself." Asquith had always kidded him about the "blue man dreams," and confessed that he himself never dreamed at all.

The memory of the dream was vivid, but it had that quicksilver quality that made it something impossible to cup and hold in the consciousness. He remembered the gleaming brass nozzle clearly, one of those nozzles that adjusted to make a fine aura of spray or a tight, hard lance of water. The dream had a sour quality, a cast of light that made him wince.

He did not want to move.

No, don't get up yet, he told himself. Stay here with Maria, staring into the almost perfect dark. At least you can hear her breathing—that's some solace.

Why of all the days under the sun was Asquith coming today?

It was as though the man had thought: what day would be the worst day for me to slither from my grave? And somehow, using some sense of timing only such madmen must have, Asquith had chosen the very worst day, and had managed to deceive him to the point that Speke had not talked him into a day a week from now, or a distant city a month away.

He rested his hand on her hip. Her slip of a figure delighted him. He would do anything to protect her, and keep secure her faith in him.

Some day he would tell her the secret pet name he had for her. It was a silly name, but it was the way he thought of her: my Little White Mouse. Embarrassing—a man of letters should be able to come up with something better than that, and so he had kept it secret.

Her brunette pubic hair contrasted with her skin to make it

appear nearly spectral. The thought of her now did not arouse him so much as make him want to lie beside her like this forever. Why was he lying here, thinking of her as someone who was long-departed? But she did have that sense of belonging not so much to another world as to no world at all, a creature separated from daily events. It was easy to imagine Maria as though he could see her only in his memory, as though she were long absent.

He crept from the bed carefully, so he would not disturb her sleep. He would look like a smashed bag of garbage when the cameras rolled. Scamp would bring that makeup whiz, though, and Bell would see bags under his eyes as a sign that he was a rumpled genius.

Besides, he had always wondered what sort of older man he would make. Would he be one of the baggy, bulky ones? Or would he grow gaunt and skeletal, one of those old guys who are all ear and chin? Today, maybe, he would start to find out.

He stared at the decanter of scotch, but made no move. In the old days he had always started his day off with a taste, red wine and bread, like an Elizabethan.

He had longed to have a biographer some day, someone to whom he could tell the story of his life. There was so much to tell, and so much to embellish. He wanted someone good, someone who could etch it into history.

Such a man was coming at last. He paced, disturbed by the approach of the man who would transform him from a playwriting celebrity, his face beside the Fritos and M&Ms at Safeway, into a modern day—but here he faltered.

A modern day what? Oscar Wilde? Not with my flat wit. A modern day Doctor Johnson? Hardly, sir, I haven't the tongue for it. Maybe he could emulate John Huston, all snarl and charm, or dig up the boxing gloves and do a knockoff of Hemingway and Mailer. He had to pretend to be something, or somebody. By himself, without an act, what was he?

Christ, where were the beta blockers that quack doled out to him in the days when he had been Speke the wreck? He yanked the desk drawer and pawed through match books from Zurich, Milan, from every place on earth, and he hadn't smoked for months.

The years before Maria had been tough. At least some of the details were hard to remember. Those years had left a smear of images: both phones ringing at once, him battling to refuse deletions in *First Cut*.

Both the song that gave the album its name and the album itself had been in "desperate need of a remix." Remix, he had said, and die. That refusal had been brilliant, since "First Cut Reprise" and "Big Bucks" both subsequently starburst at number one. His brother had even found it in an alley in Moscow, in what he had called "a really putrid-sounding bootleg." Still, his brother had grudgingly admitted, this was market penetration.

He had been known as a professional but a very ill-tempered man on the phone. Who wouldn't be grumpy, talking to people who never identified themselves and who all sounded alike? "Ham, listen, we got just a little problem with the broken bottles in the second act. The union says someone's gonna get hurt—I mean real glass. They have these sugar bottles—" All the while him thinking, puzzling, seething, and finally asking in what he thought was the mildest voice in the entire world, a voice right out of the Mother Teresa Finishing School, with the other phone bleating in his ear, "Please tell me who is this please." But it came out with a roar, not meek and mild at all and there was a long and very embarrassing conversation in which it turned out that between the pleases Speke had used the f-word to the most important human being on the East Coast. Although they did, in the end, use real empty Smirnoff bottles. The play was still running in eight major cities. People did get cut. The audiences loved it.

Without Sarah he would have gone up in smoke. Many times she had cut him off in the middle of a call to handle the call herself, and salvage with her warm honey voice what Speke had been about to wreck.

He couldn't, on this worst of all mornings, find a single pill. An aspirin. One. And absolutely nothing else.

I'll have to make short work of Asquith. Tell him how great he looks, take him over to the Outer Office, and—

Then Speke had no pictures in his head. When had he ever been able to control anything Asquith said or did? The man actually used to play with guns. Why hadn't a twelve-bore at some point whisked away just a little portion of the old cranial vault? Everyone else seemed to shoot themselves, that is, every other drug addict who fooled with guns. It wasn't right—it was unholy that someone who was addicted to six major poisons at once could still be alive.

It would be wonderful to see Asquith again, he reminded himself. They would have a nice long talk about writing songs in North Beach, using that cheap little Panasonic that, for some reason, tended to eat tapes, gobbling them into knots, a night's work turned into plastic confetti.

Will I disappoint Asquith, he wondered, and seem too sleek, too complacent? Maybe I've lost my edge.

There was a distant clatter. Clara would be up and about, attacking flour in the kitchen in the process of making her blueberry muffins. Life couldn't really be terrible, he told himself, if a kind woman was up making muffins.

It was going to be great to see Asquith again. They would indeed have a nice talk, but it would be in the Outer Office, far from the house.

First he would find out what it was Asquith wanted, before he would let the man into these walls, before he would let the old friend into the sanctuary, the world he wanted to keep safe.

·6·

Asquith was late.

Naturally. It was just like him, Speke muttered to himself. Why not torture me as long as you can? Why be punctual when you can drag this out forever?

Now and then there was the workaday sound of Sarah's office, the trill of the phone, the rattle of a printer, his career firing on all cylinders without his help. The sounds were muted, far away, muffled, as though he could not really hear them at all, but merely wished them into being.

Speke roamed the large house, paced the library, gazed at the piranha, that stainless-steel-pale fish that did not appear murderous as much as trapped. He organized his collection of antique blues recordings into alphabetical order. While fussing with the records, he discovered the rare Blind Willie McTell he had been sure a guest had filched at some point during those long drug-and-booze marathons in his pre-Maria days.

He poured a drink, and emptied it untasted down the drain, all the while feeling his insides blister and twist, scalded and punished into what he knew must be the beginnings of another ulcer.

It was no wonder. The body knew what to do: work hard. The result was a hole in the stomach, a crater in one's life.

Clara was in the kitchen, sorting through index cards beside an old-fashioned, compact Olivetti. The air was yeasty with the smell of bread. A lovely woman with a flash of gray in her dark hair, she smiled at him. Her family had lived in these hills since the eighteenth century, and Clara was one of those people who do not require speech in order to have presence.

Basil, a sheaf of fresh leaves, stood in a vase beside the sink. She was, Speke saw, typing her recipes for pesto. He had always told her she should write a cookbook, and she had always smiled and said that she could remember everything she needed to know. And yet here she was, "Spinach pesto" on the card waiting in the typewriter. It was one of his favorites, a blend of fresh spinach, pine nuts, blanched almonds, romano and what Clara had always called "mysteries." It was like blundering upon a woman writing her will.

He apologized for intruding, and Clara said, "I decided to make a file."

"Write a book. I'll put you on all the talk shows."

She looked down, smiling inwardly. "I would hate that." Then, more seriously, she added, "I just thought I might take your advice and get them on paper."

"Things written down do seem more lasting," he said. But he rarely knew what to say to Clara. She seemed always right, silent and rooted and, despite her apparent shyness, sure of everything she needed to know.

She did not meet his eyes, smiling down at her index cards. "It seemed like the right time," she said.

He wanted to linger in the kitchen, that sunny place, but he left the house entirely. Sometimes he believed that he could make things happen by a kind of magic. Sometimes he thought of someone and stepped toward the telephone and they called, right then, that very instant. Granted, that almost never happened, but it only took a time or two to make a man feel that he had a little more power than other people over the unseen.

And then, with perfect timing, as soon as he abandoned his faith in his power to make the invisible visible, as soon as he sighed and turned back toward the house, like something that had been preordained, something they had rehearsed, Asquith arrived.

Sun gleamed off a helmet, and surely this lean figure, kicking a Kawasaki into silent attention, was that of a stranger. Too agile, too young, Speke nearly thought, but then neither of them were old. And yet, this was an athletic figure, one that stepped with the loose limbs of a swimmer, or someone accustomed to hours of handball.

And that gesture, the lifting of the insectlike helmet away from the sandy hair—what was wrong with that? It was obvious after a moment. The old Asquith would never have worn a helmet.

Parking the motorcycle here would sure attract Maria's attention, and her eventual questions. Who was that tall man with the motorcycle?

Asquith looked taller, and although as thin as ever, thin the way a runner might be. His handshake was strong. A handshake—

even that was a surprise. Asquith had always greeted people with a stare, and offered them, if they were lucky, a cigarette.

And it was wonderful—it really was. To see his friend standing with his half-smile, his quick eyes, was more than a delight. Speke wanted to dance, cry out to the heavens. It was true—Asquith was alive!

Asquith studied him, and then said, with something like humor, "Here I am, back from the dead."

Speke embraced him, and he could feel within Asquith's frame a strength, a muscular thinness that made him think Asquith must run to stay in this sort of shape. He managed to utter some pleasantries as Asquith rolled the motorcycle under one of the live oaks, over the great roots.

Asquith cut him off by describing, in a calm voice, an accident he had passed on 101. "And there was a dead deer beside your gate, up by the road," he said. "A buck."

It's like him, Speke thought, to mention something violent, something dead.

There was something he had forgotten about Asquith, something all his midnight jaunts to score narcotics on Market Street had obscured. Asquith had loved the outdoors, and had, during his acting stints in Oregon, enjoyed camping near Crater Lake. So the man was not only alive, he was healthy. Speke licked his lips, and shook his fingers to get some feeling back into his body. He felt numb, unreal.

Asquith left the helmet on the motorcycle, and without this piece of armor he was more the old Asquith, wearing only a baggy shirt and jeans.

He had a way of walking that Speke recognized at once. He took his steps carefully, as though choosing to leave no footprints. He had an athlete's way of moving his arms, the limbs easy and relaxed but with a hint of inner tension.

Christ, thought Speke, people don't really change that much.

He welcomed Asquith into the Outer Office. It was a separate, remote cottage, ideal for interviews. Complete with a wet bar and a sound system, it gave the visitor the impression that he was visiting the great man in his lair.

The truth was that Speke rarely used what was, in a sense, his Oval Office. It was a stage office, not quite a fake, because once in a while he came out here to read a contract, and once a few years ago he had come out here with a bottle of ouzo and had drunk until he puked blood.

But it looked, with its ash panel, and its leather-bound Goethe, like the refuge of a noble mind, and at the same time a place of work, with a desk and a telephone. A large fireplace of green serpentine dominated the far wall, its jutting, sharp-cornered mantelpiece decorated with a single bronze Pallas Athena. Only a subtle eye would detect that the poker was in mint, unused condition. The mantelpiece itself was worth study. Its corners jutted out so sharply that Speke had hurt himself more than once bumping into them. The designer of the mantel was unknown, and Speke had decided that the spikes of green stone represented the rays of a stylized sun which supported the slab at each corner.

Asquith gazed around, with an imitation of respect. Or was it the real thing? Surely he would recognize the framed letter on the wall, a note from Hemingway to Charles Scribner, as authentic. And the Degas over the desk, all sepia and iron gray, would have silenced the Asquith of old into a long meditation. There were other things here, things that perhaps Speke would be able to show his visitor. Even the closet held its charms, never-used fishing tackle, handcrafted in Scotland, and a map of the estate rolled up into a leather case as tall as a man.

Asquith fell onto the leather sofa. His eyes were bright, and he was tanned.

Asquith had always been a secretive individual. Speke had never known the details of Asquith's childhood or his family. Maybe, Speke thought, this isn't the real thing—not Asquith at all. But there, just at the cuff of his shirt, was the scar from that frenzied walk up Grant Street all those years ago.

A silence, one that Asquith no doubt relished, and which needled Speke's insides. Asquith studied him, with the expression one would wear if spying an old movie on television, cherished but also charmingly dated.

Speke gestured toward the crystal decanter of single-malt; Asquith shook his head. But the time for casual greetings was drawing to a close. It was time for Act one, Scene one.

"You look well," said Speke.

Asquith closed his eyes for a moment against what he seemed to take as flattery. "You're keeping me secret," he said, and then, after a long pause, letting the word "secret" sizzle for a moment, he added, "so that no one will know I was here."

So, thought Speke, we are underway. At last it was the Asquith he remembered, the acerbic voice, the alert mind disguised by a mask of boredom. Although this tone was unpleasant, it was familiar, and Speke was grateful for the return of his old acquaintance, both because he was a friend and because Speke knew that he could manage this visitor after all.

"We can go up to the house for lunch later, if you like."

"You don't use this office."

"Why do you say that?"

"It's not nearly messy enough."

"I've changed a lot." Speke offered what he intended to be a disarming smile. "I'm more patient. Less messy—"

"You're a success!" Said with just the slightest tilt of the head.

Speke lowered his eyes. He would have to be very careful. Asquith was intelligent. I knew that, of course, Speke told himself. But he meant: really intelligent, much smarter than he himself would ever be.

"I am so happy to see you," Speke said. "But I want to be honest with you." He was tingling, and beginning to feel a clammy sweat that surprised him. "I think I was just a little bit nervous about your visit."

"You were always a nervous ruin, in private. People think you're a man of action, ready for anything. But I know."

"I think I know what you want," said Speke. Forget opening gambits, he thought. Let's talk.

"You thought I was dead," said Asquith, an oblique response to Speke's statement, but very much a response.

"I thought it very possible."

"Possible," said Asquith, as though disliking the flavor of the word. "You thought that something"—he made an airy gesture— "had carried me off."

"Life is confusing. I never know what to expect. And I did try to locate you."

Asquith smiled.

"If you want money, Timothy, I would hardly blame you. You deserve money." This was blunt, but Speke thought that by exposing the subject now he would render it less potent.

Asquith did not answer at once, but seemed amused. "Don't be silly."

Speke clasped his hands together, and worked his lips. This was not going to be easy. Big surprise. "Then what do you want?"

"I wanted to pay you a courtesy."

"How nice." Be careful, he told himself. Don't be sarcastic with this man. "What sort of courtesy?"

Asquith closed his eyes with a silent laugh. "Forgive me. I can't help feeling a certain amusement. You think I came here for money."

"It would be reasonable of you to expect some sort of reward for—let's face it—being such an inspiration to me."

"An inspiration?"

"Just being around you was exciting. If I needed a phrase for a song, or a splash of dialogue, I would just think of something you had said, or something you had done."

"You found me helpful, then," said Asquith, an airy half-question.

"Of course I did," said Speke. "You were someone I thought of as alive—fully alive, not one of these poor, pallid people you see everywhere."

Asquith's eyes glinted at this statement, and he took a moment before he said, "You thought of me as someone who was more alive than you were."

"Of course."

"And now you think that I've come back to claim my part of your success—my due share."

"I don't know how much I actually, legally owe you. . . ."

Asquith studied Speke with a slight smile.

"But I'll share what I have with you, Timothy. Out of friendship. I'll set you up somewhere. If you want a house, swimming pool, staff of helpful aides—that's what you'll have."

"You don't understand at all, do you?" said Asquith.

"I don't really have to give you anything, Timothy."

"That's right. You kept me alive when I was really unsound of mind. Counted out my aspirin, washed the puke out of my blankets. And I appreciate it."

"If you still need medical help, Timothy, I will be happy to provide it."

"You don't know, do you?"

"Tell me. I want to do what I can. Anything reasonable."

"It's not money, Ham. It's not anything that can be resolved by screwing off the top of one of those hand-lacquered fountain pens and scribbling a check."

"I want to be fair—"

"Years went by, and I was too sick, mentally, to even remember the plays. And when I did see you in *Newsweek,* it didn't bother me at all, or even interest me. But recently I have come to see that what you have done is stolen my immortal part—my life. I wasn't the inspiration for your plays. I didn't give you the idea for your songs. I gave you everything. All of it."

This was said in a quiet voice, Asquith's gaze wandering the room, as though seeing through the boards and plaster of the office to all the places he would never visit.

Speke could not respond.

"You were on television," Asquith continued. "In makeup so thick you couldn't sweat, talking about the black cat, my cat, the one I found. You felt, with your own brand of reasoning, that you could take credit for all the other stories. But that story, Hamilton, is mine."

"I don't understand you," said Speke.

"Don't you?"

Once again, Speke could not make a sound.

"I want it all. Everything that you have become."

"You're hardly being rational, Timothy. I've worked hard. I've spent years on this work-in-progress. I'll give you credit. I'll have my agent put out a press release today. I'll tell the world all about our friendship. I want that, Timothy—I really do."

Asquith watched him and did not respond.

Speke recovered himself, and continued, "But you won't take that play away from me. You won't take the plays, or the songs. They are my work. You lived the stories, but I wrote them, and they are mine."

Asquith crossed his legs.

Speke leaned forward. "You haven't written a word. You could never write without me standing over you, pouring the coffee and looking up words you couldn't spell."

Asquith began to speak in a new voice, a narrator's steady cadence. He began to tell the story, began the opening dialogue, the stronger, muscular young man too sick to continue through the jungle, the Indian turning to say, "If you're so weak we will go back." The thin, ironic young man threatening the Indian, the scenes unfolding as Speke sat, open-mouthed, unable to make a sound.

He told the story of the cat.

"No!" Speke cried at last. "That's not what happened. You can't do that to the story, Timothy. It's wrong! Those are all lies!"

Speke paused to steady his voice. "I'll help you, Timothy. In any way I can. But I want that play. I won't let you twist the story up like that. That's the most important play of my career, and besides—it's my life, my actual life, the one I lived. And as for those old plays, I was the one who really wrestled them into existence. You weren't there. You were gone!"

Speke was on his feet, pacing. "I carried those plays from door to door. I saw those plays from the days when they were so many sheets of Walgreen's typing paper in the bottom of a closet, to the nights when at last they were big words in lights. Writing them was nothing! Nothing! That was the easy part, the fun part. That was the joy! The rest of it, and the stuff you wouldn't have had the stomach for, the grind of getting these things out of the cardboard box and into the public psyche—I did that! I did it. I gave birth to these plays, and you—where were you? I put those songs on the radio, Timothy. It was all me."

"I'm calling my old friend at UPI. You remember Jessica Moe. She'll believe me."

"Jessica! She knows the truth. She knows how sick you are." That was rude—bad choice of words. But, of course, Jessica would believe Asquith. Jessica was one of those people who are willing to believe the worst. She had been the *Chronicle* music critic, and had called a cab for Speke and Asquith more than once. She was in New York now. "Out of friendship I'll agree that you can share— but you can't steal."

Speke had a cold heavy stone in his belly. Maybe it was true. Maybe I did steal all those plays. Maybe I didn't even cowrite them. Maybe they really do belong, entirely, to him. Is this possible?

Asquith was standing, too, his feet soundless on the carpet. "It belongs to me, Hamilton. All of it. And all of what you have become."

Speke was losing control of his breath, his heart. The colors in the room were beginning to flicker. The phone was in Asquith's hand, and he began stabbing numbers.

"She'll believe me," said Asquith, "when I tell her that I wrote all the plays—and all the songs."

"But it's not true!"

"It's always been money for you, hasn't it, Ham? Nothing else mattered. Principles, compassion, the truth. The truth was just so much wrapping paper."

Speke grabbed the cord, and tore the phone out of the wall, although it took two very fierce yanks to send the beige cable whistling into the air.

"Yes, I see how much you have changed, from Speke the thug to Speke the rich thug. I was a fool to come here."

Speke lunged for the door, and blocked it with his body. "Who knows you're here?"

"Nobody, I suppose. I don't broadcast my life. That's the trouble. I've lived underground, like a sow bug, for years. I want to claim what's mine. I want a part of the daylight. I realize how hard you've worked, Ham, and I offer you my congratulations."

"You're not leaving. You are not stealing my life."

Asquith laughed. "I'll leave by the window. Remember that time I called the police because you were ranting? You used to frighten me, Ham, but I've changed."

"Don't go near that window."

"I was going to do it nicely. I was going to tell them that we collaborated on some of them. And, it's almost true. All the ugly language, your witty use of obscenity, all the clever references to fellatio, don't appear in the rough drafts."

"Sit down."

Asquith smiled. He said, as though remarking on a mildly pleasant surprise. "I'm not afraid of you."

If he had, at that point, returned to the sofa, or sauntered over to examine the Degas—if he had done anything at all to give Speke a few moments to clear his vision and take a few deep breaths of air, everything would have been different.

But Asquith stepped toward the window.

He flung it open, the two wings of the French window opening outward. He propped one boot on the sill, rocked back, ready to bound into the daylight, and Speke caught him by one arm.

He flung Asquith—threw him, hard.

He hurled him back into the room. Asquith was light, and easy to fling, the thin body spinning like a dancer's, slamming awkwardly against the wall.

But it wasn't the wall. It was the sharp point of the serpentine mantelpiece. It caught Asquith with an ugly slap, like two hands smacked together, and for a long time nothing happened. Asquith was pale, and did not move, and Speke did not draw a breath.

Asquith's lips were blue.

It's okay, Speke told himself. It's all right. It isn't the way it looks. Everything will be all right.

Asquith stepped forward, slowly, with a lurch. He opened his mouth, unable to speak.

"I'm sorry," Speke whispered. Then, louder, "I'm sorry, Timothy."

Asquith halted, stiff-legged and staring. Both hands crept to his throat and he made a gagging sound, a retching cough, and there was a red stain at his lips.

Speke wanted to say: You're all right. Stop it. Say something.

Asquith twisted, working one arm backward, trying to reach a place on his back, hunching, coughing. Speke nearly howled, but he could not make a sound. *No! This was all a mistake!*

Asquith dropped to all fours, and vomited blood.

Speke seized the dead phone, and then there was blood everywhere, a spreading pool of it as Asquith struggled for breath in the center of an expanding nova of scarlet.

And collapsed, face down, one leg twitching.

· 7 ·

No, a voice howled inside him.

He'll be all right.

Speke swept over to his friend, and then stopped, afraid to touch him, unable to take another step. There was blood on the corner of the mantelpiece, and blood on the shirt where the stone had punctured Asquith's back. The body stopped twitching, and it was so obvious that Speke could do nothing but raise his hands to his head.

He closed his eyes, rocking in place. Everything will be fine. There's no problem at all. Go ahead—look and see.

Look and see in a minute, when you can stand to do it. Count to three. To four. Then—take a peek.

When he looked again, everything was still as it had been. The body at his feet sprawled in a way no living body could tolerate, one arm flung, palm upward, head to one side. There was a rank sewer stink, and a glistening, still-spreading patch of piss at the crotch.

The room around him blanked out. Speke was cold, stiff, unable to see anything but the sheen of scarlet. He prayed, a wordless, silent, shrieking prayer.

He lunged to the telephone, but the thing was dead, and he hurled it against the wall. And then he heard a sound that twisted his insides and made him close his eyes. No! Not this—anything but this.

It was the voice of Maria. "Ham? Are you all right?"

Please, God, anything but this! Why couldn't he move time backwards, just five minutes? That's all it would take—five minutes. His legs were stiff, and his breath tore in and out of his lungs. He began to shudder, absurd, uncontrollable trembling as he staggered toward Maria.

Don't let her see this, he prayed.

"What is it?" She still didn't see. "My God, Ham, what's the matter?"

He shook his head, meaning: leave. Go away. Now.

She said, "I heard shouting."

She carried a watercolor of what looked like a bright yellow hand grenade, and Speke could only hold out his arms and mouth at her: don't come in here. Don't look.

She dropped the painting and put her hands to her mouth. Her eyes widened as she stepped gingerly, but inevitably, toward the lake of blood.

Don't look, his soul screamed. Maria, please don't look.

She became a statue. Staring downward, her face pale, as if her mind were struggling to deny what lay before her.

Speke felt himself melt away. If only he could be a boy again, with a boy's sense of what life was. Sun, and bicycles. And little, simple sins, buying Winstons out of a cigarette machine. That was all gone now, in another universe.

She knelt, and then was on her feet. Her lips parted, and when she spoke her voice was nearly inaudible, but Speke could hear it. He heard it well.

"He's dead!" she whispered.

For an instant something like laughter ripped through him. Of course he's dead. Didn't I tell you about this little hobby of mine? I throw people around the office.

Then the laugh was gone, replaced by something cold and heavy. He anticipated her thoughts. The phone doesn't work, Speke wanted to say. I tore it out of the wall, and then I hurled it and it broke.

Shivering, she knelt and touched the multicolored wires which had burst from the telephone, and then looked up at Speke, as if beseeching him to tell her what had happened, to tell her this wasn't what it seemed. She held up the dead receiver, as though to say: you, Hamilton, did this.

There is only one thing to do. Call the police, he commanded himself. Run up to the house and—

He couldn't move.

It was an accident, he tried to tell himself. Just a simple accident. The police would understand. A troublesome visitor. People can be so annoying. We all lose our temper from time to time, Mr. Speke.

An arm wrestling match got ugly. We were practicing our old soft shoe routines. We both used to dream of being stuntmen. We were having a business conversation and Mr. Asquith hurled himself at the mantlepiece.

It was time to practice what he was so good at. It was time for him to be honest with himself. He grabbed Asquith by the arm and threw him, as hard as he could. And besides, just yesterday he had thought of doing something like this. He could not forget the taste of anxiety in his mouth, and it all came back to him now. In the back of his mind he had always wanted to do this. He had planned it all along. Admit it to yourself, Speke. Admit it—you wanted this all along.

The room swayed one way, and then the other. He felt his legs vanish, his head wander way from his body. Murder. That's the way it would look, and that's the way it was. He had murdered someone. Just like that, no trouble at all.

He tried the word out again. Murder.

"What have you done?" she whispered. "Ham, tell me what you've done."

She would never forgive him. It was self-defense, he wanted to lie. This was a dangerous man, this Asquith. A black belt in every sort of martial art known to man. He nearly killed me, but I fought him off. It was brutal. He attacked me with—

He had to sit down. He would, some day, some fine day in the future, when he could control his body movements again. Surely there was a mistake of some sort. Surely Asquith was only injured. A handful of paramedics could chopper up from Stanford and everything would be fine.

She read his eyes. Read him too clearly. She shook her head, a shiver. No, her eyes said. It's too late.

The intercom spoke in Sarah's voice. "Mr. Bell is just arriving," it said.

Bell! There was still a world out there, a universe of people and events. Somewhere someone was probably opening a letter, reading a newspaper, turning on a television.

His voice functioned, amazingly. "I'll be right there," it said, the disembodied phrase he had uttered a thousand times before sounding so normal that it was obscene. It shouldn't be possible that he could stand here and say something so banal while staring at so much blood.

Tell Sarah, he commanded himself. She'll call the police. But the thought of telling Sarah made him cringe inside.

"I'll do anything you want me to do," Maria said.

What could he possibly want her to do?

He groped across the desk, and switched off the intercom. Don't take any unnecessary chances, he told himself. And, just as quickly, he demanded: why not? Why not tell everyone what had happened? He was amazed at himself, and wanted to hoot with laughter. He acted as though he had a plan.

Tell her to call the police. Tell her to run up to the house and call the police.

"Anything," she was saying. "Ham, I'll help you. Tell me what you want me to do."

She was weeping as she said this, trembling, and Speke wanted to take her into his arms, these arms which had just killed a man.

The police. Anything else is sick. Anything else is wrong. Wrong: the word stunned him. He had committed a crime, even, he made himself think, a sin.

He had wanted to protect Maria. He had wanted to keep her from anything ugly. He had wanted to cure her of all the hard things that had happened to her in the past.

"We have to keep this secret," she said.

He couldn't form the words. He took a breath. "What do you mean?"

"I couldn't bear it, Ham." He held her, and she was trembling. "The police, all the questions, the cameras—I'm not that strong."

No, he told himself, she wasn't strong. He gazed down at her, and he knew what she was saying with her eyes. If he called the police, and if the world closed in on them with its heavy boots she would leave him.

He could bear anything but that.

"I'll help you," she said, her voice barely a whisper. "I'll tell you what to do."

It was simple, when she told him what steps he should take. It was simple, and perfect. For an instant, when he looked back at the body, he nearly collapsed, but he kept himself upright, and as he spoke, and began making decisions, it was astounding how his mind began to clear.

"We're going to be all right." He deepened his voice and forced out the words, "We're going to get away with this."

As soon as he said it, he knew that it was true.

· 8 ·

It was very simple: before they did anything else, they would have to hide the body.

Sure—that's a brilliant idea, he told himself. It was like finding a wallet. Just stick the body in your back pocket and keep walking.

It was getting hot in the Outer Office. It had never been so stifling, and he found each breath a little shallower than the one before it. His lungs contracted to two painful points and the room around him began to go gray.

The heat made the smell rise higher, each breath a whiff of urine and that other smell, the soprano shriek of blood. Speke began sobbing, but even so he was able to stalk toward the window, and lean, pushing the swinging glass doors outward, to let in the fresher, cleaner heat of the day.

The soil lay beyond, the stone sea to which he would commit his friend. It all swam in his eyes, the roots of the trees and the fallen acorns, the leaf-litter and the spill of sun through the branches. His palms were wet. This hand . . . He gazed into his palm. This hand had grabbed Asquith's arm and—

"Who?" she asked. "Who was he?"

The question echoed in him. Ah, yes, he wanted to say. That, Maria, is the question of the hour. "An old friend." It was true. Asquith was an old friend. The thought nearly destroyed him, and he had to take several deep breaths to keep from breaking down.

"Ham," she began. Then when she could speak again, "Don't let them take you away from me."

Like many men, Speke had always wondered what he would do under real pressure. He had never been tested by war, and the physical crises that shape other men's lives—accidents, natural disasters, physical handicaps—he had somehow avoided. As a result, he had always wondered how much courage he had. His character had been tested by the exigencies of his career, but now he could endure the fiercest sort of challenge, and he suddenly treasured this opportunity to prove to himself, and to Maria, that he was equal to it.

He had killed, and he would get away with it. It was that simple. He would triumph. He would have something in common with the heroic, with the lion, with the eagle. He would be a man who believed in himself. Never again would there be a ripple of self-doubt. He would know the truth about himself, and other men would sense this in him. (Speke has changed, they would whisper among themselves. He's harder, now. Colder. You can see it in his eyes.)

"Maria, listen to me. Are you listening?"

"Yes, Ham. I'm listening." Her voice was the sound of someone shocked beyond feeling.

"Do exactly as I tell you. We don't have much time."

To put it mildly. Bell already here, and Scamp on his way with cameras and a sound crew. He would let Bell stay. But Scamp would have to leave. He would think of an excuse. He would not grin before the video cameras today.

If only he could draw a single, deep breath. Or maybe that was not the problem. Maybe he was breathing too fast, hyperventilating. He turned to face her, trying to send her courage through the air. She seemed to try to respond, but, for the moment, she could not speak. He felt his legs regain their old strength as he reached her. (He's somehow strangely masterful these days—not the same man at all.)

"We have to work together," he said, gripping her shoulders, the strength of his feeling making him feel drunk, stupid and bestial.

Her eyes beseeched him: whatever you do, make it all right.

"Get the shovel from the garage." She did not seem to hear him. "Now!"

She hurried from the cottage.

He was panting hard, gasping. Alone with his triumph, Speke could not stand to look. He forced himself. This is what he had done. This is what he would live with.

He snatched the carpet from before the fireplace, a stiff burgundy and tawny wool pile that he had considered an investment. Woven by women, he had been told, in a remote village long before television had even been imagined, its earth-golds the effect of tobacco juice dye.

He rolled the body quickly into the carpet, not letting himself look at it any more than he had to, but seeing all-too clearly the blood-smeared death snarl. And then to his horror he found himself embracing the rolled-up corpse, calling his old friend's name, knowing that he would never have a whole mind again.

The body made a gurgling groan, a breathy syllable as his hug squashed air from the lungs. He let it fall, and stood slowly, then fell to the body again, rocking it and calling Asquith's name.

Maria was there, struggling with him, pulling him away, thrusting the shovel into his hands.

"Quickly," she whispered.

He staggered to the window. She was smart. She knew what to do. We'll be a team, he thought.

It was good to be outside. He dug, stomping down hard to cut through the roots of trees. The smell of earth was powerful medicine. The earth would help him. Just an hour away from San Francisco, the estate was a refuge, a secret apart from the world of cars and news. He had been kind to the trees here, and to the house. He had cleared away the brush, and had once contracted such a bad case of poison oak the doctor had given him two shots of cortisone.

He was giddy, he knew, with the rush of thoughts, but he couldn't stop them. As unlikely as it seemed, he knew without a doubt that the estate would help him. Nature itself, that unacknowledged god, would help him. This was madness, but he found himself recalling that he had donated money to dolphin research, and that he had written letters to the Senate decrying animal experiments. He had always stood up for the whale. He would become a vegetarian. Was it madness to think that his entire life would change? This was all a great blessing. It was a chance to grow. What a crossroads he had reached.

(He's always been self-confident, but now he has real presence. I wonder what happened to make him so strong?) He shivered. What was Sarah doing with Bell? The biographer would be restless, even suspicious. This was the worst possible situation: a professional reporter, a man famous for his eye for detail, not a two-minute walk from a murdered corpse.

Speke was in fine physical condition, and he was able to work fast. Strong, he told himself. Be strong.

But the soil was hard, and full of rocks and snaking roots. Tough roots, resilient ropes that the shovel could not cut. The earth was rich with stones that chimed and grated against the blade. Pithy cables of tree clung to the steel, and he had trouble wrenching the shovel out of the soil, much less making headway into it.

What a pathetic tool this was. Apparently, it had been left in the garage by the previous owner or his gardener. Speke had a gardener of his own. He could call up and ask Brothers where he kept a better shovel, but Brothers was a wise and curious man.

His palms hurt. He was getting blisters. He leaned on the shovel, panting. He didn't have time. He would have to go up to see Bell now, and excuse himself somehow and come back and finish later. He couldn't do this when the cameras got here. Those weasels followed you everywhere. He had to beg CBS not to have a shot of him flossing his teeth on the evening news a few months ago.

Who would have thought plain soil would be so difficult? It was a wise place, though—a shrewd place for a grave. It was close enough to the Outer Office that coyotes would not dig up the body, not far from the window out of which Asquith had intended his escape.

He scrubbed himself in the wet bar. Maria was already at work, wiping up the blood with a rag. Christ, blood was sticky stuff. He wanted to vomit for a moment.

But Maria was tough. What an amazing woman she turned out to be, his Little Mouse. Once again, he was struck by the realization that he did not really know her. He helped her drag the body to the closet, where it became one more object in the storage place of unused flyrods and rarely consulted maps.

"I'll finish later. I'm going to run up to see Bell." His voice was hoarse. "I'll be quick."

"Don't worry, Ham. I'll clean up."

The blood she meant. She would wipe up the blood. He could taste it in the air. He loved her, for a moment, too much to speak.

"How do I look?" he asked. "Do I look all right?"

"You look fine."

He would have to look better than fine. He would have to look perfect to deceive a man like Christopher Bell.

He hurried through the sunlight, telling himself that there was no hope at all. How could he even con himself for a second?

Couldn't you even smell it, all the way here, here in the bright sunlight? Didn't the air smell of blood, dark and salt-brewed, like a stagnant sea?

II

FIRST CUT

· 9 ·

Christopher Bell rolled down the window of his Fiat, and let the smell of the dry hills stream through his hair. He would be there soon, and he laughed at himself for being so pleased.

He had read that even when you knew where to look, the gate was easy to pass by. The house had been designed to be both sturdy and unobtrusive. According to what he had heard, hikers sometimes passed it without seeing that it was there. The house was a secret amidst outcroppings of native basalt and stands of ancient oaks. He thought of it as the sanctuary he had sought for years. He thought of Hamilton Speke as a man both colorful and heroic, a man in love with life.

But Bell was a professional journalist. If Speke turned out to be a flawed giant, then he would be just as happy to write an attack on this successful playwright. It would make no difference to him at all. Besides, scandal sold more books.

Murchison, easily the most noted film scholar in the Bay Area, had lied a bit to get Speke's attention and sympathy. "I'll give him a call and mention, say, cocaine and maybe too many trips to Reno. Speke can't turn down a cripple."

Bell had protested, briefly and insincerely. He had just arranged a book contract for Murchison, and Murchison owed him at least one fat favor. Bell had been worried that Speke would be too busy to see him, and the lie had seemed necessary.

He loved the spice of the air. The land was rugged, under an open sky. This was country at its best, the dry sun of a California summer, with its golden fields, and a red-tailed hawk skimming a hillcrest.

He had looked forward to this day for months. He had enjoyed, and endured, hundreds of assignments, but this was one which his success allowed him to choose himself, and he was going to savor every minute of it.

He was a man who loved his work. The Olivier book had been a dream come true. Haunting West End pubs for a chance to interview old actors had been exciting, and had allowed him to indulge his fondness for Guinness. Then there had been the television book, which had sold thousands—or was it millions? He had to admit that researching that project had become a grind toward the very end. He was, by nature, an active man. Spending a winter snowbound at Tahoe with grocery bags of Lucy videotapes had made him buy a pair of skis.

But because of those books, his career had blossomed. He even had a gracious letter from Olivier himself, one of the last the great man had penned, thanking him for the flattering if unauthorized *Life.*

He had worked his way up from the journalistic trenches. In his early days as a reporter he had been, from time to time, under fire. He had covered paramilitary raids on marijuana fields in which backwoods farmers turned out to be armed with Browning automatic rifles. Shotgun pellets had showered on him during gunfire in East Oakland, and a liquor store hostage affair had sent a pistol slug humming past his left ear. The ear still tingled when he thought about it.

Gunplay did not trouble him, although it got his attention. He concentrated on gathering details—what people wore, what the weather was doing, what cars the bank robbers had sideswiped before they slammed into a cement truck. Somewhere between *Sir Lawrence* and *Backlot,* the story of Hollywood's happy marriage with recreational chemicals, Bell had become a professional biographer. Talk shows had to be declined after a while, and a secretarial service employed to cope with his mail so that he could get on with new projects, new lives.

People—and this still surprised him—wanted to have Bell "do" their lives, much as aristocratic English women had wanted Reynolds and Gainsborough to perpetuate in pink and silver their smiles and their favorite gowns. Bell intended only to write about people he admired, people who made the world a better place, and Hamilton Speke was such a man.

A vulture slowly circled the road high overhead. He shifted to pass a rusty pickup. This was going to be the beginning of something wonderful. This was going to be the start of a new life. This was a book he was going to relish, the story of a man of unquestioned genius. If it turned out that Speke was a fake, a man who failed to measure up to his reputation, that would be fine, too. He couldn't lose. Either way, he had a Life that would sell.

He rolled up his window. Two yellow trucks nosed the shoulder of the road. Blue smoke slumped across the two-lane. Ragged flames ate the side of a hill, and foresters worked the fire with shovels. This was much like the fire Speke had helped fight so recently, Bell reflected. This blaze did not seem likely to become a crisis. The flames were no bigger than sparrows, fluttering.

He sped through the smoke, and then drove even faster. A small blaze, he consoled himself. Small, and under control. But it was plainly a harsh season for fire. This spare beauty could all vanish in an hour.

He had wanted to meet Speke since he was astounded by *Stripsearch* in New York. This man cracked the English language like a whip. This man understood his characters. The silence of one character when another was speaking was not simply a period of time when one character jabbered. The silence supported and protected, even illuminated, the dialogue, as silence in a symphony will give space to the cello.

He had come equipped with some interesting artifacts. Jessica Moe, an old journalist friend, had loaned him some early rough mixes from Crystal Sound Studios, and some early tapes that she said, in her dry style, "might prove worth a listen." Each cassette was reputedly Speke at a very early point in his career. Early songs, Bell assumed, and he wanted to hear them very much. The tapes had arrived yesterday from New York, and he had not taken the time to listen to them yet. He had a good excuse: why listen to recordings when you were about to meet the man himself?

The estate was guarded by a fence of iron spears. The gate, when he reached it, was supported by two blue stone pillars, and it was not locked. "We never lock it," Speke's business manager, a woman with a sultry voice and no-nonsense manner, had mentioned on the phone. "Mr. Speke thinks that would be an unpleasant symbol." He had heard a great deal about Sarah Warren, too, and had once contemplated an article about her until he realized that he didn't know enough about her, and couldn't dig up enough.

There was a dead deer near the gate, its eyes gazing up into the empty sky.

He wanted to savor this moment, his first arrival at Live Oak.

He rolled the Fiat along the gravel drive as slowly as possible. The great oaks festooned here and there with dried moss, overhung the drive. The crackle of the gravel was harsh, and Bell was afraid that he would disturb the spell of this place, as though the enchanted trees would vanish with the first abrupt sound, the slam of a car door or the bleat of a human voice.

The road was perhaps three or four miles long, but it was rocky, and twitched from side to side. Like the roads to many estates in the West, it was kept primitive, unsurfaced and weathered, perhaps to give the owner the illusion that he inhabited wilderness. It was a road both short and endless, and as Bell drove he felt all the places he had seen, and all the people he had known, recede. Forget everything, this land seemed to say. See for the first time.

And then he glimpsed it.

He stopped the car.

It was grander than it had looked on television, and television so often made small, nervous hucksters into giants. This was a noble house indeed. Bell had virtually memorized last month's article in *Architectural Digest,* but even so he was surprised. Built in 1910 by a railroad tycoon turned recluse, it had been sold to Speke just a few years ago. It had a half dozen porches, a sun room, and, the article had added, "enough gables to make it seem a place of exciting secrets."

He drove carefully, closer to the house. He snapped off the engine, and took a deep breath. He would leave his briefcase in the car. He wanted this experience to be unencumbered. He was about to learn something deep about life from this man, and he wanted to enter his presence without any trappings.

His stomach was fluttery, and he combed his hair quickly, amused at himself for being so self-conscious. He had interviewed ax murderers. He had interviewed heads of state. He hurried up the stepping stones.

The front door opened before he could knock, and he bit his lips. They must have seen him fussing with his hair like a nervous suitor. He made himself smile, and hurried forward, striding through the noon heat.

"I expected you to be on time," she said, "and here you are—exactly punctual."

Bell must have responded with something appropriate, because Sarah Warren proceeded to introduce herself.

He was hushed, drinking in the sight of the dark oak wainscoting and the Monet—the two Monets, visons of hills and poppies, a sea and distant ships. The silence of the house was profound, as though the silence itself were a sound that soaked all other noises and left a presence, a heavy, pure peace.

He had expected Sarah Warren to be something of an adversary, perhaps overly defensive of her employer's bad habits, whatever they might be. This was natural, and he was prepared to respect her for that. What he had not anticipated was how gently she went about her role as commander-in-chief.

"I've been looking forward to meeting you," he said.

"Surely not. You certainly won't want to waste any of your time with me. By the way, I enjoyed your Olivier book. You may be the only writer I've read who understands his *Hamlet.*"

Bell was surprised to feel himself blushing. He stammered his thanks.

"Mr. Speke will be a few minutes. He asked me to show you into the office just in case he was late. His real office, not the one he uses for most interviews."

He was being flattered again, Bell knew. But it worked. This was a woman capable of running a large organization and according to rumor she had turned down top-paying positions to stay where she was. She did, indeed, know everything. He could tell by the way she smiled. She silenced him with her professional kindness, and at the same time promised him that he would learn nothing from her.

She spoke in the tone of a very professional docent. "You know, I imagine, more than enough about this house."

"It's fascinating—"

"The first owner shot himself. They found, perhaps you will forgive me for mentioning, the top of his head under one of the poplars. It was during the First World War. Something to do with his health. Or, perhaps, the war. I mention this because some people seem to think this place a sort of cultural Disneyland. But it's a real place, and has seen real life."

"Does that mean that the place is haunted?" Bell joked.

"I couldn't say, Mr. Bell."

He was trying to keep up with this woman, who had such a brisk step, because he wanted very much to look into her eyes again. Just for a moment. He wanted her to give him that direct, calm look just once more.

"If I could begin by spending some time with you, Miss Warren—"

He could call her Sarah. She said this without glancing at him, and then she turned and looked into his eyes.

Bell had once interviewed a homicide detective with both his own Reeboks and the detective's Florsheims glued in a pool of blood, and he had never jotted down anything but complete sentences. It was one of his strengths: coherence.

For the moment, however, he had trouble speaking in sentences. "I'm curious about the lack of security here," he heard himself say, but this was the last thing he wanted to learn. Dumb question, he told himself. He really wanted to know why there seemed to be so much more oxygen here at Live Oak than in any other air he had ever breathed. He wanted to know which room in the vast house was Speke's favorite, and he wanted to know how a man could work beside such an alluring woman as this manager without becoming her lover.

They entered the office. This was where Speke worked. A dark desk, probably mahogany. A view out bay windows of lush green grass and fuchsias.

He wanted to sit across from her, and listen to her voice. But Sarah had the manner of a busy person being generous with her time. She offered coffee, or tea, or perhaps something stronger.

He suggested black coffee. "What was it about my comments about *Hamlet*—"

One eyebrow lifted for a moment, as though she realized that he was fishing for yet another compliment. But she also seemed pleased to comply. "You knew that Olivier made a mistake, in order to shorten the play."

"Rosencrantz and Guildenstern?"

"Taking them out of the play hurts it," she said. "I think you're right. When Hamlet loses that touch of treachery, his changing of the message his two supposed friends carry to England, he seems just a little less . . ."

"Heroic." He sensed that she had wanted him to complete her sentence. "But the play's too long, isn't it?"

She smiled, as though too kind to tell him how stupid this was.

"Of course," he managed to recover, "that's our own frailty, a failure of our ability to sit still. Not the playwright's problem, really."

When a quiet woman in white brought the tray he found himself staring at the cup as though he had never seen this sort of black fluid before.

"It's terrible of me to tell you about the suicide. I've never done that before, not to a first-time guest. For some reason, I don't know why, I wanted to shock you."

"The top of a skull on the lawn is a grim detail, I have to admit. Does the house have a history of violence, aside from that sad event?"

She answered obliquely. "This is not an unlucky place. The original owner took his bad luck with him when he died. The poor man. He must have felt so desperate." Her eyes found Bell's gaze once again.

"I imagine that there's some sort of security arrangement."

"Guards, that sort of thing? There's no need for security, according to Mr. Speke. The estate is so isolated, and the occasional hiker can pass right by the house itself and scarcely be aware of it, the trees camouflage it so well."

She was a small woman, shapely, in a gray sweater and no makeup. Her voice was soft, but so businesslike Bell did not want to interrupt her for fear of wasting her time. How could a man write a word with such a woman around?

Her eyes stupified him into asking the worst question he could have chosen. It was inevitable. His excitement, his delight in sitting in Speke's office, had confounded him. And the sight of this woman in gray, this brilliant adversary, finished off whatever chance he had of sounding like anything but an oaf.

"He hasn't been writing very much recently, has he?"

Terrible question, he told himself. Terrible, rude, clumsy.

Her smile told him everything: I will tell you absolutely nothing of any importance. "Mr. Speke doesn't discuss work in progress. Not his plays, and not his music. He keeps it to himself."

"That was a stupid question."

She was sitting across from him, however, in no apparent hurry to leave, like a fellow student sitting in an office, waiting for the principal to arrive. It was kind of her to be so generous with her time. It was only his reputation that made her linger, he imagined. He doubted that he had made a very good impression on her so far.

"It's your profession," she said. "But I know what you're thinking. You suppose I know all sorts of juicy gossip, and you've made up your mind I won't tell you."

"Will you?"

She laughed. "Tell you all sorts of gossip?"

He astounded himself—once again, he was blushing.

"I know nothing of any interest. At least, nothing that will help sell books. But I'll try to be helpful in any way I can."

"That's why you told me about the suicide. A lurid anecdote to give me the impression that you were giving me inside information. Because you do, after all, know quite a bit. Maybe more than you think."

How would he describe her tonight when he wrote up his notes? He supposed he would have to describe her as quietly beautiful, and this only showed how flimsy language was. He found himself listening, waiting for her to say more.

But she only smiled, and said, "When Mr. Speke is late he can be very late indeed."

He was grateful for the coffee because it gave him something to do with the two clumsy hands he seemed to have at the ends of his arms.

"He's been looking forward to this for a long time," she said, and then Bell realized that there was something wrong.

Sarah pushed a button on the table beside her, and listened, as though the air itself were going to make an announcement. And there was just a fraction of a second when she was distracted by something like worry.

Bell was an experienced reporter, a man who had interviewed generals and had been allowed a private moment with the Pope himself, one windy afternoon in Monterey. He had an ability one editor called the "read between the lies" canniness, which he supposed cops and real estate salesmen also developed.

Sarah was stalling. He guessed she had buzzed Speke on the intercom when his car pulled under the gigantic oak in front of the house. Something was wrong. Perhaps the intercom hadn't worked, perhaps Speke had been in the midst of some dialogue—you got used to this in working with artists.

It was very nearly undetectable under her airline stewardess calm, her executive secretary smile, and her cool eye. But she was not pleased. She did not know why Speke was tardy for this important meeting. She covered up for him with a delightful description of the wine cellar "which you must see—even though the only light there is candlelight. Mr. Speke won't allow a flashlight. Violates the virgin air, he says."

"You've been with Mr. Speke since the beginning, some fifteen—"

"Fourteen years," she said.

"When does he do most of his work?" What he really wanted to know was: do you live here, too? What would you be doing if you were not masterminding the schedule of this busy man? And what is it that makes you smile so calmly? Such a smile could only mean there was something troubling her.

He also wanted to know: how do I look to you? He wasn't bad-looking, and while his athletic build and casual clothes made some subjects underestimate him, that was often exactly what he intended. He wore a tie today, and hand-sewn oxfords, but Sarah was not one to be fooled by a costume. She saw into him, and for some reason what she saw there made her stand, and apologize. "I really want to remind Mr. Speke."

She offered him a leather-bound notebook. "Mr. Speke treasures those—letters from George Bernard Shaw to everyone from Charlie Chaplin to John Dos Passos."

She left him alone, and he did not open the notebook with its embossed gold "GBS."

He leaned forward in his chair, listening.

He heard nothing. Or was it, in truth, complete silence? Perhaps he did hear something, after all.

·10·

At last Bell told himself that there was only silence. He heard nothing. With a house this size, on an estate this big, even the magnate's parting shot must have been muted. This was a living silence, an endless pause, a tireless presence as though the air were a sentient thing.

It was a surprise, then, when Hamilton Speke strode into the room.

He was a big man, broad-shouldered, with a smile Bell suspected he had practiced before a mirror for years, but which worked nonetheless. He was handsome in a shaggy way, a thinking man's woodsman or a surgeon turned trail guide. Bell's practiced eye took in the Levi's, the custom-made boots, the open-collared shirt which fit too well to be anything but tailored. The clothes were scuffed and rumpled, easy to wear and attractive. There was dust on the boots, and Speke gave the impression of having just been out hunting.

This was the man himself, and he did indeed have presence. In a world of disappointments, Speke looked larger than his photographs, and seemed complete, comfortable with himself and with life.

Only afterwards, after the handshake, and after they had both settled into chairs did Bell realize how cold Speke's hand had been to the touch. When was the last time he had touched such a cold hand, he found himself wondering.

After the first moments, the impression of health passed, and Speke looked uneasy. It was like watching an actor drift out of character. His stage presence began to ebb, like an old or distracted tragedian who has only enough energy to say his one line and then fade. A cub reporter would not have noticed. An untrained guest would have been swept along by Speke's heartiness.

But Bell saw.

Speke fought to control it, but the nostrils were dilating, the shoulders rising and falling. Even in the air conditioning he was beginning to sweat. Bell had seen this before, in liquor distributors and cigarette wholesalers called before grand juries to deny working with the Mafia. He was watching an experienced man of considerable aplomb under a great deal of pressure.

He ran through a mental list of possibilities. Marital troubles, he guessed. He had arrived during a bad day in a new marriage. He himself had never been married, although he had frequently come close. It was just this sort of warfare that made marriage seem a good way to destroy a friendship between a man and a woman. It was also possible that Speke was in pain. Back trouble, Bell thought, or an ulcer.

He didn't want to get the interview off to a bad start. There was no rush. If today were a bad day, he would be happy to spend it walking the deer paths. The first interview was always so important.

They had been trading pleasantries. Why was it people talked about the weather? If anything, it was the one subject most likely to remind one of terrors, earthquakes, skin cancer, the infinity beyond one's control.

"If this is a bad day for you," Bell said, interrupting the description of a favorite, five-hundred-year-old oak.

Speke gave a short laugh, like a bark. "Bad? What are you talking about? This is a great day."

Bell's curiosity blossomed into admiration. The man was in emotional or physical pain, and was undaunted. "That's fine. But I hate to hurry. I'm very low-pressure."

"Bell, I'm so glad you're here. So glad. I have been looking forward to this day for months. You've met Sarah? Christ, what a woman. She has a mind the Pentagon would adore. A dynamo. A general. She knows all the secrets, Bell." Speke laughed. "But she'll never tell," and another laugh, with twinkling eyes.

Bell laughed, too. But all the while he found himself thinking: maybe it's me.

Maybe all this forced heartiness is because of me. I am a disappointment. Speke was stalwart, full of life. His immediate use of Bell's last name, an affectation both Victorian and manly, made Bell feel overmatched. How could he possibly refer to Hamilton Speke as plain "Speke"? But "Mr. Speke" wouldn't do, either.

He felt inadequate. He had not expected this, and then he realized that all of his expectations, and the months of preparation, had worked him up to the point that the real man had to be intimidating. He was not easily cowed. Hadn't the Pope himself been, actually, simply another human being?

Speke would turn out to be the great man Bell had always expected him to be, but he would also prove to be yet another human being. True, anyone who could write an album like *First Cut* and a play like *Stripsearch* in the same lifetime had to be an astounding individual. But that was no reason to keep clearing your throat like a boy in the headmaster's office.

"I've had a long morning." Speke beamed and stretched, a man working hard to appear completely at peace. "Clearing trails."

"You like to be active," suggested Bell.

Speke hesitated just a beat longer than was necessary. "I clear brush."

No, it's not marital trouble. It must be physical pain, Bell thought. Speke hurts, and yet he is trying to make me feel at home. He murmured something about unpacking, but Speke interrupted him.

"I'm going to be completely truthful—I want you to know that."

"That's fine," said Bell, attempting to beam in return.

"Completely truthful."

Bell was smiling so delightedly he couldn't respond.

"You're going to know everything," said Speke. "Everything there is to know. I'll be as honest with you as I am with myself."

"That's wonderful," said Bell, sounding, he was afraid, a little strained. No subject had ever begun the research interviews with so much stressing of how honest he intended to be.

"There's something bothering me," Speke continued. "No use trying to keep things from someone like you." He gave the most winning smile, and added, "We're having visitors."

"Visitors?" Bell echoed.

"A film crew. I wish they weren't coming today."

"I see," said Bell. Loosen up, he told himself. Act like you've spoken English at least once before in your life.

"They're making a series for PBS. Right here, this afternoon. I hope this isn't too much of a disappointment."

"I thought from the very start that this might be a bad day—"

"This is a difficult day." He offered the famous Speke smile again. "One of those days you wish you could skip."

The man was doing everything to make him comfortable, and Bell felt himself shrink. He wanted to go for a long walk, and make a new entrance in a few hours, a new opening, fresh and at ease.

How was he going to interview someone who made him feel so inadequate?

And yet he wasn't the only one under tension. Speke himself was definitely preoccupied, but carrying on masterfully. Maybe he had been right the first time—maybe it was the wife. He looked forward to meeting this woman. She must be quite a virago to have someone of Speke's mettle so upset.

Because Speke was upset, that was clear. He was a man who had just had a fight of some sort, or who had just received horrendous news.

Speke sensed Bell's thoughts. "I'm in the middle," he said, leaning forward, "of something new. Just today. Right now. This very minute, up here." He indicated his temple with a forefinger.

"That's wonderful!" said Bell. You sound like a simpleton, he told himself.

Indeed, it was wonderful, and it also explained so much. Speke was in the middle of writing something new. He chopped madrone to work off his creative frustrations. It could be the new play, the one everyone was waiting for. It might be music. Bell looked away, chagrined that he had torn this great mind away from its work. Speke wasn't in the midst of discord or pain at all.

"So if I don't join you for lunch," he was saying, "you'll excuse me."

"Of course. Please forgive me. You're so kind to even come up and see me—"

"It's a good day, Bell," said Speke, standing. "We're going to be a great team."

"Of course," Bell began, but Speke, after another firm handshake, was gone.

The entire conversation, Bell mused, had been jumpy and strained. All smiles and strange cheer. And then to be left like this, alone in Speke's office . . .

I did something wrong, he told himself. I made the wrong impression. Speke's cheer was fake, and I did nothing to reassure him.

He tiptoed out into the hall, feeling like a thief. Then he had to smile at his own joke. He felt like exactly what he was—a journalist. A professional spy.

* * *

Bell met Maria at lunch. She was even more beautiful than her photographs, but she did not speak except to agree that deer hunters should be shot. She did not eat much of her quail.

This pale woman did not seem to be the sort of tornado that would drive Speke to distraction. So Speke's work must, indeed, be troubling him, Bell mused, although the injury theory could not be completely discounted.

Through the entire lunch, through every sip of chardonnay, and every swallow of espresso, Sarah kept glancing his way. She did not lower her gaze when he met her eye, but smiled as though they shared a conspiracy.

Speke isn't the only intriguing person here, Bell found himself thinking. I should write about this woman. What is going on inside her mind? Does she take lovers? What could she tell me about Hamilton Speke? For that matter, what could she tell me about herself?

It was hard to have a rigid approach to such situations. Sometimes a forthright, honest approach worked, sometimes it developed into little more than a line of awkward questions. Ignoring the evident tension was often a good idea, but sometimes people became more and more diffident, until at last an interviewer reached the point where he could never get to know the very people he sought to understand.

They must be used to dining with Speke. That was the only explanation—they missed his company. Bell tried to rally, and certainly his tales of movie stars and scandal were of moderate interest. Everyone was pleasant. Hideously pleasant.

The key, he guessed, was Sarah. He would take her aside and suggest that he not even move into the guest cottage. He could leave, and come back in a few days. He was living in Berkeley, close to the campus library, and wouldn't mind driving back across the Bay in a few days, or even a few weeks. Speke must be writing something very big. Bell was interrupting everything simply by stirring sugar into his Italian roast, a tourist among the Disciples.

The thought of Sarah kept him seated exactly where he was. He wanted the chance to speak with her again. He wanted her cool eyes on his. He had felt this way toward a woman before, but there was something uncommonly powerful about Sarah.

She knew things. She knew things about Speke, and about the world. And, he felt, she knew things about him without even asking. She was one of those people on whom nothing was lost.

While Bell had not felt so unsure of himself in years.

Speke's hand had been cold to the touch. And Bell remembered where he had felt such a cold hand before. As a teenager, he had attended a friend's funeral. An aneurism, a congenital defect, had killed the young tennis star, and with a teenager's bravado, but with a young man's curiosity and affection, Bell had touched the hand of the body in the coffin, and it had been cold, beyond cold, still and icy in its core.

Speke's hand had been that cold.

Sarah returned to her office. It was a small cubicle with a door to the outside, where, often, she tossed bread crumbs to the sparrows and to the ever bolder squirrels.

She took a box of saltines, and opened the door, making kissing sounds to the air. Five sparrows whirred onto the grass, even though it was afternoon and most of them must have been asleep moments before. They knew her, or at least they knew what mattered to them. She was food, and a gentle voice. She crumbled the crackers in her hand, and tossed the flakes like so much seed.

The lunch had been dreadful. Maria was always difficult to read, charming to men and distant toward women. The biographer, Bell, had eyes that saw too much. What had she expected? But having such an obviously perceptive man around made her suddenly aware, as a new visitor will, of the shortcomings of her situation.

Beneath the luxury, the antiques and the art, anyone with insight could see it at once. Granted, today had been especially uneasy. Maria had been withdrawn as always, and .Sarah herself aloof. This single day wasn't the only problem. There was always something wrong. Wrong with Maria, and long before she and Speke met, wrong with this house. It wasn't haunted. Of course not—what a silly thought. It was simply not a building full of life.

Could she allow herself to think one more, slightly unpleasant thought? There was something increasingly wrong with Speke, and today it was even worse.

She loved the man. They had never been "involved," but he was so vital, and boyish, and got so enthusiastic about things like a first edition *Tarzan of the Apes* or a new video game. But she had always wondered about him, from the first day she had begun typing the stained manuscript that had become *Stripsearch*. During the nights of drunken arguments that passed for parties, she had lived her simple life in her cottage, enjoying the existence of a woman abandoned by events, although she was younger than Speke. She was married to Speke's career. His success was hers. But she had always guessed that there were serpents in the garden. She had, simply, never wanted to give them a thought. An unseen serpent was, in a way, nonexistent.

She understood the limitations of Speke, and had adapted herself to Maria's presence in recent months. She knew what she could ask Speke to do, what telephone calls or letters he could respond to without exasperation, and she knew which matters she should handle herself.

But she knew more than this. She knew there was a secret in Speke's life, a professional secret, and while she had never formulated its exact nature in so many words, she understood that it had something to do with his old colleague, Timothy Asquith.

Yesterday on the telephone the strange, thin voice had told her that surely Ham would want to share a few memories. He had given her his name, and she had recognized it.

She had never seen Speke as nervous as he had been this morning, breaking, without knowing it, one of his brittle one-sided seventy-eights. And on his way back to the Outer Office just before lunch, Speke had given her one of his smiles and she could tell at a glance that something terrible had happened. He was gray, his eyes fixed, his breathing labored. And the way he tried to cover it all made it worse. Not that he was clumsy. She imagined that he was nearly successful in hiding his trauma, whatever its nature, from Christopher Bell.

Maria was pale, too, and yet she was able to carry off the lunch with a certain flourish, as though determined to prove herself to Sarah. She did not like to look Sarah's way, and often spoke to her without looking her in the eye. Jealousy, Sarah had always assumed. There was no reason to be jealous, of course. Sarah had no romantic interest in Speke. Her interest was much deeper than that, and built upon greater loyalty.

But for the first time Sarah realized that Maria was a woman impossible to know. Many women—perhaps most women—would find Speke attractive. Dear Ham, he had so much life. So Maria's affection for her husband made sense. Of course, he had money, too, but there was something further about Maria's interest in the man she had married that troubled Sarah.

Today, though, was a day apart from all the others. What had been a household of odd silences was now a household of unease. Something had happened in the Outer Office, and Maria was determined to brave the biographer's steady stare, just as Speke had been eager to avoid it.

Bell was going to figure it all out. He was going to overturn every secret on the estate, sooner or later. Sarah herself could deceive him. She was, she had to admit to herself, capable of anything. But Speke wasn't, and Maria—but Maria probably knew nothing.

But what was there to know? There was something peculiar about Speke's career. And Asquith, who had something to do with the early days of Speke's writing, was still here, still at Live Oak. Sarah had heard the motorcycle arrive, but she had not heard it leave.

The thought of having this strange man here made her cold. She did not know why. Perhaps he would stay in one of the guest cottages. Perhaps she wouldn't have to see him very often.

She found herself glad that Bell was here. Why was she afraid? Physically afraid. As though someone were about to hurt her.

A squirrel arrived at last, bright gold on his belly as he sat up and called to her in his speak-toy, yet authoritative way. She tossed a cracker in his direction, and he fell upon it, moving in jump-cut jerks.

She loved animals. Her mother had said that it was a waste of love to spend it on simple creatures, and not on human beings. Sarah was of another view. One loved what one could. This was another thing she and Speke had in common. He was a kind man, and donated thousands to groups that lobbied to protect wildlife. She handled the checks herself.

The smell of the air, the flavor of it, was delicious, wild thyme and that strange tang of creosote some of the trees exhaled. It was hard drought, though, and she was a person who loved the sound of rain, rolling across the roof of her cottage at night. A jay joined the group, and she laughed. Perhaps all the animals on the estate knew who she was. Sarah, the lady who threw food. Maybe they knew her better than anyone, and all her thoughts and memories were, in truth, completely unimportant.

The animals could not entirely cheer her, however. She dusted the last of the cracker crumbs from her hands, and made a final kiss toward the birds. She found herself thinking that she was helping Speke hide something, and had been all along. Very soon she would have to decide whether to protect him, or to uncover the truth.

She stared, the sparrows at her feet. Yet another jay joined them, but she hardly noticed.

She put a hand to her throat. She could see no one. And yet, as she glanced away, hadn't there been a shadow, with legs and arms, out there in the woods? She looked again, but it was one of those figures visible only when just looking away, like a sound you hear only when it ceases.

She was cold, her heart hammering.

Surely in a moment she would be able to laugh at herself. The cottages glowed in the half sun, half shade. This had always been such a sanctuary. It still was, the lichen-gray branches in the sunlight. It was dry lichen and the thready ghostlike moss, all aired to fossil-like fibers.

But the place had changed. She could not explain her sensation, and tried to dismiss the fear that kept her there, one hand on the door.

She could taste the sensation: she was being watched. She knew, at the same time, that the forest was not watching her, that no creature peered at her from that tangle of light and darkness. That shadow was the trunk of a tree she had seen many times before, not a shadow at all: a cleft red oak just beyond the buckbrush.

Sometimes, her father had told her, you can't believe even what you see. He had said this solemnly, even sadly, with a policeman's weariness with deception.

As a girl she had enjoyed lying on her bed, listening to the murmur of her parents' conversation, the plaster of the ceiling illuminated by the hall light. In the wedge of electric light above her she had seen faces, frowns and grimaces in the stiff swirls of plaster. She had considered this power long gone, this ability to see things that were not there.

Now she wanted to laugh at herself. She was a steady woman,

her father's daughter. Here she was, worried about absolutely nothing. Everything on heaven and earth would be well, she told herself. There was no need to worry. A phrase from the church services she had not attended for years came back to her, and she could not begin to guess why: world without end.

As it was and ever shall be. To the Son and to the Holy Ghost. These little fragments of liturgy reassured her. But surely she did not need to be reassured. The sun was bright, and rested upon her like a great, warm hand.

When she slipped back into her office she was careful not to look back at the forest.

·11·

I t was hot, and dust rose up around him.
Speke's lungs filled with this dust. His eyes burned with it.
Each hack, each plunge, each scoop with the shovel was a
loud rupture of earth. The sun was an evil star, a white hole
pouring light so urgent it had weight, and fell with something like
a sound on the rocks, and on his shoulders as he dug.

He reassured himself. No one would be able to see him digging.
His work here was secret. The trees were thick here, but he could
not reassure himself completely. The shovel made an iron grunt
each time it stabbed the earth. They would certainly be able to
hear that.

What if Mr. Brothers decided to show up on that ridiculous
little green tractor he drove around the estate, and got to thinking: I can't let Mr. Speke dig a hole all by himself? Or, that damn
fool Speke is trying to plant a tree up by the Outer Office, or
whatever damn fool pretentious name he calls the place, and everyone with a brain knows that's the rockiest soil in the county.

It amused him in a bitter way to recall that he had long been
fascinated by the outcroppings of this place. He lanced the shovel
blade into the earth and the clank reverberated up the handle. He
coughed. This was dirty work, grime all over his pants, soil all
over his arms, sweat turning it to mud, and he coughed and
gasped, sun and earth battling him. The soil here was a jumble of
mudstone and tuff-breccias, shot through with roots.

At last he had a hole, a raw crater, roughly the right size. Whatever you do, he reminded himself, *don't think.* Don't even pause
for a second to consider what you've done. Put it all out of your
mind.

Maria panted up the slope, and whispered, "They're here!"

"They" meant Scamp. Television. The eyes of the world. Fine.
Wonderful. Let's get a candid shot of Hamilton Speke burying a
long rolled-up rug with something heavy in it, something that
gurgles and bends in the middle just like a dead body.

Speke dragged the rolled up rug, and it bent, and you could see the top of Asquith's head if you looked down the tube, but he tried not to look. He gasped, and gritted his teeth. Asquith was surprisingly heavy.

You're thinking—stop it.

The body fell into the grave—because that was, after all, what it was, a grave. However, it fit very badly. Speke had miscalculated. The hole was not all that big after all.

Mean little flies, mean little flies that bit, buzzed around his face.

He wrestled the rug and its contents. The rug had tassles that were not going to fit into the cavity, although the body—he hated to think about it that way—bent nicely if he stomped on it a little.

What was he doing? This was a sacred thing, a deceased human being, and he was cramming it into a burrow like a gigantic turd. He was trembling.

God forgive me.

He chopped with the shovel, and at last he had something the body could lie down in, because death was supposed have some dignity to it. It was like a nice, dignified sleep, or it ought to be if you weren't being buried by Hamilton Speke, the Clown Murderer of Live Oak.

Self-control, he told himself. He absolutely was not going to vomit. No matter what, it would be an exercise of will. He would not allow himself to regurgitate anything from inside his body.

Think, he ordered himself, of something pleasant.

Shoveling soil over the body was very difficult. Flat, handsome stones seemed more loving, sprinkled over the carpet. With some larger rocks over those. And then some dirt, and then some more rocks because Speke had buried some poor dead birds and a cat once, and a skunk or something always dug them up. Nothing would dig up Asquith, he promised himself.

A trickle of sweat burned his eyes. This was taking a hundred years. Scamp would be cursing and pacing up and down, and planning increasingly ugly shots, ones that made Speke look jowly, as revenge for being forced to wait.

"I'll finish it," said Maria, suddenly at his side again.

"I'm almost done," gasped Speke, stepping on a large stone to force it into place.

"You don't have time," she hissed. "Be quick."

This was a strong woman, he realized. He did not really know her well at all, he realized for the thousandth time. What a mys-

tery she consistently turned out to be. He loved her more than
ever, seeing how devoted, and how sure, she was.

It hadn't taken so long, after all. The blood was all cleaned up.
Everything was back to normal. Speke took a moment, however,
to be sure. No blood on the mantelpiece. The bronze Athena gazing out with her wise, blank eyes. The floor was bare where the
tongue-and-groove oak had been exposed by the departure of the
rug, but the rug was doing honorable duty. It was the equivalent
of an expensive coffin.

Speke himself was doing fine. Just great. Except for the racing
beat of his pulse, but that would pass. Something glittered in the
bushes, something metallic and large, like a great insect.

The motorcycle! He had forgotten all about the Kawasaki. It
was glittering there in the shade like a veritable skeleton. An exoskeleton, death's steed—but he didn't have time to bury it now.

Someone will see it. There was the helmet, staring in his direction, a phantom, decapitated head watching him from the seat of
the motorcycle.

Panting heavily, Speke trotted up the slope to meet the film
crew, gathered around a van and smoking cigarettes.

Scamp was in the shade chatting with Sarah. He gave a shout,
and ran toward Speke, arms outstretched. They looked, ridicu-
lously, like burly lovers meeting after decades. Scamp gave Speke
one of his rib-cracking hugs, and then backed away.

"Mr. Dirt. Hey, get a shot of the man of words all covered with
ranch." He pinched Speke's cheek and shook the flesh there, a
gesture Speke particularly detested. "Out planting beans and oats
and green peas. We can get a shot of you digging a canyon."

A minicam was thrust at Speke's face. "This isn't such a good
day," Speke began.

"It's a beautiful day!"

"If you could come back in a couple of days. Maybe next
week—"

"Tomorrow I'm in Milan. My street cabaret film is getting an
award. It's a great honor." Scamp shrugged. He was a big man,
bigger than Speke, and older, with graying hair and a mustache,
and an accent that was a jerry-rigged assortment of German, Italian, and Brooklynese. Speke thought he sounded like a combina-
tion of a Heidelberg scholar and Bugs Bunny. "So if I can't shoot

you today you won't be in the special." Another shrug, and then a wink.

"Maybe a couple of weeks . . ." Speke began.

Scamp pinched his cheek. "And you want to be in the special, Ham. People are begging to be in it and we say—no, to be in this special you have to be as great as Hamilton Speke."

Speke felt his fists bunch, and planted his feet. Then he realized that the camera was getting all of this, every word, every scowl.

"A man of the soil," called Scamp. "We can get you digging up big rocks—"

Scamp caught sight of Bell, sauntering, hands in his pockets. "The biographer and his subject discussing life. Having a conference on death. Jesus, don't just stand there everybody. Confer. Come on, this is journalism, for Christ sake."

"I was digging," said Speke, weakly, half-hoping no one would hear him. "Digging up a stump."

"A stump!"

He mouthed the lie again, looked away, blinking, wondering what fresh hell was next.

Directions were shouted, bellowed. Cigarettes were squashed into gravel. A hand swabbed his face, and Scamp bawled, "Leave him alone—I want him dirty. Roll in dirt some more."

Speke remembered being a simple, quiet human, long ago, in another life.

"Give us some stump, Ham. Take us to the stump!"

He spun, the world blank and empty. "I don't want to dig up a stump! I'm tired and I am hot. Would you please just give me a second to compose myself please."

Sarah put a hand on Scamp's shoulder. "Would you like some iced tea?"

Speke closed his eyes and thanked God for this cool woman.

Everyone wanted iced tea, naturally. Speke felt them all courteously ignoring him, and at the same time listening to each breath he took.

Fortunately, he knew of a stump. He knew it well. It was a behemoth stump he had attacked a few weeks before. Mr. Brothers had muttered something about dynamite, but Speke had insisted that the stump stay where it was as a challenge. He had promised himself that some day he would rip that dragon out of the ground.

Now he was going to do it on national television. When Maria appeared, he sent her back down the slope for the shovel. He was going to dig up a massif that had been commanding the estate for centuries. I, Hamilton Speke, before all of you, will with these two hands battle the world's mightest taproot.

There was a moment in which he doubted the wisdom of all of this. But it was the perfect cover-up, wasn't it? It explained why he was dirty. Bell would see the stump as metaphor for a sinuous writer's block. Scamp would be delighted to see earth fly. And he himself would not have to stand there and endure Sarah's quiet, questioning gaze.

Because Sarah was thinking. She was seeing through him, and trying to make sense of what he was doing. Such women are dangerous, he thought. Dangerous, and at the same, enticing.

He had never gotten to know Sarah as well as he should have. They had both worked to keep their relationship painstakingly professional. She had been loyal and steady, the lighthouse of his professional life. What was happening to him? He found himself thinking something very strange indeed. He found himself, for no reason, thinking that he loved Sarah.

Her eyes were on him even now. Those intelligent eyes, those eyes that saw and remembered. She'll know, he told himself. Those beautiful eyes can't be deceived.

"The stump!" he cried, lifting the shovel as would lift a rifle, and leading the tiny army down the slope to the west, past the garage, toward the stump. Sarah would realize that this was not the place where he had been digging all morning, off and on. She was thinking that even now, Speke guessed, as he brandished the shovel like a gun, like a battle-ax, like the first, ugliest weapon in the world.

·12·

That night Speke experienced the worst nightmare he had ever had.

He dreamed he had killed someone, another man, a person he knew well, and buried his body near a house where he lived.

Like most dreamscapes, this setting was hard to place but very intimate, and the man he killed was both familiar and hard to remember. Even the means of death was obscure—perhaps he had strangled the man, perhaps he had pushed the man from a height. It was hard to tell.

What was very vivid, extremely clear, however, was the sense of terrible dread. The dream was splashed with reds and yellows, and pulsed with despair. This was true, the dream said. All true.

He woke gasping, sweating and staring upward into the dark. His fingers clawed the sheets on either side of his body, and he struggled to shake the sleep from his mind. The dream would not let him go. It clung to him, until at last he sat up.

What a terrible dream, he thought. Thank God I'm awake.

It was always such a relief to crawl ashore from a dream like that.

And then he remembered.

He was icy. This time, to wake from a nightmare was no escape.

Maria slumbered beside him. He had the oddest feeling that she had not been there beside him all the while, that at some point in the night she had left the bed. But she was there now, her breathing even and slow.

He struggled into his bathrobe, and lurched through the darkened house, hating every wall that loomed, and every black doorway.

He was falling—that was how it felt. Plummeting downward, as fast as a body could fall, even though he knew he was standing upright on the solid floor, one hand out to touch the wall.

This was panic, the panic attacks he had experienced before he began therapy years ago. He hurried into his office. He hungered for the familiar, the feel of standing somewhere he knew well, somewhere he was used to commanding. His telephone. His notebooks. His computer beside his desk.

The crystal decanter was heavy in his sweating hands. The scotch splashed as he poured it, and he coughed at the first swallow. It brought tears to his eyes. He drank again, a long, stiff belt, and fell back into his chair.

He would have wept, but this was a feeling beyond grief.

A sin. He had committed a sin. He had done something unforgivable.

He blinked tears. I'll never have a normal life again, he told himself. I'll never be able to eat, or sleep, or just walk along looking at hills and trees. I'll never be able to do anything because every second *I'll know.*

And there is nothing I can do. It's done. It's permanent, forever, the most lasting thing I've done on earth.

There was no hope of controlling himself now. He shuddered, and climbed around his desk to grip the decanter again and drink directly from the crystal, pouring the scotch down his throat, a rivulet streaming down his chin.

What made it worse was the needling doubt he now felt toward his writing. He had always known that many of his ideas had been rooted in his friendship with Asquith. But now he was beginning to wonder. Maybe it *was* Asquith's—every moment. Surely that wasn't true, he tried to reassure himself.

But he couldn't be sure—not now.

Maybe, he thought, Asquith was right. Maybe I was stealing his life all along, and the last, great theft of the Mexico play was a crime too great to tolerate.

My work, he told himself, is abandoning me, and there is nothing I can do to call it back.

It was hard to tell what attracted his attention to the darkness outside. Perhaps there was a vague movement, or perhaps he simply knew, in his bones, that there was something out there. He turned, straining to see, his mouth agape, sure that he was staring at nothing but the blank darkness.

That's all there was—just the dark, beyond the windows behind his desk. The friendly dark, where the oaks and the lawn that he loved so much were thriving in the dew. He couldn't see them, because the world could only be remembered now, not seen. But everything was out there, just as it should be. There was no threat there, surely. There was his own reflection, a hulking figure clinging to a crystal decanter.

And nothing more.

Then he saw it.

Something drifted out there. It was less than a vision, little more than a thought. A vague presence, a smudge, began to coalesce before his eyes. A gray shape began to focus into a figure.

The figure was a cloud, a column of smoke. The smoke figure stepped slowly, very carefully, as though unsure of its own existence, its own power, into the light.

The stare was what froze Speke. Froze everything in him. Every gland, every follicle was crystal.

The man outside was staring at Speke. Staring into Speke's eyes.

He must have screamed. He must have dropped the decanter. He must have leaped to the far wall and continued to cry out, because when Maria was at his side, calling to him, he was hard against the wall and glass and scotch were all over the floor.

She put her hand over his mouth, and her hand was strong. "It's all right, Ham. Please be still—it's all right."

"It was him!"

"You'll wake everyone. They'll be able to hear you. Calm down, Ham. It's all right."

"It was him. Looking right at me. Maria, listen to me. He was standing right out there in the dark."

III

FLASH

·13·

Sarah was up early, brushing her hair.

She had always loved morning. A day could become almost anything. Why not believe that it might be sweet, and promising? She had not slept well, and it had seemed that horses, gigantic, airy mounts, had galloped over the roof of her cottage all night, although when she peered out through the curtain she saw no evidence of storm, or even wind.

Her sleep had been stirred, too, by knowing that not far away, beyond the lichen-splashed boulders, Christopher Bell was sleeping. The end of her present life was very near. She knew too much, although she had tried to pretend to herself for so long.

Bell's presence touched her. It was like a long stroke on a violin, a sound that grazed the mind as well as the flesh.

For some reason, feeling foolishly worried, she had crept to his cottage last night, and made sure that it was safely locked. Then she had locked herself into her own cottage. She never did that. She was not afraid, usually.

But in the night, hurrying on her self-appointed errand, she had felt herself running hard. There was something about Live Oak now that was menacing, as though the oaks had all crept inward toward the house just a few steps and now waited.

Now she shielded her eyes against the bright dawn, amused at her foolishness. She had always loved this place. The great oaks were not simply trees. They were branched monuments, and some mornings there were deer the color of the hills at sunset, red gold figures like dream deer that were so unafraid they watched her, as she approached, before vanishing into the underbrush.

Before moving to this estate, she and Ham had worked out of an office in San Francisco, like an attorney and his legal secretary. This place had meant complete peace for her, and yet she wondered if it had been a good thing for Ham.

The antics with the stump had been painfully embarrassing. She had tried to stop them as soon as she could. Ham, though, had a reputation as an unpredictable denizen of the hills, an intellectual, heroic figure, and so his public would take it all in stride.

Sarah was not so sure. The look in his eye had disturbed her. The frenzied slashing with the shovel had not been an act. He had been out of control, on the edge of some sort of neurological collapse.

She found herself in her small office, glancing into the hand mirror she kept in her desk drawer. It had an ebony frame and was, for her, a rare extravagance. She was stroking her hair and thinking of Ham in a way she had never allowed herself to think before. She had sensed such feelings in the past, and always turned away from them. She turned away from them now, just as briskly as she whisked the mirror into the drawer. This certainly was a peculiar morning. She rarely paid so much attention to how she looked. But she could not hide the truth: Ham was more than a career, more than the artist she managed.

She did not allow herself to consider what he really meant to her.

In the kitchen, Clara was sliding a tin of muffins into the stove. She was a quiet, dark woman in a white uniform, and Sarah always understood that she, too, saw much and was deceived by little. She lived in one of the most remote cottages, beyond Maria's studio.

"Have you seen Ham?"

"No, I haven't seen him," said Clara. But the way she said it made Sarah straighten from the coffee she was pouring.

"But you know where he is."

"I think he's up, going for a walk." Clara was one of those rare soft-spoken people who are as kind as they seem. Some made the mistake of ignoring her, but Sarah knew that she saw and heard all that mattered.

Good. A quiet walk was what Ham needed. "He's been under so much pressure," said Sarah.

"I think he still is."

This struck Sarah with the force of bad news on television, a bulletin that had to be believed. Clara was right about things like this. Why had she expected this new day to bring a new, more peaceful Hamilton?

The animals were waiting for her usual morning gift. The squirrels bounded across the lawn, and then paused to watch her, and to watch the bread spin through the air. At moments like these Sarah knew that human beings were not sole masters of the earth, that the triumph was well-shared by other creatures.

She did something she knew was unwise. She knew that she should go into her office and deal with Ham's correspondence. Musicians sent him jiffy bags of tapes which had to be returned with polite thanks. He received dozens of letters a day, and scripts from aspiring playwrights and screenwriters, and he answered all of them—or she did.

But as she stood, sprinkling the last of the crumbs, she decided to do something that made her uneasy.

She went looking for him.

Don't follow him, she warned herself. Stay where you are, feeding the sparrows.

The sun was hot and yet the chill of the air carried her through the light, into the shade of the woods. Insects hummed, and juncos flashed through the mesquite. Bay trees in the creek bed filled the air with their sweet scent.

She wanted to know only one thing, and then she would be at peace. She needed to be assured that Asquith was gone.

That man, that enigma from Ham's early days, had some power over him. He was trouble, and he did not belong here. She could not help feeling a deeper, more baritone sensation: that enigma was also dangerous.

This was a foolish thought. There was no real reason to believe this. But why was she so careful not to make a sound, stepping over what fragments of last-years acorns the jays and squirrels had left behind?

Be very careful, she told herself. Don't be afraid, but make no mistakes. Ham was upset for a reason, and she wanted to know what it was.

The Outer Office was a bright white bungalow through the trees. The sunlight broke into rays through the branches of a buckeye. Standing there in the morning calm she was convinced that she was mistaken. There was no motorcycle anywhere to be seen. At some point in the afternoon, or even the evening, Asquith must have departed.

Her fingertips tingled with relief. She did not sense a foreign presence. Everything was as it should be.

But then she knew that it was not. A leaf crackled. A branch lifted, and there was no wind. There was another sound in the woods nearby. Birds scattered from where someone was standing close by her and there was the non-sound of someone standing very still, holding his breath.

Speke had insisted on staying in the office, helping Maria to pluck the crystal from the floor. He had always thought such a decanter would have a certain amount of strength, but he knew that it was the high-whine in his ears, the keen of blood through his brain that had smashed the crystal, not the fall.

As soon as it was barely light, the first blue of dawn that made everything bruise-colored, grass, trees and sky, he climbed into clothes and looked, he hoped, like a man about to go for a morning walk.

"Be careful," Maria had said, and her tone stayed with him long afterward. He was convinced of it now: she had left him during the night, in the hours before the nightmare.

He stole from the house, and did not breathe easily until he reached the trees. But then he stopped. He did not want to take another step.

So he delayed, trailing upward along the path that held to the mouse hole, where he deposited the only gift he had this morning, the remains of a bag of Corn Nuts.

The morning was new, the day perfect. The lightest dew had touched every leaf, the huckleberry and the hazelnut, the sword fern in the clefts where there was always, even in the summer, the kiss of moisture.

But all of this was sealed off from him now, like the twigs and lichen of a diorama, enclosed behind glass and apart from the life he was now living. He was delaying, and wasting time, because he was not going on a simple morning walk. He was on a mission to discover whether or not Asquith's grave had been disturbed.

He told himself that dead people did not arise to walk again. Perhaps there was an existence after death, perhaps not. He was not sure what he believed. But the apparition he had seen last night was either an amazingly vivid hallucination, or an actual, living human being.

Asquith must not be dead. Proof would be a grave that was empty, with signs that an unconscious man had stirred, awakened, and fought himself from the earth.

He wanted Asquith to be alive. But the thought of a living, furious Asquith somewhere in the dry creeks and bay trees made him afraid.

Doctors had warned him that his insides would kill him if he didn't start to calm down. You must change your life, everyone had said, every specialist, every smiling professional.

Onward I go, into this glorious morning. The brave Hamilton Speke, forging ahead through the trees to find an old and trusted friend.

It didn't work. Humor was futile. He evaded his duty, and followed a deer path along an outcropping of basalt, to one of his favorite places, the place where the Indians had lived.

Go back. You are a coward.

He had played war with friends as a boy, and they had taken turns gunning each other down. He had prided himself on his ability to sprawl realistically, even to the point of lying with his eyes open, a bit of drool spilling from his mouth. Friends had invariably been impressed.

Go back, Hamilton. You are afraid of what you're going to see.

The Ohlones had ground their acorns here. The mortar holes were in the rocks, darkened with black moss. He often came here to be close to something ancient and sane. The Indians had ground the acorns from these very trees into a flour so acrid it had to be leached with hot water. And yet, the land had supported them. An entire culture, a nation of faiths and songs, had lived here, and now it was gone.

He was stalling again. He must be more afraid than he wanted to admit to himself. He hurried back, nearly running. No, he was not a coward. Not now. The old Ham would be queasy, but not the new, Killer Ham. He could do anything.

He stood still. This was the place. It was unmistakable. He stood, with his arms slack and strengthless, the blood draining from his brain, making the scene before him go gray.

The grave was undisturbed. The flat stones he had pressed into place were still there. The rocks around the site would have betrayed no footprints in any event, but he was standing and looking at a resting place which was entirely peaceful. There was no sign that so much as a skunk had come foraging.

The stone had not rolled away from the tomb. Lazarus had not stirred. Wasn't resurrection, after all, much like something vile, something one never wished to see?

Whatever appeared before me, thought Speke, it was not real. It was not Asquith.

He felt himself smile. It was not a pleasant feeling to know that you were either going mad or being visited by what would have to be a vengeful spirit.

How heavy the motorcycle was, unpowered by its motor. And big—it was a weighty hulk, the skeleton of an iron and alien race. The helmet dangled from a handlebar as Speke rolled the machine over the leaves. The wheels rolled almost silently, but with a hint of resistance. This thing did not want to move.

He balanced it at the edge of a dry ravine, a creek bed tangled with fern and poison oak. The wheels would not turn. The front wheel locked, and when he gave the machine an extra push it merely turned aside, teetering, staying where it was. Then, finally, it sank forward, rolling, twisting. There was a rush of sound, tumbling dirt, snapping stems. The motorcycle vanished into the ferns.

He took a deep breath. He had been erratic yesterday, and today he was weary, stiff, and emotionally drained. In recent years he had suffered panic attacks, an ulcer, and migraines—all the physical by-products of resounding success. But for all of his present stress, and past frailties, he never considered himself a likely candidate for a straitjacket.

He returned to the grave. If anything, in the past he had been all too sane, and had required the occasional case of Glenlivet to give him any release at all. A nervous wreck, yes. A psychotic, no.

This would have been, in normal times, reassuring. But he was confronted with the possibility that he was going to be pursued by something unthinkable.

Good news, Ham. You aren't having hallucinations. The bad news is—your house is haunted.

I'll ask Maria what to do. Thank God for her help.

The memory was torture: the memory of that dawn in Cozumel, the sun bursting above the sea, the ground, chalk white, alive with tiny frogs. That had been the morning, the single moment, when their friendship changed. Twisted. Died. He kept remembering the frogs, each creature too tiny to be real. Had they been real? Maybe it had been yet another hallucination.

Those were the days of the Black Cat, the days he had been unable to work into a play, the days Asquith had claimed as his own.

His breath caught. There was the whisper of a step, and the bright snap of a leaf. He crouched beside the grave, and listened. Somehow he had never expected ghosts to walk the earth during daylight, but life was proving to be full of surprises.

If only his legs weren't trembling so badly.

There was the sound of another step, a small foot, he judged, kicking a pebble aside.

He crept into the brush, careful to avoid the green-scarlet leaves of the poison oak. This was no ghost, he told himself. This was a living, warm-blooded human. He could see the shrug of a mesquite as she passed, because he sensed that this was a woman, and he sensed more than that as he gathered himself to confront her.

Who did she think she was, sneaking around like this? He had trusted her too long, with too much of his life. He was going to put a stop to that. But he needed her, he knew, and admired her. He would simply explain to her.

But when he fell through the brush there was no one there. A figure vanished up the trail, and he took a breath to call after her.

But then he stopped. Perhaps it had been someone else. Perhaps it had been someone—or something—quite different. Jesus, why was he trembling so?

For the first time ever he knew that the forest was not a friendly place. He felt it watching him, all the little eyes in the shrubs, the beaked, shrill little lives, the small, rodent lives burrowed underfoot, the entire mass of peering lives around him that knew him and did not hold any love for him at all.

"Sarah!" he called.

She had seen the grave. She had seen him standing there looking at it, and she knew what it was.

·14·

The sun dimmed. Brothers was burning the bougainvillea. The veined, magenta blossoms withered in the golden flames, and the air was dark with the taste of water which had, until minutes ago, been the stuff of life.

When the fire had burned long enough, Speke played the hose, spattering the flames. The smoke leaped at once to white steam, and Brothers turned over the ashes with the rake.

I will have to rely on Maria, Speke thought. I will have to do as she says.

What impressed him more than anything was his ability to forget, for several minutes at a time, what was happening. He had powers of concentration which were virtually a form of self-hypnosis.

He could stand in the morning sunlight, chatting with Mr. Brothers about the buck-to-doe ratio, and it was as though no one had ever died, anywhere in the world.

Perhaps he had inherited this ability. His father had been able to ignore everything, too. "One of the drawbacks of the mental life," his father had said, wiping his hands with a rag, "is that you have to ignore your surroundings. Sometimes, even the people in the surroundings. You have to ignore what they say, maybe even what they feel, and do your work."

An inventor, his father could stand in the garage at his workbench while the soldering iron set a rag smoldering and, slowly, began a fire. The fire department had visited Gerald Speke's garage three times, each time concluding a visit with a demonstration of how to use a fire extinguisher. The big men in black waterproof coats had always been both cheerful and condescending. The firemen had considered Gerald Speke a brilliant eccentric, and, in the clumsy file system of stereotypes so many people use, they expected him to be dangerously impractical.

Gerald Speke raised two sons after his wife died of kidney failure. She was gone before she could make much of an impression on the memory of either boy. Art, the older brother, would withhold what vague memories he retained until Ham had performed some chore—taking out the trash or making Art's bed—after which Art would say: "She was tall." Or, "She had black hair." Their father, both sons knew, mourned too deeply to discuss her, or even have her photograph on display.

Gerald Speke died, caught in a downdraft while flying his Piper Cub over Mt. San Gorgonio, when Ham had already left home for San Francisco and a series of failed attempts at college, and Art had matured into the shrewdly unhappy man he remained. The inventor left some money, thanks to a series of improvements on adjustable razors he had sold to Gillette, and a chemical system for cleaning contact lenses, which was now obsolete but had made good money while it lasted. Ham was able to live on his share of the inheritance, often in grand style, if you counted the unstinting quality of the liquor consumed, and Art had perfected his education. Speke still got a quarterly check from his father's trust, administered by a bank in Santa Monica. Even without the platinum albums and the plays, he would still have been able to live comfortably.

But Speke had wanted more than comfort. He had ached to *do* something with his life, something big, something a boy from a dull, suburban past could take pride in. He had wanted a Name. His father would have recognized the need. One gnawing sorrow in his life was that he could not show his father around Live Oak. His father would have loved the place, Speke told himself, and he would have been proud of his younger son. He had not lived to see Hamilton Speke's name on a marquee, or in *TV Guide*.

"I think we probably have a ratio of, oh, twenty bucks to a hundred does." Mr. Brothers had a wrinkled, tanned face, and a laconic manner which allowed comments about sports, weather and wildlife, but precluded anything beyond that. "That's about a Coastal Range norm, I'd think."

This was Brothers' usual phrasing, not offering what he actually thought, but what he *would* think if he were really forced to express an opinion.

Perhaps he'd found a father substitute in Brothers, Speke thought. Their relationship carried little emotional weight, but he did enjoy their sunlit conversations. Brothers uncoiled a long, green hose and allowed himself some comments on the deer population in general. "Right now they're going to be showing wear and tear. Acorn fall's about eaten up."

Then, in the midst of a simple, masculine chat, the period of distraction passed and Speke was icy again.

It's real. It happened. This day, this solid world and its peacefulness, is an illusion.

And this man, this wrinkled gardener, was a threat, just as every other human being was. Brothers' mind was not limited to strict categories, only his conversation. The estate was several miles wide, but much of it was virtually impassable oak wilderness. Brothers could figure out that there was a disturbance in the soil of the estate that hadn't been there last week.

"A few years before you came there was a little trouble with a deer hunter," Brothers was saying. "Heard his gun off to the south. One slug made it all the way to the front drive and died."

The thought ate at Speke all the way into the house. A deer hunter's bullet could reach into their lives, even in this refuge.

Maria was drying her hair. She looked paler and younger than ever, and he did not know whether to reassure her or take heart from her apparent calm.

"I think," he said, sitting on the bed, "people are going to be able to figure out what happened."

"How?" She stopped working her hair with the terry cloth, and turned to look at him. "What's different?"

"The hole." He corrected himself. "The grave. And I think I should bury the motorcycle."

"No one can see it. I took a peek."

He absorbed this thought of Maria checking up on his handiwork.

"They won't even notice them," she said, "especially if we keep away from them."

Sarah saw them, thought Speke.

Maria touched his cheek. "Don't worry, Ham. It's all over. You'll never have any trouble at all. Try to relax."

He took reassurance from her touch. But he saw how like so many other women Maria was—so many women he had, at one time or another, loved. He had always been quick to become passionate over a certain type of woman, an artistic, mysterious sort of woman who had always, in the past, seemed to melt away, dwindling to yet another human being once the mysteries evaporated.

"I know," she said, "exactly what I am doing." There was, though, something strained in the way she said this. She was opaque, impossible to read. He had never been able to coax her into talking about herself, about her past. "I only want the future, and you," she would say. His wife was a lyrical enigma. He would never understand her at all, he thought, anymore than he would understand gravity, or the electron.

Before he could stop himself, he said, "It won't work."

She took him in with a glance, and dismissed his words with a sharp exhalation through her nostrils. It was this soft derision that made him so suddenly cold. She had sounded, for an instant, like Asquith.

"You don't have any faith at all," she was saying.

"Of course I have faith," he began to protest.

"In me," she said.

He could say nothing.

"If the world discovers what you have done," she said, her voice soft, as though she were reciting a gentle verse, "I won't be able to survive it."

He reached out and took her hand. He said, after much hesitation, "I think Sarah knows something." Strangely, the person who inspired his greatest faith was Sarah, and Sarah was now a threat.

Maria folded her towel. "I wouldn't worry about Sarah," she said, in a hard voice he had never heard her use before. "I can handle Sarah."

His father had immersed himself in work. Work, his father had not had to explain, was a cure for grief. So, Speke promised himself, I'll work hard.

He would work hard on his biography. Even so, he did not want to talk to Sarah. She might ask an awkward question, or, even worse, he might offer an awkward lie. He asked for his morning muffins to be served in the office, and he looked over the subjects he had planned to discuss with the biographer.

He studied his list of favorite movies. There were so many movies he loved, and wanted to see again and again, that the list had flowed onto four pages. Surely the biographer would find this fascinating. Then there was the list of favorite musicians. He kept adding John Lee Hooker, and then scratching him off.

The intercom made a barely audible tick when it was about to speak. It made that small sound now, but then there was a long silence.

A long silence that made Speke's collar tighten at his throat. Was Sarah eavesdropping on him?

"It's someone from the police department," said the intercom in Sarah's coolest voice.

That was terrific. Just wonderful. So much for Maria's reassurance. So much for those random periods of calm. He gripped the edge of the desk. Sarah had called them, a voice within him hissed. This was her doing.

Still, he told himself, there is no need to disintegrate. Stay cool. He pressed his finger to the last remaining crumb of blueberry muffin, and licked his fingertip. He brushed his hands, and pushed the plate across the desk. The room still smelled of scotch, although the scent of sage was gradually breathing into the room through the open windows.

Sarah was waiting for his response. I am perfectly cool, he told himself. Licking crumbs off my fingers.

But he couldn't talk. Act normal, he thought. Clear your throat, shift in your chair, and ask if he had an appointment.

"Ham? Are you listening?" said the intercom.

He could dash out the windows and flee the office, make it to the garage, have the Jaguar through the gate and up the highway before Sarah and the cop ever realized he was gone. That was a bad plan, though. And he couldn't leave a cop alone on the estate. He might poke around. He knew how they did it. They poked sticks into the ground, and sniffed the dirt end.

"Ham?"

"I'm fine, Sarah. I was just in the middle of a thought. This muffin is really delicious. Did he, by any chance, say what this was about?"

The intercom went dead. She was back in a moment with, "He says he really needs to see you." Her tone said: he is listening to every word.

The news was getting better and better. Fine. This was it. How did he want to play this? Jimmy Cagney? Humphrey Bogart? A shootout was not quite the way to end his career, although Bell could make it sound romantic, somehow. It would be the second-to-the-last chapter of the bio. "Speke's Last Stand." He didn't have a gun though. He hated guns.

This was the end. Maybe Sarah hadn't called them. Perhaps there had been a note left behind by Asquith. Something like: if I don't come back by midnight call the police. Because here it was only the next day, and they were already sending men with Police Specials out into the woods.

He drew himself up, and spread his legs like a man awaiting combat with sword and buckler.

Don't make it easy for them, he thought. Make them drag you out of here.

·15·

The cop was gray-haired but youthful, one of those dapper small men whose company Speke had always enjoyed. The man sported a bright red silk tie and black Italian loafers. He could have been an assistant movie producer, except he had one brown tooth.

Speke read the business card, and ran his finger over the words, feeling suddenly dyslexic: Franklin Holub. Detective, Police, City of San Francisco.

He took a deep breath he hoped Holub would not notice. Okay, he thought. It's missing the word "Homicide." So don't panic. Did you think you'd never hear from anyone about this? An investigation was inevitable. Stay calm. Don't smile too much.

Things were happening quickly. It had been less than twenty-four hours since Asquith—since the accident. Even romance can be quick. He had met Maria at a gallery. It hadn't been entirely accidental. He had responded to a telephone solicitation to see a series of watercolors dedicated to Hamilton Speke by Maria Merriam, the artist who was all the rage. So he had naturally, out of vanity and curiosity, wandered by Sutter Street after a drink at the Redwood Room and a week later they were married. It had been fast. Fast, and very lucky. Maybe this would be lucky, too.

Of course, he told himself. Everything's going to be fine. But the man had steady, dark eyes. He sat down as though he owned the chair, and slipped a yellow lined tablet from an imitation leather folder.

"You're quite a way out of your normal territory," said Speke. He had nearly said "jurisdiction," but that word smacked of judges and gavels—of prison.

"It's a nice morning for a drive." It was worse, in a way, this attempt at pleasantry. The man did resemble a gentle execcutioner, the kind that used a needle.

"I think we usually call the San Mateo county sheriff if we have a burglar."

Of course, Speke reminded himself, there had never been a burglar here at Live Oak. There had never been any trouble at all.

"I saw you on the Academy Awards," said Holub.

"Thank you."

"Too bad you didn't make it."

That's true, thought Speke. Too bad. He said nothing, but gave one of his—he hoped—manly smiles, the kind that always worked.

"I'm here to ask you some questions about Timothy Asquith."

Hope, that fragile creature, fell dead. Speke coughed.

Holub kept talking. He would be quick, and not take any more of Speke's time than he had to, he said while he got his pen in hand. "You don't mind too much, I hope."

Speke stared, twitched, and opened his mouth. "I love talking about Timothy Asquith."

"You know him." It was not a question.

The English language slithered away, and could not be commanded by any effort. "Sure. A brilliant guy."

"Have you seen him recently?"

A tremor passed through Speke's body. "It's been years. Many years. Why? What's the matter? There's nothing wrong with him, I hope. I hate to even ask. I mean, I'm sitting here talking to a— you're a detective."

"That's right."

Holub was trim, with muscular arms beneath his French-fit shirt. Speke decided to be bold. "I'm working on a book right now. My biography. Not an autobiography—an official life." Speke was impressed with his own smoothness. "It's a pretty major undertaking."

Holub made a note with his pen. What was he writing down? "Not an autobiography?" Speke was going to have a heart attack, or a duodenal hemorrhage, or simply explode in about three seconds. He struggled to keep still.

"What I'm trying to say is," Speke continued, "I want to help. But I'm under a tight schedule."

"We think Asquith has been living in San Francisco for the last few months." Holub toyed with the pen, a black ballpoint, and gazed at Speke in a way that made him feel very cold.

He cleared his throat. "I didn't know that. I thought he lived in the East somewhere. Well, actually, I more or less assumed he was either dead or hospitalized."

"Dead?"

Keep talking, Speke commanded himself. "He was into drugs. Heavily. I don't ever expect to see him again." It was true, and, even better, it sounded true.

Something switched off in Holub, some current of skepticism. Maybe it was Speke's handsome, famous grin. Maybe it was the apparent truthfulness in his voice.

"Asquith got himself into some legal trouble. Your name turned up."

This was not as informative as it sounded. He echoed, "Legal trouble?" Speke savored the phrase and found it wanting. "I haven't seen him for fifteen years."

"He has a history of mental illness, although he struck a lot of the people we talk to as reasonably sane."

People? He knew actual people? The old Asquith had loathed conversation. He had cherished music, and the heroic wherever he had found it, but actual people had disturbed him.

Besides, Holub was telling him nothing. "Why are you here?" Blunt, but Speke wanted to get this over with, one way or another, as soon as possible.

"We're in the process of finding this man. People on the East Coast have some questions for him."

Questions. Another useless word. "You don't look for someone just because you have questions."

"That would depend on the nature of the questions involved."

This cop was as smart as he looked. Speke could be coy, too. "What's he done?"

"He's been in and out of psychiatric hospitals. Discharged once, escaped once, caught and readmitted."

Even a euphemism packs power. "Caught and readmitted." It sounded desperate, anguished. "He was dangerous?"

"They aren't sure."

"We used to know each other. I do get my share of crank letters —all kinds of people have songs they want to sell me, or . . . other ideas." He stopped himself before he added, plays, tunes, titles, whole works of art that could make a lot of money.

"Of course." The pen made a note. "But Asquith vanished from custody—excuse me, from the hospital—two years ago. He was considered criminally insane, but a low priority. No one looks for insane people any more. There are too many of them. But recently he began becoming a subtle kind of nuisance."

Speke opened his hands to say: tell me more.

"He began frightening people. He appeared in the living room of the owner of the Mason Theater, seemingly lucid as hell, but promising that he was going to prove that he was the author of . . . one of your early plays, the one they made the movie of with . . . the one about the man who killed his wife and tried to—"

"Kingdom of Daylight."

"He phoned television stations, newspapers. The same story. He wrote the songs, the plays—and he would prove it in a few days. We put the stories together, and bent a rule or two and looked into his apartment when we finally found out where he was living. He was living a comfortable life. Supported by some means we haven't figured out yet. And his place, a pretty nice one-bedroom in Pacific Heights, was a shrine to you. Your picture, reviews, articles, all over the walls."

Speke said nothing, his face, he was virtually certain, a perfect mask. He silently chided himself for being so out of touch that he had heard nothing of Asquith's recent activities.

Holub ended the silence. "The man has vanished. No one has seen him. We think his intent is criminal."

Speke did not blink. He waited.

"I was hoping, to be honest with you, that he'd called you up, or paid you a visit, and threatened you. A big name like yours would be more than enough for us to have a strong case. You can't go around threatening people. Some people think we should send him to Napa State, or Atascadero. Personally, I think a few months of exposure would do him good."

"Exposure?"

"Prison."

Talk, Speke commanded himself. And you better sound good. "But the poor guy is obviously a mental pancake. He doesn't belong in prison. Asquith was a man who had compassion for people." Speke's voice began to rise. "You can't treat a man of his sensitivity like a thug."

"Theater owners, reporters, ordinary citizens—even famous ones. They deserve to be protected, too."

"I can't see this as a threat."

"You deserve to be protected, Mr. Speke."

"He's not a criminal. Asquith had a fine mind." Speke's lapse into past tense silenced him for a moment.

Holub did not seem to notice. "You remember him well."

Speke's voice was hoarse when he said, "He was a good friend."

"Maybe you can help us understand him."

Speke considered this statement. "He had many talents. He was an actor, did a little stage magic, wrote some songs."

How much do I owe him, he asked himself. How much of my life belongs to Timothy Asquith?

"Do you realize," he said, unable to stop himself from speaking, "how few remarkable people there are—how few people are really alive?"

Perhaps Holub felt just a bit awkward for a moment. There was a pause, and then he said, "If he should call you, or drop by for a visit—"

"I'm not afraid of him."

"I didn't want to mention this, because I didn't want to make you nervous."

"I'm not a nervous sort of person."

"We have reason to believe he has more than a casual interest in you. He's not another fan and not just an old acquaintance. We think it's pretty obvious that he has some sort of fixation on you, if you really want to know. He's not just another crank."

The cop's turn of phrase was coarse, Speke thought. Holub was quick but, at the same time, ordinary. "We were friends—" He silenced himself. "We knew each other well," he added at last.

"I'm still not telling you everything. I hesitate to mention this."

Speke wanted to pick the little man up and hurl him through the window. Instead he crossed his legs and tried to look polite but very slightly bored.

"The questions we have for him."

"Tell me!" Speke wanted to scream.

"He's wanted for murder."

Speke knew that he was expected to respond, but he could only croak, "What?"

"Cut some people up in the East. Pretty badly. Real badly. Women. Always women. So what we have is a criminally insane homicide with a fixation on Hamilton Speke."

Speke stared.

Asquith, he thought. It couldn't be true. You were never really dangerous. Not to anyone else. Only to yourself. He said, quietly, "You have to feel sorry for him."

It couldn't possibly be true, he told himself again.

Could it?

"Maybe a little compassion is in order. I wouldn't know." Holub slipped his pen into the folder, but continued to watch Speke as though trying to understand him. "I'd get some security. Someone around the clock. Famous people are sitting ducks. A man like that is unpredictable. He might show up here and be a whole lot of trouble. We aren't sure. But I have a feeling, personally, that he'll show up here eventually, and that he might be dangerous."

"I'm not worried."

"I got a fax last night from Elmira, New York. He wasn't your average mental patient. Maybe I'll leave you a copy."

"I feel sorry for him," said Speke, his voice dry, shaken.

He took the manila envelope, but did not look inside. "I've never worried about that kind of thing in my life. And Asquith is the last person I'm going to worry about now."

"It's just a personal opinion, not professional. But I think this man wants to destroy you." There was an edge to Holub's voice now, an urgency that had been missing. People often adopted an artificial ease when they met Speke for the first time, wanting to make a good impression on such a well-known man.

"That's a little strong, isn't it. 'Destroy'?"

"A lot of people want to talk with this man." Holub's eyes were hard. He was trying to communicate without stepping out of his cop manner, his detective diction. "He isn't wanted for traffic tickets." He flicked a hand at the envelope. "Go ahead. Take a look at that fax."

Speke smiled, and felt the beginnings of genuine warmth toward the cop. After all, he was trying to be helpful. "Of course I will. And I really appreciate your visit."

"Be very cautious, Mr. Speke. This is a very sick man."

·16·

Christopher Bell did not believe. No god nudged the helm of his craft, and no gray-eyed goddess overshadowed his battles. His life had been a tangle of lucky breaks, accidents he had just blundered upon as a cub reporter, shrapnel that tinkled at his feet, but he did not feel he owed any special thanks to fortune. He was always punching numbers into a telephone, or hurrying across the tarmac to catch a plane.

He paced his cottage. The air conditioning exhaled neutral, cool air, and the television was on with the sound off, CNN jerking one image after another, dead bodies, heads of state, multicolored maps, yet more bodies, sodden images littering a foreign street.

I won't leave, he promised himself. There's a story here, and I'll find out what it is.

Breakfast had been a peculiar affair, muesli and moist delicious muffins and excellent coffee. Everyone was avoiding each other. Sarah had apparently breakfasted before he arrived, and Maria did not make an appearance, so he had glanced through the baseball scores, and stalled a while, hoping Speke would eventually arrive. Nothing had happened.

A beige Chevrolet had sat beside the front lawn for nearly an hour, and Bell had seen enough such cars to be able to guess that this was an unmarked police vehicle. Perhaps Speke was consulting the police about his security, or lack of it. Perhaps an old friend was an inspector and he and Speke sat around swapping crime stories.

Everyone on the estate was encapsulated within their own privacy. He had seen such behavior in the more pleasant wings of Vacaville, the prison for psychiatric maintenance and evaluation, in which placid killers and baby rapers worked crossword puzzles and read paperback westerns waiting for their medication.

Everyone here is hiding something.

Bell considered himself methodical. He tried to hide this character strength from casual acquaintances. He wanted people to think him casual and spontaneous. But he was deliberate and careful, and knew how to avoid mistakes. As a boy, he had always finished his homework as soon as he got home, before watching cartoons on television, before playing outside. He had always done any possible extra credit assignment, the plaster of Paris volcano, the collection of shells, the scrapbook of clippings about UFOs. If they studied South America in class, he raided the travel agents in town for pamphlets about Rio. He had worked hard and had developed, he thought, a certain ability.

He had learned to glean information. He was, at heart, a worker, an ant, a bee. Something told him that this would be a bad time to bother Sarah. He should wait for her to make the first move or he would alienate her. For the moment, he wanted to stay well away from Maria.

That left Clara, the silent, small woman who seemed to run the house, and a leathery gardener who passed among the trees carrying at one moment a rake, and at another a long, twisted branch as Bell watched through the window.

He sat at his laptop computer and typed up a few notes. "Must talk to Sarah. She knows everything." After a few paragraphs, he deleted everything but the words "She knows."

He wished, more than anything, that he could see her now.

There was a tap at the door, a tap so plainly feminine that Bell was speechless when he opened the door and gazed down at the wrinkled, smiling face of the gardener. "I hate to bother you, Mr. Bell. I just wanted to warn you. There's going to be an explosion."

Bell was hard to disturb. He had seen gas mains and gasoline trucks blow up, and had once seen an entire bomb squad blasted to red bits in Mexico City.

But something about the silence of this place, and his own impatience, made the gardener's words especially unsettling. The words took on an uneasy, unliteral connotation, a prophecy of emotional havoc. Or, even worse, the announcement of a nuclear detonation that would evaporate them all.

"An explosion?" Bell asked.

"Nothing to worry about. I'm going to blow up the stump with a little bit of dynamite."

Bell was so relieved he could not respond.

Brothers had the careful gentleness of a man used to a certain degree of violence, like a kindly infantry colonel. "I'm going around warning everyone. So it won't be a shock."

"This is such a quiet place," said Bell.

"Most people like that," Brothers responded, detecting his subtle complaint.

"It's very peaceful," Bell said, but his chance to win a confidant was slipping away.

He sat at his computer waiting for a stick of high explosive to go off, and his fingers would not move.

He jumped, unable to identify the source of the sudden, electronic trilling at his elbow.

His hand fell on the telephone.

It was Speke, sounding jovial and relaxed. "Why don't you come on up and we can get started?"

It was this imperial tone, the easy confidence, that made Bell realize how deeply he envied Speke. It was stronger than envy— Speke had everything, and Bell could not deceive himself. He was a man who relied on wits and energy, while Speke relied on something more lasting, something endowed by nature. He was a man the Greeks would have considered beloved of one god or another, a man carved of light.

And what am I, Bell found himself wondering. I am a man who likes his name on a by-line. I am a man with something to prove, women to win, debts and a string of former friends, people I no longer have time to see.

The unmarked car was gone. That was how things were at Live Oak. Things did not simply come and go. They appeared. They vanished.

Bell hurried toward the big house.

He's going to ask me to leave, he thought. He's going to try to get rid of me somehow, and I'm not going anywhere.

The sky was empty, flat blue. But Bell did not find himself able to step confidently. There was, he reminded himself, going to be an explosion.

"Where do you like to start?" asked Speke. "First memories? I would think that asking someone to describe his first memory would be a very good place to start, don't you?"

He wore a green silk shirt, and looked both slightly tired and unusually handsome, rough-hewn and cheerful. He presented

Bell with a dish of chocolate chip cookies. The cookies were still warm.

There was a smell of scotch in the air, and Speke did not want to sit in his usual desk chair, but lounged in the chair Sarah had used the day before.

"I have the sense," Bell began, "that my presence here makes people just a little bit uncomfortable."

Strangely, he found himself sitting behind the desk. Feeling out of place, an employee behind the boss's desk while the boss looked on, Bell switched on his tape recorder.

"Maria is moody," Speke said.

"You do want to continue working on the biography?"

There was the slightest of pauses, a tick of psychological time in which it was plain that Speke would not be unhappy if Bell had an appointment tomorrow in, say, Washington. "I want to help you," said Speke.

He believes that if I leave this assignment I will return to gambling and drugs. Bell felt the itch of guilt regarding this falsehood. Speke was a good man. "This book is very important to me," he said.

"My Life," Speke said with a wistful smile, and Bell did not know whether he was referring to the biography, or something much broader and more troubling.

He could change his mind at any moment, Bell saw. He could say, abruptly, that he was very sorry but Bell would have to come back next month, or next year.

"My own first memory," he said, "was watching my father mow the lawn."

"Was it a push mower or power mower?" asked Speke.

"Push. He kept it sharp with a file."

"Really? He filed his own blades?" Speke put a finger to his lips. "A careful man."

Bell did not say: just like his son.

"I love the smell of grass when it's just cut," Speke was saying. "Brothers has a ride-on mower, and the smell gets mixed up with gasoline exhaust. The lawn here is just so big. . . ."

"It's a beautiful lawn."

"He's going to blow up the stump," said Speke.

Bell said that he had been warned.

"I wish he had just gone ahead and blown it up. I don't know about you, but my stomach's very unsettled. I sit here waiting for an explosion."

Bell admitted that he, too was nervous.

"I just had a visit from the police."

"I thought so."

"Another sharp-eyed person," said Speke.

"Nothing serious, I hope."

"What could be serious, out here in such a wonderful place? Tell me: did he say how long it would be before the detonation?"

"Not really."

"Not even a hint?"

Bell smiled, shrugged.

"I wish he hadn't told everyone. I'm sitting here, waiting for this horrible blast. This could go on all day. I can't sit still."

Bell found himself fidgeting, too.

"I'm a wreck. I can't even concentrate on what I did this morning, much less the first thing I ever saw in my life."

They both listened in silence.

At last Speke burst out, "I can't think. I'm hopeless." He drummed his fingers on the arm of his chair.

"It looks like you have a blister on your hand," said Bell. "From your bout with the stump."

Speke closed his fists. "I'm not nearly as stiff as I thought I'd be, after my exertions."

Bell warned himself: keep the questions coming. At any moment Speke could decide that the interview was over, that all interviews were over indefinitely. "Do you find yourself reading other playwrights?"

A quick change of subject was often rewarding. But Speke merely attempted to smile, and said, "Of course. There is so much talent out in the world. I hate people who only read dead playwrights." Something stopped him. Perhaps it was the anticipation of Brothers' dynamite, making both of them stare toward the window.

"Things keep going wrong around here." Speke lowered his voice, as though confessing. "Little things. There was a videotape I was going to watch. It's been sitting on the television for days. Suddenly, I can't find it."

Bell caught himself about to say, "Someone moved it." No need to sound flippant, he warned himself.

"I keep turning over things in my mind. The stump, I mean. I keep thinking about the taproot. I think I probably made a fool of myself."

"It was very entertaining."

"You think I'm asking you to reassure me, but please don't. Please. Let's be honest. Christ, I don't want to sit in here. I feel as though the ceiling is lowering itself down on me."

Bell began to reassure him, when Speke said, "Don't most people—most successful people—have security guards these days?"

There was something boyish about Speke's need to know, about his need to hear advice, that touched Bell. "Maybe," he suggested, "we should go outside."

When they were in the sunlight, Speke forged ahead, as though stump fragments could rain down any moment.

"I'm not usually so nervous," he said, pausing so Bell could catch up with him. "Not usually. I used to be an emotional mess, of course."

Bell had noticed how people use the phrase "of course" as a way of diffusing information that was usually not a matter of "course" at all. "I know the feeling," he offered.

"Ha! You don't know the kind of shape I was in." Speke said this nearly with pride. "I was a wreck." He spun and seemed about to grab Bell. "Do you know what I want to know? I want to know is Brothers a malicious man of criminal intent, or what? Telling everybody an explosion's coming. 'Hey, I'm going to blow up a big thing.' And then—nothing. I'd like to wring his neck."

Speke put both hands to his mouth and bellowed, "Brothers—blow it up!"

They both listened, but there was no answer, and no sound but the birds.

"What sort of man is Brothers?" asked Bell.

"I can't stand this," Speke said, spinning again to confront him. "Can you stand this?"

Bell began to say something like: it is a little unnerving.

"I think I'm going to lose my mind." Speke said this very slowly. Then, suddenly, "He killed a man. Brothers. In Korea."

They entered what looked like a larger version of one of the guest cottages. Inside was some weight lifting equipment, an old-fashioned barbell and a wall-length mirror above a gray wrestling mat.

"I bet you think I'm still a wreck." Speke unlooped a jumprope from a hook. His feet were quick. He was plainly in decent shape, and the rope was a white blur. He was also, Bell thought, as close to some sort of emotional collapse as anyone he could recall.

"So you don't think," said Speke at last, panting heavily, letting the rope fall. "So you don't think I'm a complete ruin of a man. But I feel like one. You want to know how theatrical I felt when I knew you were coming? I didn't know how to act. That was the problem—I didn't know which version of me you would like most. Hearty Speke. Philosophical Speke. Speke the athlete."

He tossed what looked like two large, red plastic teddy bears tied together. Bell caught them.

"Speke as tough guy. Put them on."

This wasn't exactly Bell's usual interviewing technique, but he had done a story on Olympic boxing, and had gone a few rounds with a bronze medal light heavyweight without feeling too clumsy. "I boxed a little in college," he said. "Middleweight. I'm more light heavy, now."

Speke stiffened. "What was that?"

"I didn't hear anything."

"No explosion?"

Bell shook his head apologetically.

Speke said, "Let's box."

He was apparently one of those men who simply *had* to be doing something, every single moment. Bell was wary of such men. He did not want to trade jabs with this big, lively, nervous genius. He hated the sound of his own voice. "I will if you want to, but I'm really not that interested."

"You feel sorry for me. You think I have to act like something— that I can't just be myself."

"I certainly don't feel sorry for you."

"You think you'll beat me up."

"It just seems silly." Bell shocked himself, confronting Hamilton Speke so bluntly. "I've boxed enough to realize I don't like jabbing people in the nose, and I don't like being hit."

"You're afraid of pain?"

"I'm rarely afraid of anything."

Speke jabbed at the air. His hands were quick, and he was light on his feet, too, as he boxed the image of himself in the mirror.

He turned toward Bell and snapped a fast jab, nowhere near his jaw, a half humorous non-punch.

But Bell had the very clear insight, as certain as a punch itself: Speke would knock me out cold with no trouble at all.

A thump.

Not a big noise at all. A thud, metallic, softened by earth, with no resonance. A flat, deep sound that both of them turned over and over again in their minds. The silence that followed it was thick and dull, as though sound no longer traveled through the air.

Was that it? Bell wondered.

They didn't move. Speke's head was cocked, and he looked like a sparring partner stunned by an uppercut in the very recent past. He met Bell's eyes.

He whispered: "That was it."

Bell found himself breathing again. He had been, without knowing it, holding his breath.

"That," Speke whispered, "that stupid little pop was it."

They laughed. As soon as one stopped, the other started up again, and they both laughed all the harder.

It was wonderful to laugh so hard, and afterward they strolled back through the heat, to the office. Speke vanished, to reappear unscrewing the cap from a bottle of scotch.

Bell's pocket tape recorder had run all the way to the end, and he turned it over. He didn't know—maybe somewhere between waiting for the explosion and staggering with laughter there would be a phrase, a quote that illuminated Speke's soul.

Speke savored his first sip. "The best thing ever invented."

Bell sipped. Scotch was not his drink, but this was an important moment. They were getting somewhere.

"Some day, before we finish the book, maybe we can go a few rounds?"

"Sure."

"I'd like that. I sure as hell can't box with Mr. Brothers."

Bell felt a surge of compassion. Speke was lonely. He had no real friends. He needed a playmate, someone to wrestle, to race, to climb trees and go swimming with.

He was more like a boy than a man, it seemed just then.

And then he said something that shook Bell, in a low voice. "You don't think a place can be haunted, do you, Bell?"

Bell couldn't answer.

"By a ghost, I mean."

"No."

"You aren't superstitious at all, are you?"

"I don't waste my time." The statement, Bell realized, was more self-revealing than he had intended, and Speke seemed to acknowledge this with a steady gaze.

You are not, Bell thought, going to escape me, Speke. You can dance and move, but I'm going to find out what sort of man you are.

Speke was thoughtful. "I don't, either. I absolutely do not believe in ghosts." He stared as though Bell had disagreed with him and added, "I just don't believe in them. And yet, this place. This house, this land . . ."

Neither of them spoke for a moment. Then Speke added, "Maybe we don't know anything at all, Bell. Maybe the few things we do think we know are completely wrong."

And maybe we wax philosophical, Bell thought, when there are subjects we would rather avoid.

He learned several things that day. He learned that "Speke" was not pronounced "speak," as most people did, but to rhyme with "spake," as in "thus spake." Half the people Bell knew pronounced Speke's name incorrectly.

He learned that Speke was not the high-strung, uneasy man he sometimes appeared. At the same time, he was not the hearty self-assured individual he so plainly wanted to be. He was complicated, shot through with contradictions. Bell found comfort in this. He, too, had a hidden nature.

Soft splinters of wood were everywhere, and at the heart of a great broadcast of black and red shards of tree was a crater, an inverted cone of space. Dark, wood-rich earth was flung in all directions, a nova of wreckage.

Speke put his hands to his face. "No!" he breathed.

He crept to the edge of the blasted humus. He gazed, as though unable to believe what he saw. Then he shook himself, and attempted to laugh. "I knew it would be gone, Bell, but—to see it gone like this, so suddenly . . ."

Bell was about to say something about the power of dynamite.

After all, what had the man expected? But when he was about to speak he decided to say nothing.

There were tears in Speke's eyes. "I didn't realize," he said, "that I would feel this way."

·17·

The stars were so crowded they seemed to make a sound, and even a smell, a dry, sterile whiff. Bell sat on the porch of his cottage, feet on the front steps, playing back today's interview.

There was one ability people had that impressed him almost more than any other, the ability to tell by looking at a fragment of a person, a figure dashing around a corner, the torn scrap of a snapshot, the identity of the person observed. We know who we have seen, and at the same time we know which people are strangers. Even sheep can recognize their companions from slides flashed on a screen.

So, Bell reasoned, I should be well on my way to understanding Hamilton Speke. And yet—I'm not. He sat listening. On one side of the tape, Speke worried about the explosion that had not yet occurred. "I'm hopeless." He did not respond to Bell's comment about his blister. "I hate people who only read dead playwrights," his voice said.

With a little hard work—what one of his editors had called "old-fashioned hammer and tongs application"—Bell believed that he could understand anything. Give him an hour with a dossier, a half hour with a court transcript, and he would know the man he was after.

Speke baffled him. But there was something else, something he was ashamed to admit to himself.

Speke was, in a subtle way, a way impossible to define, frightening.

He heard her first, before he saw her, and he did not for a moment mistake her for Maria. She stepped through the wet grass carefully, as though creeping her way across a narrow walkway over an abyss. She was so exactly the vision Bell needed that he could not speak.

Her eyes were cool in the porch light, and as before seemed to see into him, and to understand him better than he understood himself. She studied him, and yet did not approach any farther, as though there were a circle of magic surrounding his cottage.

"I think we should talk," Sarah said at last.

She joined him on the steps, and when she spoke, her words and the sound of her voice cured something in him.

He was not surprised. He had known from the very beginning that she knew the answers. But it was more than that. Where Speke had been fragmented, Sarah was coherent. Her peace challenged him. Speke had been unable to tell the story of his life as anything but disconnected, lively anecdote. Sarah sat next to him on the cottage steps, and told Bell that she had sacrificed her life to this man and his career.

She summarized her life so succinctly that it was nearly an act of violence. "I did not pursue anything but the publication of these plays, and these musicals, because I believed in them. And while I traveled a little, and had the occasional lover, the work of Hamilton Speke was everything to me."

Why was it, Bell wondered, that she seemed to be speaking of a time long past?

"There's an owl that flies over the cottage sometimes," said Sarah after a silence Bell was reluctant to break. "He makes a wonderful sound, like a manuscript falling through the dark."

How austere her life had become, Bell thought, how many years she had spent on the campaign of building up the reputation of Hamilton Speke.

"He's not what you expected," she said after a long silence.

"I don't know what I expected, really."

"You're disappointed."

"No, I can honestly say I'm not disappointed. Although it's weird how often the word 'honest' seems to crop up the last couple of days. I'm confused."

"Life is all confusion. That's dumb. I don't mean to be philosophical. But, Christopher." She stopped. It was the first time she had used his first name, and she seemed to want to test it carefully.

She did not speak for a long time, and Bell supposed that she was about to suggest that he leave and come back in a few weeks, or, perhaps, give up on the book altogether.

The bitter voice in him, the voice of insight, whispered: everyone wants to get rid of you.

When she spoke again, she said, "You know, I hope, how you can believe in someone even when you see their shortcomings."

Bell was surprised. He had expected to eventually discuss the bad side effects of genius, the stories he already knew and cared little about. Drinking, temper, wild nights, chasing nubiles through the woods. That sort of detail fleshed out the portrait of a human being. But he had expected Sarah to be reluctant to share such tales, and yet here she was, hinting at something she could hardly bring herself to discuss.

He did not want to push her. Perhaps she was testing him, to see if he would make a capable ally. Perhaps she was probing him, to see how overeager he might become.

"The police were here this morning," she said.

"I know." Go slow, he cautioned himself. He listened to the night sounds: wind, and the passing overhead of a pair of wings. "Do you know why?"

"I'm not sure."

"But you can guess?"

"I don't like guessing."

Sarah loved the hush of night here at Live Oak. She was thankful for his silence. She was about to make a decision that would change her life.

"My father was a cop," she said. "A detective. He worked on counterfeiters. It amounted to endless stakeouts, and my mother and I were alone constantly, and yet thinking of my father. Even his absence had a weight." Was it fair to use this man who was, after all, such a recent friend, as a confessor?

She continued, having gone so far. "It became a life of being two places at once. Where I really was, sitting while my mother sewed, helping with the ironing, while my soul, and my mother's, were really out there somewhere with my father."

She sensed him listening, and felt that his silence encouraged her, tugged her forward. "I grew accustomed to being alone, working by myself, taking care of my own life. I was too proud to settle for the life of a cop's daughter. Even a smart cop, which he was. A smart, gentle, kind man. He was killed in a bar." Even after all these years, this was a hard statement. "He went in looking for a suspect. His partner staked out the back, out by the dumpster. They expected the suspect to bolt and run out the back. Instead he hit my father with an ax handle." Again, the words were too hard.

Bell put his hand over hers.

She made herself continue. "He was hit once, in the side of the head. His pension saw me through college, but wasn't enough to get me into graduate school. I wanted to make something of myself, and I did. An English major can teach or take up computer programming. I ran a typing service. Stop me if I bore you. I sound tough, but I'm not. I'm tired of having a story to tell, and nobody to listen. Not much of a story, but it's my life. Boring, right?"

"It's fascinating."

"But you have to say that, don't you? It's your fault. You must bring it out in people, like a priest or a psychiatrist."

"And he brought you manuscripts to type, and you typed them, and a career began for both of you."

"He wouldn't like this, you know—the two of us talking. The old Ham wouldn't mind. But the Hamilton Speke of the last day or two would find it very unsettling." She gazed up at the stars, and then continued. "But I am, really, a cop's daughter. He used to show me counterfeit bills that he'd confiscated, packets that were going to be used as evidence. 'Look at this misery,' he'd say. 'Look at this misery and deceit.' Have you ever seen a counterfeit bill?"

"Not to my knowledge."

"There is something eerie about counterfeit currency. It looks just fine, usually, when you first glance at it. But then you look again, and there is always something wrong. The color is off, or the lines on Franklin's face are thick, and it's spooky. This isn't real, you think. This isn't the real thing at all. And you have a chill inside."

A creature somewhere in the dark made a sound, a cry of warning or even pleasure. She continued, "Ham doesn't make sense to you, does he?"

"Not really."

She did not speak for a while. "In a few years they'll probably make a TV movie about Ham and me. But the truth is a little flat. We were never lovers. I knew right away he was a big talent. I had tears in my eyes as I typed *Stripsearch*. It was even better, really, before he revised it. The work was the product of someone who knew the truth about people. Maybe knew them too well to function as a normal person. Anyone with insights like that would have to do something violent, or self-destructive, from time to time. Life itself might be a crisis to someone who felt things so deeply."

"Speke—Ham—doesn't strike me as self-destructive. He has a temper, I imagine."

"It used to be worse." She gave a short, soft laugh. "It used to be terrible."

"But something is left unsaid here."

"What's unsaid is this: it would have been better if you had never come here. But you're here now. It's too late. The process has begun."

"I can leave. No, I mean it. I can delay the book indefinitely—"

She touched his lips with her fingers. To silence, but also to tell him something.

When she spoke again, there was a timbre in her voice she had never heard before. "Ham is a man like no one else you will ever meet. Something happened very recently. Something very bad."

"And you aren't sure what it is?"

"I used to think this was a place of refuge, a haven, an enchanted forest."

"I think it is."

"You have faith in yourself. I didn't know if I could trust you," she said softly. "I still don't know. But I've reached a point in my life when I don't know anything anymore. I don't know if you're a kind man, or a weak one, or what you believe in, or what you hate. I'm going to take a risk. It's time."

He touched her face in the light that rose, strangely, from the hills of the estate, and fell from the stars, and seemed to play in the air about them.

Inside, in the special silence of the cottage, his hands were steady, and gentle and knowing as he undressed her, as though they had both known each other for a long time, for centuries, since light first fell. What are clothes, she thought, but clumsy pictures of human beings, maps of our lives, that we snap and button around our lives, our true selves, living beings hiding within fictions?

* * *

They both slept, but it was not like a sleep she had ever experienced before. She felt a third presence in the room, someone she had always known, a friend.

Survivors of shipwrecks, bobbing alone in lifeboats, are sometimes convinced that there is someone with them, and after they are rescued call out that their companion, too, be taken aboard. She had heard that lovers sometimes sense a third presence in the room, but she had never had this experience before.

Bell was awake, too. She reached for his hand, and his hand met hers in the darkness.

"I have so much to tell you," she said.

·18·

Even as he dreamed that he was killing someone he knew the truth. This time it was not merely a nightmare. It was the truth. It was the knowledge, beating in him like a new, ugly heart, a diseased, pumping organ. The truth pulsed through his body, his blood turning to cold iron.

He had killed.

Maria was asleep beside him. Her breath rose and fell, evenly, slowly. She was strong, and untroubled by what they had done. "They." Speke gave a dry laugh, a silent croak. What he, Hamilton Speke, Lord of Live Oak, favorite of audiences around the world, had done by his own hand.

But strength did not communicate itself to him. Her faith did not help him now. She slept.

What sort of person is this woman? he asked himself. How can she go on so calmly? She seemed to have resigned herself to reality completely, like a well-adjusted prisoner, a woman who thoroughly understood the limitations she faced.

He climbed out of the bed. He needed a pill, but something had happened to all the sleeping pills in the house. They were all gone, completely. He had been certain of a few old valium, so ancient they were damp-crumbled, but this afternoon he had fumbled through every medicine cabinet in the house, and found only Alka Seltzer and antihistamines.

Sleep was nothing more than a habit. He would learn to do without it. The bathrobe captured him, confining him, and when at last he fought into it, something ripped. Forget it, he told himself. Put on clothes.

Before coming to bed he had read the fax in the manila envelope left by Holub. It had been, to his relief, nothing remarkable. Grisly, but not remarkable, especially if you did not believe what you read. The fax was a mistyped hodgepodge, a report evidently from a detective's files, of a series of murders. Speke didn't like reading about violence, so he had scanned it, hastily. Mutilation, blood. This was the sort of subject he hated. It was awful the terrible things that could happen. Wounds so many centimeters deep, sharp instruments. He didn't like gore, and besides, he did not believe Asquith could do anything like that. Some murderer chopped up a few very unfortunate women over a period of several years. One woman had been killed by a slender instrument thrust through the top of her skull. That was ghastly, and terrible to even think about. It had nothing to do with Asquith, Speke was convinced, and he had not finished reading every page.

When he had tugged on a shirt and a pair of pants, he made his way from the bedroom. He was going to forget all about medical advice. This was a time for scotch. Scotch and television. The two stalwarts of his life, his two favorite drugs. They would see him through the night.

The piranha was asleep, its ax-blade body drifting easily in the huge tank. The tank made a pleasant gurgle, one that in any other time Speke would have found soothing.

He waited outside his office, listening. This was the only room of the house he felt was truly his, and yet it was in this room that he had seen Asquith's stare. He fled the office, and switched on a lamp in the television room.

He stopped, unable to trust his eyes.

The tape had, in fact, vanished. He had been very frustrated. But here it was, back again, right where it was supposed to be. He had to pick it up to be certain that his new tape was back again, shake it, read the label in the very poor light. It was Kurosawa's *Seven Samurai,* a movie he had seen in a revival house in San Francisco years before. In fact, he had seen it with Asquith, who had slipped a half pint of tequila into his Fanta, swallowed a couple of big red Seconals, and had fallen asleep hours before the band of marauding brigands choked on their last sword.

The tape had vanished. But now it was back exactly where it had been for days, waiting for him to watch it. That used to charm him—the effervescence of this place. Now it seemed shifty, unsettled. He had been looking forward to seeing the tape for quite a while, but hadn't had the opportunity. Not, he told himself, with all the annoying little distractions of his life recently. The movie was sitting on the television, waiting as though it had been there all the while—invisible, perhaps.

He had ordered the tape just a few weeks ago, but now that afternoon on the phone to the distributor in North Hollywood seemed like a distant epoch, a moment in the Devonian when dragonflies ruled the earth. It had been a day in which his mind had been untroubled enough to think of things like old movies.

He drank scotch, tilting the bottle, and when the liquor was gone—it did not take long—he put the empty bottle beside him on the sofa, as though anticipating that he might need a handy weapon.

Where would I be, he wondered, slipping the tape from its sleeve, without television? Imagine, he thought, Walter Raleigh, imprisoned in the Tower of London without a television.

He slipped Tape One into the VCR, and settled into the sofa. I, Hamilton Speke, do intend to sit out the night with my sword at my side. I will be as steady as a samurai, and I will think of nothing at all. Not a thing.

The screen fluttered and purred. Speckles of static streamed by. Speke folded his hands. The speckled tape illuminated the room with moon-gray bursts of light.

When he saw it, he did not realize, at first, what he was seeing. Surely that wasn't a face. Surely that wasn't a dim visage forming slowly out of the streaks and speckles of static.

Surely it was not Asquith's face.

It stared.

Asquith's face stared at him, and even when he blinked, and leaned forward, and shook his head, the face remained. Speke fell to his knees, still gripping the empty bottle.

Stop looking at me! his mind shrilled.

And then it was gone.

It's gone now, he told himself. See—everything's fine. The face is gone.

A nightmare has a special quality that lets the dreamer know: this is a dream. It was like the difference between videotape and film. The quality of light, the intensity of hues, the texture of a dream are unlike a real, actual event. Speke knew that he was awake. He knew it just as he might know when he heard a recording of Fats Waller or Billie Holiday that he was experiencing a voice from the past.

He was awake. This was not a dream. He knew that much. He lifted the bottle, holding it like a club, and stared around at the room. Where else would Asquith appear?

He seized the remote control with unsteady fingers, and rewound the tape.

There, he told himself. There's nothing there. Just a speckle or two of static. No reason to be upset.

He held his breath. The stare was there, but so dim you could almost not see it. Speke pushed "pause," and the face seemed to be composed of shadows, half-grays and blurs. Someone else might not be able to see it at all.

But it was there. Asquith was there.

Speke forced himself to move deliberately. He stood, feeling the stiffness from digging the grave in his shoulders and thighs. He balanced the bottle carefully in his hand. He gripped the bottleneck, swung the bottle back, and hurled the bottle into Asquith's face.

There was an abrupt burst, and the television glow in the room vanished. Everything went black. The silence was imperfect—there was an electronic buzz. A metallic stink drifted to where he crouched, hands on his knees. There was the dullest light from the walls themselves. Bits of glass glittered on the carpet.

He crept, as silently as possible.

Don't move. Don't take a step. What is that in the tank with the piranha?

Nothing. There's nothing there.

Maria was awake, sitting up in the bed.

"I'm just putting on some clothes," Speke whispered.

"What's the matter, Ham?"

"I couldn't sleep." He buttoned his shirt and snapped his pants. "I heard a noise."

"No noise." He stepped into his boots, tugging first one, and then the other. "A perfectly quiet night."

"What's wrong? There's something wrong, I can tell."

"There's nothing wrong. You want some sort of signed statement from me, is that it?"

He had never spoken to her like this. "I'm sorry, Maria. Please forgive me. I didn't mean to shout."

"You haven't seen him again?"

"I'm sorry, Maria."

"You have." Her tone was definite, sure.

Speke didn't respond.

She streaked past him, a flutter of nightgown and a light step. He put out his hand to stop her, but she was gone.

He caught up with her in the office. She switched on the light and raced to the windows, fumbling at them, flinging them open.

The scent of the damp earth, and the night hush, drifted into the room.

"There's nothing there," she said. "I told you, Ham. It's in your mind."

"I never said I saw him outside."

"Where else did you see him? Ham, tell me. What's happening?" Her voice did not sound surprised, or even anguished. Despite her words, she seemed to have been through this before.

"It's all right, Maria. Everything is fine. Do I seem upset?"

"You're trying to act calm, but—yes. You seem upset."

"I'm upset, okay. I admit that. But I'll be fine."

"Ham—I'm worried about you."

He held her, and she was not trembling. "There's nothing to be afraid of."

"Ham, I'm afraid of what this is doing to you."

"What's it doing? Disturbing my sleep? Making me a little restless? That'll pass. I'll be fine. Everything will be just fine."

He snapped off the light, and the darkness made them huddle together.

"I'm going out," he said.

She stiffened, and for the first time seemed anxious. "Stay here, Ham," she whispered, but he imagined that he heard another message behind her words: go out, and make sure it's safe here.

He stepped through the open windows, onto the dew-fresh lawn. There was the slightest wind, a rustling in the trees, a sound like great lungs slowly inhaling oxygen, and just as slowly letting it go.

With each step, he knew exactly what he was doing. He was not taking a walk. He was not going forth to revisit the terrible place. He was setting forth as though to an agreed-upon meeting, a rendezvous. It was a short walk, just a nighttime stroll. He was walking, however, from one world to another. He was stepping from the walls of logic to the chamber where he had taken a life.

It had been a clever joke: put the face of the dead man on the videotape. That'll give old Ham a shock.

But who would do such a thing?

Why can't I close my eyes, utter some charm, and be a child again? Why can't I slip back down the staircase just a few days, when none of this had taken place. He had been avoiding the Outer Office. Normally, days would go by and he would have no reason to visit the Outer Office, but now he had no practical excuse. He had been, simply, afraid.

He was afraid now, turning the knob, half-hoping he had locked it, determined when the door swung silently open. He was frigid in his bones with the realization that what he was doing was dangerous. He was afraid, but he was also angry.

The phrase stitched him: playing with my mind. Someone, or something, was playing with his mind. He did not believe in ghosts, and yet like any rational man he had to admit to himself that the world was a strange place, rich with possibilities.

If ghosts were real, wouldn't they tend to haunt the place where they died?

How innocent the Outer Office looked. Here, leaning against the wall, was Maria's watercolor, that interplay of yellows and greens Speke had seen as an unlikely hand grenade. It was, he saw now, a pineapple—not one of her better pieces.

The mantelpiece was glossy in the light from overhead, the stone an unearthly green. Speke forced himself to touch the corner of the mantelpiece. Here, he told himself, his hands trembling. Here is where it happened.

He knew that if he touched the stone itself it would awaken the powers of the air.

There was a step, a whisper, foot pressing a dry leaf. Or was it, perhaps, the whispered sound of his own name. Surely, that's what it was, that breathy syllable.

"Ham."

Asquith stood, pale in the light from the cottage.

Staring at Speke with those glittering eyes.

·19·

She had so much to tell him. And yet, it all seemed to slip away from her, and nothing mattered except the two of them, lying exactly where they were.

Playing hide and seek as a girl had been like this, her face pressed against fermenting leaves, so still she was someone pretending to be dead among slain bodies, escaping searchers who were very nearly not playing at all, hunters prodding bushes for the kill.

Perhaps a sound woke her. A shout, she thought, or a voice in a dream. It was hard to tell. She held her breath, and she could hear only the quiet footsteps of her own heartbeat. How peaceful she was, drifting in and out of sleep. Surely there could be no harm, anywhere in the world.

She listened, but there was only the huff of the wind above the cottage, in the trees. The sound had been something in her own mind, she decided, a cry to stir herself.

What sort of shapes had she seen in the plaster of her ceiling as a girl? Faces, of course, swollen-cheeked cherubs and grinning buffoons and benevolent grandees, all made of nothing, of light and trowel-swirls. The mind will search for a face anywhere, and see it where there is only textured chaos. And what did her parents talk about, out in the living room, in their adult lives? She recalled only the lift and fall of their voices, casual, affectionate.

Such a precipitous affair was not common for her. But she did not question what she was doing. Her father would have understood: Chris was a man you could talk to. It was time to tell everything. She shook his shoulder. It was perfect dark, except for the dimmest gray around the curtain. A single bird raised its song, like the squeak of a tin box from which morning escaped.

She snapped on the nightstand lamp, blinking against the sudden spill of light. "Chris, I have to talk to you."

"Sarah." Like a name spoken in a dream.

"I have to talk to you. Wake up."

He smiled sleepily. "I don't want to wake up."

"We'll go to my place. I'll make coffee, and we can talk. I want to show you some things from my files."

He sat up, suddenly alert. "What is it? Sarah—is something wrong?"

"Yes. But now I know what to do."

His body was tense. "What happened?"

She laughed. "It's not an emergency."

He seemed to sense it, too. There was a cool current in the air, a trickle of unease. Had there been, after all, a sound in the darkness outside?

He squeezed her hand. "You startled me." Then, "I must have been dreaming."

She could not speak for a moment. She had too much feeling: gratitude, passion, sense of purpose. She had always believed that she had a special obligation to Hamilton Speke. She felt it now— loyalty, but also a loyalty to the truth. "I have so much to tell."

He stroked her hair. "You're the most alluring woman I have ever met."

How wonderful he looked, tousled and sleepy. How silly she must look, she told herself, but that didn't matter.

"Lures deceive," she said. She meant it as a light verbal parry, but the heaviness of the truth she was about to share silenced her, and she looked away.

She tossed aside shyness as unworthy. She crept from the bed, and, in the dim light, dressed herself, slipping into her clothing like an actress assuming an accustomed role.

But the role was different, now. She could share the truth with someone. They both dressed, as unself-conscious as children, except that she thought: just like children. Real children, she knew, would never have such a thought.

They stepped through the dew-dampness to her cottage in the barely stirring light. There was a scent of sage and tinder-dry wild rye and wild oats, and an extra scent she had never been able to identify. The smell of silence itself, perhaps, silence and light, steeped in the earth.

The kitchen light was cheerful but too bright for a moment. "Don't think I brought you here just to make you coffee. I don't believe in impressing men with my ability to provide nourishment."

He smiled, a smile that rose up through him, and suffused his face, and his eyes. "You can impress me in more ways than that."

Her knees were weak for a moment. She had to look away.

She adopted her most adult tone. "I'm too reluctant to tell you anything so serious," she began.

"Take your time. We don't have to rush headlong into seriousness."

"First, I want you to read something. Just a single page of typing."

She found the page in a folder in the bedroom, and hurried back into the light.

"A double-spaced page of printout," mused Chris. "Dialogue. And some . . . stage directions?" He looked at her questioningly, and then he read for a moment.

It did not take long. When he was done, he set the page on the table, face down.

The words were impossible, but she forced herself to speak. "It's Ham's recent work."

He did not respond. He smoothed the paper before him, like a man clearing haze from a window. "He's supposed to be working on something about traveling in Mexico. Everyone's been talking about it for years. *The Black Cat . . .*"

"He's been working on the same scene over and over again, two young men lost in the jungle. He writes the same stage directions over and over, the color of the light, the offstage sounds of waves, parrots. He deletes, rewrites, rediscovers, forgets what he has written. The sound of the surf, what the men are wearing. He writes it again and again, each time slightly differently."

"The play isn't nearly done?"

She turned to the coffeemaker. She poured, and asked, "Do you want a cup with a right whale on it, or a harbor seal?"

"I don't know. That's a hard decision. How can I face a question like that so early in the morning?"

She gave him the whale.

Then she lowered her eyes. "I don't think the play exists."

"He's stuck. That happens to playwrights, and biographers, too."

"There's something wrong with Ham." The time had come at last, and she could not continue.

He waited.

"When I first read the early plays, I knew they were magnificent, and I admired Ham so much for being able to write them."

She stilled that nervous flutter in her breast. She waited, though, before continuing, "And he has never disappointed me, personally. He's generous, spontaneous. He loves life. I admire, him, Chris. Very much."

"But there is something wrong with him these days," suggested Bell.

There is, she thought. Something very wrong. The next words choked her. She couldn't possibly utter them. She whispered, at last, "I'm beginning to wonder how much of the old plays he actually wrote."

Bell blinked.

"I never questioned it for a long time. For years. But then I realized that all the plays were written on the same cheap drugstore typing paper, with the same ribbon, and they all looked—felt —like manuscripts which had been produced about the same time. But that was only a glimmer of doubt . . . a hunch."

She had once thought she would never be able to voice these suspicions. Now everything was changed. Still, she chose her words with care. "What convinced me was when he showed me things he had begun to write, things he started during the last year or two, after all the original manuscripts, even the screenplays and the songs, had been depleted."

Bell glanced at the sheet of paper face down on the table. "And that's a sample of his recent work." He pursed his lips. "It's well written, though. What there is of it."

"I kept telling myself that I was wrong, and I was able to suppress my doubts."

"Didn't Speke realize that you were . . ." He searched for words. "Suspicious?"

"Ham is so important to me." She was surprised at the way her voice shook as she said these words. "I don't care who wrote the plays. Does it really matter? I'm concerned that the man, Hamilton Speke, is in trouble, and he needs my help."

"He must have written the plays." Bell looked around the kitchen, as though to make sure the room were still there. "You're suggesting a kind of hoax."

"No, I'm suggesting that we don't know anything about Ham's

creative life, not really. We don't know where the plays came from, and why they've ceased."

"What you're suggesting is outrageous."

"You misunderstand me—"

"Just for the sake of argument, who wrote these plays if Speke didn't?"

She was quiet for a while. So much truth all at once amazed her. Her confessions should change the color of the light, or the color of the walls, but the morning continued to dawn slowly, gradually.

"So who wrote them?" He was gentle, but he put out his hand to touch her arm. "Sarah, who was the playwright?"

"I gradually became convinced that somewhere in the past he had a ghostwriter." There it was: that word that she had kept secret so long. "But I didn't know who." She waited for a moment, until she was certain that he was beginning to believe her. "But I have records that go back fifteen years, and a name that came up just a couple of days ago stopped me short."

She was reluctant to leave his presence, even for a moment. Her bedroom, when she reached it, was dark and quiet. The bed had that look of neat neglect, unslept in, witness to no passion. She tugged a drawer, and slipped the piece of paper, Speke's recent effort, back into the darkness.

She hurried back into Bell's presence, as she had when, as a girl, she had been afraid of the dark.

Don't stop now, she told herself. Keep going. "There's someone here. Someone on the estate—someone secret."

He was plainly a man used to absorbing news. "Hiding?"

She could not even nod. Her voice was hoarse. "I think so. I'm not sure—but I think he's still here."

Bell was leaning forward, his eyes searching hers. He looked shocked, fascinated, even more mystified than before.

"There's a name from Ham's past, but I'd completely forgotten it. I never thought of this man as anything but a character in a few wild tales of Ham's early days. This man—Timothy Asquith." She paused, as though his name might be an evil incantation. "This man called, and Ham agreed to see him in the morning, just before you got here. Asquith arrived, but he didn't leave."

His expression said: are you sure?

"He rode a motorcycle in," she continued, "and he didn't ride it out. I've searched, and there is no sign of it anywhere. It was red, like flashy lipstick, and easy to spot. It's hidden well. In fact, I think it's buried."

"Buried?"

"I saw Ham in the woods, putting the finishing touches on what looks like a grave. That's what it is, in a manner of speaking. A motorcycle's grave."

Bell shook his head, amazed or incredulous.

"It all made sense to me: Speke needs his ghostwriter back again, but he has to keep him secret, because he's so proud. And, after all, he does have a reputation to protect. Asquith is still here, somewhere on the estate."

Bell gazed into his coffee cup, and then met her eyes. "Is that possible? Could a person hide here, out among the ticks?"

"Speke is dry. He has no ideas. He's desperate."

Bell shook his head. "He wouldn't be keeping Asquith against his will—"

"That's not what I mean."

Bell sighed, a sound of masculine uncertainty.

"You don't believe me," said Sarah when she could make a sound. Her hope was a curl of smoke.

"The problem is worse than that." He put his hand over hers. "I am beginning—just beginning—to believe you may be right."

She leaned forward, as though she might be overheard. "I think Asquith is out there."

He bit his lip against a question he seemed unable to ask.

"Hiding. Asquith is out in the woods somewhere," she said. "Watching us. And he has some sort of power over Ham. Some dangerous power."

"Maybe he's back to renew the old partnership."

"I don't think it's that innocent."

"I still need some convincing." He was struggling to put it politely. "You have to admit that there's a good deal of supposition here."

"My father was a cop. I know about trouble. Granted, I don't have any proof. But I think Asquith is here to do harm. To Ham, and just possibly to all of us."

· 20 ·

Speke could not take a single step, could only stay where he was, unable to make a sound.

Asquith stood beyond the window, and did not move, did not waver or flicker.

The flesh of the face was the color of the electric light that fell upon it, and the surface of the skin was blistered, broken, with the first eruptions of decay.

Or was it? The vision held itself back, at the very limit of the light. Shouldn't a ghost seem, somehow, transparent? Speke forced himself to breathe, listening, watching, aching for an owl's keenness, or a cat's. This was a bad time to make a mistake. Listen, he commanded himself. What sort of being is that out there? Out there, in the dim light from the cottage.

Wasn't adulthood a surprise, its contradictions, the lingering childishness of one's own nature, the paradoxical nonsense of success? Why, then, shouldn't a ghost baffle expectations, too?

"Asquith," he whispered.

The silence was a response.

"What do you want?"

The figure was a stain in the air, a smudge on the otherwise perfect darkness. The apparition was almost like someone who wasn't there at all.

But he was there, and more—there had been a sound, the breathy hush of grass depressed by a foot, the snap of a stem. Don't lose control of yourself, Speke commanded his quaking arms and legs. Stay calm. Stare back.

It was certainly exactly like the living Asquith, a human presence barely illuminated by the light from the cottage. There was a chiaroscuro effect, a gilded line of head and shoulder, eyes glittering in shadows. The spectral figure stepped back, shifting away on its legs just like a living man. He was fading to black again.

And Asquith was gone.

"Come back," Speke said in a low voice.

That made it worse. It was bad enough to have a hallucination.

It was madness to actually talk to it, and he was not only speaking, he was shouting. "I can't help what happened. I didn't mean to kill you."

Then he stopped himself. He was sweating, but the strangest feeling powered him forward.

He stumbled, flung himself to the windows and threw them open, but by the time he gazed at the patch of light they cast upon the earth, he saw only his own shadow and a few vague branches.

It was hopeless. The ground here was the same obdurate stone as always. He knelt, searching in the bad light, aware that any moment a dead hand could fall upon his shoulder. The hand would be cold, he knew. Perhaps even cold and wet.

This was the grave, its stones impossible to make out in the darkness, its presence a vague scatter of rock in the night. This was the light from the window. This—he put out his hand—was the jagged stone of the earth here, fragments that reminded him that earth was created by an explosion, a series of explosions, fire and storm.

But at least the stone was real. He was reassuring himself that the world was real, and that he was awake, but he was also realizing something else.

Asquith, he whispered. And he laughed.

Because it was funny—he had just been looking for footprints. He had just been imagining a hand, corporeal, with flesh and bones. This was because he did not believe that the apparition was a ghost.

He didn't believe it. He never had believed it, he told himself. Not really.

He wasn't a child any more. He still had nightmares from time to time. A waking, struggling corpse could disturb him, scare him, do everything but convince him. It wasn't real. Everything was going to be just fine. He still had his native intelligence. He wasn't going to let fear turn him into a cowering animal. He had pride. Don't worry. Everything will be just terrific.

"I know you, Asquith!" he hissed.

No sound answered him. Of course not. What did he expect, an echo? A long-range conversation? I feel, he told himself, strangely lucid. Strangely peaceful. Perhaps a human being can only feel so much terror before something snaps. You are being watched. Act calm. He closed the windows, and turned off the light, telling himself to take his time. The dark alone won't hurt you, he reassured himself, although he took a deep breath when the door was shut at last, and he could follow the trail up the hill.

It really wasn't much of an act. He did feel calm. It was a peculiar, stunned sort of calm. But it allowed him to feel certain of one or two things. Hamilton Speke was not such a fool, after all. It was time for the truth.

Why was night so slow to fade? The stars were still vivid, the black perfect, except around the edge, where the east had gone gray. The gray of dirty dishwater, the gray of granite. How weak light is when it first dawns, he thought.

He would use his wits. He laughed, a rusty grunt like the sound of the garage door. The darkness held the stale, leftover heat of the previous day. He fumbled in the garage, groping for a light switch and finding cobwebs.

He grasped the familiar shaft, then turned and groped back into the dawn. The shovel was like an old friend. Good old spade, thought Speke fervently. My favorite weapon.

He understood why Beowulf's men had names for their swords. It was only right: you could talk to the steel that would save your life. You could talk, as a driver might speak to a stalling automobile, willing life into iron.

We have work to do, he breathed.

It was still too dark. He wanted daylight. He wanted the shovel in his hands under the sun, and what he wanted more than anything was the truth. And he knew exactly how to get it.

He was going to dig up the grave and see what, if anything, lay under those stones.

· 21 ·

Bell and Sarah shared the growing dawn. From time to time he asked a question regarding Speke's friendship with this actor or that director, and returned to a subject that increasingly puzzled him: why Speke had so little regard for security. "To be famous these days," Bell said, "is to court assassination."

Sarah enjoyed answering his questions, but she savored most that inner silence that ensues after confession. Bell, on the other hand, enjoyed quite another sort of feeling.

He was secretly ecstatic. This was going to be an amazing story, he thought. Talk about scandal—he could expose Hamilton Speke completely.

He sipped his cooling coffee, and tried not to let Sarah see how pleased he was. He tried to look pained, concerned. What sort of herbs did Clara grow in her garden? Did any of the wild animals on the estate ever suffer from rabies? All the while he ached to call his publisher and tell them to get ready for the most astounding biography ever written about a contemporary figure.

If this were all true. That was the catch. This was where his methodical cast of mind, his training, slowed him down to a step-by-step grind. If you are going to write this kind of book, he knew, you have to be completely sure your facts are anchored.

How, Bell wondered, will I broach the subject of a ghostwriter when I talk with Ham? Start by mentioning ghosts? Maybe the bluntest approach was the best. Tell me, Ham, which words did you actually write yourself? Go ahead, underline them. It shouldn't take long.

Was that wind overhead, on the roof of the cottage? For a silent place, a sanctuary, there were too many hushed movements at Live Oak. This was a place where very little made sense. All paths here twisted, and each silence seemed destined to be eroded by a whisper, a rustling in the dark. This estate was enchanted, but something solid in Bell was uneasy. He liked things to add up. He liked his facts in order, and his shirts ironed. He liked the fresh starch of common sense. It was time to return, for a while, to the world, the real world, the one beyond this estate with its tangled trees.

Clara grew thyme, Sarah said, and basil, and tomatoes which attracted the sphinx moth larva, the big green worms which Clara killed while singing the softest, saddest sounding songs in Spanish. Rabies, Sarah said, was supposedly endemic, and bats and skunks were rumored to suffer from it from time to time, but there had not been a case discovered in San Mateo County, she had heard, for more than a decade.

The cold coffee reflected his face, a dark, quaking caricature. He returned to the subject that flickered inside him. "It's not as simple as it seems," he said. "We need proof." Surely, he meant to say, you can discover evidence for me. He added, "You know Speke better than I do."

"He needs our help."

"I need more evidence." This, he knew, sounded brittle, and betrayed too much of his purely journalistic interest. Bell pushed the cup away. "What do you know about Maria?"

Sarah considered his question. She recounted the bioparagraph many people could have rattled off, but then she was quiet, as dissatisfied as he was. This list of galleries and art institutes was scarcely knowledge.

"I have a bad feeling," said Bell at last.

Maria was watering the nasturtiums as he and Sarah descended from her cottage. In the morning sunlight white fire sputtered from the watering can, and blisters of water scarred the dust. There was the scent of soil, and spice of wild flowers.

How cute, Sarah remarked to herself. Maria never did such a thing as simple as watering flowers. She either closeted herself with her watercolors, or sat listening to tapes with her earphones, tapes labeled "Surf Sounds" or "Thunderstorm, New Hope, Connecticut." This display of horticultural enthusiasm, missing only a bonnet to make it something out of Renoir, was for Chris's benefit, Sarah guessed. In one of those insights which can never be wrong, she thought: Maria is trouble.

It was rare to have any insight at all into what Maria might want. Maria smiled. This was not a kind smile, nor a smile of greeting. It was a smile that said: you see me looking so pretty.

Sarah wished her a good morning, and Bell said something cheerful about the watering can. It was a large green metal can, with a spout that sprinkled the nasturtiums prettily, but, Sarah suspected, inefficiently.

"I don't think it's an antique," smiled Maria. "Just something for a person who enjoys solitude."

"Why not use the hose?" Sarah asked. Indeed, the can was already empty.

Maria ignored the question, and said, "I see you two are getting to know each other."

"Sarah is very helpful with some background material," offered Bell, with as much gallantry as seemed required.

"Ham says she knows everything," said Maria.

"Oh, hardly," Sarah began.

"Ham is under the impression," said Maria, "that Sarah is the mastermind behind his career."

"He may be right," said Bell.

"Sarah, we must have a talk soon," said Maria, managing to shake a few last drops from the can. The can made a low, metallic rumble, a hollow grumbling surprising from such a relatively small container. "In fact, I think we should get together for a long talk. Something I think we've both been putting off for too long."

"Actually," said Bell, glancing at Sarah, "I was just about to suggest that Sarah and I take the day off."

Sarah started. He had mentioned no such plan. Whatever could he mean?

"Or maybe," he said, "she's too busy."

"I think it would be a marvellous idea," said Maria. "Poor Sarah spends every day in that fusty little office. It would be so nice for her to spend the day away from here. Her eyes get so red, sometimes, from looking at the computer. It's so kind for you to suggest that, Mr. Bell."

The dapples of sunlight were sharp-edged, brilliant razors.

"I haven't been away in—" Sarah stopped herself. There was no use in elaborating for Chris what a spartan life she had been leading lately. True, there had been the affair with the photographer, and those romantic, if too-brief, interludes at the St. Francis Hotel in the City. And, before then, the trips to Paris, always a five-day jaunt, too short, too rushed, because she had to hurry back to open Speke's mail.

Maria plainly was delighted to have Sarah take the day off. "Take three or four days off, or even more, Sarah. I think you should take care of yourself."

"Good heavens," Sarah heard herself say. "I would think you want to get rid of me."

Maria laughed. "I think it's a delightful chance for some fun."

"Fun." Sarah savored the word. What a puerile, empty word it was, smacking of balloons and cheap plastic toys. Fun indeed.

And yet, the thought of a few hours more with Chris weakened something in her, her resolve softening as under the influence of champagne. "For the sake of my health," Sarah suggested, in her brightest, sweetest voice.

"You start to make mistakes when you're tired," said Maria.

It was unsaid, but as vivid as the beads of water on the circular leaves of the nasturtiums. Maria would get what she wanted. This sudden shift in the emotional climate baffled Sarah, and yet logic was useless.

Don't go, her inner voice whispered. Stay here. Don't abandon Ham to this woman. Where had this thought come from? Maria was, as far as Sarah knew, a true and faithful wife. She loved Ham, certainly. And Speke would stand by Sarah, no matter what Maria might say.

Besides, there was that silly word: fun. It might be, after all, fun to spend just a little time with Chris.

He took her hand when they were alone, their shoes squeaking on the dew-rich lawn. The shade of the poplars spilled over both of them. "I think we'll both think more clearly away from this place."

That was certainly true. She was pleased that he sensed it, too. But she did not respond.

"You'll come with me, won't you?"

She hesitated. "The sky here isn't like the blue over any other landscape," she said. It was nearly a confession. She was amazed to hear herself speak like someone under hypnosis, in a truth-serum trance. "It soaks up our thoughts, and even our dreams, and at night I sometimes hear things. I heard the voice of my father, once, laughing, telling a joke I could almost make out. As though there is another world, but so dim that we can never see it."

He absorbed her words, gazing into her eyes with a measuring look, as if trying to estimate her weight. Then he turned away. "I would enjoy your company," he said, studying the glittering ferns, realizing he was about to be rebuffed.

"I should stay here," she said, but her voice lacked conviction.

It was one of those moments that change everything. Whatever he said next would alter her life, one way or another.

"Please come," he said.

Exactly the right words.

He added, "There's something I have to find out, and I want you to be there."

Then they were a man and woman with a secret, and they behaved accordingly, speaking so that a spy, listening from a distance with a shotgun microphone, would hear only polite chat.

"It'll be cool in the City," she said.

"Yes, it usually is this time of year," he said, hopefully.

"I'll bring a sweater." Nonchalant, as though her knees were not weak.

"I thought lunch in the City would be nice. And then there are a few places we should visit."

"You mystify me."

They were inside, and the hush of the house made them feel the need to say as little as possible. They were lovers, now, not only because they had shared a bed and pleasure last night. They understood something about each other.

Clara must have sensed it. She wished them a good morning, and then said that she had made muffins especially for the two of them. "Corn muffins, with some more of that blackberry bush," she said. "From out by the Indian rocks."

Then Clara, a woman who had long ago accomplished the most unobtrusive manner of any human being alive, turned back at the doorway. "Maria waited for you," she said.

She did not speak again for a moment, as though listening for a distant footstep. "Out by the flowers," she added.

This information was hardly a surprise, Sarah thought, and yet she was grateful to Clara. She and Bell sat and shook out their napkins. Sarah had that feeling that troubled her from time to time. She did not know Clara well, after all these years. She was

one of those quiet people who change a room deeply by entering
it, or by leaving it.

The room shrank, just slightly. Clara had left it, and, like someone who drifted on the air, Maria entered beaming, carrying a
large white rose, a great fleshy blossom at the end of a black wire.

· 22 ·

S peke stood over the grave.
    Go ahead, he ordered himself.
    Start digging.

The day was already hot. The scent of the air was dry and clean, like fresh bedding, both sterile and promising life. He cringed from what he was going to ask himself to do. And yet, there was a thread of determination, a dry, hard iron within him. He had no choice.

The shovel worked as though on its own. The blade rang musically on the first stone. He tossed the stone away. Another shovelful grated, a hard sound that made him pause. They'll hear me, he thought. Work quietly, or everyone will know.

The shovel knew what to do. It worked carefully, surgically, paring away first the larger stones, and then the gravel. He pried earth from within the shifting figure of his own shadow. The dust lifted into the air, and hung there, drifting nowhere.

A dozen voices chattered in his mind, warnings, reassurance. He couldn't do this. A superhuman couldn't do this. It was asking too much. The memory of their times together was sharp, vivid, more real, in a way, than the years that had followed.

Night after night Asquith would despair, rumple his hair, swear that he needed a drink. And Speke would pour him a couple of fingers of Southern Comfort and urge him to stay alive. "We need people like you. Do you realize how boring most people are?"

"I'm bored," Asquith would moan. Or: "This is all stupid." Or: "I can't possibly continue waking up, trying to figure out where I am. This is a complete and utter waste of time." Spoken always with that theatrical flair, Asquith's standard stage diction sharpening each T, making his melancholy, or his hangover, the stuff of tragedy.

"You have to believe in the future," Speke would say. "You have to believe in yourself." He actually mouthed such trite encouragement, and he believed it, in his youth and his enthusiasm. He had felt honored to be the companion to such a great soul.

A vibrant soul, but hardly an easy one, on himself or on others. A ballet could move him to tears, and the casual discourtesy of a waiter could have him brooding for days. Asquith had possessed a characteristic way of listening, eyes closed, head tilted against a wall, drawing hungrily on a cigarette. And a characteristic way of answering a doubtful opinion with a glance. Occasionally he had made coffee for both of them, or poured Speke a beer, and such a homely gesture had always touched Speke.

Don't do it, he told himself now. You know what you'll find.

I have to be sure. I have to be absolutely sure of what is going on. Because I don't believe in ghosts. I don't believe Asquith's spirit is out there in the woods. I think Asquith is still alive.

I know he is. All I have to do is keep digging, and I'll prove it.

He knew very soon that he was wrong.

The smell was worse than he had anticipated, an odor like a shriek. The smell made him pant, and he nearly dropped the shovel several times.

He's here. He gagged for a moment. He's in the grave. I was deluding myself. Playing little games with my mind. Asquith is rolled up in the rug, and he is rotting.

Speke gagged. This stench tells the tale. There was no need to keep digging.

He let the shovel fall. The carpet was a vague shape under the last remaining earth. Cover it up, he told himself. Cover it all up, and go on with your wasteland of a life.

But something rallied within him, that old, tireless courage that had caused so much trouble in the past.

I don't believe in ghosts. There are certain rules that we have that keep us . . . sane. There are certain truths. One is that dead people do not get up and stroll around, not at night or at any other time. This simply cannot be Asquith.

The thought broke over him with the strength of hunger, or sexual desire: he should run away. It was such a wonderful thought. There is that farm, he recalled, near Avignon, where they grow the red Rhone wines. He'd spent a summer there once, after spraining his back in an athletic affair with that television actress. Why not an extended visit now? How about that flat in Edinburgh, that chateau near Chartres? He had spent time in so many wonderful places. It was time to seek refuge. Ham, you can't stay here any more.

Was Maria calling him? Christ, she can't show up here and see what I'm doing.

Pick up the shovel and finish the job.

What do you mean, finish the job. I'm done. It's all over.

Uncover the carpet, and unwrap the body. You have to be sure.

I can't do this. I need a drink. This is fetid air. Every breath coats my lungs with a stink I'll never be able to cough up as long as I live. Death pus—my lungs are slimy with it.

All through his days with Asquith he had suffered nightmares of the staring dead. His rational approach to the subject of ghosts was one he had acquired over years of adulthood, and he would not relinquish it now. He had a characteristic he knew was unlovely but real. He liked a fight.

A black chip floated in the blue, like a defect in his vision, a carbon fleck in his eye.

Finish the job. *Look at the body.*

I'm a human being. He was my friend. I can only ask myself to do so much. It will destroy me to look upon his rotting face.

Maria was, indeed, calling him. Or maybe it was a hallucination —he couldn't be sure.

The black chip drifted closer, a pair of black wings shaded with ash white. The graceful half-circles continued, the wings passing over the tops of the oaks as Speke watched. Another pair joined it, high above. The most graceful bird of flight, the vulture passed a folding, pliant shadow over the stones.

Certainly that was Maria's voice. It was far away, but unmistakable.

She was coming closer. If she sees this—and smells it—she'll be shattered. She'll see the vultures. They might as well be skywriters, spelling out in formation: dead animal. Spelling out: dead man. Spelling out: look what Speke did.

He stooped to pick up the shovel just in time to see a vulture gliding from an unexpected direction, its little withered head glancing back and forth, a leathery nub of a head, like the hard butt of a corncob.

The bird's voice was a grunt, a creak like a very old and very large trunk opening in a dark attic. The large bird was to eat the dead, without even a song. But what sort of song can we have, Speke thought, we who attend the dead?

Finish the job, Speke. Look at the body, Speke. Stop wasting

time, Speke. Worthless jerk, Speke. Pathetic staggering killer. Go
get a drink. Go get a bottle. Get half drunk and then you can give
Asquith a French kiss.

There are no such things.

Why not?

As ghosts. No such things.

He had been denying something. He had been denying it very
masterfully. But he could not continue to pretend: he was about
to throw up absolutely every single thing he had ever eaten. Every
spoonful of strawberry yogurt. Every pink shrimp in every scoop
of dip. It was all coming back. Every last corn chip, every last
beluga egg.

He had been the one who was never seasick, even on that ferry
from the Yucatan to Cozumel, that pitching, staggering slab of
wood and puke. No, he had held his own. But now—this was
different. He had been a young man then, and a man who still
thought himself a good person. Still, he walked with something
like presidential grace, the dignity of a second inaugural address,
or a summit meeting. He reached a poppy that had lost its blossoms, and was reduced, far past its prime, to a green shrub. He
bent over, and retched.

Was that sound a step, that whisper, that rasp of footfall on
dried leaf?

There was no one there.

I need to take a break. I'll come back, after a little break. Half
time for the weary athletes, just a bit of an intermission. My lords,
ladies and gentlemen, the bar is open for your pleasure. The
dancers all need to rest.

He experienced a thought he had never had before. Not on
those long sweaty hungover mornings in Mexico. Not after one of
those knuckle-breaking parties here on the estate. He thought:
maybe it would be better if I died.

The powerful, strangely pretty syllables subvocalized themselves
on his lips: suicide. This was not a sophomoric fling at despair or
morbid philosophy. The idea of suicide, the flash of certainty that
accompanied it, was foreign to him.

He shrank from the sensation gladly, but it left him feeling
weaker. Weaker in spirit than he had felt in his life. In a short
while, he thought, urging himself to attend to the business at

hand, I'll drag Asquith out of the grave. I'll look at him so I will be one hundred per cent sure that he is dead. But not now.

Find out where Maria is. Make sure she isn't about to burst upon you. The chatter of an emcee played itself in his head: We'll be right back so don't go away.

The black wings far above made the slightest rustle, the creak of plumes as the birds kept themselves from falling to the earth.

· 23 ·

He could feel it—Maria was slipping along one of the paths, and he had to stop her.

But as he hurried toward the house he could see no one. He held his breath and listened. He had the itchy sensation that he was in the company of someone, but there was only sunlight and heat.

He knew then that it was his need to speak with Maria that had tricked his hearing. Maria was not calling his name. He was calling hers, over and over again, in his mind.

He stopped. He wanted to fall to the ground, slither through the dry weeds and hide. Someone was coming. The smell of the grave could not be detected from here, but whoever was lightly stepping along the path had to be stopped.

He gave a cry of welcome.

Sarah gasped and put her hand to her throat.

He apologized for startling her. He was always glad to see her, but now his enthusiasm seemed to surprise her, or trouble her. She stammered, "I looked everywhere. I'm sorry. Please forgive me."

"For what?"

Her voice steadied, and she continued, "I looked everywhere for you, Ham."

"But you knew I was out here, didn't you? You expected to find me here."

"I haven't been spying on you," she said, quietly.

Speke could not respond to her steady gaze.

She continued, "I was just speaking with Mr. Bell."

"Christ, I've been awful. The man must think I'm the rudest creature in the world. I can't begin to talk about myself, Sarah. Maybe he should . . ." He should find another subject, he nearly said. "I hate to keep him waiting."

"He understands."

"Does he?" Speke wondered. A man who understood so much could be a great deal of trouble. "Have you seen Maria?"

"She's in the garden, I think, or in her studio."

Sarah was deliberately not saying something, Speke could tell.

"It's very peculiar," he said, trying to make it sound amusing. "I kept hearing her voice, calling me."

"I didn't hear her," said Sarah.

"No, I decided it was my imagination," Speke began, but then realized she was saying something about going to the City today with Bell. She wanted to know if that was all right.

"You're leaving?"

"For the day."

She was aware that he sounded very happy, and was, he thought, a little surprised, even offended. But it was perfect. She should elope with Bell. That was all there was to it. She should escape with Bell, and never come back. They should have wonderful lives together, and leave this place to its fate.

He took her by the arm, and guided her along the path, back toward the house. "You've done so much for me," he said.

"Ham, are you all right?"

"Fine."

"What's wrong with you?"

"I'm trying to do more exercise. Get in better shape."

"*GQ* said you were an exercise maniac."

"That was a little unkind, wasn't it?"

"You need me here."

"You should travel more, Sarah. You've done too much to help me."

"I'll stay."

"I want you to go. Get out of here. I insist."

It was the ideal solution. With Bell gone, there was no one to fall into the grave by accident, and no one to ask any questions. Besides, she really did deserve a day off. Poor, hardworking, steadfast, trusting Sarah.

"Ham, please. You're obviously under some kind of stress—"

"I'm a man of iron these days. Everyone knows that." He made an extravagant wave. "All my troubles are in the past, Sarah. All healed, long since."

She did not respond.

"I'm a healthy man," he said.

"Be careful, Ham."

"I'm like a rock." He kicked a knob of serpentine out of the path. "Besides, you want to go to the City. You have a spark in your eye."

She did not speak for a moment. "I can't look after you this way, Ham. You have to turn to Maria for this kind of help." She considered for a moment, and added, "You have to turn to yourself."

"I have my inner resources." He could not meet her cool, caring eyes. "I just had a little trouble working up some notes for the biography. I was writing about my dreams. My nightmares. The really ugly nightmares I had when I was a kid. Kids have worse nightmares than grownups do. They have to visit all the horror for the first time, a world of fire and violent men and earthquakes. They almost can't do it. It gives them terrible dreams."

"Ham, it's all right. Whatever you think is wrong. It's all right. There's nothing that can't be survived, as long as you have your body and your mind."

Sarah still believes in me, Speke told himself. She still believes in life.

Inside the house it was cool.

The lounge was silent, that deep quiet that soaks in the footstep and the voice. Have a drink, a voice said, a serpent uncurling in his belly. Go ahead, you deserve it.

He put his hand on the crystal that held cognac, but did not take a drink.

There was a splash in the aquarium. The piranha had snapped at nothing, apparently, breaking the surface of the water. Speke loved the quicksilver bright fish, and he loved the house, this refuge, this citadel of rooms he could enter like a boy, ever surprised at what he found. But he knew that he had neglected this house, and his life, in a fundamental way.

I'm wasting time, he nagged himself. Delaying the inevitable.

The firearms had vanished from this room long before he arrived, pilfered perhaps by servants or nephews decades ago. Guns were frankly evil, in Speke's view, and he was happy to have not so much as a twenty-two on the estate. He had used the mounts for a display he knew was in doubtful taste, oars from Hitchcock's *Lifeboat* and a spear, with a rubber head so old it was gray and stiff, from a Johnny Weissmuller movie.

The steel-bright creature pulsed peacefully in its tank. He never mentioned this to guests, but the piranha, for all its hatchet blade fierceness, was a vegetarian variety, and had never tasted blood.

Maria, he thought-whispered, where are you?

She must be in her studio, as Sarah had suggested, and he had promised her he would never enter that cottage uninvited. After all, they had both agreed, an artist needs that extra measure of privacy.

He often had imaginary conversations with his father. His father merely listened, in his fantasies, preoccupied as he had been in life with some tiny, intricate piece of work. Speke was, as usual, sour with the realization that his father would never listen to one of his songs. Would he have liked my music? Possibly not. His father would certainly not like any of the foul language spat between the characters in the plays. His brother Art had commented on Speke's fondness for what Art called "the fuck word."

Look at you, he told himself. You are wasting time. You have left unfinished business. This inner voice was like a talking computer in an early scifi movie, the voice an electric pencil sharpener might have if it got smart.

Wasting time, hurrying from room to room looking for your bride, mooning over your father, muttering about your brother, riding the ancient hobby horse of the many things your family could not, or would not, do for you.

Sarah looked into the room. "Are you sure, Ham?"

"Go, please. And have a wonderful time." He laughed. "Bell is so lucky." He silenced himself, because he did, to his surprise, feel a wrench of jealousy.

He laughed at his own feeling of emptiness as she left, at his own desire to call her back.

If I have a gift, he told himself mockingly, it is a rare talent for stalling. Procrastination. First the book, now the movie. Gentlemen, I see no reason why we should completely dig up and unwrap Mr. Asquith's corpse all in one morning. Why not wait until the afternoon? Gentlemen, a day is fit for any shape. It's like water. It knows all outlines, all configurations. I think a stroll among the prize roses and a drink would be in order. And then a survey of the library and a drink.

What a strange man I am, such an unlikely alloy of stubbornness and self-deception. We never really know that one person we will never meet, who carries us every heartbeat of our lives. Ourselves, that living shadow, eludes the hand. Jesus! Was this the day Brothers was coming? Or was he here yesterday? He doesn't come every single day. Or does he?

What if Bell falls into the grave while he's waiting for Sarah to put on her going-shopping outfit? He might go jogging while he's waiting, and get Asquith all over him. That would certainly look bad in chapter one of *Speke: The Life*.

The window opened with difficulty. Tires crackled up the drive, and Bell's Fiat caught the morning sun. But the sky beyond the ridge of trees was sprinkled with wheeling birds.

Don't let them see them, he prayed. Let them keep driving. Don't let them stop. Surely they have to see the tangle of vultures beyond the trees. Maybe—was it possible?—the wind would rise, and they would smell the body.

The green car slowed. They smell it! Of course they did. You can't leave a body that size half dug up.

Then the gears shifted, the engine finding a lower, stronger note. Speke scrambled to the drive in time to see the Fiat vanish around the curve.

For the moment it was not Maria he needed. He wanted to call to Sarah, to call her back to his side.

But it was too late.

What was it that called him back to the grave so suddenly? Was it the spinning shape of one of the black birds, or the snap of teeth in the distance, so far away he could not have heard them. He found himself running. Unseemly, this rush, he told himself. But he couldn't help it. There was a sound that he recognized from a corner of his mind, a corner that understood animals and hunger, and the kill.

He stopped, panting hard, and put his hand out to the branch of an oak to steady himself. This can't be, he thought. Surely I'm mistaken.

It was not the snap of teeth, not even a growl. Something more subtle than that, the rasp of animals taking nourishment. The secret, furtive beasts were feeding.

Branches snatched at him as he charged through the undergrowth. What he saw made him scrabble on the ground for rocks. Black wings flapped upward. He shouted something half-speech and half-howl, and flung a stone at the two slinking, dirt yellow, long-tailed coyotes.

Then he froze, unable to take another step.

The coyotes had dragged the body from the grave.

The body was completely out of the earth, now, and the carpet had unrolled. The corpse was exposed, lying in the bright morning sun.

Speke could not breathe. This was worse than he could have dreamed. This was far worse than any of his childhood nightmares.

Something horrible had happened to Asquith's body.

IV

STRIPSEARCH

·24·

Sarah had forgotten how the road out of Live Oak snaked back and forth. Sometimes a root lifted itself out of the packed earth, or a stone like the helmet of a man buried upright. Though it was no more than three or four miles long, the distance it traveled was, in a way, much farther than that. It wended from a place which, like a psyche, had its own coloration, its own logic, to the land beyond the forest, the land of straight roads and common sense.

"A road like this could drive me crazy," said Bell.

She said nothing, but she did not agree. The road was like language, defining and delineating, and all the while passing by all that which is not named. She could not suppress the thought, happy as she was to be leaving with him: stay here.

They reached the gate. The Fiat coughed, and nearly stalled. The gate was open, but even so there was a barrier, if only imaginary, that clung to the car for a moment. A branch in the drive, perhaps, or a half-buried stone.

Then they were on the two-lane pavement, and Sarah felt diminished for a while, shrunken and empty. They were back to the world. The real, empty world, with its speed limit signs. There was, she knew, in a sense only one road in the world, interconnected, many-surfaced, a beast of seemingly numberless tentacles. In truth, they were well-numbered, and mapped.

Bell drove fast. It was not the speed of nervous haste. This driver knew what he was doing. The highway beneath them was smooth and nearly without texture under the tires.

There was, as counterpoint to his conversation, the emptiness of the bland, paved road, and its hum beneath the tires. The fields were drought bleached.

As Bell drove he talked about himself. Occasionally he would pause in conversation to pass a dump truck, or a flatbed laden with earth-moving equipment.

Most men she had known enjoyed talking about themselves. She didn't mind. In this case, it was almost embarrassing to admit to herself how much she enjoyed the sound of his voice. She wanted to learn everything she could about him, and his voice reassured her that this trip away from Live Oak was exactly the right thing to do. She enjoyed the way he hesitated, carefully selecting the word that would define or explain, without telling too much. He spoke like a man used to typing paragraphs. He was careful, deliberate. He was even, she guessed, a little secretive. Bell would make an excellent spy.

"You're not at all what you seem to be," she said at last.

He didn't respond. Both hands tightened on the steering wheel for a moment. "What do you mean?" He tried to laugh.

"You act like a man of action. Ready to do anything."

Another fake laugh. "You mean you've figured me out so soon?"

"You're careful. You like a plan of attack. You can read a map."

Why did she think, just then, of Ham? She wanted to hear Ham's laugh. She was quite silly, she consoled herself. She heard Ham's voice every day. She was fortunate to be with this bright man, her new lover.

Christopher Bell was everything she needed.

Her mother would have wanted to know all the usual information regarding Christopher Bell. Who is he? her mother would ask. And Sarah would answer, satisfying even her mother's curiosity. Married to a cop, her mother had begun to think like one. Everyone was a suspect, everyone was a "party in question," or "an individual under investigation." Sometimes it had been difficult to think of the right answer, because her mother, while she rarely looked anyone in the eye, made few mistakes. She always knew.

Her mother had always had those busy hands, folding towels, putting cups onto hooks, smoothing, straightening. Even when she drowsed post-stroke her hands were busy, patting and soothing the coverlet until the moment she could do no more.

And now Sarah wanted to tell her mother exactly who this man was: a companion. An ally. A man who knew how to do things. Her father would have admired him, because he had always admired good writing, and, strangely enough for a policeman, he had always been a reader, with a favorite quote from Thoreau or Mark Twain tacked to his cork message board. Sarah remembered particularly Twain's description of Lake Tahoe photographing the sky, words her father had written in ballpoint in his efficient half-print, half-cursive.

Her mother would have said: a companion is a good thing to find in a man. By this she would have meant: what do you feel about him, really?

Is it possible you can really love someone you have known for only a few days? Or was love something Sarah had long ago abandoned, something her mother knew, but which Sarah had surrendered, a language her family had spoken but which Sarah had never articulated as an adult?

Love, her mother would have said, smiling skeptically, is a possibility. But see what you're thinking about, Sarah. The sun is bright on the hairs of his arms as he drives. A sinew twitches there in his forearm, for an instant as he changes lanes. You see what I mean?

Perhaps her mother would be right. What she felt was old-fashioned libido—sex, infatuation.

Sarah was wise to all the disappointments of the heart. But infatuation like this was like remembering the old language, the mother tongue, and being fluent again, the words returning to her in phrases, the phrases in sentences, in poetry.

It was wonderful to be in the City again.

Holding hands with Christopher as pigeons burst above them across Union Square, she forgot every unhappy memory. She knew only his warm hand, and this sunny/cloudy day. It had been more than a year since she'd paid a visit to San Francisco. She had been a slave to the telephone, the appointment book. This was a return to life. They had a croissant in a cafe with a green awning, and sipped delicious French roast coffee while he told her what he intended to find out.

"This is partly just an excuse to escape the estate for a while," he admitted. "With you."

Why did she feel, for a moment, disappointed? This man was, after all, a journalist. But she could see that he was one of those people—and they were usually men—who did not like to waste time. Perhaps he was not a romantic, after all. "But you have another reason for escaping Live Oak."

He glanced into his coffee for a moment, like a man consulting notes. "There's too much we don't know." He did not have to add: about Hamilton Speke. About Maria. About everything, it was developing, that there was on file regarding the man with the famous smile.

Sarah had faith in her own judgment. Over the years of keeping Speke's books, and answering his fan mail, she had learned to trust herself. She had acquired some of her mother's sense of things. Sarah knew things about the world, and about herself.

"I know this about Ham—Maria changed his life," said Sarah. "The day he met her, when he came back from the gallery, alone, he was singing until midnight, playing old records, dancing, raving to Clara and me about this wonderful artist he had met. I could hear his old records as I went to sleep, Fats Waller resounding through the trees. She changed his life." The way you could change mine, she thought. "He hasn't had a serious hangover in months." My own addiction, she reminded herself, is to work, and a kind of brittle solitude.

"Did you resent Maria?"

"Possibly. But I think I was happy for Ham. He was so full of life."

"You are either a very good person," said Bell, "or the most facile woman I have ever met."

"Why not both?" Because it was true: her cool demeanor sometimes disguised confusion, and, once in a great while, even passion. She knew that she could both keep a secret, and tell a lie.

"Because I trust you," he said. "And I hope I'm right."

She touched his hand.

But even then she thought: Ham would like it here. He would love watching all the people hurry by. She wanted to laugh at herself. What a silly person she was to think of a man she saw every day. What was wrong with her?

Maiden Lane was a short walk away, with its galleries and shops of diamonds and gaudy, expensive dinnerware. They paused beside a planter of hybrid begonias. The street was alive with glamor, the charm that deceives. Sarah was not deceived. This charm was a way of making people with money feel flattered. On this street of shop windows and well-dressed shoppers they were close to uncovering a secret.

The brass plate said "Please ring bell," and Bell pushed the button and introduced himself to the electronic voice as Christopher Bell, "the writer. I called earlier today."

The lock made an inelegant buzz, and they ascended a carpeted stairway.

Sarah held back. She could not imagine why. She was never shy, and always sure-handed with people she did not know. She found herself thinking: leave this place. Don't take another step.

You don't want to know the truth.

"I'm so pleased to meet you, Mr. Bell," said the woman in black. "I'm Erika Spyri. This is my gallery." She flicked an eye at Sarah, but Sarah wore her coolest expression. For the moment there was no handshake, and no one smiled. "I'm pleased to meet such an important journalist, Mr. Bell. I've found some of your criticism of television and theater nothing short of brilliant."

Bell told her that he was living at Live Oak, writing Hamilton Speke's biography, and that this was Hamilton Speke's personal assistant, Sarah Warren. Erika Spyri's hand was cool and hard, the touch of a wooden saint, one of the abstracted, preoccupied saints, not one of fire and steel.

Sarah saw what was wrong.

Erika blinked frequently, and held her head stiff, touching her hair with her hands in quick gestures. She needed reassurance. The woman was struggling to conceal anxiety, or perhaps an even stronger emotion. "I am so pleased to meet both of you," she said. She met Sarah's eye again, and her look said: please leave. Leave now. I don't want you here.

Bell complimented her on the gallery's appearance, but compliments were not, for the moment, being entertained. "I know that you could hardly write about Hamilton Speke without delving into the nature of his marriage," said Erika brightly. Nearly too brightly, Sarah thought.

"You must know Maria quite well," said Bell.

She did not respond directly to his remark. "A marriage is so often a matter of some mystery, to outsiders." She paused. "But we don't usually help with research ourselves," she added smoothly. "We aren't really organized to assist even when we would like to."

"I don't think you'll find our questions terribly taxing. And, of course, your gallery will be mentioned in the book."

"That will be very pleasing," she replied, politely but with no trace of joy.

The gray carpet contrasted with the brilliant splashes of color on the walls. Erika led them on a tour of the gallery, a way, Sarah guessed, of showing how successful it was, and how little time she had for them. It was also a way of avoiding conversation. "Maria's one of our more successful artists. I think people find her watercolors soothing."

Maria's work had a room to itself, flower shapes staining the paper like blossoms just beginning to dissolve. Sarah did not find them soothing.

"But, of course, living near Maria, and near Mr. Speke, would allow you to know her much better than I ever could."

Sarah was thankful that she herself wore no makeup, and that she wore simple clothing. No one could compete with this swan, this smile, this amazing voice. And yet she heard herself respond, "I'm charmed by Maria. It's such a joy to have her at Live Oak."

To her own ear this sounded strained. There was a hesitation. Erika was about to make a decision. "Such a joy," she said at last, "that you want to learn more."

"If it's not too much trouble," said Bell. Sarah gave her best smile.

Something had worked. Bell's charm, and Sarah's presence, and perhaps a dash of Erika Spyri's business sense. A command was given, and coffee was served in an office furnished in black leather.

"This is exactly what we need, all of us. The study of a happy marriage," Erika said. "A successful artist and a very successful playwright. People love reading about successful people, don't they?"

"I'm especially interested in her background," said Bell.

Erika Spyri had perfect lipstick. She did not bother to sip her coffee. "There is a question of discretion."

"Of course," said Bell. "There always is."

Erika was choosing her words. "Maria has asked us not to respond to any questions about her past."

Bell seemed to ignore this statement. "I've seen the lists of shows, and awards. But," he said, "I need to know something about her childhood. Her teenage years. Her young adult years." He gestured, a wave that meant: you know I'm being entirely reasonable. "I can't write about her relationship with Hamilton Speke unless I know something about her."

"But my dear Mr. Bell, you probably know her much better than I do."

She did not have to say: the two of you are not here researching a book. There is something troubling you. "This is difficult," she said. "This is what happens sometimes. Someone wants to know the provenance of a painting, and the owner has asked me not to divulge his name. A wealthy man might need to sell a Bonnard to raise some spending money. You know where that leaves us—in a difficult position."

Erika met Sarah's eye. Sarah understood her glance. It said: this man chooses not to see, but you understand. There are secrets I cannot tell.

"I certainly wouldn't want to put you in a difficult position," said Bell.

There was quiet laughter. No, we certainly wouldn't want that.

Then Erika looked upward, and away from them. In another human being this might have seemed mannered. But it was plainly nothing more than her way of beginning to share a secret, or several secrets.

"She doesn't like to talk," Erika began. She gazed at her own nails, studying her hand. "I thought at first she wanted to give the impression of being a mask, an enigma."

"Many artists are complicated," said Sarah. Meaning: get to the point. And yet, she felt a certain compassion for this woman. Something held her, kept her from talking freely. It was as though they were being overheard.

Erika's voice was silk. "But the fact that you, who should know her fairly well, have to come to me—this tells me something. This tells me how secretive Maria truly is. I didn't mean to say 'secretive.' I meant to say 'private.'"

More quiet laughter, but without humor. Sarah knew that Erika did not choose an incorrect word without purpose. And she guessed, how she could not be certain, that Erika was relieved to be able to discuss, however discreetly, something that troubled her.

"The truth is that Maria seemed to come from nowhere, bursting into the art world in the East, perhaps ten years ago. She had been recently widowed, a young woman of quiet attractiveness and a really amazing ability with watercolors. A gallery in New York began showing her work, and then there was a review, and then another, and in a few months everyone needed to buy a Maria Merriam. They were simple watercolors of flowers—who would have thought it?"

Erika considered her desk top, her nails. "Then she vanished a few years ago. Completely dropped out of sight. There were rumors of travel, marriage, dramatic artistic sulks. But the art world forgets. Maria was not the first glorious moth to flit in and flit out again. It was, I think, troubling to some of us. But"— Erika gestured with an open hand, what could one do?

"And then several months ago I was astounded and delighted to see her here, in this office, with new work. I was delighted enough to welcome her, and to avoid asking awkward questions. She came, as far as I know, out of nowhere."

Erika watched them both, studying the effect of her story.

"So you don't know anything about her, really?" asked Bell.

"I've just told you a good deal. I know that it is what you already knew." She looked away, and seemed to listen for something far in the distance. "I don't like mysteries," said Erika. "I detest them. Let everyone tell all their secrets, all at once, and how bored we would be once we heard them. Then we could sweep them off into the dustbins and start our lives all over again."

Sarah used her most soothing voice. "If it's something shameful, of course, Mr. Bell wouldn't dream of writing about it."

"Of course not," said Erika, with the most careful of smiles. "Of course he wouldn't. And the truth is nothing shameful. Besides, nothing really *is* shameful, after all. No sins exist any more. There is no real embarrassment these days. Unless, of course, the truth is very painful, or there is some real reason to keep silent."

Erika rose, and adjusted a black venetian blind at the window, quite unnecessarily, Sarah thought. The blinds had been, as they were now, perfectly unruffled.

"This is a difficult moment for me. In a minute or two I have clients—"

"Of course," said Bell.

Erika hesitated at the window. She lowered her voice. "If only we could tell the truth about people by simply looking at them. But the face is a disguise, isn't it? A mask." She turned, and for the first time her face wore a simple, unguarded expression. "I don't believe you are here because of the book you are writing."

"Biographies are my profession," said Bell.

"I can't say any more than I have. Even the slightest possibility of danger to Maria or to this gallery—"

"What possible danger could there be?" asked Bell.

He was listening to the words, Sarah realized, but he was not hearing what was being said. And her own first impression of Erika had been accurate. She was more than anxious.

She was afraid.

Sarah touched Bell's arm to silence him. "There's a threat," she said, meeting Erika's eyes, "to all of us. Isn't there?"

Erika's expression said, for an instant, "I don't know what you are talking about."

Then she put her hands flat on the desktop and said, "Then you already have guessed." She did not speak, listening once again to far off sounds. "I'm not certain," she said. "I am only using my judgment, my sense of Maria, and her life. If I knew, without any doubt at all, I would call the police, regardless of my own safety. But this is precisely why I am talking with you."

Bell sat, all attention, but Erika was speaking to Sarah when she said, "The woman the art world knows as Maria Merriam is a very frightened creature named Maria Asquith."

Sarah could not speak for a while, feeling her soul contract. When she could draw a breath she said, "Please tell us every- thing."

· 25 ·

I t's good, Asquith thought, to be more than alive.
It's delicious to be more than human. He closed his eyes
and drew hard on a cigarette, just as he had years ago between acts, the fellow actors declaiming, the words reaching his
ears translated by distance and the heavy drapes into something
not heard at all but remembered.

"He's beginning to guess," she said.

"As I expected." He yawned. How delicious this cigarette was.
How could half-decayed leaf taste so full of life?

"He's digging up the grave," she was saying, "just as you said he
would."

He closed his eyes against the smoke, as he had years ago, listening to Speke read what he had just written. "I am so pleased,"
said Asquith. He didn't bother to tell her that he had watched
Speke plunge the spade into the rocky ground, just as he watched
so much else that took place here. He lifted his hand to touch her
hair and she flinched, and he made a little kissing sound of reassurance because he wanted her to know how well she was playing
her part in this finest theater.

"It's all going the way you wanted, isn't it?" she asked.

"With your help, my dearest, the play unfolds."

He had come in from the woods to avoid the heat. From the
trees, from the dusty pastoral backstage, he had been able to
watch everything.

"You're not unhappy," she said, in a tone that was half question.

His poor sister. So afraid of what he might do. "It's going so
well. I'm so proud of you, my little actress. You would make a
magnificent Ophelia."

She did not meet his eyes. "You won't really hurt anyone, will
you?"

Out of love, Asquith thought. Only out of love, the loyal compassion he felt for each one of them, even the man he did not
know, the stallion to Sarah Warren's mare, the journalist. Even he
drew a special tide in Asquith's soul.

He made his voice a purr. "All these months we have worked on this delight, and you still need to ask."

"You're changing."

"From what to what?"

"It's wonderful, in a way, Timothy. You're becoming the way you used to be. When you were happy."

"Oh, *happy*." He pressed out the cigarette carefully, and waited while she opened one of the skylights to dilute the smoke. "Yes, I do recall being happy."

She wiped the ashtray carefully. "I only want to be sure that you won't go back on your word."

"No," he said, luxuriating inwardly with the lie. "Of course not. I won't hurt any of them."

"He's not a bad person, really." Then she would say no more, because he turned to eye her. The studio had that tang of pine and the florid stains of her art. He felt the walls confine him, closing in. He sat, sipping soup she had stirred up for him on a hot plate, but he missed his little camp beside the spring.

She added, "I know he was unfair to you."

"Worse than you can imagine," he breathed. Was he so unfair, though, Asquith wondered. Had Speke really stolen the essence of his life? There was little question that Speke had typed late into the night, paper scattered over the kitchen table, but he had always been happy to stop and listen to one of Asquith's stories, or to applaud as he improvised an improved version of *Turandot*. Why did such a lovely opera have to be so dull? Asquith couldn't recall the details, at this point, but his new version of the opera was an astounding improvement. Speke would listen and laugh approvingly, and then continue into the dawn, his typing two-fingered but powerful, hammer punches that worked the typewriter sideways on the table so it was always about to fall off.

Perhaps, in the cosmic view, it didn't matter how much of Speke's work he had inspired. What did it matter how much of Hamlet's dissemblance was written by Shakespeare and how much by an assistant or a colleague, or even miswritten by the memory of an actor? An actor can improve a line, as Asquith knew, and besides, there is that other factor in the writing, the life of the work itself, the power of the man playing Hamlet for the eighty-second time to ad lib a quip more deftly than the poet, even though the half-phrase might be ever forgotten in the joyous white noise of the applause. The work works its way, a tree uttering its leaves.

But Asquith did not find himself quite capable of taking the cosmic view. This was no longer a battle for possession of the plays. That was a swamp without a passage, a Grimpen Mire, death to even hounds. Now he knew only great love for Speke and his household of stalwart cheer. Great love, and another sort of feeling, a dark intention much more powerful than any form of human affection.

"I know he deserves to suffer," she continued.

"But you've come to like him, haven't you? Go ahead, admit it. Everyone likes Hamilton Speke. Animals, children—the world was made for Speke and his like."

Her voice was uncertain. "He's been kind to me."

"Of course he has."

Of course Speke was kind, kind as the rain, kind as the rolling summer wind. Such vitality could only be admired. And envied. Envy was the desire to possess amidst a certainty that possession was unlikely. Asquith would, in time, master this estate. He was embarked on a play to catch the sanity of the King. He could not win Speke's love. He would win his life, his soul. Such theater was starlight itself, or rather the light of those invisible stars, the ones imploded to the point that time itself collapses in their cores.

This little theater past, he would move into the second and third acts, make love to the beautiful, capture the hope of the King of this sunny land and blow it all out, out like the little candle flame it always was.

Such a long shadow they cast, the celebrated, their images coined and emblazoned beside chocolates at the checkout line. The televised semblance, broadcast across a continent, parts its lips and shows its teeth and millions of picture tubes on televisions beyond imagining show teeth, a sea of incisors, a vast, many chambered fly's eye of manly joy.

Did Lucifer feel the injustice of it all, that eternity carried the children of God and merely washed the breakwaters of others? Did Lucifer regard with an even calm the unfairness of the sky as it rained life on some and half-lives on others? The hawk banks, lifts a cry. The scorpion scuttles.

But Asquith was kind, and even knew himself to be wise. All inside him was night, and no one beyond his sister had ever loved him. He wanted only to let the day see how truly it misjudged the dark. Public preening over one's future is not the best form of eloquence, and commerce with the unseen millions was not the only grasp on hope.

Hush, gentlemen players. Listen: the crowd in the pit, the rump-fed and the lousy both, fall still. The Actor steps across the boards, mastering the light. The light plays upon him, warms him, but does not go beyond the skin, which itself is merest lubricant and paint.

Within is the dark from which all art proceeds. And this dark loves what it sees, these frail ignorant, these poor citizens of the day.

This is all to be mine, says the Artist. The shadow turns upon the victor, the real shadow, the darkness within, and begins the battle, the endless one, the war it always wins.

·26·

Speke could not move. Something very bad indeed had happened to the body.

He was unable to do more than stand there in the sun with the sound of the great, dark wings ascending into the sky. The air, the light itself, seemed to flutter, ascending, leaving him in a fallen world.

Something terrible.

He took a step. His chest shrank, ribs squeezing his lungs. Terrible. He would never take another breath again. This was it. His life contracted to a knot. His heart stopped.

He took another step. Then quickly, leaping, stumbling, he nearly fell upon the body, and struggled to keep himself from collapsing over it.

Even when he saw the truth, and comprehended it completely, a part of him clung to the irrational discovery: he's turned himself into an animal.

The shock made him almost gleeful for an instant. But not quite. It was too horrible. Asquith would do that, wouldn't he? Turn into a beast? Of course, Speke knew this was madness. And yet, there it was. The body had ebony hooves, and tawny skin—a hide. Dark eyes that were no longer eyes streamed black ants. This transformation played over Speke in a series of heat waves, each wave hotter than the one before it, until he was about to collapse.

But he did not collapse.

Hamilton Speke can handle a shock, he told himself. He looked around at the fluttering poison oak, and the yellow, past-prime Scotch broom, at the scribble of wild thyme.

"Maria!" he rasped.

A deeper breath brought a bellow: "Maria!"

He staggered to the lawn, and called so loudly the poplars seemed to sway with his cry.

Maria slipped from her studio, but did not bother hurrying toward him, until she saw his arms waving.

But there was no time to consider that. "He's not dead!" he cried. "Not dead!" It was a song, a cry of joy from the bottom of his feet. And it was also a cry of fear, although the fear was irrational. "Not dead! Asquith's alive!"

For some reason she was pensive. She was more than pensive. She held herself back, not wanting to hear this.

"It's all a joke!"

"What do you mean?"

He wanted to shake her. "It's very simple. He's not dead. The body in the grave isn't him."

She put a hand to her breast.

"No, it's not somebody else. It's not a person."

He ran, and when he turned she was following him, but halting along the grass, not running at all. "Hurry! It's all right! I knew he wasn't a ghost. I never believed it for a second."

A large animal, a giant coyote or some other carnivore, crashed through the underbrush.

Maria blinked through the stench, and stood well away, but close enough so she could see the hooves glistening in the sunlight.

Speke gestured. What did I tell you?

A joke, but what sort of a mind would play such a prank? What sort of person was his old friend, after all? There was the slightest pepper of fear in his soul. But for the moment, that didn't matter. Joy gave him power. Using the shovel, he worked the body back into the grave, welcoming the flies, the smell, welcoming all of it as a gift, the most wonderful gift he had ever been given in his life: the return of his future.

Only as he buried the body, working with more vigor than he had imagined possible, did he become aware that Maria was still standing quietly, one hand to her breast.

"Don't waste time with that," she said, so softly he could barely hear her.

"I'll never waste a moment again in my whole life," he beamed.

She glanced up, as though she heard something far off, at the house, and once or twice seemed torn, wanting to run, needing to stay.

Speke did the job right, no half-measures. Earth, then stones, then larger rocks, until he had a prize grave, the noble resting place for one of Nature's creatures. Not that the work made it impossible to think. Far from it. It gave him time to think. To surmise, because what he knew was very simple.

What he concluded was not so simple, and not such an uncomplicated joy, although it did not diminish his sense of overpowering relief. Asquith was alive, and that meant that Asquith had buried the deer. Clever Asquith. What a wily man. You couldn't trust a man like that, but the truth was that Speke was no longer a murderer.

"The smell," she said. "Didn't that discourage you?"

"Discourage me! Hell, yes, it discouraged me. But the coyotes came. God, I love animals."

Maria looked away.

What could possibly be the matter with her? Why wasn't she relieved? "So he's alive," said Speke. "The best discovery I've ever made." But his voice was losing strength in the face of her downcast eyes.

"Why did you have to look?" she whispered, but Speke could not believe what he was hearing. He took a step closer. "Why did you have to know so much? You couldn't just let it lie?"

Speke could not speak. Why did I have to recover my life, and discover that my old friend was alive?

Then she started, spun as though she heard a step, and Speke himself was nearly sure that he had heard something from the house, or from the garage. A door shutting, perhaps, although acoustics had always been peculiar here at Live Oak. Clara was outside, beating a rug, perhaps.

"You are a good person," said Maria. "You don't mean harm."

Speke could not understand her shaken expression, her reluctance to celebrate. She gripped his arm, and it hurt. "You have to go," she said. "You can't stay here."

Speke gazed into her eyes without comprehension.

"I am beginning to imagine," said Maria, her voice trembling, "what he's going to do now."

· 27 ·

S arah sat with Bell in the twilight of a cocktail lounge, considering how little she had known until now.

The eye, her father had taught her, is the easiest thing in the world to deceive. To look out upon the world is to see surface, illusion. "Never," he had said, "believe what you see."

Sarah had trusted her eyes. She had believed that what she saw was real. The eye, she thought sadly, stunned, groping her way through her feelings, is fooled by nearly everything: the courtesan, the cheat. Even in total darkness it takes what comes. Wake up, it calls to the bored stone of the skull. Wake up! And it always wins, always wakes the hand, which has wandered as far as it can get, and the soul, which has seen enough. She should never have been deceived by her eye's innocence, this orb of water, this first to be deceived, this star.

Her father would say, emphatically: don't believe a thing.

Sarah felt herself wake, as from a trance. "We have to leave," she said, her voice nearly a whisper.

Ham was one of those rare human beings worth serving. He was one of those people who seem dressed in richer colors. She had been right to spend her days helping such a man. She knew, in her bones, that he needed her now.

It had been ages, it seemed, since they had left Erika Spyri's office, but they sat there in silence while Bell did nothing but jot down his thoughts. Erika had ushered them into the street, whispering, darting her eyes from side to side, and then she had left them, plainly relieved to be ascending once more to the routine of her office. Even as she sat there in the lounge Sarah felt a current of compassion for Erika. It was a terrible thing to be afraid.

Bell's black notebook was cluttered with jottings. His pen made the slightest whisper on the paper.

"We can't stay," she said.

He said, without looking up, "Let me finish my drink."

She was about to agree: of course. Finish your drink. Maybe he was right. His manner said: What's the rush? But inside, she seethed. She was motionless, but she knew that she was very close to throwing her glass of sherry at the far wall.

She usually loved the sound of a piano. Music almost always lay calm, warm hands on her, like a homecoming. But today the music was like unwanted affection, reassurance she did not believe or want.

"For someone who refused to divulge a secret, she managed to tell us volumes," said Bell. He snapped his notebook shut.

As much as she was charmed by his presence, his voice, and the way he moved, she could not sit still.

Everything is wonderful, said the music. The rest of the world is a dream. It was one of those outdated and yet potent pop tunes she could never quite name. "Stormy Weather," perhaps, or "Cry Me a River," something before her time and yet a part of it, too.

"You don't like it here," Bell said.

She could have loved it here, actually. Salted nuts, muted lighting. She felt the *frisson* she had experienced here once, years before, as a teenager when she had considered that some day she might fall in love. This was romance, of a sort she had long ago imagined to be the stuff of teenage novels and ads for champagne.

But now she wanted to run from this place. This was not the moment to smile prettily, and Sarah knew she had a pretty enough smile. There was a warning signal bleating somewhere in her marrow. An alarm, insistent, painful.

The pianist ended one song with a glissando, and then his fingers began toying with another tune. You see how delightful life is? said the music.

Don't believe it, the alarm said. Warning warning warning.

The alarm said: Maria Asquith.

The alarm said: Ham is in trouble.

"I think well here," Bell explained, nearly an apology. "I've interviewed mayors, senators, and gangsters here. A Columbian druglord sat right where you're sitting and talked about the Cal/Stanford game."

Certainly Bell would feel exactly as she felt. Certainly he would understand what was happening. But her fear was so visceral that she couldn't articulate it, and thoughts which cannot be verbalized tend to slip away.

"I don't see what there is to think about at all," she said.

He misunderstood. "Maybe not. A man might naturally be attracted to the sister of an old friend—"

"Ham doesn't know who Maria is."

"He married her—"

"She lied to him."

"This doesn't quite fit together, Sarah. Why would she do that? I mean, think about it: most of what Erika just told us is purest conjecture."

"Believe me, I'm right."

He frowned, earnest, deliberate. "But how can you be sure?"

It was difficult to keep her voice steady. "It's pretty obvious. Ham doesn't understand Maria."

Bell leaned forward. His posture said: Go on, I'm listening.

"I saw it happen," Sarah continued. "I saw. But I didn't really know what I was seeing." Her inner voice said: fly. She silenced it with an effort. "Ham was ecstatic when he first met her, out of control, practically, with—well, with love. He introduced me to Maria as though he were allowing me to at last meet the Good Fairy herself, as though I would faint dead away from the sheer honor of it."

"You're jealous."

"This isn't some giddy hunch, Chris. I know Ham."

"And how did Maria seem when you met her?"

"As she always seems. The sort of look and soft laugh that stuns men and that women find less than consistently charming." But, she told herself, you were fooled by Maria, too.

"Do I seem slain?"

"Ham wouldn't have been able to keep a secret under such circumstances. He blurted out everything he knew about her. He can't really control his feelings that well. He's too full of life. If he had known that Maria was Asquith's sister, he would have said something, or let something slip."

"I'm not so sure," Bell said. "It would be a natural way to get his old collaborator to spend more time with him. The brother-in-law as partner—it makes sense."

"That's not what happened. Ham was deceived."

"How do you know?"

She did not answer.

"And why would Maria deceive him? There's no reason. And if Maria deceived Ham, then so did her brother. And yet you say that Asquith and Ham are probably heads together right now working on *Stripsearch II.*"

Sarah took a deep breath. Bell was, despite his good sense, a calm thinker of the worst sort. Not a clumsy thinker, and a natural skeptic. For this reason, conclusions did not come quickly to him. This, no doubt, made him an excellent journalist, each fact a pinch of ore to be mentally weighed. Assaying the truth was not Sarah's habit. She was either ignorant, or enlightened. And now, without a doubt, she knew the truth.

"I think we've been outfoxed," Bell was saying, "all of us, including you. I don't know whether to laugh at Ham's cunning, or tear up my notes in exasperation. Except, I'm too stubborn to quit. How can I write a biography about such a wily fake? A charming charlatan. Unless he expects me to hide the truth, which I have no intention of doing. I'm capable of writing a hostile biography, if that's what it turns out to be."

She had trouble controlling her voice. "He deserves your affection. And some of your faith. There's some kind of trouble. Something wrong."

"Okay, fine—you may be right. Even when I trust your judgment, I find myself balking. Professional habit, I suppose. I need more information." Bell, sure-footed, calm, frowning with the responsibility of what they had discovered, seemed to wish he had a map he could unfurl on the table before them, a chart he could study. "All that whispered wild talk about the homicidal brother is completely unsubstantiated. It could be nothing but Erika's imagination. I can't believe it." He shrugged an apology.

Sarah detested the sound of the piano.

Bell selected a salted almond. "I need to know more about Asquith. He's probably nothing more than a very bright guy with an ego that really isn't very hungry. He doesn't mind Speke getting all the glory, and all the paychecks."

"That's ridiculous," Sarah said. "Maria is trouble."

Bell interlaced his fingers. He had to admit that he didn't understand Hamilton Speke anymore. And Asquith—who was this mysterious *eminence grise?* But Sarah had just said something that he understood. "She is trouble. Don't worry," he added with a laugh. "She's not my type."

"What type is yours, exactly, Mr. Bell?"

"I hope you're never mad at me, Sarah. You have a glance that would lay a tank battalion to waste."

"Then I suppose you wouldn't stand much of a chance."

"Not a ghost." Then, "There was a strange, mechanical quality about her interest in me."

"Mechanical," Sarah repeated, drily.

"As though she wanted to charm me simply to distract me."

"Tell me one thing, Chris. Are we going to sit here forever?"

"I'm trying to absorb what I've heard." He added something that should have been a warning. "Erika has started me off on a very interesting path and I want to take my time."

"I can't stand it here."

"So," said Bell, "we've established that Maria slithers and licks the air and in every other way acts like a serpent."

"A legless lizard," Sarah agreed.

"But what does this mean?"

Sarah pushed aside her drink, so hard that sherry spilled across the table. Its scent was nutlike, the odor of oak and something else, something both tantalizing and poisonous. She apologized, but then said, "I can't sit here any more."

She was on her feet, and was about to leave without him when she saw him thrust currency just beyond the small lake of wine. His movements were slow. His words, though, when he reached her were reassuring.

"You're right," he said. "We have work to do."

· 28 ·

Maria clung to his arm, and she was weeping. "I've done something terrible to you, Hamilton."

Speke wondered at her words. Had she been unfaithful to him? "It's all right," he tried to reassure her. "Whatever you've done, I'll make it all right."

It was hot. The sunlight had weight, like a radiologist's lead blanket. The heavy sun draped over his shoulders, and made it hard to do more than stand, absorbing what she was saying.

This should be a happy moment. His own life had returned with the fact that somewhere his old friend was still alive. There was no guilt, there was only the sunlight and a landscape restored to hope. He understood that Maria was frightened, and he forced himself to be receptive to what she was so desperately trying to communicate.

"He told me I could never trust you, Hamilton. But I do trust you. Please believe me—you should leave this place."

She was afraid of Asquith. That was clear, and yet Speke wanted to laugh. Asquith! Why be afraid of a man he had nearly killed?

Death had been vanquished. Nothing else mattered.

And yet, Maria was afraid of Asquith, and Speke himself could not shake this peculiar chill that wended upward in his bones. "He wants to destroy you," Maria wept.

When Speke interrupted her, he was surprised that his voice was reasonably steady. "Where is he?"

She did not answer. Instead she replied, "Don't you see what's happening? He's going to destroy everything."

She spoke with authority, as though she had seen all of this coming. The color of the sunlight faded for a moment. His voice was a rasp. "You—" It was impossible. He could not say a thing like this. "You knew, all along."

She wept.

He ran his fingers through her hair. He held her for a moment. "Where is he?"

Now he was beginning to feel his feet anchor themselves into the ground, his boot heels digging in. Maria turned away, and would not answer. He folded his arms. His entire past would have to be reconsidered. Maria and Asquith were a team he would never have imagined. It wasn't possible, even now. Could they have become lovers? At night, when he was watching old movies? Once reality unravels, anything is possible.

His voice was calm. "I'll protect you, Maria. Whatever has happened, and whatever you've done. I won't let him hurt you."

"Hamilton—" She turned back to him. There is so much you should know, her expression said. "He used me."

Ugly words. With ugly implications. "He's a deceiver," Maria went on. "He uses people. It's his way. He can't help it, because he really doesn't have a life of his own."

She continued, "He made me meet you. He encouraged me to marry you. It was all his idea. Your whole life the way it is right now—it was all his plan."

These words made him close his eyes for a moment. Speke felt her words, and understood them, and when he opened his eyes again he felt the world flicker, as though he would faint. Asquith the mastermind, Asquith the magician, had deceived him in every way.

The air was stone. Each breath was acid. He could taste the strength of Asquith's envy. He, Speke, had fulfilled the dream: he had lived, his name in bright lights, his words treasured. He had achieved what amounted to immortality, a life that extended not into eternity but around the world. He was Someone. And Asquith had never lived, in a sense, choked off from even ordinary, private pleasure. Speke had spent too much time on the telephone, too much time giving interviews, too much time sitting for publicity stills while strangers fussed with his hair and adjusted the lights that cascaded over him. But he had been offered life, and he had taken it.

He bit his knuckle, hard, wishing for enough pain to force him to concentrate. He felt concussed, lost to his senses. Isn't it astounding, he found himself thinking, that even now my heart goes on thudding away in my chest? Don't deceive yourself. Your life with Maria was an illusion. Reality, that steady rod of iron, is twisting out of shape, alive and writhing, a serpent.

"I forgive you," he said. "Whatever he made you do, I love you, Maria." It was funny, in a bitter way. Asquith had known the sort of artsy, mysterious woman he would find irresistible, and had turned his life inside out.

"Stay here," Maria said. "Please don't do anything. Wait!"

She left him, the sound of her footsteps receding to silence.

I must have been so easy to trick, he thought. So simple— blinded by my own faith, my own ceaseless belief that all would be well.

He had the strangest impression that Asquith was everywhere at once. He had the impression that Maria had gone to bring Asquith forth to take a bow, that an invisible audience would burst into applause as Asquith, dressed as Pan, as a Jack o' the Green, as the very devil of the woods himself bounded nimbly to take a long curtain call.

There are many things I don't know, old friend, Speke said, addressing the presence of Asquith, the ozone sting in the air around him, the still platinum stalks of the foxtails beside the path. But there are things you don't know about me, which you know only how to ape. I love. I love Maria, I love this place, I love the people here. I love Sarah—yes, it was true. I am a man of heat.

And this gives me a strength you can not share, old colleague. And yet he was afraid, too, even as he was certain. If Asquith could do so much, if he could craft Speke's life so the very vessel of his days began to sink around him, then Asquith was like night itself.

Maybe, he told himself, Asquith was not the man he once was. Maybe he had changed. Maybe this new adversary was not spite, not envy, not vengeance, but something worse. Maybe it was the hatred the lifeless must always feel for the passionate.

She was back, panting, struggling for the breath to speak. "He's done what I was afraid he'd do—"

"What?" he heard his voice ask.

"The telephone doesn't work," she said.

He had never seen her like this—tear-stained, wild-eyed. He wanted to utter something soothing about the telephone, about how funny phones were. Nothing to get excited about, he wanted to say. "Of course it doesn't work. That's the first thing Asquith would do, and the easiest." Think like Asquith, he told himself. What else will he do?

But something hard stabbed his palm. The car keys. She was forcing the keys into his hand. She dragged him by the arm. "Get into the car and get out of here. Go!" Her fingernails dug into his flesh.

"He's done something to the car, too," said Speke. "Go see."

She snatched the keys from his hand, and streaked toward the garage, wrestled with the door, and, somewhere in the dark of the garage, flung open the car door.

She cried out.

He caught her in his arms, at the edge of the shadow of the garage. "It can hardly be a surprise, can it? Don't worry, Maria. I know the way he thinks."

He knew without even slipping the key into the slot in the half-light of the garage. He knew before he even turned the key. He did it only to assuage Maria, looking back at her with an I-told-you-so expression. It was useless. All twelve cylinders were silent iron. Speke settled into the leather seat, and the ignition that always coughed power gave a metal click. A dry, steel cluck. The single tick of a large, broken clock that meant: nowhere. Nothing.

The car was dead.

"I would do the same thing," Speke offered, with a grim lilt in his soul. This was a game Asquith was playing, and he was beginning to recall the rules. He gazed under the hood for a moment, but the cavern of the engine, and the expensive, cold-iron intricacies could hold a dozen severed cables. His untutored hands groped in the dark for an obvious sliced connection, but the car was not going to be coaxed to life by him. A sheepdog has more mechanical talent than I have, he told himself. It had always been a sort of comfort. He had always turned to a mechanic and said: as long as it's fixed. He had never had to wrestle with the details of solenoids and distributors, except as words on his copy of the bill.

Asquith's game was an ugly one, but wasn't he, in the long run, Asquith's equal? Couldn't he beat him, even now?

Let us see what else our old adversary has been up to, thought Speke, with a sickening certainty that he knew exactly what would happen next. Brothers wasn't due to come today, but Clara's bronze-brown Buick was parked under the pepper tree, where she always parked it, where summer after summer of pink seeds and leaf litter and bird droppings had gradually worn the finish to the same basalt tan of the stones of the estate.

Maria seized his hand. "Go up to the road. Hurry. Try to flag down a car."

Clara's car would be disabled, too. He was sure of that much.

Her car was always unlocked, and the keys hung in the ignition, a metal Saint Christopher on the key chain. The keys tinkled, but nothing happened. Speke fumbled for the hood release and pulled the small black handle.

Wasn't this going a bit far? To hurt my car is one thing. It made a sort of rough-and-ready sense. Speke recycles cars like Budweiser empties. Trash his Jag.

But this was an assault on Clara, and Speke did not like that. Clara was innocent. The hood gave a rusty creak, like the alarm of a beast, the distant note of a bull elephant. The old car smelled like so much stone: old petroleum, old rust. Clara didn't deserve this. The bright copper gleam contrasted with the glaze of aging rubber and road grease.

Speke slammed the hood, very hard. The radio antenna quivered.

Asquith was not playing an extended joke. Asquith was playing for life, and for death. Speke could feel it now—Asquith was watching, as the tragedian might watch from stage left, in the shadows among the drapes and cables, waiting for his cue.

I am an actor, too, he thought. In my way, without your polish, Asquith, without the acid you could deliver with each consonant. My gift was always instinctive, knowing what the characters would say because I was a human being and had wept and laughed. Asquith had always known only wit. Cunning Asquith had understood only the mind diseased. Asquith had understood why the arsonist in *Flash*—the play *Variety* proclaimed was "still burning records in New York and London"—worshipped fire. The arsonist in the play loved fire so deeply he eventually burned alive.

Don't run, Speke counseled himself. Don't even consider such a thing. This is your land. You are master here. You know he's watching.

He couldn't keep himself from gazing along the line of trees, over the concrete block of the wellhead, over the bottlebrush and the toyon and the buckeye, the silver-dollar eucalyptus and the Russian olive. To the California bays in the dry creek and everywhere beyond, everywhere with their huge, still, wrestling branches, the live oaks.

Beyond the garage, far down through the woods, glittered the lake. A quail far away twisted off one of his calls. The air was hot, and redolent with the exhaled flavors of the wild oats and the foxtails, the thistles and the thyme. The dry perfection, the hills in their summer coma.

I'm trapped here. Caged within a spotlight, an airless zero.

Then he knew how ridiculous he was being. Of course he could walk the few miles to the road. But why should he? He was master here! This was his land. He wasn't going anywhere.

He turned to his wife. He thought of her this way, as an extension of his body, a deep, vital organ. Asquith had failed. She was his.

"No, don't go in there, Hamilton, please don't go. You don't know how he is," she gasped. She was hyperventilating, eyes wide. "You don't know what he wants to do. He wanted to do much worse things to you than try to trick you and deceive you. He wanted to do everything he could to wreck everything that was yours. Hamilton, please don't go into the house."

He cupped her head in his hands, and kissed her tears. What power Asquith must have, he thought, to capture a woman and keep her like this. "If he's in there, I want to see him."

"I hated you, too. I hated you!" Her voice was like a leak in an airhose, a hiss that was more scream than whisper. Speke could not move for a moment. "But I know you don't deserve this, Hamilton. I can't hate you any more."

There was a thought as sickening as a snapped bone: madness was not impending. It was upon him. There had never been an Asquith. Asquith had never visited, and Speke had buried a road-killed buck in a psychotic delusion, a holiday from reality. Maria wasn't saying the things he heard her saying. He was having a complete, sunlit hallucination.

Stunned, staring straight ahead, Speke strode through the heat, into the cool vault of the house.

Was it possible that he could have so completely lost his mind? What test was there, what way to determine what was real. Once he had eaten some very bitter mushrooms, curled fungi black and withered as dead tadpoles. "Powerful stuff," a fellow partygoer had said, sprinkling them into his palm. "Powerful" was an understatement. They had been crippling. He had spent the day watching television simply because he could not trust himself to go outside where there was traffic. Better to stay inside, he had told himself, although to this day ads for certain detergents made him feel a giddy horror.

Asquith had never been strong enough to wear the heavy cape of fame—the love of strangers. Asquith could hide, and he could poison a life he could never have captured and kept. But Speke knew his own strength. He was sunlight. He was laughter. He could feel it in his lungs, his bones—he could save Maria from all that had happened, He loved her.

Asquith had lost his mind. Lost his mind, and his power to love, long ago. Early one morning in North Beach, he had walked naked along Columbus Avenue. So early only pigeons and a street sweeping machine stirred on the street, along with Asquith, blood streaming down his arm, trickling from a bite he had taken out of his own flesh.

I don't know, Speke told himself, what is real. This is what Asquith must have wanted: he wanted to strip everything away. So let it be stripped, Speke thought, all illusion, to an empty stage set, a landscape of stark light and cutting dark. Let it be simple: this was a contest between faith and hope over spite and cruelty. Light was stepping forward to battle the dark.

Speke had no weapon.

Nothing but his anger, and his love.

· 29 ·

If Asquith was in the house, hiding, soaked into some recess of the interior, Speke would find him.

He called Asquith's name.

The house was his. The house was home, and affection. The house was knowledge that a future was possible, a human future.

He stormed through the sun room, that beautiful airless place, the hall, that carpeted, ferned atrium, and bounded up the stairs. He burst into one bedroom after another. Each chamber was a page from a decorator's brochure, the air in the teak room scented with tung oil, the bunch of dried rose petals in Maria's study surrendering the ghost of a perfume into the air. He was, he knew, violating each uninhabited, perfect room with his anger.

But he knew he was right to do what he was doing. He would not be cheated of his life, cozened into a lesser world. He wanted to rip the air itself. He kicked open a door.

"Asquith!"

The chimney of a hurricane lamp shivered, chiming. A spray of baby's breath trembled at his tread. He had not been in this room for months. It was delightful, colonial American, hand-finished maple, great oval rag rugs. One of these rooms was supposed to be Empire, all spindly legs and mother-of-pearl inset rosewood. He couldn't find it, and then, when at last he did, he broke one of the chairs, tossing it aside. The leg was pink where it had fractured, like a thing of flesh. There was no air.

No, he thought, this is wrong. His search did not have to be this frenzied. Take your time, he told himself.

He called his old friend's name. And as he searched, the fury returned. He threw open doors, whisked dresses off their hooks in closets, and there were many closets, walk-in rooms of empty, unused shelves, and others crowded with stylish silk *frou-frou* from Milan, clothes Maria had just bought, a brass hook from each neck.

When he had exhausted the upstairs, he pounded downstairs to the office. To the bar, with its princely piranha. To the dining room, and into Sarah's office, where he fumbled with that phone long enough to realize that this receiver too, was dead.

"Maria!" he called. He stabbed at the intercom, and heard his voice echo in distant rooms. The two-way system told him that the house was empty. It had mikes so sensitive you could hear a fly whine in a far-off room. Except that at this moment there were no flies. No distant footsteps, no stifled laughter. No one but one confused, sweating, angry Hamilton Speke.

The intercom was dead, too. Of course.

Hamilton, said a sweet, soft, smart-ass inner voice. Hamilton: you are losing your mind.

There never was an Asquith. Never. He was never here.

Christ, he thought. Where is Maria?

Be steady, he commanded himself. Stay calm. Move step by step. Asquith wants you to panic. He might be listening even now. Don't give him the satisfaction of seeing you like this. Take a deep breath. Remember those breathing exercises that were supposed to stave off panic, the ones the therapist taught you? Asquith wants the old, ragged Speke to come back, the Speke who chewed tranquilizers like antacids. He wants you to be as sick as he is.

I was just an ordinary kid. I had a bicycle, and a paper route. It was California suburbia, lawns and friendly dogs. I wanted something more.

I will be all right, he told himself. I'm taking big, deep breaths, just as the therapist instructed me to do when I felt a panic attack and couldn't get my hands on the one-hundred-and-fifty milligram beta blockers.

Asquith had taken the sleeping pills, too. And the tranquilizers. He had cleaned them all out. He squirreled them away, and probably swallowed them all himself in one great belly-bloating party. That's all right. Hamilton Speke didn't need chemical solace. He was here like iron.

But there was something wrong. Something very wrong. He stepped into the corridor. The house was too silent. An instinct, a hunter's guile, perhaps, came to him from a prehistoric part of his mind. This quiet was bad.

"Clara?" he called.

Maybe, he thought, she can't hear me from here. She occupied her own world, the kitchen and her recipes, her drying herbs, her muffin tins. Maybe she had left the house altogether. That's it—she's not here.

He called her name again, and there was no answer.

Not here, he told himself. There's no question about it. She's gone.

This silence was very bad.

Clara was still here. He could tell. That same instinct, that same hunter's savvy, returned to him. The woman he thought of as the unacknowledged guardian angel of this place, the sentinel that kept it safe, the woman who would know where Asquith had been hiding, was somewhere in the house, and almost certainly right where she always was—in the kitchen. Asquith was cagey, but he had always needed that extra toke of hashish to keep plodding, that extra slug of cognac to stay bright.

Asquith had met his match. He was up against Hamilton Speke, two-fisted, life in his lungs. "Clara!" he bawled into the shadowy walls of the hallway, knowing that by now she should have heard him and responded.

He shrank back into the office. His instinct told him: find something in here that you can use. Put your hand on a weapon.

Sarah's office was hot, stuffy, glittering with tiny toothed objects, staplers and staple removers like fanged robot snakes. Why did Sarah need three sets of those? And what a strange invention they were, really, nothing like the elegant solutions that his father had brought into being. *We've got the answer to the staple problem, sir. We'll bite them off with one of these.*

He was cold. There was nothing that resembled a weapon here. Besides, he was unnerving himself. There was no need to find a weapon at all. This was just another form of giving in to fear.

He needed to see Clara. He needed to wash dishes with her, and help her dry all the cups in the sunny kitchen.

Clara.

He crept carefully, very quietly, down the long hall. You see, a nasty inner voice said. You see? She should have heard you. She's only at the end of the corridor, behind a door.

Bad quiet.

He lunged at the kitchen door and the broad white door swung open.

The room was silence and light.

There—you see how foolish it was to worry. You were silly to get so upset. Everything is just fine.

The kitchen was sunny, yellow walls and Spanish tile gleaming. The door was on a spring and swung back and forth, a trap that hid what it had just displayed several times before working its way to the closed position.

Speke slumped, panting, in the hallway.

He had been overexcited, nothing more. There were no problems at all in the kitchen. None at all.

Except for that one little detail that didn't quite belong. That one little smudge. Well, it wasn't exactly a smudge. It was not a smudge at all, really, so much as a handprint. It had been a dark, sticky looking handprint. It was nothing more than a jam handprint.

Nice, tart jam.

Go ahead, he told himself. Take another look. Open the door and take a nice long look. But it wasn't his voice nudging him forward. It was that nasty, wise little voice that knew everything too well.

I should call the police.

Sure, said the little voice. Go ahead and call the police on your brand new AT&T state-of-the-art telephone system that somehow just doesn't seem to work all that well.

Go back and find a weapon. Something hard and heavy, something that could kill.

His hands were numb, and his arms did not obey the command to lift, and push the door. The door wasn't heavy. It was a single swinging door. There was even a window in it, through which yellow wall was visible, a small window, just big enough for one servant to see another coming with a brace of roast pheasant.

Just big enough for Speke to step to one side and see the jam handprint. It was clear and very bright, at the bottom of a cupboard, down by the gleaming floor.

He slumped to his knees. This wasn't happening. This wasn't real. But if it isn't real, then I might as well go ahead and look. Right?

Asquith has met his match, right? Isn't that what you were just telling yourself? Or maybe the dark is powerful, so much more powerful than the light. He told his hands to move, and very slowly he climbed up the wall, and carefully, very gently, pushed at the door.

Even then he didn't look. Whatever you do, he told himself, don't look. You could make a mistake if you look too soon. The early evidence might prove misleading. Wait until you step all the way into the nice yellow kitchen, until the swinging door has done its pendulum routine and has shut all the way and then, only then, take a nice long look.

He was shuddering, deep in his muscles, like a man up to his chin in ice water. His arms and legs had no feeling, limbs lost to hypothermia.

Turn around and look. Turn around and take a look at Clara.

Because that's who it was. He could tell through the back of his head, through his shirt, through his skin. There was a smell.

It was not the smell of blueberry muffins.

He turned his body. He closed his eyes, but it was already too late. It was already much too late, and a moan was rising from the bottom of his lungs, rising, and increasing in pitch and volume to a cry.

Clara was everywhere.

· 30 ·

Splashes of shadow slipped over him. Asquith melted from tree to tree, making his way quickly into the woods.

He stopped to listen. The brush around him was busy with the keen and blurt of tiny lives, and there was a dry wind, a sturdy breeze, beginning to stir in the upper branches.

Hamilton no doubt still believed that he was Asquith's equal. He could easily imagine Speke's reasoning: I am the man of life and reason, and with a little perseverance Asquith doesn't stand a chance.

Poor man, so full of trust. Hamilton Speke had always had too much faith, and too little understanding of the ways of darkness. Speke thought the world was good.

He clung to yet another tree for a moment, looking back toward the house. He heard Speke's cry, calling the name of his old partner. Asquith's senses had always been more keen than the senses of most athletes. Most men were so clumsy, although Hamilton was keen enough, in his way. Asquith was trembling inwardly, alive to the great power he had over this place.

Yes, dear friend, you really are finished. Look hard, Hamilton. Search from room to room. Enjoy the last moments of this sunny chapter of your life.

Asquith did not need to run, now. He slipped along a trail of his own making, a path no eye could detect but his, his feet seeking stones and the pithy, sun-baked loam because he knew that while Hamilton Speke was not a skilled tracker he was not, at the same time, a stupid man.

His own play, the great work of his life, was proceeding magnificently, and it was satisfying how little was surprising him. Of course Maria had divulged all, taken in at last by Speke's overpowering warmth, his genuine animal liveliness, his beauty. He had not overheard her, but he had seen it in her eyes. She was beginning to fall under the spell of her husband.

As Maria had told her inevitable tale, Asquith had played his game of love. It had only taken a few minutes, just a few perfect moments, slipping like pearls, and the woman had been so fortunate as to die in a convulsion even as he slipped into her. His spasms had thrown her body against his, and he had crooned into her the faith he had that the journey she took, the tide that swept her outward, was far more blissful than any joy she had ever experienced in this page after page existence some people prized.

He trotted downhill, dodging boulders and down-swept branches, leaping the man-thick roots of the ancient oaks. He fell panting beside his hiding place, his camp, with its smudge of campfire ash and its discreet roll of sleeping bag.

He stood still, listening.

Soon, he knew, she would slink to his secret place, and lie to him, pronouncing a complete falsehood, bringing him something, candy or a thermos of coffee as a distracting gift. Asquith waited for her approach, and listened to the purling waters of the spring, a moss-greasy fault in the rock that leaked water and made it hard to hear the approach of anyone, but did after all allow him both water and a comforting cool against the heat.

In all he was that sole man against a kingdom, much like Hamlet, but what had Hamlet to do but feign madness, while Asquith was enacting the tireless, noble carriage of a murdered man.

His audience was select, even tiny, that one man who would most appreciate such theater. Well, hardly appreciate. But such a play was working on Hamilton Speke as on no other human being. Asquith knew his audience. So a little hardship was itself a kind of pleasure, and despite his fastidiousness where human beings were concerned, he had always loved the feel of getting really earthy, asleep and slowly waking to the rustle of dead leaves under the ear, a temporary forester turning by the hour more and more the dusk of wood and clay.

One does need a cup of coffee, and a portable propane stove loses its gas until at last there is nothing to do but make a fire, small, secret, out of old wood that exudes so little smoke it is but another exhaled breath into the air. All he had to do was swallow some of the chemicals purloined from Speke's dispensary and the forest had a new lord, a magician.

Real theater had never been so delicious. Playing Hamlet in his theater days had not quite met his glorious expectations. Enacting the antic disposition in Chico during a festival of moths had been amusing enough, the feathered insects thumping off the spotlights, spinning in the radiance amidst Ophelia's mad scene. During the instructions to the players, hardly a great speech but a sensible one, how could he speak of not sawing "the air too much with your hand, thus" while a blizzard of moths rose up and into the light, including the light of one's countenance.

Asquith came to call it the Insect Tour, his last days as a working actor. One critic had blamed his dead end as an actor with the trite dismissal, "too many drugs." Fair enough, perhaps. But the bugs were real, not hallucinations with little legs. As he lost touch with who and what he was, he experienced most acutely the various venues—one peculiar theater after another. There was the county fairground in Paso Robles before a one-third house, the audience waving their programs against an onslaught of June bugs, "flying tanks" the director called them. There was that little theater in Needles during a plague of darkling beetles, the black carapaces underfoot everywhere, the mildest scent of iodine released with each footfall so it hardly disgusted after a while. The beetles thrived only at night, a flashlight spying the slow insects moving with no sense of impending danger. Hamlet sought a man who was not passion's slave in a land that crawled.

The exoskeleton masters the earth. Everyone knows that. This seemingly endless tour of Hamlet, though, taught him everything worth knowing. He starred—it was not too grand to be true—in the Avalon Ensemble financed by the estate of a Hollywood widow who needed to lose money for tax reasons. The tour did lose money, bleeding cash even as Hamlet learned the trick of the sword fight, the little prick of the poisoned foil that even at a touch must draw blood. You could buy the same Gorepak at the magician's shop in Disneyland, but somehow the glint of the steel, the flowing white sleeve just-blossoming with scarlet, did not look like art. It looked real. One touch, and the mirror was held to a fairly sanguine nature. People took in their breath. The front row winced. It was all in Hamlet's own surprise, not knowing at first what has happened, that flare of disbelief, replaced by realization, replaced by further disbelief. A wound is like a word, it can be misunderstood, mastered, forgotten. Remembered again. Pain is the silence that carries our egos forward, lilylike on black water. Memory is a constellation of microscopic cuts.

Ophelia had to die. That was something Asquith had always known, and that was something Hamilton had never quite understood. Ham would have said "Oh, sure, we have to live with bad things happening," meaning that we have to learn to accept it, endure. But Asquith meant that it *had* to happen, was required as food is, and water, and defecation, because without it there was no life.

So the best copulation is somehow homicide. Forget rape, that ugly trespass, that assault. Rape was never erotic enough the few times Asquith had accomplished it, knees on the muddy asphalt, trussing and stuffing the grocery shopper, half the time not even achieving the necessary penetration because it was all so obvious. Rape lost its appeal. It was a political act, the vigorously and stupidly male over the supposedly weaker sex. It could in no way be considered an act of love.

Sex with men had its virtues. There had been a few male lovers, most notably that ex-Marine in the hotel in Santa Barbara, and then that truck driver in Jersey City, of all places, the one who rear-ended the just-purchased used car, his sister's, and had to go back to his walkup for the insurance papers. That was fun, the nose breathing and nearly gagging while someone else's bell got rung. And that boy—well, boyish—tennis player from Iceland, he had claimed, but then later Asquith had heard the same voice in Lincoln Center, just after the opera singers sang gospel music and everyone was feeling light-hearted. It was on the way out, and the voice had asked someone nearby, "What is that French phrase that means 'Dazzle the bourgeoisie'?" in a High Midwest accent, Chicago, perhaps.

Men were worthy of that special sort of love, too. At some point he had realized, with the same turn of self-acceptance everyone must reach, or should, regarding their sexual natures, that only one thing provided the release, the sweet burst, the consummation which was more nearly the chief nourisher in life's feast than anything else in bed or out.

He used to wonder as a little boy: why do they do it? Murderers who kill a dozen nurses, one after another. Why do they bother?

The first was that thin, nearly emaciated, would-be model who had fled the photographers lights for a little quiet in the small town Asquith had chosen, one so much like another, each a sheet of paper with the same watermark, the abandoned mill, the re-opened mill, the mill going on reduced hours, the men on their coffee breaks huddled, drinking coffee too hot to sip because time was running out and it was January.

She had arched, like a gymnast, and he had read about such pleasure before, in a study of Hindu sexual practices, the man who can have an orgasm while merely glancing at the departing figures of women, hurrying under the open arms of trees.

He cut her. Even the void of her bowels, and the fluid, neither water nor mucus, that flooded from her nostrils, gave him great fulfillment. They were rude details in themselves, but they were like the lingering evidence of a great passion just consummated. And he believed what someone told him that Jung himself had come to understand: that dying is itself a keenest pleasure.

So it was fair. He was a lover. He gave pleasure. It was by killing that this pleasure was given, but this was honorable, as an act of love. If it was kind to put a sick beast "out of its misery," how much finer it was to put a woman into ecstasy and out of this diurnal plod.

No doubt Hamlet regretted missing the scene of Ophelia's death. But then, Hamlet was, as Asquith had discovered, a limited man, caught in both court intrigue and his own responsibility to the dead. Asquith suffered no such limiting text. Like Goethe, his field was time. His faith was illumination. He loved. He took life.

But Speke. It had all been so easy for Speke. Women responded at once to his laugh. His laugh! Who would have thought the laugh was a feature of a man's desirability, but Speke had laughed and women had loved him, easily. He was one of those men who stride into a restaurant followed by gazes, not only the glances of women. Men liked him, too, as one might like a prancing horse or a winging hawk. Speke had color, hue, tone.

And Asquith was one of those on whom gazes never fall, one of those figures humans glance away from. Babysitters tightened their grips on toddlers' wrists when he made his way from the bus stop.

He had wanted Speke's praise, Speke's attention. Why wouldn't Speke laugh at his jokes? He would, to be kind, or out of the cheerfulness of his own nature, enjoying Asquith's imitation of this famous dictator, of someone afflicted with that famous disease. But Asquith knew that even his humor was flat. Speke was alive, and gave life, and Asquith was a shadow, one of those people no one can like. He sensed it in himself, as one can sense the thinness of one's singing voice: he was quick, smart, eager, and impossible to love.

Only Speke had enjoyed his company—Speke, whose eye would brighten at the first syllable of one of his plans, because Asquith had always schemed, he had no shortage of ideas.

He listened, trying to discern through the splash of the spring, that little leak of water, whether or not Maria was coming.

There was no one. He sank back, comforted by his reflections.

They had lived in a duplex, he and his sister and their mother, a woman who was at last too weary to drink and simply gazed at the television, a permanent lipsticked smirk on her face. It had been, at one time, a sneer of rebellion, the expression of a woman who could handle everything.

It became the tic of a woman who knew what she had lost, and saw the house she lived in, the housing development around her, and even the sky as a place that had abandoned her. She asked her children to leave quietly and come home quietly, and peered outside from time to time, growing more and more anxious at the end of every week until the check from home arrived, in the jagged marching scrawl of her father, just enough to live on, punitively meager sums of cash intended to encourage her to get a job and marry and quit these one-night interludes with her social inferiors, men with blurred tattoos and gold outlining their canines, men whose favorite stories were of brawls and drinking, and women who hungered after them unfulfilled.

Asquith knew how these men toyed with her, and how little they loved her. Once in a while, the sofa springs done squealing, the last of the bourbon measured out, Asquith as a boy, with his boy's sense of propriety, knowing when to leave the grownups to their rough play, would toddle forth. One of the men would be there smoking, watching television, a cop show or boxing, or an old movie, Gary Cooper mouthing words with the sound off while Asquith's mother slept hard, each exhalation a groan as though even oblivion was a form of boredom.

Some of these men were kind in a distant way, knowing the trespass they had committed against a son's feelings toward his mother. Some of them tousled his head, or gave him a quarter. One of them gave him a Tootsie Roll, one of the big kind, one end just opened. And one of them, a man with dark eyebrows, tugged down his pajama bottoms and gazed at his boy's parts, critically, until his hand slid up his boy's legs and found brief, not unfriendly, play.

Asquith had liked these men, even the ones who touched him, even the ones who hit him with big knuckled hands. Joy, he learned, often meant pain. As a young man he had sought this affection with one or two other men, men just a little older than himself, as an act of nostalgia, hoping in the embrace of half-drunk pickups to find that old household satisfaction, the sticky coffee table, the squashed unfiltered cigarette and the erection all intermingled in his head.

So sometimes just turning on the television, just watching the news, endowed a certain arousal, because he associated sex with the television on in the background, as a man might like the sight of black panties or a jockstrap, or find the rumble of a bus or a plane arousing in a drowsy sort of way.

His mother had bleached out, and vanished, like the old painted face of the giant cheerful Eskimo that had, long ago, advertised Eskimo Pies, only to be one day so faded to a Last Supper illegibility that it was a relief when the fence was torn down.

She was discovered by Asquith himself, folded over into that position people called fetal. But she resembled nothing infant, nothing promising. She was, in death, a doll, carved and knitted wickedly to resemble a caricature Mom, a woman smiling with the g-forces she'd ascended through to reach what she had always wanted, the same status as the empty can, the crumpled wrapper, the package both marvelous and trash.

His sister had wanted the traditional funeral. Maria had always played the beads of a normal psyche—however frightened, however pathetic she had become. So they called ministers, Lutheran, Methodist, stabbing at one Protestant denomination after another, until they found a Presbyterian minister with a tan and a linebacker's shoulders who conducted a service in the suburban cemetery that was all sun glare, and made Asquith believe in, if not God, certainly the importance of a well-kept lawn. The first time he kept down enough peyote to kill the cerebral anthill he saw that this was an insight, not ironic at all. God, he saw, was a lawn, well-kept because nourished by its own water, a fertility that was green growing out of green under a sunless sky.

Asquith knew that he and Speke had wanted the same thing. They wanted to be more than their backgrounds intended.

Speke's childhood had been more comfortable, but the bland or-
dinariness of their daily lives as youths was what weighed upon
them both. They wanted to be alive twice, alive in the vitality of
their craft, and alive in the minds and the loving fantasies of
strangers. They had both wanted to be people of greater dimen-
sion, men who could be, if not immortal, certainly spread far
across the horizon during their lives. But Speke had succeeded,
and Asquith knew too late that only Speke had the ability, the
instinct, to endure this 3-D life and not be dissipated by it. Asquith
had bled inwardly from the very start, from Speke's first review,
from the first glance of the first groupie outside the recording
studio in San Francisco.

Her step could not be mistaken. Maria was here. Leaves whispered, and he stepped forth to meet her.

"I brought you some cookies," she said.

He accepted the plate from her hands.

He sensed her watching him, hesitating. She added, "Are you
all right?"

"I have never felt better in my life."

"You look flushed," she said, and he drew back from her touch.

It was true that there was a transformation at work in him, a
simmering in his skin. "The phones don't work, do they?" said
Asquith, sampling a chocolate chip cookie.

"You know they don't. And the cars won't start."

"Are you angry at me?"

"I'm afraid."

The cookie was delicious. "Thank you for bringing me these
treats. They will help to sustain me, I think, during this long day.
This is going to be such a busy afternoon." He paused, and then
added, "I know that you've told him all about your marriage—
that it was not exactly arranged in Heaven."

Would she lie, he wondered. Would she look him in the eye and
do what he had so long expected? She was tempted to tell the
truth, and disappoint his sense of knowing exactly what would
happen, and when.

"I don't want him hurt. I don't want any of them hurt, Timothy. Not Sarah, or Clara, or Mr. Brothers."

She had been in all things so obedient. She had even worked on
the distraction of Bell, an attempt to deceive that thoughtful biographer.

She was so worthy of his love. Soon, he promised himself. Soon he would let her partake of that great bliss, as so many others had before her.

But for the moment he delayed, savoring the cookies, admiring them, at the same time recognizing that the hand which had prepared them had experienced its last, greatest pleasure.

And she was waiting for his response. "What sort of person," he said at last, "do you think I am?"

She had the grace, or the sweetness of habit, to smile, and he was weak with his love for her, his sister, the only person in the world with any loyalty to him.

Dear girl, he thought, you cannot imagine the rapture that will be yours.

·31·

Christopher Bell had always thought of himself, with pride, as a man who could get things done. His favorite daydream as a teenager had been of a newspaper reporter in a ditch of possibly poisonous and certainly giant leeches, hammering out a dispatch on a battered—always "battered"—Royal portable, while bullets screamed and whined overhead.

He had become just such a reporter, more or less. But then there were days like this. Some days things went smoothly, and some days you ran into one wall after another. He felt doubly foolish, because he had really hoped to impress Sarah with his many connections. After all, Christopher Bell was a name that made people run to their faxes at CNN. He could call London day or night and find people willing to swim raging rivers to help him. But not today. Today he was a mere mortal. So much, he thought, for teenage daydreams, and for adult hubris.

Again, he hung up the phone and tore through his book for another number. "Just a couple more calls. Won't be a minute." He sounded lame to himself, pathetic.

Sarah folded her hands with a patient expression, trying to make him feel better, he supposed. He could see, however, the tension behind her smile. He wanted to be dramatic. He wanted to say: I'm getting to the heart of things. Watch me: I'm lopping the very head off of this mystery, and with one stroke. I have powerful friends, friends with mega-connections, friends with databanks in Kiev and Tehran. I have friends with secure telephones in Langley, Virginia, just itching to help me out of any kind of trouble. I'm more than a biographer. I'm a journalist.

"You'll have to get your facts the old-fashioned way," she was suggesting.

"Torture captured prisoners?"

"You'll have to ask Maria." A hint: please hurry.

She was right. Sarah was being patient, trying to appear calm, and he was going absolutely nowhere at the speed of light.

She had those eyes that seemed to look at him from far away.

She made him nervous, actually caused him to fumble, made his lips stiff.

I wish she wasn't lingering there, watching me.

Bell endured yet more robot operators, and when someone human answered he spoke. But no one was "in." No one was "at his desk." His friends at the *Chronicle,* his librarian friend at the university in Berkeley, everyone in the East Bay with a computer and a modem was out to lunch or off to get a haircut. L.A. was a desert, New York a black hole. These were workaholics. These were people who got red-eye from staring at the computer twenty hours a day. These were facts freaks, people who lived on instant coffee. Nobody was in the office.

All he wanted was facts. Simple information. That's all he wanted. He wanted to confirm Erika Spyri's industrial-grade gossip. That's all it had been—simple gossip. Just because some giddy gallery owner thought someone's brother was a lunatic . . .

He turned to Sarah and gave her what he hoped was an encouraging smile. "Just another minute."

She smiled, nodded. He could not take his eyes off her for several heartbeats. He had never known a more seductive woman, and she was all the more attractive because she seemed partly unaware of her power over him. He had a vivid splash of memory: her breast, the dark triangle of hair, her quiet cry.

He would do anything to help this woman, climb mountains to rescue her, battle rabid grizzlies—anything. And the one thing he did well, gather information, make calls and take notes, he could not manage at all.

She made him nervous. Why didn't she go sit down?

Bell had trained himself to wait, and people who did not know him well thought him a very patient man. He was not patient at all. He seethed, nearly always, with energy, but, like a bottle of champagne shaken hard, unless the cork is loosened no one will know how much pressure is really there. After awhile the gas is reabsorbed. Sarah, it was clear, could soothe him with a touch, a glance. He needed a little soothing right about now.

This was a nice, civilized place, not such a bad place to wait for a while. The lobby of the Clift Hotel was a reasonable place to make a few phone calls. If only she would go over there where there was a nice chair and not sit there fuming. He could tell she was fuming. Why didn't she go flip through a magazine?

Another busy signal.

He hung up the phone so hard a young woman at check-in glanced his way.

Sarah was watching him as though he were a prize mantis at an insect show. Her patience had faded, and her hands were no longer folded. She was twisting a tissue to pieces. He gave her a hectic smile, showing, he knew, too many teeth.

This isn't very impressive, Bell, he warned himself. She's going to think you subscribe to the Curly, Moe and Larry Information Service. All this uncertainty ate at her. In her case, however, it wasn't the uncertainty that bothered her so much as what she seemed to know. Bell hated this sort of tangle. Give him a machete and half an hour, or a telephone and a credit card and he would have them out of this jungle. Usually. But today he could leave a message after the beep.

He tried another number.

Sarah waited. The wait had become her entire existence. She endured the passing minutes with the dull lack of patience of a person who has been manacled. Here I am, she found herself thinking again and again, waiting. Doing nothing. Watching Bell mismanage his telephone calls. She would be happy to knock a hole in the lobby with her bare hands, and run through it. She knotted the kleenex in her hands. It was worn to white powder. Kleenex dust sifted downward, onto the brightly polished table before her. Bell was punching buttons on the phone like a man who was used to instant gratification. So this was what the logical mind was like when it was frustrated. He was flushed and youthful, and, at the same time, suddenly unattractive.

When he glanced her way she smiled. Her smile encouraged him, she hoped, to both effort and speed. Mostly speed.

The hotel had that desultory but impressive pace of a place where people had plans. Leather suitcases were trundled past, uniformed men hurried to push elevator buttons, their uniforms not implying military crispness or the authority of law, but simply that the customers here were getting what they paid for.

He'll never get off that telephone. She had never enjoyed sitting around for long periods while nothing happened. Her father had laughed at her impatience as a girl. "Ants in your pants again, Sarah?" he would say with a smile. She enjoyed swimming on her vacations, long strokes carrying her beyond the surf in Samos, and she enjoyed walks, the Luxembourg Gardens brilliant, black elms and white sand. She liked horses and snow. She ran her office like a command center. She made things happen. She would not choose, if she had a great deal of money, to spend her time showing off her latest clothes in a hotel lobby.

That sense of trouble kept flicking on and off, an alarm she could not silence. The memory of Maria's eyes needled her. She reminded herself that Maria had wanted them to take this jaunt into the City.

What was Maria doing this very minute?

"Asquith," Bell was saying, and he proceeded to spell out the name.

Sarah folded her arms and ground her teeth. She had to be sympathetic, in a way. Chris responded to a chaotic world with the powers of his intellect. What we need, he no doubt believed, are more facts. Well, facts had a place. On a sinking ship, though, Sarah would not care to sit around for the final report. Facts could wait. Give her a good life jacket.

But, she thought, men are like this—nearly all of them but Hamilton. They were not the macho goofs some women seemed to think them. They did, though, spend an unnecessary amount of time spelling names and jotting down numbers. Only a man would invent a saying like "let's get our ducks in a row."

Bell wasn't saying anything quite that demotic, but he was insisting that someone had to be around somewhere if he had been there a minute ago. His voice had an edge to it. Had they paged the photocopying department?

Her father would have liked him. Her father had prized rational procedure. Even polishing shoes was a methodical business. He called it the Sunday Shoe Review: cans of Kiwi polish lined up, light tan and cordovan and black, and the various cloths folded and waiting to be shaken out and used, beside a coarse brush and wood-handled buffer.

The cop and the newsman. Maybe they were more alike than she had suspected. Sarah did not understand the respect the world had for news, for information of all kinds, the stream of faces and names. Sarah was rooted, more simple and, she guessed, deeper. Information can be misleading, or simply false. Facts could be inaccurate, or lies. She believed in the evidence of experience. If something did not make sense, then there was something wrong.

Her impatience made her thoughts quick. She had the intelligence of a cat. The intelligence that let the chipmunk snatch the crust of bread, and let the quail escape the fox.

There were foxes at Live Oak. She had seen one once, a cat-sized, auburn creature so confident in the early dawn and his own prowess that he did not bother to startle, like a deer, or make a beeline in another direction. He actually paused and took her in, and then merely altered his trot to take him more quickly to a tangle of mesquite. So small, and so fine, she had been astounded that this was the wily reynard of the tales, the figure of cunning. She had run to tell Ham about it. He had laughed with delight.

Bell hung up again. "Let me try one more person." He hesitated.

Go ahead, thought Sarah. Try the president. Try Moscow. But be quick. And she experienced another, nearly treasonous thought: this reporter, this gatherer of facts, laboring like an ant after crumbs, was not fit to write the biography of Hamilton Speke.

"It's a woman I hate to bother," he was saying, talking to himself, it seemed. "Someone who knows Speke, actually, but who hasn't been well lately." He hesitated. "She sent me some of Ham's early tapes and I haven't had a chance to listen to them yet. I've been more interested in the actual human being than something from the archives. The story is that she's burned out. Some kind of personal problem. She doesn't want to hear from people. My question is: am I 'people.' "

"You're not."

He gazed at Sarah, barely seeing her.

"Call and be quick about it."

She could tell by the way he hunched his shoulders, leaning eagerly into the phone: he was getting what he wanted at last. He scribbled some notes, and she was embarrassed to eavesdrop simply because of the intensity with which he nodded, and the way he tilted his head, as though the connection were weak and he might not hear every syllable.

She tried eavesdropping anyway, sidling around the table, but it did no good. Chris was not doing the talking. Now and then he would say "Uh-huh."

Hurry up, Chris, she tried to mentally telegraph him. Hurry up, don't get someone's life story. Let's get out of here.

Bell was asking more questions. More questions! When was this? What did he say? And he did something that made Sarah strangle the last fiber from the Kleenex—he switched ears. That could only mean that ear number one was tired, and he needed a new, fresh ear. It could only mean that this conversation was far from over. It meant they were staying here for a long, long time.

Chris put on an I'm-hurrying-this-won't-be-a-second expression. Her growing suspicion was well founded. There was without doubt a real flaw in his character: he was slow in the most grinding way.

Oh, it could be a strength at times. Her father had been methodical, too, loving nothing better, it seemed, than sorting screws and nails in the garage, a glass jar for each type: Phillips, wood, molly bolt, brad, two-penny, upholstery, bulletin board tacks for his Twain and Thoreau. He had hoarded a row of jars of rarely used fasteners. The task of sorting was an end in itself. Bell loved gathering information because he was a gatherer. Making notes was what he loved to do. The act of understanding itself was an accomplishment.

There was only one man in the world she wanted to see.

She missed his enthusiasm, his wild It's-Raining dance, his excitement when he saw the first poppy, or when he saw a skunk with three babies by the well. Her father would not have liked Ham at first. Ham was too unpredictable, too lively. Ham would have won her father, though, with his enthusiasm for the cottontails at dawn, or his hatred for whoever it was that shot a deer with a thirty-eight and let it escape and die days later in a dry creek. Her father, like many cops, had less than love for the cruelty of gunfire.

Ham blundered, got nervous, lost his temper. He made mistakes. He was not a notetaker, not a man who would be, necessarily, cool under fire. In danger, he would probably run away, and laugh at himself for doing it, and then, just as easily, lose his temper and run immediately back to the danger, fists swinging. He was neither brave nor cowardly. He loved life.

She realized, standing there in the hotel lobby, refusing to sit, fuming, why she had stayed so many years with this man who was neither husband nor brother.

It was like reading a passage in a novel, or hearing a snatch of music, and suddenly weeping, and realizing: I'm sad. I'm sad, and I didn't know it.

Watching the well-coifed travelers, the bellhops, and Bell's earnest, eager pen, she realized what she felt for Hamilton Speke.

Christopher Bell was a rare figure of a man, and "loving" in a way that aroused and satisfied her. But Ham was mythic, a blundering human who was life itself. He erred, cursed himself, laughed at himself, and more than anything he *saw*. He saw the colors of the sage and the deer, and heard the cries of the birds. She missed his voice.

She tried to send a mental message to him, but she found herself, to her surprise, thinking a prayer. "Let Ham be all right. Let nothing hurt him."

She tucked the demolished Kleenex into her purse. She had suffered with Ham, and she had seen him hurt himself with booze and a problem temper. She had endured the trespass of a new wife, never understanding what she really felt toward him.

She was more than his manager. She was more than the woman who opened his mail and reminded him to tuck in his shirt before ABC arrived. She was the only human being in the world who understood him, who wanted him to live the sort of life only he could, laughing and hurrying in with the gleeful news that there was frost on the lawn.

She had always wondered why she had felt this strange loyalty toward him, and why even the insight that he was not a great playwright after all did not shake her faith in him.

When Bell hung up the phone at last he stayed by it, unmoving, as though stunned with what he had heard. His hand flipped the notebook shut, and fumbled as it tucked the book into his inside pocket.

"You got what you wanted?" asked Sarah, reminding herself to be ever cheerful, ever polite.

"We better hurry," he said. "What I found out is bad news."

Bad news, thought Sarah, with a certain irony. You found out that we have to hurry. I started thinking that in Erika Spyri's black leather office. I've been convinced ever since the Redwood Room. She herself had never needed "information." She had her mother's judgment, or was it her father's? Slow to waken, now that she knew the truth she was alert and ready.

But she did not speak. She had just discovered who she wanted to see more than any other human being in the world, and all she could do for the moment was treasure the memory of his voice.

Don't worry, she breathed to herself, to him. There's something wrong, Ham—I can feel it. But don't worry.

I'm coming home.

V

THE BLACK
CAT OF
LA GUADAÑA

· 32 ·

Speke closed his eyes, crouching in the kitchen.

He pressed his eyelids together so hard he saw lights, and thought: this could not be Clara. The thought was definite: Not Clara. This was another one of those macabre jokes. Surely that thing he had just seen wasn't human at all. Once again, just like the body in the grave, this was some kind of animal. That's all. Nothing more than that. It was just another one of Asquith's tricks with a dead deer.

Now, he told himself. Look now.

He made himself wait a long moment, a long hesitation on the high dive of reality.

He opened his eyes.

His mind came and went like a pulse. He pulled himself to his feet, and reality switched off and on, like a mercury switch. He clung to the butcher block table to keep from falling, and he heard the great panting, as of a huge beast, a loud shuddering in-and-out of breath.

The light was magnified to a nearly blinding glare. The kitchen faucet gleamed, a truncated arc of sterile chrome. He had been stripped of his humanity, and he was a frightened beast, now, a creature of no name, no past, no hope.

It was Clara.

Innocent. The word hammered him. Clara was an innocent person, a good person. And the kitchen was black-red with the wreck that had been her body.

The refrigerator made a low, interior chuckle, the mutter of digestion. The presence of this death, and its scent, shocked his body into knowledge. He had to do something. He had to take revenge. He had to strike back, in Clara's name.

First, he thought, cover her. Cover the woman, the broken, besplattered thing that had been a human being. He found himself in a bedroom, tugging at a quilt, dragging it, the mantle of cloth sweeping behind him until he hesitated again outside the kitchen.

Asquith was someone—something—he had never dealt with before. Envy did not commit such deeds. This was not spite or the desire to reclaim one's life. Everything, every option, he told himself with a nauseating lucidity, had to be reconsidered.

When he stepped into the kitchen again he gagged at the sight. The room was hotter now, the smell of flesh ripe in the air, not putrescent but wet and heavy. Death was ascending here on the estate, a sick power breaking over the sky, and he was not equal to the battle. He had thought himself strong. He had been mistaken. He was strong enough to struggle against anything alive. He was not strong enough for this.

The big quilt hovered in the air over what was left of her. He whispered her name: *Clara.* He had never known or understood a thing in his life. It was that simple: he knew nothing. All his knowledge vanished. He had enjoyed his fame, the glee of seeing his name in advertising and on marquees. He had watched videotapes of this talk show, and that interview, until the tapes got streaky. Stick the mike in my face and watch me talk.

The quilt settled over the rise and fall of the body, and its thickness blotted up the blood, growing sodden as he watched, islands and continents of fluid fanning out, the weight pulling the quilt down around what it hid.

And there was so much it could not hide. A human being, he saw, was only so much meat.

He clung to the table, gazing at the knife cuts scarring the wood. He was amazed that he could still command his hand to move, and that it would obey.

On the sun-yellow linoleum lay a thing, unrecognizable and bloody, and for an instant, as his eye fell upon it, he knew that this was some strange, geometrically perfect organ torn from Clara.

Then he realized what it was: a cleaver. That's all it had taken to do the job, an ordinary object, because Clara had been only a creature, after all. Undone by that wedge with a handle, that inert thing.

Wading through nausea and a yellow haze that seemed to ascend upward from the floor, Speke grappled with a drawer handle. Must find one, his mind ordered him, must find one right away.

His hand sought a weapon. The tool his hand fell upon was, he knew, an innocent thing in itself, wood that had never felt or dreamed, steel that was, in human terms, equivalent to nothing.

Clara, I should have protected you. It's my fault that fiend was here in the first place.

And then Speke had a thought as definite as a splash of ice, a thought that struck him as cruel and at the same time thoroughly honest: thank God it wasn't Sarah.

He closed his hand around the handle. To him this common implement was death, and life. To touch it steadied his hand. The handle was worn by use and by dishwater into the gray brown of a mule deer's hide, of driftwood. Three brass rivets were coin-bright. Ten or so inches of molybdenum steel, the blade was heavy, a slender, daggerlike counterpart to the cleaver.

Speke nearly dropped it. What are you doing? he asked himself. What are you thinking?

Its similarity to a weapon was no accident, Speke saw. What cleaves flesh in the battlefield is not only brother to the kitchen implement, it is the same tool. The dining room is an extension of the slaughterhouse.

You were so glad Asquith was alive.

The ancient hunter sense rolled forward in his soul again, and he found himself looking upward, as though trying to make the ceiling and the walls invisible with his gaze. The thought para-lyzed: what if he's still in the house.

And as soon as the thought occurred it stung with all the venom of the truth. He *is* in the house—of course he is. And he is waiting.

For you.

Good, Speke breathed. Good. I'll make him suffer.

But at the same time it was sickening. Don't you remember those documents Holub left with you? You barely cast your eye over them. It hadn't seemed important that Asquith had slaugh-tered innocent women.

He reminded himself of something especially ugly: Maria had something to do with this. Maria, the woman he had sworn to understand some day, this new, sudden stranger.

He would have left by the back door. He would have taken the few strides, and let his hand fall upon the knob—except that the knob was thick with gore, and with hair, a glistening protrusion, a brass knob becoming animal, glutinous and raw.

It was just as well, it was better to stay in the house. If Asquith was in the house he wanted to corner him. Let's get this over, Speke thought. The swinging door squeaked more and more slowly, and more and more quietly, until it was still.

Clara—I want to talk to you. You should have had a priest. You should have died with a prayer. All the things he should have said to her stung him, the appreciation he had always felt and never uttered.

Animal. We are animal, and mortality is not an idea. It is real. He had never realized what a treasure Clara was. It's so wrong to kill, he thought, except it wasn't a thought at all. It was like having the wind knocked out of his body, empty of every breath ever taken, empty of sky, of life. This is the truth. To kill is a terrible thing.

Red jam.

There was a click, a creak of floorboard or hinge somewhere above and beyond him in the timbers of the walls. Don't make a sound, he told himself. Hold your breath.

In here—he's in the house. This house was life itself, and the dark creature that had been, long ago, his friend Asquith was here somewhere. Speke crouched, holding the knife before him in a way that surprised him, in a way that told him how frightened and determined he was. The knife played easily in his hand, balanced and ready to do the terrible thing he had just found so appalling.

Two conflicting thoughts sandwiched him: make it to the road, to the highway. Get help. And the stronger urge: stay here, and fight.

Avenge Clara.

What I need to do, he said to himself, nearly speaking aloud, is get into a very large room. A room where it would be very difficult to have him lunge in at me. This hall, for example, he said, think-talking to himself as though to a child, is a very bad place to be. There are too many doors. Any of the doors, including the swinging door behind him, could burst open at any moment. So you should creep, as he was beginning to creep, and slip into the very large room, the lounge, with its great high ceiling and its calmly bubbling aquarium. A natural fortress. For the moment, however, he stayed where he was.

"Asquith," he whispered.

There was only the vast, non-answer of the house, silent and solid. Walls are not only refuge, they are also confinement. There was no oxygen in this air. None at all. Something had happened to the atmosphere here in this bad light, in this hall with its doors and silence.

"Asquith," he said, in a full voice.

It's worse when you talk, he realized. It really is. It makes the silence deeper, and it shows how really frightened you are, because that's all you are, and you can't pretend to yourself. You are all taken over, completely, by fear. Isn't that right, Ham? Have you ever been more afraid?

The house gave a creak once more, the big structure adjusting just barely to a change in pressure. This was not the weight of a footfall. Outside, in the world under the sky, a wind was rising.

He has Maria. He has her, and he will hurt her.

"Asquith!" he called, a bellow so loud the hall reverberated.

Maria is in league with Asquith. That has been on your mind, Hamilton, admit it. Once you begin to doubt, there is no end to it. You know Asquith can do anything, including seducing any woman he desired. Perhaps you always sensed that your Mouse could as quickly leap from one bed to another. Jealousy is love's shadow.

What power could Asquith have had over Maria? What control had he exercised for so long?

And why?

Speke surprised himself by slamming through the door into the bar. In one, smooth movement he dragged a massive oak captain's chair to the door, and wedged it under the knob. To his amazement, when the chair was in place, he realized that the knife was in his teeth, like a pirate's blade.

The steel had no flavor at all at first, until it warmed to the temperature of his tongue, his breath. Then it did have a flavor, a faint tang, the sullen absolute of steel.

Asquith could descend those steps to the rest of the house, the four steps that led to the dining room, the sitting rooms with their dried lavender and their Degas prints. Perhaps Asquith was even now tearing through his files, cutting up his software, urinating or bleeding or defecating all over everything.

There was no end to what Asquith could do. He was like water, and could take any shape. He was a serpent, who could be any configuration at all.

But you're safe here, Speke promised himself, here with your old friend, the gleaming piranha.

Aren't you safe?

Asquith could sprint through the atrium, like a guest in a hurry for that first martini. But otherwise there was no need for concern. All present and accounted for, Captain Speke. I'll put his head upon the battlements.

But Asquith could do anything. Asquith *knew*. This was the genius that Speke had recognized in him. He knew that when one character was speaking, the others were silent, and that this silence played and worked upon, supported and shaped the speech of the actor who spoke. Silence itself was a substance, the air intaken before the utterance, and more—the earth upon which language stepped.

It was this silence that held Speke now. This silence that buried him standing upright, sword in hand. The piranha, pale as the knife, took a turn in his quiet world, both imprisoned and liberated from all care.

He hurried through the rooms of the house again, but this time he moved deliberately, confirming the truth. The creak and murmur of the roof was only the wind. The house was empty.

He stood before the front door, and then opened it, letting a gust of dry wind into the hallway, a leaf scuttling at his feet.

Before Sarah comes back. Because it was Sarah he kept returning to in his mind, as the piranha kept nearly stroking the glass of his world with his mouth. Sarah was at once the home he wanted to protect, and the one person he knew he needed to see again in order to remain sane—to remain himself, Hamilton Speke.

The trees swayed in the breeze, and then the breeze ceased, barely stirred, tossed again, alive with light.

Sarah. The thought of her surprised him, this faith in a woman he had come to see as a part of his life like a sun, or moon, or gravity. He had never thought of her this way before.

The rules of the game came clear to him again. Asquith wasn't coming. Asquith was waiting. Asquith has all the time in the world, an eternity to wrap around your neck. You have to go out there, where he is. Asquith hides, you seek.

He wore the knife in his belt, like a Jacobean courtier. This game was one he had played before, in another age, in another life, with another Asquith. He stood at the front edge of the porch, drinking in the sunlight, the rise-and-fall tumble of the wind. Stay here. This is a position of strength. Show a little military strategy for once in your life. Stop bumbling around. Stand your ground.

Asquith is watching. He holds all the power. The outside belongs to Asquith. The house is a place he can only steal into, trespassing. The house is order, and trust. The woods are chaos, and they belong to the dark.

Maria's studio, the cottage he had promised never to enter uninvited, was airless and warm, a room scented with the sap of still-moist pine and the electric presence of clean, perfect paper. Her flowers were scattered, tumbled here, pinned to a board there, and all of it seemed like a tomb unsealed after three thousand years.

Asquith had been here. He could not guess how he knew, but the hunter in him sensed it. Asquith had been here, sitting on this chair, drinking soup from this mug, perhaps.

He had to force his way into Sarah's cottage, and before he had the door broken away from its frame he knew how pointless it was. Asquith wasn't going to screw his way between the floorboards like a silverfish or a spider.

Speke's legs were strong. The door was redwood panel and forged brass, but it splintered, and he entered Sarah's refuge, and stood there, well aware that what he was doing was both futile and important. He was claiming the cottages, one by one. I am master here, he was saying. I belong here, and you, Asquith, do not.

There were two cups, washed and turned upside down on a clean white towel beside the sink. One of the cups was decorated with the emblem of a whale. Speke stood in the doorway to the bedroom, gazing at the well-made bed, the ordered beauty of the simple, even spartan, bedchamber.

The two names were linked now in his mind: Bell and Sarah. Of course. It could hardly be a surprise. But he put his hand out to the file cabinet to steady himself.

It sounded like the squeak of a screw in metal at first. A squeal, and he had a thought he must have plucked from the collective memory, from a book he had read, or a movie: something being slaughtered, some beast.

A beast was in agony, death agony, far off, beyond the trees, somewhere in the woods. It was the nature of the estate to distort the sound, and make it come from every direction at once.

He sprang from the cottage. He sprinted down the path toward the Outer Office. It was a long run, and when he burst into the office it was empty. There was the desk, and the naked floor where the rug had once decorated the office, the gleam of the mantelpiece and the never-used poker.

Again—a scream, somewhere in the woods.

This was not a farmyard shriek. This was human. That's what humans were when you slaughtered them, when you butchered them alive. They were hurt animals.

But he did not know where to run. The screams had stopped, and the trees writhed in their unmoving contortions, the forest enigmatic, a place of secrets.

Asquith had Maria. Out there somewhere, almost too far away for the cry to carry. This was not the sound of someone feigning agony. This was not the sound of someone pricked with a knife.

A woman was being killed.

· 33 ·

"Isn't there some other way we can go?" asked Sarah.

Five trucks had double parked on Geary street, and traffic in downtown San Francisco had halted. Two traffic helicopters rattled overhead, hidden, except for an occasional glimpse, by the buildings.

"I don't think so," said Bell ruefully.

"There has to be."

"This is the way," he said. "I'm sorry. I can't stand it, either."

It *was* the way, and there wasn't much he could do about it. She realized that. But there was something strange about his manner. He was keeping something from her, she could tell. And it wasn't only the information he had gleaned from the telephone. There was something else going on behind his smile, a secret intention that made him guarded.

Bell braked—it took no effort, since they were barely rolling—to let a parked Volvo work its way out in front of them.

Sarah clenched her fists. She couldn't believe how slow they were going. His courtesy struck her as untimely, at the very least. But she began to reprove herself. It was possible, after all, that she was being unfair, suffering nothing more than an emotional hiccup. Her father had believed in the stakeout, and if the suspect fled, in going through the motel trash cans, if need be, to find out where he might be going. She could easily imagine him telling her to let things happen and not get upset. "Slow sometimes gets you where you want to go," he would tell her.

But, she asked herself, wasn't Chris absurdly slow, painfully deliberate? Even now he was letting cars drift before him, waving politely. He was making even less progress than anyone else on the entire street.

It was strange how someone so charming could seem so plodding. She tried to say it nicely. "We could go a little faster, don't you think?"

"Are you saying that through clenched teeth?"

"It seems to me you aren't really trying."

"I can't really do much about that taxi right there. And that double parked—whatever that is, that truck full of rolls of paper."

"Try." They were rolls of paper, she saw. Giant rolls of what looked like shelf paper.

"I am trying. This is me making every earnest effort to travel forward. See—look." He shifted out of first and then back again as a string of pedestrians jaywalked before them. "I've never known a woman who made me feel so—"

She guessed that he had been about to say "inadequate," but had not been delighted by the word's broader implications. "So I begin to irritate you," she said, as though in mock despair. "After such a short affair."

She wasn't despairing, but she was continuing to see her relationship with him in a new, afternoon light.

"My mind," he said, "isn't on my driving."

She could not say a civil word, so she made no sound.

"I spoke to a woman named Jessica Moe," Bell was saying, trying to saw the Fiat into a new lane. "We used to get along pretty well."

"And?"

"There was some sort of murky story. I didn't get the entire tale. But I got enough. I called her, and lo and behold she talked."

And talked, Sarah did not say.

"The thing with Jessica is: she's very reliable."

"An old girlfriend?" suggested Sarah. What did she care? she told herself. Her romantic interest in Chris was suddenly muted. She could think only of Ham. But she knew what "reliability" meant to Chris. Reliable meant believable. It meant: facts.

"I worked with Jessica briefly," he said. "There was a big drug story in Oakland. Enough cocaine to fill Squaw Valley was intercepted at the Port of Oakland. There was gunfire, drug-sniffing dogs, everything but flying elephants. But that wasn't the story. One-third of the cocaine was missing a month later, and that got everyone's attention for about two days. During one of those two days I met Jessica."

How interesting, said Sarah to herself, grinding her teeth.

"Jessica has a knack for digging up the secret everyone else misses. Someone pilfered hundreds of kilos of warhead-quality cocaine that was supposed to be state's evidence." Bell was attempting a breezy tone but failing for some reason. "She was free-lancing at the time, but she had been working for *Newsweek,* and right afterward she worked for UPI, which was I think a little bit of a desperation move for her. She's one of those people who get cold sores from worrying."

Perhaps he was hoping for some conversational encouragement from Sarah. She offered none. Still, she sensed that Jessica was, in truth, a source of information, and she had the strangest prickling sensation in her stomach.

"Well, I liked her. She was very serious and smart in a way that's good to be around. She made everyone else work hard, just to keep up. But she irritated me, too. She was so slow and deliberate about everything. She was so painfully methodical, running after bleeding gunshot victims to make sure she had the name spelled right. And she was always on the phone. It drove me crazy. She was good at her job, though. In fact, she encouraged me to write the Speke book. And she sent me some artifacts, the old tapes I mentioned."

Sarah nearly rolled her eyes. She had never known such a prosey human being in her life. "You knew her fairly well."

"I knew her professionally. We had a beer together now and then."

She gritted her teeth because of the green and white cab insinuating itself in front of the Fiat. Bell had the good sense to lean on his horn, and the cab seemed to take this as express, written permission to force its way even farther.

"She knew Speke and Asquith," Bell continued, "in the early days, when they all lived in North Beach. She developed a theory, all by herself, that the solid, energetic and compassionate Hamilton Speke might not be—just might not be—the playwright who penned *Stripsearch.* She had known them both, and she had remembered Asquith as being shy to the point of agony, and Speke being very protective of him and, at the same time, very outgoing. Asquith was the genius, she thought, and Speke was the man who could get things done. She had a hunch, the sort of guess that might end up as a snappy six inches in a book review tabloid or Book-of-the-Month Club selection, or might end up as nothing. Her thesis was: what if Speke hadn't written the plays?"

"She thought up this theory out of a vacuum?"

"She's smart."

"She sounds more than smart. She sounds psychic."

"She says that it's a thought that would occur to anyone who had known the two of them. She didn't think it too much insight to at least be able to wonder. Apparently one or two people have even written about the possible collaboration—"

"Where? Who?"

He shrugged. "This is what Jessica says."

Traffic churned forward, a crude imitation of progress. "During the last few years," Bell said, "she's been living in New York. She did some reading—the New York Public Library has several cubic meters of Speke. The Asquith bibliography was a blank sheet. What happened, she wondered, to the man so sensitive that seeing people gave him sunburn?"

Then, as a light turned green, traffic quickened, cars skittering from lane to lane. At last they reached the freeway, but as soon as they ascended the on-ramp, traffic clogged again. Sunlight glittered off back windows, and the Fiat wedged into another lane, only to be stuck behind a beer truck.

"Jessica is methodical," Bell continued. "She found Asquith, living in rural Pennsylvania with his sister, and phoned them to beg an interview. The sister was very much against it. But when Jessica begs, she gets. Asquith, when he heard her theory, was delighted. More than delighted. Too eager—in fact, he came to see her before she even had a chance to plan a trip to see him. He came uninvited."

A large arrow composed of flowing spots of light directed cars left, into one lane.

"She didn't enjoy the interview?" Sarah prompted. All of this was, despite her exasperation, fascinating, vital.

Bell was being deliberately laconic on this point. "Not too much."

"What happened?"

"She didn't say, but knowing Jessica—"

He hesitated, aware that he was telling Sarah how well, in fact, he knew this fellow reporter. At the moment Sarah didn't care if Jessica Moe were Bell's secret wife.

"I got the impression," he said, "that he was very strange. Possibly even dangerous."

"In what way?"

He shrugged. "Her conclusion was that Asquith was brilliant

enough, but that he could not have written the coherent plots, the consistent characters, the stunning dialogue in any of the plays. He was too—I think her word was 'twisted.' She decided that Speke was the playwright, and dropped the project as a dead end."

Traffic had stopped. Sarah folded her arms.

"Then she began to hear from Asquith again, and when she explained her decision—and she is very forthright—he began to ask if he could pay her a visit. And the basic point is—Jessica is terrified of him."

"So she's not avoiding people."

"No, but she'd do anything to avoid seeing Asquith. She was sorry she'd ever thought of him again. She was only too pleased to warn me away from him."

Sarah went rigid, her fist gripping the door handle. "Where are we going?"

His voice was tense. "This was something I was afraid to mention."

Bell had wormed the Fiat into the wrong lane. The San Jose turnoff, which they should have taken, was three lanes away, across a small legion of immobile trucks.

"What is this, Chris?" Her voice was cold, and Bell shrank against the door.

"We have to go to Berkeley."

She stared. This was impossible. This wasn't happening. She could feel veins protrude in her neck. She could feel a great surf of color wash through her.

"I've made up my mind," he said in a thin voice.

She dug her nails into the cloth of her skirt. Whatever they did, they were stuck in the jam, and it would be fifteen minutes before they would reach the next off-ramp.

"I want to get organized," he said in a burst. "I want to know exactly who Asquith is before I have to deal with him."

He must have misunderstood her silence.

"You have to see my point," he continued. "Jessica said there was some work by Asquith in the UC library, a pamphlet, a one-act play. It's my chance to do a little extra research, Sarah. It's a chance to get some facts on Asquith and really figure the guy out."

Figure the guy out, she echoed to herself. She felt herself turn to cold steel.

She did not know anything about Asquith. For all she knew, Maria was as great a threat. She knew only that she belonged with Ham, and that every moment away from him was agony.

Still, her silence seemed to encourage Bell. "Look, Sarah," he said in a steadier tone, "I know this is practically a character defect of mine. I can't help it. I don't like to take any kind of action until I get my ducks in a row."

The vision of glittering rear windows and chrome swam for a moment in her eyes.

Before she could stop herself she was out of the car.

· 34 ·

As soon as he entered the woods, and hurried through the shadows of the ancient trees, Speke realized his mistake. The outside belonged to Asquith. He could be anywhere, armed with anything. The shapelessness of this place was to his advantage, and the sinuous branches and the multifoliate green seemed to be almost his doing, as though he were a primal force.

Asquith had those magic hands, that quickness that could turn anything into a weapon. He had even turned Speke's mind against itself. The birds announced it in the shrubbery: the entire sky was a spotlight Asquith could play on him, savoring every moment. The wild, open scan of possibility was Asquith's.

Within Speke, a voice of caution sounded: go back. Don't take another step.

The scream had been bait. Come out, Asquith was saying—come out where we can really play, unconfined by any rules. Because there aren't any rules any more, Hamilton, he could imagine Asquith saying. There are no rules, and nothing human. This is life against life's enemy. And you lose.

There was a whisper in the grass behind him.

Speke spun. There was an instant spice of crushed grass blades, and, when he continued into the woods, the scent of the dry herbs and grasses all around.

The trees seemed to creep forward for an instant, the path shrinking to an earthen ribbon. He had loved this place once, long ago, because of its magic. This was a place where anything was possible. He could hear Asquith in his mind, as clearly as a snapping stick: admit it, dear Hamilton. You were prepared for everything but this.

Maria. He listened, hard, to every sound, every flaw in the silence. Maria, wherever she was, made no sound at all. Someone who had been really hurt would still be uttering some sort of gasp, a whisper, some sort of sound—not this vacuum of human sound, this fluttering, heat-splashed silence.

It was amazing that branches still inhaled the wind as always before, and that leaves skittered across the bare patches of dirt as always. Sparrows bounded across the open path, and the sky was the same color as it always had been. The sky, the blank, bright heavens had always seemed kind before now. That had been only an illusion, the misjudgment of a child. The sky was empty and without love.

This was Asquith's triumph, the greatest theater any human had ever performed, turning the bulk of nature against one man and the people he loved. Speke made himself take a slow breath. Be logical. Take things very slowly. Review your situation. Take a reality inventory. Palms icy wet. Legs wobbly. Guts churning.

He had nothing to do but to search, hunting carefully through the place he had once found a sanctuary, a countryside of refuge.

"Maria!" he called.

He searched along the path, pausing beside the stones where the Indians had ground the acorns into flour, generation upon generation, until the holes were sunken into the gray of the stone.

He called again.

He climbed through the woods, into places where even the deer did not wander. He knew that Asquith must have chosen one of the springs as his command point, the staging area for his circus. Asquith had always felt at home among trees, whether in the scrub and thicket of jungle or the steep, spanning spread of oaks. Speke recalled how the old Asquith had lived, but this new Asquith was a stranger.

The spring whispered, sounding so much like human speech that Speke hushed his breath and listened. Then he felt his way carefully forward, inching, knowing that Asquith could burst upon him at any moment.

It was with something like pleasure that he studied the tight-rolled sleeping bag, camouflaged but still there, if you knew where to look, if you knew your quarry. Here was the fuming spoil of a campfire, although what seemed to be smoke at first glance was only the stir of ash that his step gave forth.

There were crumbs, faint golden dust on the carpet of dried leaves. An ant was just discovering one of them, and a fly was just arriving to scribble the air over yet more crumbs, and then Speke saw what lay beyond the poison oak, the dark sill that reflected the trees.

Blood.

Asquith had not bothered with finesse this time. He had used this jagged stone, a wedge the size of a loaf of bread, but tapered at the end that was now blood-bright.

But there was no body. Maybe—was it possible? Maybe this, too, was a ruse. It's not too late. I could run, of course, up the road to the highway. But that would give him a few miles of scrub and woodland to follow me through, preparing an ambush. Maybe he was up there already, in the manzanita, peering.

The blood was fresh, blue transparent bubbles winking in its surface. Beyond the pool there were spatters of it, a trail, bright splashes that said, as though Asquith actually spoke the words: follow me.

Maybe this blood was more stagecraft. Maybe it wasn't real. Speke took refuge in the old actors' rule: act as you would feel.

The pebbles of the path crunched under his feet. For a while he followed the gouts of blood, but then they dwindled, and gradually there was no blood to follow. It didn't matter, because he had already understood that the next act would begin exactly where the play had started.

Maybe the blood had been squeezed out of a tube, and the tube was flat and empty now. Maybe he had Maria trussed up, and could tweak a scream out of her without really hurting her. Surely Asquith was basically a sick person, not an evil one.

A lizard skin glittered on the pale gravel of the drive. He carefully avoided stepping on it, but it cringed away, that empty wraith, that tough, translucent leather, as though it knew.

He didn't like this silence.

He stood unmoving. He ran his eyes across the tree line. The house was up the slope to the left. Wind tossed and stilled itself.

Women. You butcher women.

You planned it all along, this slaughter. Let's put Speke on a spit and watch him sizzle: hurt the people he loves. Maybe you always knew you would have this delightful vacation. Bring a packet or two of stage blood, and have a wonderful time, driving Speke slowly to the point of madness, or maybe to the point of drinking himself to death. But you forget that I am not the same man I used to be, drinking you under the table in Cozumel.

It hadn't been a table, and it hadn't been a contest. It had been so wonderfully hot. The skin was coated with a second dermis of water, and that sweat had made it possible to drink tequila Sauza by the liter. They had sat under an areciba, a thorny tree that seemed to hold itself with some disdain away from the two of them. They had watched the sunrise.

Except it hadn't risen. It had burst, exploded above a line of creamy thunderheads, and the two of them, who had been drinking all night, honing their drunkenness to a religious edge, had been too paralyzed to perch on their blue Honda motorcycles, too stricken to even stand. They could only gaze across the coral rubble at their feet and the smear of scarlet sun on the water. Then the rain had come, an early morning storm that was like the air turning to falling coins.

Then, just that quickly, the rain was gone, and parrots squealed through the air, steely cries that skewered the mother-of-pearl radiance. And the ground was covered with tiny frogs, frogs little bigger than grape pits, thousands of them, so the two men had been afraid to take a step. Had it been real, or had it been the booze, the monument of intoxication they had slaved to erect all night?

He missed his old friend. Nostalgia lanced him. It was more than nostalgia. It was friendship, deep friendship, a feeling toward Asquith he had forgotten during the events of this day. He wanted to ask his friend—were the frogs real?

He wanted to have a drink with his friend. A nice, long drink, like in the old days, one of those drinks they would have after popping amphetamines all night, a nice long walk down liquor lane, the sky growing bluer by the drink. Let's sit and talk over a half gallon of Smirnoff, Asquith. Let's have a meeting of the drink-stunned minds.

Then we'll see you handcuffed and jammed into the back seat of a deputy sheriff's Chevrolet. All the good in you I helped create. The bad is your fault, but I brought it here.

It was all an act, this standing in the growing heat, playing to an audience—unseen, but very perceptive—of two. Yes, you see how unafraid I am. You see me here, lord of lawn and tree.

Speke felt himself walking, observed the yellow oak leaves on the path, and the wrinkle of a lizard's track in the dust, but he was astounded.

What are you doing? he asked himself. You can't meet with him there, not where you thought you killed him, where you wrapped him in the carpet.

Where else? Where else should I lay a madman to rest, or a ghost, except where it all began? They would sit and they would talk. It would be like the old days, except there would be no typewriter. What would be hammered out would not be Act Five. It would be the truth.

What would his father have done in a situation like this? That solitary man, who loved his sons by being absent from them, repairing yet another burned-out centrifuge—this situation would never have happened to such a rational man. A psychotherapist had once offered the opinion that most of Speke's ache for success was directed at the mother he never knew, and the father he had always been in the process of losing. And Art, his brother: what would Art advise him to do? Art was an expert on everything, wine, Beethoven, da Vinci. He loved nothing better than calling Speke on the phone to read him a bad review of one of his plays, or complain about the crude mix on one of his albums. The last time he called was to report that he had been unable to find the soundtrack of *Stripsearch* in the Macy's record department. "You ought to complain about this," said Art in his best I'm-only-thinking-about-you whine.

Asquith would be in the Outer Office. Speke was sure of that. He'll be the star. All eyes on him. Because it was I he always wanted to impress. Asquith was a toxic drum, dropped into the sea. My plutonium. My creation.

He'll be there.

He reached the secluded shelter of the Outer Office. He put his hand on the knob. The brass was warm. It was a warm day, even a hot day, perhaps the hottest in months, but he had not been aware of the temperature of the air. He studied the earth, the scatter of leaves and unraked twigs.

He was looking for footprints, and he did not see any. The knob slipped from his grip, and slipped a second time. His hand was boneless.

He opened the door.

Athena gazed down with her usual introspective wisdom and her blank eyes. Hemingway's note, the Degas, all looked as though they had been hung in place just ten seconds before at the command of a director who even now was impatient to begin.

Speke sensed the presence before he saw it. Each detail in the room sharpened in his eyes. My stage office, he thought. It was as unused for real work as the desk and chair in a soap opera. The serpentine mantelpiece gleamed, and the mint-condition poker seemed newer than ever before, as though Clara had been at work here just this morning with her Brasso. The bare floor glistened where centuries ago the carpet had been dragged away.

The room was not, after all, empty.

Of course not, Speke thought. I never expected it to be empty. But his blood was stone.

There was the figure of a man half-hidden behind the curtains, the full-length drapes before the large windows. This figure was so taken, apparently, with the view out the window that he could not spare a greeting.

The figure gazed out into the woods, a shrouded half-presence. This specter did not move.

"I'm glad to see you," said Speke, and his voice was strong.

I am still your equal, he wanted to say. I can still match you, dream for dream, act for act, because while you have all the cunning I have all the life.

There was no movement. The ghost behind the curtain gave no sign of having heard. If anything, the curtains were drawn in slightly, the phantom clinging to the cloth as to a robe. Then, soundlessly, the curtain shifted. A fold spread, then narrowed. A foot shifted. The curtain began to part.

His hand ached for the hilt of the knife, but his limbs could not move.

The figure stepped from behind the curtains. The sight of the face was what seared Speke, and stunned him so that he knew he would never move or speak again.

What stood before him was a hulk, hands blistered, face an eruption of wounds, eyes bright within a corrupted mask.

·35·

"I'm not getting back in."

She recognized her own voice, and yet it surprised her. She had not sounded this way ever before.

They stood on either side of the car. The traffic, breaking up, surging forward like a thaw, was backed up behind the green Fiat. There was a blast as someone close enough to see that this was not a mechanical problem but something merely human, an argument, punched his horn, and then kept his fist on it for a while.

"I'm sorry—" Bell said.

"I mean it."

They had spoken simultaneously. Bell gestured, a shrug of surrender, apology, admission of his own stubbornness, but a gesture that also meant: you are overreacting.

But she was not overreacting. Her whole life she had been underreacting. She had spent years in a detached, ironic, responsibly muted frame of mind and now the lights were on.

She was amazed at herself. She had never seen the sky so bright, or realized how coarse the surface of the freeway was, seamed with tar. This portion of her planet was rough car-stained concrete. Having gone so far, she was free. She had seen this look of peace on accident victims who were not hurt, or hurt only slightly. They had nowhere, suddenly, to go. They could surrender with a kind of abrupt enlightenment: a plan was only so much air. Reality could twitch and wreck everything and, at the same time, liberate.

Standing in the cool air and the bright warm sun, cars surging past, she saw how little she had understood her own heart. I will change my life, she thought. It was that simple: what I have been, I will not be again.

She was surprised at the force of the promise to herself. There was none of that self-mocking skepticism, that "sure you will" with which she had greeted such resolutions to lose weight or learn French.

It was over. I will never be the same.

A traffic helicopter muttered across the skyline. A driver at her elbow asked if she needed any kind of help. For some reason the tone of his question implied medical assistance, or something even more dramatic. Did she look deranged?

"No, but thanks," she said, as though engaging in a moment of cocktail party small talk. "I'm fine."

Then the self-doubt, her old shadow, started in again. It knew it was beaten. The act of standing in the middle of a freeway had abolished it to a recess within her psyche. Her old muted self had been arrested, but it still had a voice. You will change from what to what? Her doubt voice was very much in the accent of her mother. Will you abandon the strengths you cultivated over the years? Will you expose yourself to becoming unsure of yourself, not knowing what your opinion is on art, faith, food? Heavens, Sarah, you won't know what you know, will you? You'll be estranged from yourself.

Honestly, Sarah, you can't just change into a different person, her mother would say. Honestly. Her superego scolded her, a Shadow Mom that would not shut up even as it was losing the fight. Gradually, the Mom voice began to win. It was no longer nagging. It was preaching. Her new, bright day was about to become sicklied over.

A blue light flashed in the distance, an emergency vehicle struggling up the shoulder of the road. So often in the past such urgent lights had meant nothing personal. Somebody else, they had always said to her, is in trouble. She had always winced, inwardly, at the sight of a racing ambulance, but she had never been in quite this circumstance before. She made out the distant shape of a Highway Patrol car with something like a thrill.

I, she reminded herself, am the emergency.

She slid into the seat, and slammed the door hard.

For a moment she was tempted: lock him out. It would serve him right. This sort of urge was quite unlike her, and yet there it was.

He got in with an expression of gratitude, and waved to the cars behind them that, yes, they would all be moving soon, and that, yes, he knew they were all there smiling peacefully behind him, cursing them both. Bell, civilized and manly, ground the gears trying to get the car moving again, and killed the engine.

He made an elaborate show of not talking. Whatever she had

felt, whatever she felt now, was fine with him. He would concentrate on driving.

Bell was frightened of his own passenger, his lover, the woman he thought he knew. He had the most peculiar sensation in his belly. She could have gotten run over. But it wasn't only her safety that made him feel weak. You just don't *do* that. She'd interrupted traffic. The outrage of standing outside the car, the breach of traffic decorum, making a rhetorical point by standing arms akimbo in the middle lane of the Bay Bridge approach, completely drained him of speech.

And she had seemed so rational. She had intimidated him with her calm. She had become suddenly a new person. It was amazing. You just never know a person at all. You just never can tell.

Don't think—just drive the car, he told himself. Don't try to understand, and no matter what, don't start arguing with her. Don't criticize her. Don't question her. Don't say a thing.

The green sign said: Last SF Exit.

It took, perhaps, a minute. They were lost. There was no other way to put it, although he worked to come up with another word. Misguided. Malrouted. And it was his fault. Bell got them lost in a district of warehouses, somewhere in a South-of-Market canyon of loading docks and piles of flattened cardboard and what looked like cubes of crushed houses, blocks of plaster bristling with wire and splinters. Water glittered in gutters. Morning glory snaked over and around a mountain of used tires.

"Where are we going?" she asked, as though trying to regain some of her former cool. "If I may ask."

"I just took a wrong turn or something."

"We are wasting time."

"I never get lost," said Bell.

"You're lost."

"But I mean, this is the first time. You do it to me. You make me nervous."

She had to feel a bit sorry for him, in the midst of her adamantine fury. She was making things worse even when she folded her arms and didn't say anything more. He was preoccupied with making no mistakes, and in doing absolutely nothing at all to offend her further, and all he could do was turn left into a street that began wide and empty of traffic, and became at once a truncated avenue into a brick wall.

At a Chevron station a burly figure stretched forth a long arm in the direction Sarah would have gone anyway, and Bell hopped into the driver's seat, shaking out his dark glasses again and snapping the car into gear.

Be kind to this nice man, said the Shadow Mom. The Mom Voice used a pet phrase, a phrase from years ago: don't be such a pill. "I'm sorry I'm so tense," she said. One of the reasons the light was brighter, and the clouds softer, was Chris. He had awakened her to life, after all. "You shouldn't have tried to deceive me."

He licked his upper lip, choosing his words carefully. "I just wanted to track something down about Asquith. I don't care about it," he added quickly. "Not now."

"What was it," she inquired, attempting to sound less-than-venomous, "that you wanted track down, exactly?" Her father, too, had used phrases like "track down." For some minds life was a series of problems, of solvable problems the mind was equal to.

"Some very early writing of his. A one-act play he wrote just before he met Speke, a work for two voices. Jessica said they had it at the library. I was curious to compare it—" He broke off as he maneuvered the car into the fast lane. He continued, "Compare it to the work we all considered Speke at his best."

"I know you want to help Ham, too." She was attempting to reassemble some semblance of her ordinary manner. There was no purpose in riding in a car with a man she wanted to bite. And he had, perhaps, in a stubborn, deliberate, wrong-headed way, wanted to understand what was happening. In that sense, he wanted to help Ham. It was clear, though, that more than anything, Christopher Bell wanted to help his book. More than anything else, he was a journalist, a man whose profession was the crafting of contemporary histories. The biography was taking a fascinating turn, she knew, and he wanted to follow it.

He cleared his throat. "He's the most intriguing person I've ever met," he said, plainly grateful to be able to hold a reasonable conversation with her once again.

Bell was intelligent, and warm, but he was not the heroic intellect she had imagined him to be. He had an exciting story. That was all that mattered to him. She forgave him that, but Bell could not be loyal to Ham as she was. She asked, "Even now?"

"Even more so now." He worked the car into the right-hand

lane for the 280 turnoff. He gave a self-deprecating laugh. "When I first saw *Stripsearch* I knew that I should be a playwright."

"The movie or—"

"The play. The movie was great, too, but they had to add some scenes that could be shot outside. Like when they go to a playground, just so they could sit on the swings and have the same confession scene that in the play took place in the bedroom. The play made me more nervous, you felt so shut in with the characters."

Here they were, she realized, continuing to believe that Speke had written *Stripsearch*. He *had* to have written it. The feel of the play, the impatience of the characters, their insistence on getting more out of life than ordinary day-after-day existence, more than the television schedule and the financial page offered, was so much like Ham.

"Ham used to drink, you know," she reminisced out loud. "I don't mean the way he does now. I mean very heavily. He used to start before breakfast. It got so that his liver began to swell. He was frightened. One day it looked as if a balloon were swelling up inside his body, like a weird pregnancy. I think we both thought of his body as made of iron."

"Iron can rust."

She ached to see Ham. To hear his voice. She forced herself to make conversation. Talking about him made him seem, somehow, closer. "He's always taken an Elizabethan view of medicine, not quite taking it seriously, seeing his body as a metaphor for something else. 'The organ of courage in me is sick,' he said, but he cut back on the tequila sunrises before breakfast. It hurt me to watch him do that to himself. I nagged him quite a bit. Then he went on a marathon drunk in L.A."

There was no other way to put it, she supposed, but it was wrong to use such a coarse phrase regarding a man like Ham. It was like something her father would have said about one of his old friends. "They had him closeted with screenwriters trying to create a plot around 'Big Bucks'—a movie based on the song. And he drank so much they didn't know what was wrong with him. He had hallucinations, cockroaches made of glass. It was obvious by the time he got back here that he was going to drink himself to death, and I locked all the liquor up and kept the key."

"Did it work?"

"No. What worked was when he realized how much I cared. That worked." She gazed out the window for a moment. "And then Maria came. She cured him completely. Oh, there was always the triple scotch before dinner, and he still did odd things like celebrate the Greek Orthodox Easter with a bottle of ouzo. He drank, but it wasn't going to kill him any more. But I thought for years that he was basically fun loving, and liked to drink because he liked to laugh. I misunderstood, or maybe I lied to myself. He drank because he remembered Asquith." And I could have done more to help him, she thought. I could have done much more, and I will. I promise you, Ham. I'm going to help you.

But it was all too late. Whatever could have been between Ham and herself was all in the past, a river unnavigated, a trail grown thick with jungle. The earth reclaims. A life with Ham was a possibility she had never considered. Had he, she wondered, once been in love with her? It was possible, on one of those nights clipping critical studies out of the *Washington Post,* "Random Notes" out of *Rolling Stone.* Maybe he drank because he was so close to a woman who was determined that their relationship be unnaturally professional, a priest and a nun against the world. Even priests fall prey to love, she thought. Many priests drink.

Bell was driving fast, she knew, but the car did not seem to be making any progress. Buildings floated by with a dreamlike sluggishness. Overpasses loomed majestically, deliberately.

"Sometimes you spend years," she said "and then one afternoon you find yourself looking out at the trees, thinking that you haven't been awake for a single moment, that it has all been lost on you." I should have been his lover, she thought. We should have been married. It was my austerity that put him off. The eyes so many men had described as "cool." Cool, sure-handed Sarah, expert at every matter but herself.

But Ham had mistaken her, too. Or perhaps he simply didn't want her, sexually, the way he wanted Maria.

Her nails dug into her palms. This drive had never taken so long before. There was San Francisco Airport way off to their left, and the blur of eucalyptus, leaves glistening in the sunlight. And then the lumpish, awkward statue of Father Serra, pointing enigmatically westward, toward a ridge and a mass of trees. She kept feeling that they would be too late.

Too late for what? she asked herself.

Too late to help Ham. That's why they kept talking about him, creating him with words because they could not actually see him.

They left the freeway. Tree shadows flashed over the car. The highway to Live Oak had always seemed to Sarah to be a simple county road, two lanes that speared the hills. Now it was endless, twisting, writhing, more curves than she had remembered, a slow pickup truck, and then a horse cropping grass among the thistles, its rear jutting into the road. The highway stretched, elastic, surreal. They would never arrive.

Sometimes she ran across an old friend at an airport, or in the rare luncheon in the City. "Do you really work for Hamilton Speke?" they would ask.

It was easy to understand their respect for him, even their awe. Speke was one of those people who seem created by nature, or the gods, to be more alive than the people around them. For such a person fame was an easy garb, a comfortable clothing made of light. Fortune, joy, generosity—these had all come to him.

Now the time had come for him to claim his life, wrest it away and become an artist again. She did not believe Asquith, whoever he might turn out to be, was half the creative man Hamilton Speke had been, and would be again.

"What is he really like?" old girlfriends would ask. She had always murmured some pleasantry, unable to state simply what she really believed: that Speke was destined to be great.

She clenched her hands together, tightly, like someone praying fervently, even desperately. Her fingertips were icy. Soon, she told herself. We'll be there soon.

There they were—the last familiar gnarled oaks, the outcropping of boulders.

At last. But what she saw confused her, and her lungs tightened in her chest.

No sense, she told herself. This makes no sense.

She shut the car door behind her. The ugly clunk of the door was the only sound in the stillness. Numb, and unwilling to guess what was happening, she bit a knuckle, hard. Had Ham gotten security-conscious at last? It was possible. But this did not look like something he would do.

But of course, it must be some whim. Something he had done to —to what? Ham would not do a thing like this.

The black iron gates to Live Oak were shut, and chained, and the chain was locked.

"Security guards?" Bell asked. "Maybe some sort of precaution . . . ?"

They both approached the chain as though it might be alive. The padlock was large, the chain old and made to tow dead trucks, or drag ships. The black links of iron looked strong, but they did not look like a professional security arrangement at all.

She looked to Chris to say something but he simply fingered the padlock, as though its mechanism might be touch-operated. This was the way his mind worked, she saw yet again. He had to see and touch and consider every little detail.

"We'll have to get in," he said at last, in a voice that apologized for stating the obvious, "some other way."

The chain shifted, just slightly, as though it writhed at the sound of his voice. Its subtle movement silenced both of them for a moment.

"This is the only way in," she said.

"There has to be some other—"

Her voice was shaking. "There really isn't any other way at all. No roads, no trails. Nothing. There's this iron fence, and then when you get off the road it's all scrub, all undergrowth." She could not add: virgin and thick, and full of poison oak.

Even if she called out, Ham would not hear her voice from here.

Bell shook the gate. It made a low, iron rattle, but did not appear to move. "I'll have to lean on the horn—let them know we're here."

"Chris, I don't think you understand."

She was too cold to move, frozen in the heat of the sun.

Trouble. She could not mouth the words.

Ham was in trouble. She could see it in the color of the air, in the rise and fall of the oaks as they shrugged in the breeze.

Something—an ugly, crushing blow, as unjust as the fury of a brutal god—was about to annihilate Hamilton Speke.

·36·

Asquith's face was blistered and seared. The skin glistened, corroded with flesh-rust. He was a heretic rescued too late from the pyre. The body had been burned, it seemed, and released from the stake just as the flames began to digest the flesh.

His carriage, however, was easy, his body relaxed, one hand falling lightly upon the back of the desk chair, a man ready to return to his studies, an executive poised to interview yet another underling. His eyes were alight, the same old Asquith eyes, the eyes that had watched him from outside. The eyes of a dead man who was without doubt very much alive.

He did not move. He did not speak. Presence, his body seemed to say. I have presence, and you—what are you? You are a mere man, a clumsy, artless member of the audience. You have life, but I have magic.

If nothing happens, Speke found himself thinking, if nothing happens, then all will be well. If we both stay like this, eternally.

"It doesn't really make me feel uncomfortable," Asquith said. His elegant enunciation contrasted with the scathed mask of his face.

Speke reminded himself to keep silent. Trading words with this apparition would evolve quickly into a losing contest.

"I have been, if you will forgive me, taking codeine and other ameliorative drugs from your own medicine cabinet. They are most soothing, really. But there is one thing we must understand from the outset."

Speke did not take a single step, and he did not glance away for even an instant. As long as I do not move or speak, he reminded himself, he has no power over me.

"The knife," said Asquith.

Speke tightened his grip on the wooden handle of the kitchen implement. But even this much of a response was a weakening, a giving-in. Stillness and silence are my shield, he told himself. This is not the old Asquith. This is something new, something beyond all experience.

"You don't really think it's necessary, do you?"

Speke did not move, although his spirit shrank within his body. Asquith was feeling his way into the room, and into Speke's soul.

The blistered mask of Asquith's face creased for a moment in something like a smile. "Surely you don't believe that I'll do anything to hurt you."

Do nothing, Speke cautioned himself. Don't answer him.

And yet, he had to marvel at the thespian clarity of Asquith's speech, the precise diction, the strong, clear voice of the most well-trained actor.

"I am a bit like Giselle, awakened from the dead to dance the night through. I do wish I had a weapon, too," said Asquith, almost dreamily. "I could never tell when you would lose your temper."

Neither of them spoke, Asquith gathering the silence about himself as if a counter-ploy. Then he lifted a hand to his face and fought the desire to scratch. "It got this bad within the last few hours. It's like being simmered alive when the drugs wear off. It turns out I was building my lean-to with it, and I didn't even know it." A quick laugh. "I was probably building my cooking fires with it. And I thought I knew the outdoors."

Speke said nothing.

Asquith trembled. "Put the knife down, Hamilton." His voice was sharp.

Put on a show, Speke reminded himself. Put on a demonstration of calm. "Where," he said, "is Maria?"

"She is quite happy."

"Where?"

"You want to know all my secrets at once, don't you?"

"Where's my wife?"

"She's safe, Hamilton. I promise you. She's perfectly all right. She is, actually, quite fortunate."

And the blood, Speke thought.

Asquith must have read his eyes. "I've tricked you before with a little gore. I tricked you again."

"I want to see her."

"You will, very soon."

"What is it you have to say to me?"

"I'm afraid of you, Hamilton. I know how angry you must be."

Why, even now, did he feel compassion for Asquith? "You should see the kind of people who can help you."

Asquith leaned forward, transfixed by an idea. "Let's start off our conversation by being on an equal footing." Asquith smiled through the reddened mask of his face. "Throw down your knife."

He's going to kill me, Speke said to himself, with the same dull clarity with which he would think: it's raining.

Asquith continued, "Walk back to the door, and throw it away, or I won't talk. I'll just turn around and walk out these windows. It's not fair, you with a butcher knife, and me—nothing but a wrecked body."

Speke was horrified at what his own hand did just then. He was appalled at the action of his own limbs. He stepped to the brilliant brass and iron poker, unhooked it from its stand, and set it on the desk, within easy reach of where Asquith stood. The glittering instrument seemed to hum, like the single prong of a tuning fork.

"You are a brave man, Hamilton," said Asquith.

It was not courage, Speke marveled at himself. It was some power Asquith had over him. He felt a deep need to reassure his old friend, as though they were somewhere far away, in entirely different circumstances, years before now.

Asquith waved him into the chair in front of the desk, an emperor about to release a minister. "We might as well talk, since that's what you wanted."

Moving slowly, Speke crept into the chair, but not until he shifted it just out of reach of any quick gesture Asquith might make. Asquith observed this, and showed his teeth.

"You see," he said. "I made no move to hurt you. I am harmless."

"I've never seen a worse case of it," Speke offered. He couldn't help it, somehow consolation seemed appropriate. He had, actually, seen a case nearly as bad. A neighbor had been burning weeds, and had inhaled smoke. He himself had once needed medical help with a nasty episode.

"I was foolish." Asquith studied one of his blistered hands. "Poison oak." He said the words slowly, with wonder. "I do believe I am losing my mind."

Speke sat poised on the edge of the chair. Your mind, he thought sardonically, was gone years ago. He did not say this, however. Instead he said, "Clara." Just that—just the name. He could not let himself keep silent any longer. The outrage was too great. This is the business at hand, he told himself. Do not be distracted, and do not let Asquith worm his way into your trust. The man kills.

The name meant nothing to Asquith.

"Clara!" Speke bellowed, slamming his fist into the arm of the chair. I am the dangerous one here, he realized. Asquith is right to be afraid.

"Who is that?" said Asquith, like someone answering a call.

Speke controlled himself, blinking tears. No need to bellow. He could handle Asquith. "The woman you killed."

"The woman I killed," echoed Asquith drily.

"She was a kind, gentle person," said Speke.

Asquith seemed not to hear, shivering and starting to scratch the raw flesh of his arms, and then restraining himself. "She was my sister," he said abruptly.

Speke stared. "Clara?"

"No, heavens no." A snicker. "Maria. She was my sister. I planned all of this, for a long time."

"A long time." Speke said it woodenly, as though recollecting a phrase in a foreign tongue.

"I was quite brilliant, I think. Even your courtship was planned by me, the master puppeteer, the lynchpin of the masque. The invitation to her gallery, all of it. I planned it all. My sister was bait, continued to be bait, and at last was bait even today. Her cry got you out of the house."

Speke had to look away for a moment. Perhaps he had tried to believe Maria was lying. Perhaps he had tried to convince himself that Maria might still be innocent. Certainly she could not have anything to do with Asquith, he had thought.

His breath was ragged. He was broken. His beloved Mouse had tricked him from the very beginning. Had she ever loved him? It was bad enough to have one's future evaporate. But now his past was shifting, fading away, his recent past, his love. His tongue was foul, his stomach a cold, black wad.

"If it makes you feel any better," said Asquith, "I think she gradually came to love you. It's true. She came to love you, against all that I could say. You are that sort of man, you see, like King David in the old tales. No matter how he sinned, and how much punishment he required, God loved him steadfastly. There are people like that, Hamilton. You are one beloved of the sun itself."

Speke could say nothing.

"And I. I am a dissembler, an adversary, one of life's shadows, the sort that must make do with a life behind the baseboard, under the foundation."

Asquith's blistered hand crept toward the poker. It stroked the length of the shaft that lay on the desk. "I knew you would be easy to deceive. You have no idea that there are other people in the world, or what they are really like. Hamilton, you were always so trusting. You believed the world was good."

Speke's voice was broken. "I loved her." Why, though, did he use the past tense. Didn't he still love her?

He shook himself. He had to pay attention to the business at hand, this ugly business of dealing with Asquith, dealing with the truth. He had to go forward.

"You don't want to hear more," said Asquith. "It will make you sick."

"I want to hear all of it," said Speke in a rasp.

"You don't."

Speke waited.

"I planned to at last arrive at your estate, your lovely estate, subject of so many magazine spreads, and feign my death at your hand. For it to work, I had to take the worst possible day, a day on which your schedule was especially difficult, even aggravating. I chose my day, with Maria's help."

He waited, perhaps for applause. "Go on," said Speke.

"Are you interested in self-torture, Hamilton?"

"It's not self-torture. You are causing the pain, and I can take it."

Asquith gave a hard little laugh. "You were always the strong one, and I was always weak." He paced, as though standing still, or sitting, caused him agony.

"I had an aggravating schedule," Speke said, to urge the confession—or the speech of triumph—forward.

"I had to provoke you in some way, which was easy enough. You think your old days of bad temper are over, but they aren't at all. I'd hoped for something a little more convincing than a mantelpiece. A blow to the tummy, resulting in a burst spleen, convulsions, bloody foam—I was ready to earn an Oscar. But, I did what

I could with what you offered me. My leap into the grave with the cry 'It is I, Asquith the playwright,' with the same sort of Halloween stage makeup I used in my expiring sweet prince days was all so delicious. You can do miracles with little bags of blood. Do you think it was easy, keeping myself alive on stage-corpse breaths for half an hour? More important than fencing or tap dancing. Underappreciated. Notice, I don't say how to 'play' dead. This wasn't play."

He started, as though recalling something particularly painful. "Buried alive. And buried so carefully, I thought I was going to suffocate while you tamped the rocks over my head so gently. I nearly died."

He interrupted himself to savor the presence of his dear friend. He gazed upon Hamilton and knew at last how much he wanted Speke to admire him. That was what this was.all about, this little encore, this coda. Love me, Hamilton.

Speke kept himself steady—and aware. He had already become entangled in a conversation with his adversary, and he played out silence like a line descending far into the deep.

"The deer," Asquith continued, "was a bright stroke, unplanned for. I had seen it on the way in, by the gate."

"The face on *Seven Samurai* . . ."

"I had my doubts about that. It wasn't really my style. A little too obvious. Maria did that. Your tape splicer, your video cam. It was simple. It had to work. It simply all had to work, so that I could torture you. We took all the pills out of the house, and I determined that I would gradually drive you mad." He winced as he slipped his hand into his pants pocket. He pried the lid off a vial of pills. "I'll swallow a few more of your pills. Maria emptied the house of them. Thank you. I would have suffered even greater misery without them."

"I might have attacked the ghost and ended up really killing you."

Asquith was chewing three blue pills and four large, chalk white capsules. He swallowed, without water, and coughed. "Maria would soothe you—" He coughed again. "And keep you just this side of doing that. My plan was that you would gradually drink yourself to death, or start mixing pills and booze when Maria finally reintroduced the drugs. 'Oh, look what I found, some nice pills,' " he said, in an excellent imitation of Maria's breathy reassurance. "Then, there was your ulcer. Or maybe you wouldn't die. I didn't care, as long as you suffered.

"All along," Asquith went on, "I really just wanted you to feel the kind of agony I feel. That's all. I wanted you to deviate just a little from your ridiculous mental health, and see what it's like to be someone like me."

He paced and did not speak.

"What did you hope to accomplish?"

"I saw you smiling in magazines, smiling on television, smiling in your sleep, probably, because you were a success. Success! Do you know what success—fame, money, glory—mean? They mean that you are alive, really alive, while I was not even a person any more. They gave me drugs that made me drool, uncontrollably. A drooling zombie. I, who could play the Goldberg Variations both drunk and blindfolded. Do you remember that favorite trick, Ham, that magic trick that so amazed you?"

"Which one?"

"The old Houdini trick with the needles and the thread. I can still do it, I suppose. You put a pinch of needles on your tongue, and a thread, and swallow water from a glass. Remember? Then you put your fingers into your mouth and pull on the thread, the glittering needles dangling from it in a row. It took only what all magic takes, or most of it. Planning. Preparation. The needles already threaded, tucked into the cheek, the disorganized needles all sleight-of-tongued into the other cheek. It's not easy to deceive, but it's easier than an actual miracle would be. It's easier than real power, real life."

"Revenge."

"Something greater than that. Your soul in exchange for my emptiness."

"Spite. Ugly spite."

"No, it's something more celestial than that, Hamilton."

"Are you happy?"

"Yes, let's swap cute words, shall we? I'll say 'celestial' and you'll say 'spite,' and then you'll ask me if I'm happy. We'll make a song of it."

Speke stared, biting back a response. Color flushed the room. Control yourself, he commanded his body, but he couldn't help it. His fists were hard, and he had trouble sitting still. "I always did the work. You were always afraid to believe in work. You thought it would amount to nothing."

"You may be right, Hamilton. I can't tell any more. Were the plays mine, or yours, or someone else's, some other entity neither of us can claim?" Asquith gave a quiet laugh. "You aren't afraid of me, Hamilton, are you?"

Speke waited.

"It was always so easy to manipulate Maria. She was, you see, afraid."

"What do you suppose I'm going to do?"

"You will try to destroy me."

"I'm not as sick as you are."

For an instant, a moment so brief it was almost undetectable, Asquith's eyes flicked to the poker on the desk. Speke sat on the edge of his seat, confident he could react at once to every move Asquith made. The poker lay still, although something made it shiver from time to time, perhaps Asquith's step as he paced. The iron behaved as though something magnetic in Speke made it point directly toward his heart.

"I was hoping," Asquith was saying, "to come to an understanding. Just a little understanding with you. Everything has unraveled."

"You are dangerous," said Speke quietly, controlling his voice with the greatest effort. He remembered the fax Holub had left, the one he had read so carelessly. He remembered the black jam that had been Clara. "How many other women have you killed?"

The words were terrible. He at once regretted uttering them.

"An understanding," Asquith repeated.

"What sort of an 'understanding'?" asked Speke.

Asquith was weeping now, but managed to stop as he said, "I've begun making one mistake after another."

Speke was surprised by a further burst of compassion. He had to remind himself not to take his eyes off Asquith for a moment. But it was difficult. The old Asquith was in there, somewhere, his old friend who was now suffering so terribly.

"I'll tell the world what an inspiration you were," said Speke. "I think it's time for everyone to know how much our friendship meant."

Asquith turned away, and gazed out the window, just as he had stood when Speke first entered the room. He was no longer weeping. He looked upward through the glass, pensively, as though watching something.

"You don't understand," he said quietly.

Speke struck at the air with his fist. "I don't care about the plays any more." His voice was ragged, but he continued, "What are they worth to me, compared with this horror?"

"Hamilton," said Asquith, spinning to face Speke. "You miss the point entirely."

"You have a future, Timothy." A tremor of compassion made it hard for him to speak. "They'll hospitalize you, and I'll do everything in my power to help you. You deserve my help. And the truth is—we can help each other." Speke could not continue for a moment. "The new play is not going well at all, the play about us, about our life together."

"The black cat was mine," said Asquith.

It was difficult to speak. "I know that—"

"But you can have it." He considered Speke, as if reflecting over the words Speke had just spoken. " 'Hospitalize,' " Asquith mocked. "Do you know that at one point I drank so much aquavit that I stopped breathing? When I woke up my lungs were full of fluid. They had to practically teach me to breathe all over again. I used a Triflo II, an Incentive Deep Breathing Exerciser. You have to learn to inhale more and more deeply to get three blue balls to spin up within their little plastic tubes. A toy, to keep the patient from developing pneumonia. You have no idea who I am, what I have done, and what I am doing," said Asquith, in a tone of amazement.

"You can have years ahead of you, Timothy. A future. You can have what every living creature has a right to expect—"

"You don't understand," snarled Asquith, and seized the gleaming poker. He slammed the iron shaft into the desk, and the room seemed to leap. There was a gouge in the desk, a bright puncture in the dark surface. "You don't understand anything about me at all. I am not the old Timothy Asquith, your friend. Not any more. I am something else now, something that wants what it cannot have."

He did not release the poker. He held it in one corrupted fist. Speke eased himself to his feet. The span of iron waved in the air, like a baton, like a magician's wand, as though it had a will of its own, apart from Asquith's body, as he continued, "I loved you,

Hamilton. And you have no idea what that means, do you? Think of it: love."

Speke watched the poker. Urged by the need to distract Asquith, and also by the need to know, he asked, "Those little frogs, do you remember them? They were real, weren't they?"

"Maybe you are the only person I ever actually loved. Hamilton Speke." Asquith shook his head slowly. "I give up, Hamilton. I quit entirely. I give up on being a human being. I want to be something else, some other sort of creature, something far more alive." He turned again, and gazed out the window, looking upward.

Something out there, Speke told himself.

"Yes," said Asquith. "I do believe that the frogs were really there."

There is something out there that troubles Asquith.

"Don't you like this last soliloquy, Hamilton? Remember Stanislavski's caution: 'Has my imagination initiative?' I could not have done what you did. I could never finish a single scene, a single act. Hammering the plays into works that could float upon the light, and not sink. Knitting life into a costume. Answering one question after another on the trashy beach of publicity, but most of all believing in it, having the faith. The plays are yours, the songs, all of it. You deserve them."

Speke could barely whisper. "Where is Maria?"

"She's entirely happy."

It was all but impossible to ask. "Where is she?"

Asquith gave that otherworldly glance, that actor's start—the ability to hear the far off bell, the warning carronade, the call that lives only in the empty, white spaces of the script.

What, Speke wondered, did he hear?

When Asquith spoke again, he said, "She's just outside. My loyal sister, netted by her fear of me, and by her love. She is outside, dear Hamilton, in the arms of a tree, where no harm can ever befall her again."

·37·

The chain that fastened the gate was a living thing to her, something monstrous, an iron, writhing knot. Sarah tugged at it, knowing that would be futile.

It had looked black and new-forged, but when she put her hands on it she could see the dark glaze of years of dust on the surface of the links. The dirt was clawed where someone had dragged the chain into place, up the drive, from the direction of the house.

Someone desperate had done this. Someone determined to the point of remarkable strength. Someone who wanted Sarah to stay far away.

She had to hurry to his side, and there was no way in. It was a harsh joke, a vicious lesson. Love was nothing compared to a Gordian tangle and a steel lock.

"We can dig under the fence," in a tone so definite he sounded cheerful.

"The spears are sunk far into the ground," she said. "They are made to deter people who might want to 'dig under the fence.'"

"Then it's hopeless," he replied. When she did not answer, he added, "That's what you're saying, isn't it?"

She dusted off her hands.

"We can climb over," said Bell, with just the least touch of doubt in his voice.

Her fist closed around one of the spears. The thought of scaling the gate made her wince. The top of it was lined with black spear points, not mere ornamentation. The iron fence along the road to either side, too, was a line of black spears.

"Don't even try," she said.

"I might be able to make it."

She had always found the black spears attractive, in an unremarkable way, without really noticing them. Now they were arrayed against her, weapon upon weapon keeping her from where she belonged, and what had been intended to be decorative would serve just as well to do harm. Ham had never given a thought to security, but someone had, in the past.

And someone in the present. Someone who wanted to be alone with Hamilton Speke.

Her chest was tight. She trotted, her eyes searching, along the fence. Bell followed her, and she could sense his desire to argue with her. The trails were secret, impossible to find, and the heat was increasing, the pavement at their feet fluttering with heat waves that soared before their eyes. Sarah had sometimes wondered what it would be like to walk off into a distant mirage, into the place where the land melted and became mercury. Now she knew. The sunlight wavered before her, pebbled and fluid. Mirage began a stone's throw away, just ahead of them, a smear of silver wings.

"It's not really an emergency, is it?" Bell panted behind her. "As far as we know?"

She spun to face him, and her eyes gave him her answer.

"We can go to a farmhouse. Make a few phone calls—"

"I don't want to wait. I want to be with Ham now."

"We'll have to tear our way through, then," said Bell, sweating, squinting, hands on his hips. "Dig our way under the fence no matter how deep it is."

This was the sort of decision her father would have made, after adding up the situation, making a list of the facts. When nothing works, you have no rational option but to resort to violence. It was the dark side of masculine intellect. When calm analysis failed, load the thirty-eight. She did not despise this reasoning. It had the heft of logic, after all.

She knew better. "Tearing through" would result in becoming lost. The creek beds and culverts of Live Oak would lead them nowhere. Tomorrow the two of them would both have poison oak, and might well still be lost somewhere between this road and the lake. And digging under the fence was not possible. The cable television company had spent an entire day drilling at the buried foundation of the fence with a jackhammer a few years ago. The salt-and-pepper granite buried in the ground wore out one air compressor, and three drill bits.

Bell sensed her disapproval, and dogged her steps, working himself, she could tell, into an argument in favor of leaping the fence, which would have been a painful ordeal of worming up the iron shafts to the black, iron points. And even if they made it over, there would be no way through. Perhaps he was on the verge of suggesting that they pile back into the car and drive to the sheriff's office or back to San Francisco, or all the way back to Berkeley.

They hunted along the shoulder of the road for a quarter of a mile, and when the iron fence ended a stone wall began. The wall itself would have been easy enough to climb. But the woods there seethed with dense, virgin undergrowth. The brush was a tangle of branches, stiff, writhing fossil snakes, white looming limbs scarred with dead lichen, massive grandfather oaks centuries-old roped with lifeless moss, and in the undergrowth a mass of blackberries, like living barbed wire, and the scarlet, fluttering leaves of poison oak.

They paused again beside a brilliant, late-season poppy and a crowd of star thistle. The light was fragrant with herb scent. Bell frowned, like a man cheated into living in a world that made no sense. This was what happened to all such human beings, Sarah thought with compassion. The rational people are determined to understand, and what they learn baffles them. The trail is lost, the barroom dark, and the adversary who fells the hero is never a worthy enemy. The hero lies broken, and the victor scrambles away into the dark.

She was not as patient as she seemed. She was not patient at all. The huntress may seem calm, she knew, but she is not. There was something very wrong about this. Ham was trapped in there, somewhere, by something sinister. The sight of the chain still reverberated in her stomach, a cold, ringing knot of steel.

"Sarah, please talk to me for a second."

"We're looking for a trail."

"A trail," he echoed doubtfully.

"We'll find it."

"Of course we will," he said skeptically. There was something very nervous about his voice. They were both dressed for a day in the City, but Bell had loosened his tie, and Sarah wore, she was pleased to reassure herself, what her mother would have described with some humor as "sensible shoes."

"A deer trail," she said.

His silence meant that she had scored a point.

She added, "There has to be one that reaches the road, because I've seen deer here, browsing on the shoulder."

He even smiled. He was eager, now. He had a plan, he knew what to look for. Bell was the sort of man who required an agenda. Even so, there was an unsteadiness about him.

He jogged along behind her. Give him a schedule and he was all action. "You can pass them and not see them at all," she called. "They run parallel to the road," she panted. "Well into the estate, but we need one that—"

She stopped herself, and hurried back to gaze over the top of the chest high wall. A fly flicked off and on like a tiny electric light as it circled in and out of the shadow. There in the scribble of brush was a long wrinkle of bare earth.

The way in. They had both passed it in their hurry to find it. She called Bell to her side, and they scrambled over. Even so, iron points set into the stone wall caught her clothing, and there was a minute tear as the medieval-looking rampart caught and held her briefly.

"Stay on the path," she whispered. She did not know why she spoke so softly. For some reason she was afraid of being over-heard, as though the very ticks in the brush were spies.

"What happens if we lose our way? I mean, how lost can we get?" Bell tried to sound bouncy, ready for anything, but she could tell that somewhere within himself he was shaken. The im-agery of this place confounded him, the black spearpoints, the shaggy trees. Bell was a man of information and flash-communica-tion. As some people might be afraid of heights, or of confined places, she sensed that he was afraid of being lost.

We can become very lost, she wanted to say. We can lose our way entirely. It was the truth. Hikers had wandered on the estate for days, even struggling within sight of house and not casting eyes upon it, until they found themselves at last, torn and bone-tired, either on the surface of the highway or beside the lake.

This is a place that deceives, she wanted to say. This is a place of voices in the night, of shadows that spill where nothing casts them, and of light that pools from no source, not sun or moon, but the own, sole magic of this place. This is like the soul, the psyche. This is a place like no other, unmatched, unique, roped with power, and frail.

But she did not say this. Bell, with his gentleness and his

strength, and his need for facts, would want to understand, but he would not. He would want to fumble for his notebook and write "magic place," believing only that this was her own, impressive but irrational view. He would want to possess Live Oak by understanding it, and she knew that understanding was impossible, and was an effort that did nothing more than dilute such a place of its color.

Instead she pointed to a flourish of poison oak, and he nodded.

The trail lost them. It did not take long. She spied the two prongs of a deerprint, and then another, worked with the trail down the slope, and then they stumbled over a wash of round granite stones. The skeleton of a tree rasped against them, and the hum of wasps was the only other sound.

They hunted. The trail could not have vanished, completely. It was only a path, with no will at all, and it was crazy to think it might.

Then she realized that the deer, being practical creatures, would follow the creek bed for a while, before meandering off again on their own.

"We have to go back," Bell panted. "This is crazy."

"We're lost," she said, and to her it was a challenge she knew she could overcome.

"I'm going back."

"You'll never find your way."

"Sarah—" he began, panting, sweating.

"Follow me."

She ran, tottered on a rock and looked back.

He wavered, unsure.

She urged him downstream after her with a wave of her arm. She hurried forward, eager, balancing over the scabs of old algae on the stones. A junco flashed its white tail feathers where a bay tree had let drop a scatter of blond leaves, and the air was delicious with the scent.

Here—where the trail resumed.

She was running fast, now, with the speed of a child, and with a child's sure-footedness. She was amazed at how well she bounded over this rock, this fallen tree. Her hair streamed behind her, and the past-blossom lupine whispered at her feet.

There was a crash.

She froze.

Before her, startled, frozen to statues themselves, three deer stared at her, into her, looking hard. The sound had been the sudden leap to their feet from where they had been drowsing in the dry leaves. Bell panted behind her, and the two of them gazed upon the deer as though the animals were a trio of unearthly beings.

Black eyes, and black snouts, and ears as large as human hands. The deer drank in everything there was to know about Sarah and her companion. They did not even want to shift a single hoof for fear of making a deadly error.

Then the buck turned, both easy and cautious, and made an impossible leap, out of the culvert, and over the branch of a tree, which he barely ticked with an ebony hind hoof. The others followed, nearly silently, like a sound track that was out of synch with the picture, or badly dubbed. The deer were gone when the sound of their rustling was still in the air, and the branch swayed, slightly, where they had vanished.

She had known that the estate was large, and that it was, in a sense, prehistoric woodland, but with all her respect for the land here, she had not realized how Live Oak sprawled. They ran, splashed with heat, stroked by shadow. She could not run any farther. She would have to stop. Her feet were tingling, and her lungs burned. But she did not stop, although she left Bell far behind, his footsteps distant.

She ran until at last the peak of the roof and the tall green columns of the poplars were visible through the oaks. The last bushes whipped her as she hurried past, and she reached the clearing.

The lawn hissed under her feet. She should never have left him, and she would stay with him always, no matter what happened. Maria could do nothing to hurt Ham now. Sarah wrenched at the front door, fumbling, until she got it open.

The house was cool, and with the sound of her footsteps the walls seemed to inch outward, the cavern of the hallways taking her in.

She could not utter a word. She was breathing too heavily. She called for Ham, but her voice was broken by her panting, and was hardly a voice at all.

She called again, her voice clear, now, and insistent. Her response was no sound—silence, except the very distant gurgle of the aquarium. There was no response from the upstairs, or from the sunroom. She called for Clara, because she knew that Clara would answer at once.

There was only the hush of the great house around and above her. It was the quiet of old walls, old, horsehair plaster, and great redwood timbers. The place was empty of everything but its own stillness. It was both wonderful and chilling, like realizing that the earth will continue after one's own death.

Her breath was steady now. Everyone must be gone somewhere, she felt, feeling like a child trying to piece together an explanation for a place that was, subtly, but undeniably, dangerous.

And then she told herself that she was being childish. It was too quiet, and yet for the moment she was so thankful to be here that she convinced herself she was untroubled. Surely everything would be fine, now that she was here at last. Her fears about Maria were fears, only. All would be well. If only she could see Ham, and know that he was safe.

So, she thought, I am alone. She had always thrived on solitude. Quiet had nourished her. But this was not the right kind of silence. This was a silence that soaked the color from the sky, the oxygen from the air.

The piranha flicked, a steel blade transformed into a fierce, supple life. Ham's office, when she reached it, was empty. She tried to read some meaning into the clean desk, the chair kissed with the print of his head.

She touched the intercom, and heard the reverberating silence of the house for a few heartbeats before she realized that what she heard was the mere silence of a broken instrument. The hard, solid silence. As an experiment, a gesture in the interest of merest curiosity, and perhaps as a possible check to see if the entity that had provided the chain had provided even worse mischief, she picked up the phone.

She had guessed as much. She had not expected the phone to work. This was predictable, this dead instrument at her ear.

The French windows swung open at a touch, and there was the green lawn, the cheer of distant birds, and all was well. Ham must be off somewhere, hiking, or perhaps working on the play at last. And the chain and the dead telephone meant nothing at all. She hesitated, trying to lie to herself, and failing, and then she stepped into the heat.

There was no sign of Bell. He had been right to be afraid. He was lost, now, the poor man, and once a person is lost, she knew, it can be a long time before he sets foot again in a place of refuge.

When she first heard it, it was a pretty sound, much like the sound of celebration, discordant but merry music—the sound of something breaking. A sweet sound, surely a happy noise.

The tinkle of breaking glass.

She put a hand to her lips. Time hesitated. The Outer Office, she thought. It's happening in the Outer Office.

She began to run down the slope of the lawn, toward the continuing sounds. Or were they sounds? The noises were so faint she could hardly make out what they were. Not breaking glass at all, she decided as she ran. Surely not. Sounds shifted here, a rattling leaf rasping like an ugly song, music resounding from nowhere. That had always been the way of Live Oak. The air whispered, the trees murmured, the very sky was alive.

She told herself that this was not the sound of breaking, of splintering, of violence beyond the trees.

Until she heard it again.

· 38 ·

What was it about the black cat, Asquith wondered, that had so aroused his desire to own it? And not only to own it, but to prize it, and hide it away where no one could see it and covet it in return.

Certainly its appearance had been remarkable enough. A cat carved, or chopped, out of black obsidian, it had been just the right size to carry without effort in the hands, even slippery hands, moist with the humidity of the jungle.

It had taken a long time to find the place, on a branch of land, a coral tumble the locals called "La Guadaña," the scythe, an arc of land that sliced into the sea. The Yucatan had many such sights. It was an old, man-made hummock of rock yet unexcavated, tangled with the copper-scrub brush of jungle growth and the lairs of snakes, serpents that straightened underfoot and vanished, leaving the barest track. The place was a stew of lizards and the leaping punctuation of mosquito larvae in the foot-size pools between the chalky coral boulders.

Ham had not even wanted to struggle out there through the undergrowth. The two of them were having such a wonderful time, he argued, drinking and calling to the parrots that flung overhead. A few of the bright, metal-green birds were attracted to him. He had always understood animals, and they had always responded to his voice, his gifts of, in this case, bits of tortilla. From time to time the two travelers lurched into town to buy Lomotil at the Clinica Guadelupe, a place with green walls and green asphalt tiles and a green welcome mat with crisp new rubber stipples for the wiping of street mud from the shoes.

They found a man with a yellow-headed parrot that said, in English, "drop dead." This man had worked for Americans in New Mexico, setting up microwave stations near Taos, and he was both amused by these two long-haired young men and eager to show them, for a price, "where the secrets are still lying for anyone to pick up."

"If they're so easy to find they would be found," Speke had

argued, cheerfully but with a certain lively force. "He's tracking us off into the swamps of Quintana Roo to show us something made in Mexico City, or Korea."

The beach life had been seductive. The village was both trashy and prosperous, a broad concrete and mud avenue of Valvoline signs and a burro with what looked like white eyeliner browsing under a bridge. The police in their blue and white pickup trucks had been unsmiling but friendly, once the two Americans established the fact that the owner of the abandoned boat yard did not mind their campfires. The truth was, the retired owner of the yard had sold all of his boats long before, and kept the white sand raked so that his pet grackle was the first creature to make tracks across the white beach each morning. The black bird had been beautiful in his dark plumage, but the *urraca* was not as dark and beautiful as the obsidian cat Speke and Asquith were to find.

The owner of the grackle made a steady profit selling the two Americans, and a few other international wanderers, tequila and Oso Negro gin *destilada seca,* but one day he encouraged the two to take the advice of the man who had built communications systems in the desert. "You dig," he said. "Who knows what you might find? It's not easy."

Being told it was a challenge was all it took to engage the interest of Hamilton Speke, and they had hacked their way with those machetes which seemed at a glance too rusty to slash the ropelike brush. The steel was keen, quiet. Once there, stumbling up the ruined pyramid, they tied a hammock overhead, and cleared a camp with the blades, snakes unknotting and vanishing at the touch of their shadows.

Speke had always maintained that the locals had left it there, as a gift, implying that it was both wondrous and a fake, but it was like him to think such a thought. He always assumed that strangers liked him and were planning ways to give him a pleasing surprise, while Asquith knew that the world was populated with men and women who knew his kind at a glance. They had lived, it seemed, on booze and Bimbo brand *donas,* the little packaged doughnuts, some powdered with white sugar, some coated with chocolate frosting. The air was heavy, creamy, sweet, and after a while the mosquitoes would not sting through the coating of perspiration. Insects whispered, scuttled, fled. Sometimes Speke would sear a white-fleshed fish over a fire, and they lived the time both searching and pretending to search, both avid and not caring, until one day Speke climbed out of the virtually Etruscan rubble of the rocks and dropped the moss green statue in Asquith's lap.

It looked lumpish, deformed, a monster made of jungle slime. Washed off, the green and coral white gave way to perfect black, rough-hewn, the glass carved into the scallop-shaped divots glass always leaves when it is crafted. They had their find, an idol, a little feline god.

A treasure. It was, Asquith had breathed as soon as he examined it, a fake. Speke was more cheerful, even manic. Fake or not, he had argued, it was theirs. And it might well be authentic. Hamilton had argued for a trip to Merida, or Mexico City, to have it verified, but Asquith had wanted to bury it somewhere nearby while they decided what to do with it, to keep it away from robbers, or from the whims of the things themselves, which so easily vanished or got lost. While he voiced doubts, it was clear that he wanted to believe that the cat was a genuine treasure. This had led to their great disagreement, after their wondrous celebration. It had led to the end of their friendship.

Speke stood before him now, and lifted his hand to take Asquith's shoulder. Where is Maria? his eyes asked, and even though Asquith had told him the truth, Speke was slow to understand. "I'm not going to play your game, Timothy. I want you to tell me what you have done with her."

My game, Asquith wanted to laugh. But that wouldn't be fair. Because this was, in a way, a game, after all, as was most art. "She is out there," he said. "Go look."

There was doubt in Speke's eyes now. Anxiety was making him slow, and deliberate, the same feeling that caused some people to become frantic.

A jaguar god, Asquith mused now, as Speke stepped through the French windows of the Outer Office. It had almost certainly been authentic, he thought as he waited beside the desk, one of the many Mayan idols strewn in the jungle. The vegetation there was so ingrown and so infested that it healed over even famous monuments, closing in over parking lots and highways. It had long ago swallowed the remains of that symbol of their youth, and their friendship, the black god.

I always wanted to write a play, Asquith thought, about the two lost young men, so recently successful with Ham's first songs that they could live in idleness and discovery like that in the heat. I wanted to write the play, or the screenplay, complete with music, that would convey the affection I had for Hamilton, and the wonder of finding such an astounding, rough-hewn miracle in the lime gray earth. This was going to be my crest-jewel, the tale that made up for years lost to illness, and to fear.

But, Asquith told himself, the tale had always been Ham's—it had always belonged to the world of light. And I was wrong to ever imagine otherwise, to believe that I could claim even so much as an episode as my own.

Speke was out there in the woods now, and Asquith was waiting for him to make the discovery. Why hadn't he seen her yet? She was not far from the Outer Office. Surely he had found her by now.

Asquith cut at the air with the poker, a fencer readying his thrust and cut. The iron hummed.

He eyed the poker. It seemed, just then, less a weapon than something magical, Aaron's rod, a caduceus from which the snakes had fled. He made a sound, part cough, part laugh. Come back, he called to his old friend with his thoughts. Hamlet, mortally stung, will yet fight to his death.

Only please be quick, dear Hamilton. See her soon, make your discovery, and get all of this over with. The audience is hushed, hankies in hand. The ushers are frozen in place at the exits. All eyes are ours.

Be quick.

Speke saw trees. He saw a place of tree browns, tree grays. That was all. Where was Maria, he had asked, and Asquith had indicated that she was out here.

This was bad. This was a trick.

But as he failed to see her anywhere, he began to see that the living Maria was hiding. She must be. Dread stirred, and became relief. That was it—it was another part of the game, the rules of which kept multiplying and unfolding, the further dissemblance of Asquith, both Lazarus and magus.

Surely it would be all right. There would be limits to how evil Asquith had become. Speke had always believed in life, in the basic light within the core of even terrible events. "Maria?" he called softly, increasingly convinced that she was here, watching, waiting, Asquith's sister but, at the same time, the wife and lover of Hamilton Speke.

Come out where I can see you.

That morning in Cozumel, the puddles chalk white from the hard rain on the coral soil, Asquith had taken Speke's hand. They had been celebrating all night, drinking down their joy at discovering the obsidian cat.

Asquith had taken his hand. Held it, and, like a man lifting a glass to his lips, he had kissed Speke on his knuckle. The very knuckle burned, even now, the knuckle of the forefinger of his right hand. It had been plain in Asquith's eyes: he expected to be kissed in return, there, on the lips.

The tiny frogs had scattered around them. There was so much life that unless you were very careful each footstep killed one of them. It was the impossible multitude, as well as their tininess, that had made them seem unreal. There were too many of them, he had thought, the way sometimes he stepped back from a television screen, struck by the thought: there are so many people.

There was so much life in the world. Speke rubbed his knuckle into the palm of his hand, a man trying to erase not his future, and not his past, but his own character. The little frogs had come out with the rain, and vanished with the heat, a kind of living smoke. The parrots had spiraled through the light, with cries like steel given the gift of joy. Iguanas had marched through the scrub like ugly aristocrats. The air itself had been an extended body, as warm as blood.

When Speke had responded by turning away, Asquith had strode into the excavated tumble of stones, stepped forth with the black cat and accused Speke of stealing. He stole Asquith's time, and his affection, and all the while he was oblivious, knew only his own happiness, his own faith, his own belief that the world belonged to Hamilton Speke.

Asquith had lifted the black cat high into the sunlight, so high the glass god glittered.

And then it had all ended—all of it.

Maria, his prayers called, louder in his mind than any call could have been. Maria, please come out. The game is over. It was always going to be over soon, and it was always going to have a happy ending.

He heard them first, the living static that surrounds the wound, and feeds upon the blood. Even as he knew that Maria was hiding, or perhaps merely bound somewhere, clamped into silence, he began to hear the tiny songs, the keen of insect wings.

He put his hand out to a branch, grasped at it, and missed his hold. He found the branch again, and kept himself upright.

Time to come out, he called in his soul. Time to come home and be safe. He followed, step by step, the ceaseless thrumming of the flies.

Not like Clara, his inner shriek said. Not like Clara. It won't be anything like what happened to Clara. You'll see. It will be all right.

The roots, the stones, the scattered acorns, of course, and the clawed, worked-over grave. But there was nothing there to give him any concern. Everything is sun and air, he thought. There is nothing wrong. The light from the sky played on the sharp, cinnamon brown stones.

And then he saw her.

·39·

At first she looked like part of a tree, a forked, treelike growth, an oak turning into a human being. It was easy, for an instant, to believe exactly that: a tree was turning into a woman, blossoming into a human form. This transformation was curious, and even amazing, and it was an illusion he struggled to maintain even when he began to realize what he was actually seeing.

He reached up to take her into his arms, but she was too high, and her face, a twisted, blackened gargoyle, looked down into his. Speechless, he stretched his arms upward. A cord cut into her blue neck, and attached her to the great, smooth-barked branch of an oak.

Even when he called to her, she did not respond. This isn't what it seems; it's another trick, he tried to tell himself. It's only another joke.

But the cold stone weight in his blood told him the truth. She was nothing like herself at all. She was transformed. She was no longer human, this woman he had never really known at all.

Her name was his heartbeat, his breath: Maria.

Blood and other fluid had streamed from her body, and spattered the ground beneath the tree. Already there were flies. It was the sight of the flies that snapped him, that and the sound they made, the relentless, pointless hum, that endless nearly soundless syllable they made, that tiny, mindless keen.

The idiot chaff of the world had her. Flies, the little, mindless flecks, tasted her eyes, and Speke did not know where he was. He did not know his own name, and whether or not he had a past. He was not a man anymore.

There was only the strangest sound, a shriek, as of a voice torn. That, and the strangest lucidity. He observed himself with a sickening detachment. There had been blackouts before, during his drinking days, nights that were holes in his life, holes so complete they seemed never to have happened. Waking after such a night, it seemed that time had, somehow, healed itself, sunset welding with dawn.

But this was something entirely different. He forgot everything, and everyone. And yet, he knew. He lived the present like something years gone, or like something far in the future, something that had been foretold and inevitable.

Speke threw himself through the half-opened French windows. The window frame clung to him. Glass shattered, shards of it skittering underfoot. He stumbled, and recovered his footing.

The knife was in his hand, the light off the steel nearly making a sound, a crystalline peal. Asquith cut at him with the poker, but it was not, both of them seemed to understand, a serious attempt to defend himself. Asquith thrust again, and it was a fencing pose, the tragedian's flair for the rapier, that allowed the poker to ring against the knife, withdraw, and strike it again, virgin fire tool against kitchen implement making a crisp, metallic music.

"The final scene, dear Hamilton, strewn with noble corpses." Asquith stabbed with the poker, and Speke reflexively fended the heavy weapon to one side with a stroke of the knife.

"So you see at last," said Asquith, smiling, or was it a grimace? It was the expression of a man looking into the blast of a sudden fire. "Endgame. I win. You mastered life, dear Hamilton, but I mastered everything else."

The poker whipped the knife from Speke's hand, and sent it spinning far across the floor. The heavy iron lashed again, humming through the air, an arc descending toward his skull.

He caught it, seizing it with both hands, wrenching the poker from Asquith's grip, and hurled the tool to one side. It spun, describing a gray circle through the air, and punched the wall just beside Athena.

It was an embrace. He grappled with Asquith, finding a grip on Asquith's crusted neck. His thumbs found the life in Asquith's throat, a leaping thing like a trout, and he caught the living creature under his thumbs, and pressed, pressed hard, seeking, and finding, the little jerking thread.

He held the quivering fiber of Asquith's life.

This wasn't happening, and yet it was. It was the only event in his life that mattered, the only thing that had ever actually taken place. This embrace, this grip. There was, in this vivid dream, a struggle. Asquith fought back, his fist striking Speke's forehead, knuckle crunching against his ear, his jaw, bringing the barest of taste of blood to his tongue.

Asquith flailed. He wrestled free. He slipped as he picked up the desk chair. He hurled it, but Speke caught it easily. Another pane of glass crashed, and the chair flew, as though by its own will, dancing on one leg, out the open window.

Speke caught him again, by the arm, and wrenched that limb so hard the joints popped. He felt now that he would never release Asquith again. They would be locked like this forever. Even Asquith seemed to understand, and to surrender, Speke's hands at his throat. His hands clawed and grappled at Speke's face briefly, but they weakened and began pattering about Speke's eyes like large, warm butterflies.

Asquith's expression was blissful. His lips twisted, as though with speech. Yes, his eyes seemed to say, I have put up a fight, but it was all to establish myself before this audience as a man who was a hero—flawed, betrayed by even his soul, but in the end a human being of noble nature.

Speke did not release his grip on Asquith's throat. Asquith made a sound, a rasping, airy utterance, and one of his arms waved up and down, a referee signaling an obscure but outrageous penalty.

This was further magic, the adept at his most skillful, both hero and clown. This was yet another role, the escape artist in agony. Speke thought only of Maria, and Clara, even as he was aware of Asquith's contortions. He watched himself, aware as he might have been aware of a television in a hotel room next to his own, hearing without listening to the tattoo of Asquith's feet on the floor.

There was a bright sun inside him. It rose. They say suns never rise, that the earth falls, continually, toward the star, and away from itself. But this sun rose, white and blinding. Speke had the impression of squeezing so hard that Asquith's spine was a knobbed cable in his fists. He saw only a distant face, blurred and unreal, a charred and twisted cartoon that became with every hammer of his pulse less and less human.

Speke took a breath.

He stepped back, and a heavy burden collapsed awkwardly away from him, and sprawled. Speke's own throat hurt, and he coughed. There was a silence in the room, a flat, total quiet, worse than a blast. There had been a roar, but now there was nothing. The sun in his head faded, dissolved in the sky.

There was a smell, like the soil of a hospital room. Speke put his hands to his lips, to his eyes. He groped his own head with his hands.

He took another breath. The roaring noise, he realized, slowly, had been his own voice. He tried to take a step, but could only shift one foot forward, like dragging a large, heavy stone.

A room. Of course—he knew exactly where he was. He had always known. The gray and white veins of the green serpentine shivered in his vision. Athena was eyeless, staring with those two planets where there should be irises and pupils.

He wanted to talk to Asquith. He wanted to ask him a few questions. Where was his old friend? He would call and his friend would answer. They would understand each other. They would help each other again. He would never forsake his old companion.

Sarah's hand was cool, and it was strong.

He worked his lips, and yet no words would come.

"Maria," Sarah said, not a question, a password.

Outside, Speke said, forming the word soundlessly. She is outside. Go look. Go look, and tell me none of this has happened.

She left, briefly, and then she returned. She knelt and examined the sprawling, gaping creature at Speke's feet.

She put her hands to her face, and her silence was like a word—like a prayer.

Speke felt a tiny, dry laugh twisting deep within himself. I can bury Asquith yet again, he thought. This entire play can be leafed back, page by page, to its beginning. It will all take place, over and over, scene one and the final, silent scene both encased in the same cover, held by the same spine, enclosed within the same darkness into one single point in timelessness.

She took his hand. "Come on out," she whispered. "Come on out, away from this place."

· 40 ·

Speke's father had never expressed a belief in God. His blueprints and his drafting table, his rolls of solder and his C-clamps had been, apparently, faith enough for him. And yet, from time to time, their father had taken Art and Hamilton to church, the big, purple-carpeted Methodist church with the pipe organ that vibrated the floor beneath their feet. The services were dull and stately, the minister black-robed and gregarious, shaking hands at the church door after sermon and collection and the final, sparsely voiced hymn. God had seemed to the youthful Speke to be associated with the prosaic, the microphone clipped to the minister's robe, the freshly mimeographed program that stated which family had paid for the splash of lilies beside the Bible.

Somehow, though, he had gathered that there was an illogical, even impossible, last court of appeals, a dumb wall which could be addressed, in a heartfelt apostrophe which did not even need to be heard. God was what was not there, a deep absence, and because Speke had learned that what was missing, or at least not apparent, was responsible for much of life, it did not seem completely foolish for even a faithless man to pray.

He prayed now, as Sarah led him into the sunlight. But this was not a prayer of supplication, or for forgiveness. This was a deeper, more anguished cry, almost devoid of coherent thought. It was the nearly wordless question: what have I done?

These hands of mine: what have they done?

Outside, where Sarah led him, the patches of sunlight flowed over their bodies, a stream of light and shadow, as if they had wandered before the flowing images of a movie projector.

Speke could not speak to a human being. He needed to speak to time itself, to the earth. And what language could he use to address the universe? He himself was the memory of a memory, a dream dreaming. Every hope he had ever entertained had vanished. Life would always be very simple, from now on, very simple and entirely empty.

"I'll take care of everything," said Sarah. "Don't worry."

Thank God, he found himself thinking, for Sarah.

Still, he could not respond. He could only take her hand again, as she was about to leave.

"Don't worry," she repeated.

Speke was beyond worry. He was washed up high ashore by everything that had happened. He did, though, feel gratitude for Sarah. She did what she had to do, like someone experienced at this, well-rehearsed for this sunlit scene.

He could not shape the words, but the thought twisted in him: her help was a treasure, but it was too late.

The names were wounds, the secret names for vital organs in his body that would never heal: Maria. Asquith. There was another thought, one that nearly stopped his heart: was it all my fault?

Christopher Bell was no longer lost. He knew where he was. He was at last within view of a building. He couldn't tell which building it was, because he had wandered way off not only the deer path, but off the dirt and gravel road to the house, too. It was the truth, he had to remind himself. It was the glorious truth. He had found the road and had lost that, too, sure that he knew a shortcut.

He gave himself a certain ironic praise: you're doing just fine there, Bell. Way to go. Now you get to explain to Sarah how you got lost behind a manzanita bush or a tree trunk and couldn't find a gas station. Twice. You got lost twice. Not counting getting lost in San Francisco. It wasn't fair to count that. Let's let that stay off the record.

He knew where he was definitely now, though. There was the peak of a roof, the flash of white walls through the dark trees. He was coming up, scrabbling and climbing, on the Outer Office. Congratulations, he told himself. At last you've found something. He couldn't approach it directly, though. A rotting tree lay in one direction, and a picket of poison oak in another. He had to work a detour, swing wide around the cottage, and trudge up what was a slight slope but seemed, at his point, steep enough.

The flies made a long chord of cello music, a low hum that stopped him. This was more than a snag of flies in the shade of a tree. This was a chorus. There is something there, he told himself. Something over there. There is something up in that tree.

She was a work of insect bodies, the flies tracing and retracing her so thickly he could not make out her features. But he knew who it was.

Speke, was his first thought. Speke did this. The thought was unjustified, and he knew it was concocted of shock and prejudice, but there it was. You start to doubt someone, and anything seems possible. He was hyper-rationalizing, he knew, to compensate for the shock. And it was a great shock, even though he had worked alongside homicide detectives, and he had seen bodies so decayed that arms came off when the cops tried to lift them.

This was different. He had to tell someone. He had to make a telephone call. He had responsibilities. He had known this woman.

He sprinted, slipped, and a branch scratched his face. He blinked. Someone's arms were around him, and he could not escape. It was someone strong, someone who held him at arm's length.

Speke gazed upon Bell as a man might gaze at his own brother after years of separation. It was good to see this biographer. It was good to have him here.

"You need to help us," he said, and Bell backed away, then looked a question at Sarah.

"We have to cut down the body," said Sarah.

"Are you all right?" Bell asked.

"Be quick," was her sole response.

Bell's eyes narrowed. "What have you done?" He directed this question to Speke, but Sarah answered.

"Do what he tells you to do," she said.

Speke stood shivering in the splashes of sunlight as Bell climbed the tree and cut her down. The knife made a fine, breathy song as it cut through the telephone cord. Speke did not want to hear it, but he could not deafen himself to the whine of steel and plastic, the subtle squeak as of a serpent fighting the blade. It set his teeth on edge, and yet he could not look away, and he could do nothing but cringe at the tune the steel made until the body nearly fell, dangled, and then did what it threatened to do, as Bell strained, clinging to one dead arm.

For a while the tree clung to her. He strained to reach upward to catch her.

The body fell. Joints made a butcher shop creak, and air was forced out of the dead lungs with a sound like a moan, a love making sigh. The arms flung, lifted, fell into a new position. Dust was suspended in the air. A sparse tangle of flies settled over her.

"It's all right," Speke heard himself say. He meant: she can't feel it. He also meant: it's not all right. It's terrible beyond belief.

That thing there, in the dark moist pool of fluid. That can't be her.

"Come away," Sarah said.

She stayed at his side, a presence like the strength of a body-guard, steadying him. Good Sarah, thought Speke. She should have been spared this sight.

Bell slipped from the tree. He and Sarah were trembling, and Speke felt sorry for them. These two brave, good people had not expected this. Most people live their entire lives and never see such violence. But she sustained him. Sarah's presence was like cool water, and he was thankful that she was there. He was more than thankful: her voice, the very whisper of her step, was every-thing to him now.

He directed Bell to Brothers' tool shed, where Bell found what they needed, something with which to conceal her body and de-feat the busy flies. Maria was stretched out on the dry leaves, and Bell covered her with a plastic ground cloth he brought back folded into a tight triangle, like a plastic, post-funeral flag. Maria's shape was visible through the translucent cover, a woman frozen in a spill of ice.

The sound of the flies was audible, but farther away and scat-tered, the hum of an electric shaver far off, or the breathy purr of a computer.

"I have to talk," Speke began.

Sarah put her hand on his arm.

"It's all right," he said. "I want to tell you . . ." He could not continue.

"We'll take care of everything, Ham," said Sarah.

Bell, whose face was blanched and pinched, said only, "Any-thing we can do," in a harsh voice.

Speke could not feel anything but gratitude for Sarah, and for Bell. But the gratitude faded, and was replaced by the granite escarpment of horror. This was real, he told himself. This was really happening. Sarah's eyes told him that. This was no dream.

The law would arrive. He knew that the sheriff would be here eventually: he knew the specialness of this place was about to be lost. There would be detectives and reporters, and not the friendly sort of journalists. It didn't matter. There was only one last thing that did matter, and it was easy to accomplish.

To his surprise, it did not take long at all. He was not aware of the words he chose. He was aware only of uttering the truth, the liberating, and painful truth.

It was amazingly easy, telling the beads of this narrative, this tale that was not only his. It was like telling the secrets of a stranger. Maria had deceived them all, but Asquith had been the great magician, accomplishing far more than Speke could have imagined. Explained in human speech, as he sweated in the sunlight, it was all so simple. Ugly, but simple. Sometimes, especially as he said their names, he had to pause and wait for his speech to return.

Why was Sarah's touch on his arm so steady? Hamilton Speke did not, in a real sense, exist. His lies, and his self-deception, had led him to this day, in this heat, with three people dead.

The last news blanched them, silenced them, took away their breath. "You don't know about Clara," he said, half question, half regretful discovery.

Whatever else you do, do not go into the kitchen. News that should never be spoken. Words that should poison the air.

"You'll be all right," said Sarah at last, in a voice almost too soft, too broken to be a voice.

No, Sarah, Speke wanted to say. He could not talk for a moment. The speech that had played out the facts had been the last words he ever wanted to speak. He patted her shoulder. No, he thought. Sometimes faith is pointless, even wrong. I will never be all right. My life, he could not bring himself to say, is over. It's only right. I have done too much.

He stiffened.

They gazed at him without comprehension.

He scrambled over a ridge of roots. No! he told himself. It can't be!

Lord—say it isn't true.

This was what he had feared ever since he first saw Live Oak, and walked the grounds in the healing sunlight. This was the dragon that had always hidden in the woods. He could do nothing but tell himself that it wasn't true, trying to deceive his own senses.

He sniffed the air again. There was no smoke at all, he told himself. Not even a little bit. Then, just as definitely, the scent was back.

It's not possible, he told himself.

He buried his head in his hands. When I look up again, all will be well.

Everything. My entire life will be wonderful, and Maria will be alive again, and Clara and Asquith. He wanted to weep, and not just a simple shedding of tears. He wanted to fall to the ground and gnash the earth, chew the twigs and branches, let himself dissolve into complete oblivion.

Instead, he lowered his hands. He took a deep breath, and there it was still, a dark spill in the air. This place was never meant to last. You never did belong here. You thought this was your home, just as you dreamed that Maria was yours.

These trees, this air, belonged to no one. Of course, he thought. It was only right. Asquith was in a way still alive. In a way, he could not die. It was wonderful, a miracle wrought by a man with no faith. Asquith had mastered everything that was not life, and that was a great legion indeed. "Can't you smell it?" Speke demanded.

Bell stood like a man unable to trust his eyes or his ears. He looked shocked beyond thought, haggard and blanched. "What?" he said, but it came out as a whisper.

I will take command, Speke told himself. There is nothing else to do. "I'm going to need your help," he said, laying a hand on Bell's shoulder. He did not recognize the sound of his own voice, this tone of authority.

"Anything I can do," said Bell again, his voice broken to a whisper.

"Don't stop and think—just do what I tell you."

"Anything—"

"We are going to fight."

Bell did not respond, was afraid to respond, gazing with a look that was lost, even frightened.

Speke laughed. He saw how he must look to Bell, a disheveled figure delivering a senseless battlefield rant. Perhaps Bell was not the sort of person who rallied to a challenge. Perhaps he was a man easily confused by events.

How dull-witted the biographer seems, thought Speke. How slow to understand what is happening. Perhaps I misjudged this man completely, thinking him keen, equal to my life's story. Look at him, even now, looking to Sarah for help. Tell me what to do, Bell was asking her with his eyes. Tell me what is happening.

"Before Asquith died," said Sarah, "he set fire to the woods."

· 41 ·

B ell followed Speke's command. He had, really, no choice.
There was something about Speke that made a man obey.
He ran toward the road, for help. But suspicion bit him,
and kept biting. There was no fire. It was entirely in Speke's imagination. *Don't leave Sarah with Speke.* It was a non-fire, a figment, a
phantom. He couldn't smell any smoke. It was too hot to run, but
he ran anyway. The drive was littered with acorns, brunette teeth
so hard he nearly slipped on them.

Stay on the road, he warned himself. Don't stray for even a few
steps.

Bright Mr. Bell. You were so smart. He had dreamed of a stim-
ulating project, and here he was. He would not, of course, be able
to turn any of this into coherent chapters. He had discovered a
new life, and it had nearly destroyed his talent. Speke was neither
genius nor fake. He was something beyond human, wonderful
and terrible at the same time. The next biography, Bell told himself, will be about someone long dead, someone who can do nothing but stare at me from photographs.

It was like a man reaching a tripwire, and barely catching himself. He stopped running.

I am a fool to leave her with him. *Speke is dangerous.*

Speke, he thought, must think me a total ass. Speke was going
to kill Sarah. A ridiculous thought—and yet, there it was. His lips
were chapped. Sounds were strangely crisp. The yellow white rye
at his feet made a fine, high noise with the wind.

Stay here. Speke had gone mad. Bell put his hands on his hips
beside the drive, in one of the deer paths that ran parallel to the
road. His breath was heavy, but soon settled to its normal rate. He
listened, and sniffed the air. He was sure of it—there was no fire.

So what now, he asked himself. What should I do?

There in the dust of the deer path was the single print of a very
large cat. It was a big print, nearly as wide across as his hand.
There were no other prints, simply the single kiss on the ground.

It was exact, proud. It struck Bell how a thing can be only itself, and not any other creature.

Distinct, and deadly. The red branches of the mesquite looked different to him. The gray leaves, the writhing, copper branches hid another world. A world that deceived, that disclosed treasures and buried crimes. It was a world he would never understand.

What should I do?

As a youth Bell had promised himself that he would never be like his father. He wanted a big life, a life of color, of scope. His father had been a deliberate man, an accountant whose hobby was the sharpening of shears, knives, and mowers. It was a life of numbers and carbon steel. The whetstone was his father's favorite tool. Now, his father dead just five years, Bell realized that he had inherited his father's skills, his father's temperament. He was a man who craved the fine edge, the sharp fact, the plain, tungsten truth.

He did not want greatness, and he did not want to capture life. Not any longer. He wanted to flee this place, and never return. That was what drove him now. He ran, hard. He ran until the cramp returned, that steel stitch in his side. He forced himself onward. He had one, simple need: escape. He was not seeking help. He was running away, defeated.

He clung to the gate, panting, his eyes closed.

This was the barrier that had blocked them earlier in the day, so long ago. Ham had not known about this chain. Bell had conveniently forgotten, but now here he was. There was no way over the gate. The words fell within him with masochistic solemnity: no way. There was a taste like iron on his tongue.

The black iron spears might have been greased. He could not find a grip. He kicked, fought, climbed, and slipped all the way back.

Again, he grunted his way halfway there. And slipped nearly all the way back, all the way to the dust.

He had one thought: leave this place. Run away. The place is too much for you. It has defeated you.

Just climb and escape, that's all, and forget everything else. This place is magical, and you are not. Speke is a giant, and you are just another little man. He slipped, but battled upward. Until, elbows bruised, shins aching, he found himself at the top of the gate.

Go ahead.

But Sarah had been right. You couldn't climb over this fence. The spear heads were sharp, and several times he nearly lanced his scrotum. He wanted to flee, but there was no way to escape. He was trapped at the top of a row of spears, and could not fall either way.

His own nature was revealed to him. He could not embrace life, after all. He need a telephone, a phone book. He needed a computer, a row of books. He needed a cross-reference on this. He couldn't survive intellectually naked. Confusion was not his element. He felt the child in him return, baffled, even scared. His inner voice was a piping, immature reed, a boy imitating an adult. This doesn't add up. What's the agenda here? Just a little information. That's all he needed.

There was no way over the gate, and it was just as well. He let himself fall inside the gate and panted, sweating, determined to run back to the house and save Sarah's life. At the same time, he felt the injustice of his position. Too much was happening that made no sense. He was confused. Some people lived quiet lives. They made coffee and read the newspaper. Some writers hired researchers, and did all their work from a desk overlooking San Francisco Bay. He was a field man, and didn't mind work. But he needed to double-check his facts, and that's exactly what he couldn't do now.

He would run back and save Sarah. He worked to convince himself. Lying here in the dust was an act of cowardice. It was probably too late—she was probably already dead. And he knew that whatever the battle to be fought, he was lost.

And then he smelled it.

The smell was dark, the scent of earth turned to poison, the smell of life turned to heat and light.

Bell clawed, wrestled, humped his way to the top of the gate. The sky was flawed in the distance, against the horizon. A fabric stretched into the sky, soiling the blue.

Wind stroked his hair, and hissed through the dry grass, and he could smell fire as he balanced on the row of black spears, took a breath, sweating, unable to tear himself away from the heads of the spears. Clothing tore, the crotch of his pants or the seam along one leg. A spear head was cold against the flesh of his thigh. He teetered, wanting to fall, trying to keep from falling.

Can't make it, a voice nagged him from within. You can't make it—don't try.

Until he fell at last. Earth met him with a clap, and he rolled. As a cub he had followed the Oakland Fire Department, and he knew how to drop from a roof onto bare concrete. My breath, he found himself thinking, is knocked out. I'll be able to breathe again soon.

But he couldn't sit up, and he couldn't crawl. He kicked at the dirt, and could go nowhere. Hurt, came the electric thought. I'm hurt.

I can't move.

Speke ran up the slope and Sarah followed. The shadow in the air was closing around the two of them, as though the air were becoming not gas but a solid, coalescing from gray dust to dark, impervious stone.

The air around them shook, trembled, and then began the perceptible shift, dragged inward toward the woods. He had always awaited this enemy. Now it was here at last. Speke felt the strangest glee. Fighting a fire like this would be a war against death. A war against the army Asquith had scattered in the woods like the teeth of a dragon. He could only partly understand the fierce pleasure he felt. He was awake again. There was something to fight for, he sang in his heart. A reason to battle. And a great, iron joke. Asquith isn't defeated at all, not even a little bit. He is alive in the fire.

There was no sight of the flames yet. There was only the tumult, as of a riot, an army gibbering and insane, wrenching and wrestling the oaks.

The garage door would not open. The old wood door creaked, the nail heads groaning beneath their bright, ever fresh paint. The hinges complained. The handle pulled loose. Speke felt the strength of his arms, his legs, his back, the power of his life.

He could hear the fire now, fierce applause.

Brothers' toolshed would not open, either. Bell had slammed the door, it seemed, so hard the wood was jammed. Speke pulled so hard that implements in the interior clanked softly, shifted by his effort. He wrenched, and with a shriek the door tore open. In the half-dark of the shed he found a shovel. He called to Sarah, but, to his surprise, she was just behind him.

"You don't have to stay," he said. "You can run up the road—"

Her fingers touched his lips.

He found himself holding her in his arms, surrounded by the shafts and dimly gleaming blades of the only weapons they had. It was always going to be this way, he knew. He had reached a chapter he had read long ago, but then deliberately forgotten. She had always been intended to fight at his side.

Outside, the fire came on. The two of them slashed at the sun-bleached foxtails, the drought-stiffened stalks of thistle. A grasshopper flicked through the air, rattling in its flight.

The heat rumpled the air. Distant branches writhed in the spidered sky. The two of them worked without speaking, the shovels making bell-like thuds against the hard clay. Their shadows were muted, blurred and erased by the shadow of the smoke.

She chopped a milkweed, clearing a path, a firebreak of dust and severed wildflowers. The dust floured her arms, and she worked in a fog of chalk.

They were not fighting to save Live Oak. They were fighting chaos itself, the void that waits to thaw and flood, the black fire that consumes every human hope.

· 42 ·

They cleared a long strip at the edge of the woods, a long rip of raw earth. The fire was creeping closer. He could hear it, now, snapping, tinder bursting.

Heat. The sun was a hole filled with it. Every breath was choked with powdered bleach. His tongue was a dry, dead, dust-saturated leaf. He was using, he realized, the same shovel he had used to bury Asquith.

His weapon, his still nameless blade. This battle was prehistoric, a struggle that had always gone on, long before his own life, and would continue long afterward. He used this tool to cut a firepath around the cottages, and when he looked up Sarah had a long scythe, like a mower in a classical etching, and she sliced the brush with a high, ringing sound. The brush shuddered for an instant, and the blurred shapes of small animals burst passed them. They were rabbits, abandoning the woods, he knew, but they might have been sprites or demigods, driven to the point of frenzy.

For some reason the fire was holding off, simmering beyond sight. It was like a deliberate enemy, stealthy, the soul of malice. Speke had the uneasy sensation that it was creeping just below the surface of the land, roiling under their feet. Still, he could see no flames, only the powerful countryside of smoke, billowing into the air.

The work made it hard to think, and hard to remember. Work, he told himself. Fight. The enemy was still only a rumble, a distant avalanche, and the singed flavor of the air. The quaking air around them swept upward, now, hauled toward the sun by the rising heat.

He needed Sarah. He had been stupid to pretend otherwise. How could a man be stupid for fifteen years? Stupid was the only word for it. Stupid and oblivious to the truth. But that was all in the past. He could not think about the past.

The dust rose about them, earth rising upward to become a part of the sky. Speke took her arm, interrupting her mowing. A last spring of sliced oats sang from the curved blade, and rained to earth. "There's nothing more we can do," he said.

If the firebreaks they had torn so quickly did not stop the fire . . . He leaned on the shovel. The thought was too ugly to complete.

"It'll be all right, Ham," she said. She was gray with dust, and her eyes were gleaming. She bore the scythe like the spirit of life.

It will be all right. That was her refrain, her repeated promise. He had always disliked easy optimism. The giddy faith many people had that good times were just around the corner had always struck him as childish, or even stupid. Some promises, Speke knew, are false, and to believe in them is dangerous. Part of him wanted to laugh. How could it be all right? We're going to die here! But her faith was steady, cool, honest. She seemed to believe, as Speke did, that the fight was everything, the refusal to surrender all that mattered.

"You'll see." Her voice had always been like soothing medicine to him. The sound of her strengthened him again.

He found himself smiling, his face a mask, he knew, of grime, soot, clay. Just like hers. As he worked he uncovered lost secrets, an old shotgun shell, a weathered husk with a black copper tip. Two old shells, forty-five caliber he judged without giving them a second glance, tossed, ancient and spent, from the shovel. He overturned a dry divot and a centipede writhed for a instant before it vanished, and at one point the translucent pod of a rattlesnake's rattle, long abandoned by the snake itself, spun to a stop at his feet.

The shovel dropped with a clatter, and her scythe fell. He put his arms around her. He never wanted to leave this place. But the place he wanted was not the land. It was Sarah. It was this moment, this inner landscape.

A surreal flock tossed in the branches. But these were not birds. The fire had come.

Other flames flung across the firebreak, as easily as tossed coins. Smoke boiled under their feet, and the fire danced before them, around them.

They beat it down with their tools, stamped the errant fires that sputtered on the lawn, but then with a rush a crowd of flames forced them staggering backwards, eyebrows singed.

She shouted something, warning or encouragement, he could not tell.

The Outer Office was hidden behind a leaping tangle of flames. Maria's body, and Asquith's—the fire had them both. The knowledge was a blow to the stomach, to the soul. The bodies were burning.

"I'm going to climb the roof," he cried.

She leaned forward, eager, hungry for his words, straining to hear like someone in a blizzard. He directed her to one of the garden wells, far away from the rumble of the fire. "And then you run," he cried. "Take one of the deer paths. Run away! Save your life!"

His old friend had won. But he had not won entirely. There was still a little fragment of Hamilton Speke left. He used a ladder from the shed, propped over the door to Sarah's office. The roof was even hotter than the ground, and heat waves fluttered off it, making the chimney seem to dance. He slipped, and nearly fell, but caught the peak.

The hose snaked away from his outstretched hand. He could not reach it. The thing was trying to escape. The nozzle bounced along, down the shingled slope.

He plunged after it, nearly rolling from the eave. And caught it.

"Turn on the water," he called, his voice lost in the wind.

The hose rasped and twitched. There was a gurgle, but no water. The sky dirtied. Ashes circled downward. The air tasted foul. In the amount of time it took to inhale, the world grew dark.

A long drape, like fine, dark silk stretched across the sky. It extended over his head, far to the north. The sun tightened into a hard, red coin.

Ashes rained on the roof, fine white dust that covered the hairs of his arms. A larger ash spun to his feet, smoldering. Another spat and sizzled, until his foot killed it. An ash licked his eye, blinding him for a moment.

"There isn't any water coming out of the hose," he called.

Her voice responded, a cry far below that he couldn't make out.

"No water!" he called.

A long ribbon of gold worked the hillside to the west, beyond Sarah's cottage. It ran like a liquid thing, unpeeling perfect blackness. The black streamed white smoke. Wind gathered in the trees, as though the plants were breathing, taking long, deep breaths and letting them go.

Wind! His jaw clenched. The wind is rising. It was driving the fire closer, whipping it forward.

"Water!" he cried, the wind snuffing his voice.

It was in there, far within the estate, a secret lake, an aquifer buried and ripe with promise, a sliced melon of cool far beneath the heat. He uttered the word again, for the sound of it, for its magic: water.

The hose choked, and then gushed a fountain of warm water which was, almost at once, cool. Good well water, Speke said to himself. Of course Sarah would know how to get water from the land—that was exactly the sort of miracle she had mastered long ago. Water from the inside world. He wanted to talk to it, call to it, scream to the water to come on and help them, water god, long-ignored though he had been. They needed him now.

Surely Bell would have alerted a fire crew by now. Surely help was on its way.

Sarah leaped to the roof from the top of the ladder. He tried to wave her away. "Run!" he called. "Don't stay here." The house will be surrounded soon, and then what will you do? Save yourself while you can.

He did not say this. A sound silenced him before he could utter the words. There was an explosion as a tree, a stately blue gum, flashed into flame. They both watched as the fire poured to another eucalyptus, and wrapped it. The speed was amazing, even beautiful. The tree was a spiral of flame. There was a report like a shot as the heart of the tree split.

This is how I die, then, he thought. Fighting for my house. He would fight well. If only Sarah would run, while there was still a chance. The fire had chosen a tough man to seek out and destroy. This is going to be hard for you, fire, because I don't fear a thing.

As he thought it, he laughed. It was true. Death meant nothing to him. How could it? He grinned into the smoke and sprayed the smoldering ashes as they fell. Death was attacking, and he was killing it wherever it fell.

Let it come.

Sarah folded her arms and gazed into the wind that drove the fire. She wanted to be nowhere but exactly where she was. She blinked her eyes against the smoke. If this was the way Hamilton Speke was to die, she would go with him. She had been a stranger to herself for too long.

The fire surrounded the house, and began to close upon them.

· 43 ·

There was no time to lie there, he chided himself wryly, blinking up at the sky, thinking how hurt he was.

Bell dragged himself to his feet. He took one step, and then another. The ankle was not sprained, and his ribs were probably not broken, either. They only felt that way. But this was no time to stand, feeling his shirtfront like a smoker who has misplaced his lighter.

He limped to the center of the road. The surface of the two lane reflected the sun. The asphalt absorbed much of the light itself, but gave off so much heat that the double yellow line withered and floated in mirage only a few paces ahead of him.

A car had to roll along this road eventually. He began to run. The first few steps were awkward, but then he found his stride. A car would be here soon, he told himself. He could smell the smoke with every breath now. They would burn to death. The thought choked him. Surely any moment there would be a car, and he would flag it to a stop.

The mirage ahead of him did not look anything like water. It looked like gulls made of aluminum foil, flames made of shivering ice. With every step this silent ice escaped ahead of him. So much depended on a sole, running man, sprinting down the center of a highway, over rabbit skins with wire-thin bones, over ancient roadkill identifiable only by a stain on the road, a pinch of hair or a glittering scrap of reptile skin. He had, he gradually realized, no plan. He did not know where the nearest ranch might lie. He knew only that the road was empty. There was not a single car.

Another pancaked mummy passed beneath his feet. He had never realized what a desolate place a highway could be. He stopped, panting, sweating on the crown of the road, when his cramp bit him once again. He forced himself to run. There was no time to stand still.

Burn to death—the thought made the air whistle in his throat. Surely a car was coming. Any minute now. Someone had to use this road.

Bell shouldered through the heat as though it were a thickening gel. Each step was a loud *thwack* on the gray surface of the road.

His thoughts were fragments. Surely soon. A car. Any time.

The road was empty.

Speke shot down the sparks as soon as they danced on the roof. The hard stream of water blasted them away. It was all burning. The Outer Office was gone, with the two bodies. Sarah's cottage was fuming, ropes of smoke writhing from the peak of its roof. Anguish made him tighten his grip on the hose, forcing the water into a hard, white rod that played and broke on the curls of smoke.

He looked back at Sarah watching it all, straddling the divide of the roof. She caught his eye.

Her glance said: Don't worry. We'll survive.

She watched with the kind of serenity she had before now only imagined. She descended the ladder briefly to pluck the shovel from the lawn, then carried the shovel up the ladder and used it to flick sputtering ashes when they fell out of Speke's reach. She sent them spinning into the range of his water, or off the roof, then returned to her post at the peak.

As a girl she had been fascinated by the life of Joan of Arc. Perhaps the reason for this was quite simple. Joan was a young woman who fought like a warrior, with fighting men behind her. Her father, she must have imagined, would prize her all the more if he could see her leading men to battle. This fascination alone had brought her to consider, as a teenager, a Catholic conversion. Joan of Arc's last word had to Sarah always been something of a mystery. Surrounded by the flames, lapped by the fire, clothes and flesh licked clean, her last word, as the flames possessed her, was the single name: *Jesus.* Sarah had always wondered how this last name sounded through the crackling prison. Like a shriek? Like a prayer, offered up in absolute faith? Like a call for someone, something, certainly her own champion, to come at last?

People who heard her last cry were shaken, changed for the rest of their lives. Just after her death the faggots were tumbled aside so the crowd could see the partially consumed corpse and see that their champion was dead. At this moment, Speke battling the rain of hot ash, Sarah hammering a red spark dead with the flat of the shovel, she was stung by yet another spinning ember that fell from the sky. Only one small burn, she told herself. Nothing more than that.

The spark left a black smudge on her arm, and it seemed to Sarah now that Joan's cry was just another human cry out of agony to a sky which responds to nothing.

Speke turned. "There's still time."

She stood at the very ridge of the roof line, where it fell away to either side. She did not answer.

"For you to run," Speke added. His tone said: I know you've made up your mind, but I have to say this anyway, for my own conscience.

She smiled. Sometimes, she saw, it doesn't matter what you believe. It only matters that you act as though the faith were real. Heaven takes you in its loving arms, or it doesn't.

She climbed downward toward another plume of smoke.

It was a pickup, and it was coming fast. Bell flung himself into its path. The driver did not see him waving his arms, dancing, crying out for the vehicle, for time itself, to stop. The truck came on, hard.

At the last moment the driver hit the brakes so hard that blue smoke billowed from the tires, and the truck swung from side to side.

Then it hit him.

· 44 ·

"Are you all right?"

It was a man's voice. Strong hands brushed Bell's hair back from his eyes, and touched him gently, knowingly.

"I'm fine," said Bell doubtfully. He shifted his legs as he lay on his back, staring at the head that eclipsed the sky in his vision. It was a grim test: arms worked. Legs worked again. Let's lift the head a little.

The pickup had braked so successfully that the hood had brushed him to one side, virtually all the momentum spent. Still, he had been flung backwards, an impromptu lesson in physics and comparative weight. There was a smell of rubber sulphur in the air. The road beneath his body was gritty. Bell ached to stand and walk around, but at the same time he was partly stunned and he knew his body, and his mind, were not working quite properly.

And then he remembered the fire. He fought to stand, to speak. "Speke . . . Sarah . . ."

"There's a fire," said the man, and it was then that Bell realized he was talking to Brothers, the gardener. "I saw the smoke. Called the county."

Brothers helped Bell to his feet. From far away, sounding strangely metropolitan and out of place in the hills, came the sound of a siren. There were several sirens, the urgent rise-and-fall sounding thin and distant. Bell had always believed in the powers that solved emergencies, the police, fire departments, surgeons, airline pilots. He had always admired the men shoveling sand into sandbags against the flood. Perhaps that was one of the reasons journalism had attracted him. It had been a chance to interview rookie cops after a shooting, a chance to interview actors with greasepaint still caking their wrinkles. It had been a chance to be a part of what he had always thought of as Life.

But now his only thought was: too late. It's all too late. His fundamental faith in hope, and in human accomplishment, withered in him. Life had run through his fingers once again.

Sarah was lost, and so was that man he would never know, that lively enigma, that amazing human being, Hamilton Speke.

Bell drawled something about the fire sending a "plume you can see from Soledad to Tamales," but he thought only: too late.

The ashes fell. It was a rain of the fine, spent residue of life, and it coated the wet shingles of the roof.

Speke had grown up with minor fires, as though his childhood had been a preparation for this day. His father had not been absentminded. There had been fires in the garage where he worked; his father had never explained why he took so little notice of the fire department's suggestions, and why the fire extinguisher was always lost in a pile of flower presses, or hanging on the hook with a mysterious puncture in the base, the sort of wound only a bullet or a spike could cause.

Perhaps his father had been fatalistic, nearly desperately so. Perhaps that last flight through the thermals over San Bernardino had been more than just a little suicidal. Perhaps windsheer is an adjunct to human failure. Perhaps a beloved dead wife calls to a man of reason in a way he cannot understand, and causes him to seek death in ways he admits to no one, especially to himself.

She must have been beautiful, this mother he could not remember. He had always pictured her smiling, looking down at him and smiling, as though in each memory of her he was still an infant. To remember my mother, he came to realize, I have to forget my own manhood. There are many ways to be beautiful, and she must have had them all, this absent woman, this half of his childhood he would never know. Often he found himself wondering, what would she think of me? And what, if we met in some plane out of time and space, would I think of her? Would we disappoint each other?

But I am not like my father, Speke had always reassured himself. I embrace life with both arms. I am not secluded with my number three pencils and my designs for improved valves for pressurized deodorant. And yet, standing there, seeing that his house was about to burn, surrounded by fire on all but one side, he understood that he had deliberately chosen such a place. Its fragility, the fact that it could vanish in smoke, surrounded by drought-prone brush, had made it all the more precious. Perhaps, Speke thought, we value most that paradise we can lose.

The trucks, when they arrived, broke through the line of fire and tumbling smoke.

First Brothers and Bell careened to a stop on the lawn, then a stream of green county trucks. Men with orange hardhats spilled from the vehicles, and there was a clatter of spades and a surprising lack of speech.

Speke leaped, and half-fell, down the ladder to direct them. Ordinary time was stripped away, leaving a sequence of heat and smoke. The men worked, shoveling a naked firebreak across the smoldering lawn.

"The house," Speke called, or perhaps he didn't call it at all. Perhaps he thought it so desperately that everyone heard him.

Save the house!

At one point during the afternoon, airplanes, graceful shapes like sharks, dived at the fire, disgorging gouts of orange. The orange plumes started as precise, well-defined spouts that slowly fattened and dispersed. Men ran, orange with powder.

Through it all, he came to believe that the house was lost. It was logical, it was even just. He had done harm in the world, great harm. This was being taken away from him, exacted from him by the mindless twitch of the flames.

The wind continued to shower Speke with fine ash the size and color of eyelashes. They collected in the hairs of his arms, clinging to his sweat. Now and then one blinded him for an instant. The men stooped, and shoveled dust, surrounded by a rain of burned fur. Speke shouted encouragement, his voice a rag, and at one point Brothers stopped him with a crowbar nearly as tall as a man, and thick, a great, iron lever.

"We got a problem," said Brothers. He waited for a moment, as though counting his syllables.

He looked down at the ground, and smoothed a spent ash with his shoe.

Oh, for a man of words, Speke nearly said.

"Someone had a chain on the gate," Brothers said. "We had to crash through. Damn near wrecked one of the county trucks."

Speke spat an ash from his lips.

"That's not the only problem," said Brothers, hesitating.

Speke waited.

"I think," said Brothers, lowering his voice, "that we have a death." He jerked his head in the direction of the Outer Office. Then he looked back and studied Speke with a gaze of worry and curiosity. Brothers could not add: tell me I'm wrong. His glance said: tell me its not true. "Is anyone missing?"

Speke grabbed a pick from the smudged green of the lawn and gave what he hoped was a manly nod. Understood, he tried to say. We'll deal with it later.

"There's a body," Brothers said. "You can—you can smell it in the smoke."

It's nothing but a deer, Speke wanted to say. It's nothing but a trick.

Brothers stepped before him, and asked, "Where's Maria?"

Speke tried to talk, couldn't, and then tried yet again.

But something in Brothers' character, or Speke's look, prevented further questions. Brothers hurried off to wrest at things with his lever, wellheads, Speke imagined, or flaming timbers.

Perhaps it was only his imagination, but there did seem to be a number of men using dashboard radios. Several men stopped work to gaze off in the direction of the Outer Office.

Speke endured. He was still fighting. He would not quit. But the faith, the power of belief, was waning. There was nowhere else to retreat. It was afternoon, but dark. The engine of another dive bomber surged overhead. The darkness streamed above them.

Sarah stood on the gables, watering the roof.

The Outer Office had completely burned, showing scarlet, blazing ribs. The building, however, seemed fueled from within. The roof fluttered fire, and the blazing lumber fell inward. The fire finished its work quickly, and then it did not die. Their bodies were caverns of flame—he tried not to think this, but he could not escape the knowledge. Asquith was about to step into his life again, as a presence that would have to be explained, an absence that had weight and charred form.

The men battled everywhere he looked, but the wind was strong.

Speke bounded up the ladder. He used his most commanding voice, the voice that never failed to win respect from man, woman, and beast. "You have to leave, Sarah. I'm sending you away." His voice was strong, but he wanted to beg her: please. Please go.

Her eyes were bright, and she did not answer.

His voice shook. "I'm not going to lose you, too. I won't let it happen."

"I'm staying here." Her voice was crisp and definite, like a wire of gold.

"If I lose you . . . I can't bear it. . . ."

She cast the hose aside, and the writhing thing cast water in one direction, and then another. She held him, and then kissed him, her lips on him with the fervor of someone resuscitating the dying.

He let her hair stroke his lips. He whispered her name like a word he had struggled to recall for years.

Sarah, he thought—after all this time.

"I don't think we can save the house," he said at last. "What do you want us to try to save from inside?"

She touched his face. Her hand was pale against the grime of his skin, and her touch was strange, strong and calm. He had never felt a touch like this, like a hand out of another world.

Manuscripts, she wanted to say. All your manuscripts. The art. Everything. Save everything.

"It's time," he said, through tears, whether caused by grief or the smoke she could not tell. "I'll get anything. Anything you want. Just tell me what it is, and I'll go in and get it."

Still, she could not respond.

"Tell me what you want from in there, Sarah!"

"The house is saved," she said.

"No," he groaned. Reading her expression, he said, "I don't believe that any more. This is stupid optimism, Sarah. The house is going to go, and when it starts it won't take any time at all. Think of all the art. Think of—" Words failed him. He made a wild gesture. "Think—"

But he stopped himself. He had her. That was all that he wanted, and all that he could rescue. The rest of his life was gone, finished.

Sarah understood. The house should be saved. But, she knew, if the house were lost, what did that really matter? Ham was what counted.

"There is one thing you can save," she said. "Not that I'm giving up hope . . ."

He was too eager, shaking her. "What? Tell me!"

"It's a symbol."

He leaned forward eagerly.

"Go in," she said, "and use the white net beside the aquarium."

He did not have to say: yes?

"Use one of the smaller bowls in the cupboard."

He blinked in the smoke.

"Save the piranha."

Speke studied her for a moment, and then he laughed. He laughed so hard that one of the men on the lawn adjusted his hardhat so he could gaze up at them.

After a while there were shadows again, and late afternoon sun made the shadows long. The earth was a mat of black, and white streams bled from a hundred places.

Long before sunset men from the sheriff's department came, and men from the county coroner gathered around the dark, spent place that had been the Outer Office.

Speke's eyes stung, his contact lenses fogged with smoke. There was time, fifteen minutes he supposed, before the house itself began to burn. There was time to step into the house and to see it again, to inhabit it once more, however briefly.

· 45 ·

Outside, cop radios jabbered in the darkness.

There was a residue of fine ash over the tops of books, and on the dust cover of the computer. Speke had glimpsed the men in suits, dark jackets and dark pants, the men in black shoes and wool blends whose presence meant: a few more minutes and they'll be done with body bags and have their list of questions.

They would have many questions. Many wonderful questions, and he would sit still and tell them all. Fire and the law. They went together in a kind of visceral logic.

There will be questions, and then handcuffs. Maybe that was logical, too, the theater of the law. They would march him manacled before the flash cameras and the mikes, to the police car. Speke sat in his office, rubbing Pliagel over one of his contact lenses. He rinsed the flexible, collapsible lens with a squirt of saline solution, and lifted the tiny, inverted disk to the surface of his eye.

He blinked. His vision was new again.

It was all theater, all of it a stage, all of it imagery to be consumed. He shot a peek out the big windows of his office and he saw hardhats in the dim distance, around the garage, and heard the snap and bite of yet more flames somewhere in the dark.

He could feel it in his bones: there was a fire somewhere in the house, maybe in the floorboards, maybe in the lath and plaster of the walls. Smoke began to foul the air yet again. You see, he hissed to himself: I told you. You can't rest. You'll never be able to rest, ever again. The house is not out of danger yet. And what difference does it make? It might as well burn. They will take it all away from you. They should. It's only right. After all: you killed.

He pressed the lid over the saline solution, and thought, Which of my lawyers will I call? My contract man will be useless with this sort of case. Thank God my father never lived to see this night.

He had lived a childhood of simple prosperity. It had seemed normal to him, unremarkable, his life drifting just as a childhood should. But as an adult one morning, walking up a ravine near Oaxaca, passing goats and rotting garbage, the rattle of the automated looms in the distance, he had realized that his childhood had been Southern Californian, convenient and without disease or violence. He had washed the dust of newspaper ink from his hands and watched television, waiting for his father to come home from the Hickory Pit with the thick-as-cardboard paper plates laden with pork and potato salad. His small, quiet family had not been rich, but the bicycles leaning against the garage walls were always the newest ten-speeds.

His favorite cartoon character had been Popeye. His brother had preferred the Road Runner. He and his brother had walked along the beach, peeling jellyfish from the wet sand. The dead, glutinous creatures left the trace of a stain on the sand from their purple markings, like those make-believe tattoos one could buy and apply to one's wet—usually just-licked—forearm. The purple dapples of the jellyfish left a transfer pattern like a starburst, a nova, an exploding sun. It was as though nature could not endure an ugly thing, but even in its randomness and blind reproduction achieved symmetry and hue. His boyhood had been one of unremarkable comfort, a life of late dinners while the sprinklers danced water over the bermuda grass outside. His father had been kind, quiet, always quick to encourage, to help find the puncture in the bicycle's tire, to up the allowance when the paper route became so successful Hamilton could not squeeze all of the newspapers into his canvas bag and decided to quit.

Why wasn't I satisfied? Speke asked himself. Why didn't I plan on becoming a realtor or a car dealer, a lawyer or an engineer? My father could have gotten me a job with Ford or IBM, especially toward the end when *Time* ran that thumbnail bio of him under "America's Brain Trust," next to cardiologists and weapons specialists. Neighbors and friends had always liked me. Any number of friendly neighbors would have given me a start in retailing, distributing, investing. I could have had a wife and kids, a normal wife and normal kids, kids who need braces and break arms playing soccer. Instead I wanted something that life can never offer. A life of magic. And I got it. I got it, and then I lost it, because it was always too much to hope for, too much to want.

But he had wanted life—not to be simply alive, but he wanted that version of immortality, life multiplied, that success can bring.

He avoided the professional voices, the matter-of-fact discussion tones and almost surgical caution of the kitchen. He peeked out one of the upper windows and saw Holub's car, gleaming amidst all the sooty trucks. Television lights were set up, glaring blue-white beams illuminating the still smoking coals. And there was still a fire to be fought. What a show it must be, carried live.

Like a planned demolition, the garage was consumed. For a few moments it was a scribble drawing of itself in tangerine and scarlet, until it sagged. Someone thoughtful, perhaps Bell, perhaps Brothers, had rolled the Jaguar out of the garage and down the drive, nearly as far as it would go and not be surrounded by fire-stripped trees.

How convenient, thought Speke ironically. That meant that if a last remaining fork of fire should reach the car, turning it inside out with heat, we'll all be able to watch. It'll be carried into homes all over Northern California. This news next: The Lives of the Rich and Burned.

Even now he had a sense of humor, an inner, dry laugh, the old itch of something that passed for wit. The fire became a tradition. There had never been a time in which it had not laid seige to the house. There had never been a time before now, the air of each room ripe with smoke. He carried the fire extinguisher from room to room, sure that somewhere, hidden, unseen, there were more flames to fight.

The Hemingway letter had already burned in the Outer Office, along with the leather-bound Goethe. Speke loathed the thought that flames could consume the Monets here in the house. Those paintings were more than stretched canvas on frames. They were portions of a man's soul.

The tube of the extinguisher dangled, its nozzle a brass sleeve that swung wide and knocked against maple bedposts and mahogany wainscoting as he hurried from room to room.

When her voice interrupted his search it paralyzed him and he could not respond. "They want to talk to you," she said.

He didn't even understand her for a moment.

She looked radiant, peaceful. He tried not to look broken. Yes, he thought, of course they do. A nice long talk, Mr. Speke. A couple of things you can help us with. His breath caught. It was all so cruel to Clara. And Maria, and Asquith. All, fundamentally, his fault. He squared his shoulders. He would not embarrass himself.

"That's fine," he said. His voice sounded solid, serious but not overly concerned. It's good to know, Speke thought, that I know how to keep up appearances. Then he added, "Stay with me, Sarah. Please."

He was by her, hurrying outside. It was time.

The wind was dead, and the lawn was trampled wet in the spotlights. There was a lunar look to the woods, in the opening-night lights. The landscape resembled another, more foreign moon, the moon of a distant planet.

He sensed the eyes watching him. People had always watched him. Both men and women had always found him the one to follow with their eyes. He waited on the porch. Sarah joined him, and a tiny thread of calm took its place in his soul. He could not make out where the knot of cops waited, the ones that would arrest him. A phrase came to him, perhaps something out of an old gangster movie: facing the music.

Poor Sarah—she had no idea what the world was really like. Good calm Sarah expected cops to be like she was, steady and understanding.

But her father had been a policeman, Speke reflected. Perhaps she had seen this sort of arrest before.

They stepped off the porch, into the heat of the lights. He had done all he could. His eyes were two sores in his face, and he could not take a deep breath without giving a great cough.

The crush of people made progress difficult, although the crowd made way for them. A camera flashed, and another. Someone asked a question. He was quiet, and merely gazed at the charcoal-dusted lawn. It did not seem to be day, or night. They stood on an island that had no time, smashed lawn crisscrossed with TV cables.

There were atolls of ash, pure, carbon black. There was a new smell, too, of clean, empty air. Black grass smoldered. Feet left white footprints that curled with smoke.

He endured what he knew was only the beginning of his new, ugly public role. Even now he could sense it: people saw him and believed in him. He was strong, broad-shouldered, important to the people around him even in defeat.

A figure stepped to his side. "I don't think you need to worry about these people, Mr. Speke." The man's tone was respectful, reassuring. "I'll tell them everything they need to know."

Speke gazed at the gray-haired man wonderingly. He was the only man here in a glowing, pale suit. It was a well-cut suit with black buttons, and there was not a single ash anywhere on it. The man smiled, showing a brown canine in his otherwise perfect teeth. His tie was silk, green lizard patterns, Speke noted dumbly. Or were they iguanas?

"It's Inspector Holub," Speke said, his memory working with the jerky determination of a steam shovel. "Come forth to tell all."

He had meant it, in his numb state of mind, half ironically, but Holub gave a short, quick nod. "I'll do that," he said, in his crisp, humorless cop voice.

"I'm ready," said Speke.

Humorless, but not without compassion. "You better go inside and wait," Holub said. "We don't really have to talk out here. I just thought you could help us with something. Something that doesn't make sense to us."

Speke found himself still holding the fire extinguisher. He let the weaponlike object dangle at the end of his arm.

Perhaps Holub expected him to offer some advice, or further comment. But Speke only stared, and Holub read the stare like a ringside physician gazing into the eyes of a boxer. "I'm sorry we troubled you. After what I've seen," Holub added, "you're lucky to be alive."

Speke did not understand. The sequence of events did not make sense. Luck, he mused, had not been a major factor in recent hours.

"Wait," called a voice. "Wait, Ham, don't go in yet." A bright light, a germicidally blinding light, raked him, then found him, then held him, and he was, momentarily, unable to see.

"Look back here, Ham, and look up at the sky with a real—wait, Ham, don't go in. Please, Ham, you look terrific."

He should be surprised at the sound of his voice, his brain told him, but he was not. He could barely croak, "How did you get here, Scamp?"

"Saw it on television in L.A. What a deal! It's on CNN, Ham. Everybody feels so awful about this. Stand there just a sec."

"What is it, Scamp? What do you want?"

The big man was a silhouette, snapping orders in his Eastern European/Bugs Bunny accent. "Standing there and looking. Just standing and looking. You're surveying the disaster manfully.

Talk about grit. It's wonderful! Mr. Strong. Mr. Life. That's it, Ham. We just want you."

The black cat had not quite resembled a cat, in Speke's eyes. Asquith had insisted it resembled a cat, so that is what they agreed to imagine it was. It may or may not have been authentic. What it was, however, as a prize, as a souvenir of hard work in the sweat-slime, made it something to treasure. Authorities he had questioned about it years later, sitting in first class or sipping martinis in stylish cocktail lounges, had been inconclusive. The Mayan pantheon was complex. The black jaguar may have been a pre-Columbian treasure, or it may have been something altogether different, a hoax, or a more recent carving lost or tossed away as worthless.

The jungle heat had been oppressive. Oppressive, and unending, a permanent strata of heat underlying the day. When night fell, the lower, more enduring heat remained. The air had been saturated with futility and dead power, like something left over to be claimed or ignored entirely. The coconut groves were weedy and cluttered with downed fronds. The sand was sugar-bright, the parrot fish easily visible in the clear water. Indians slept on the beach beside the half-constructed hotels, their camps rolled blankets and sores of ash on the white sand.

Day had weight, and night an even greater presence, a smell, the funk as of rotting cheese of decay and the sharp, almost citric, odor of garbage fires from town. The top ten single from what was to be the album *First Cut* paid for all of it, and they could have lingered for months, or even years, turning record company checks into pesos.

But they had that moment, that instant of affection and rebuff. Speke's rejection of Asquith led to the cat being hoisted high over Timothy's head, both of them so drunk they were at once slow and clear-headed, intoxicated to the point of sanity.

Asquith had held the cat high, and it glittered in the sunlight. And he threw it down, with full strength, against a coral boulder. It should not have shattered. Coral is soft, and the cat's shape was rounded, spheres and jagged arcs.

It broke, with a strange lack of sound. Bits rolled, came to rest, each one smaller than a human tooth.

Asquith had sunk to his knees, and then entered a long period of virtual catatonia, a trance that lasted for over an hour as dawn advanced to full day.

They had never discussed it. Speke cleaned up the broken black glass and walked all the way to the road, where he scattered it in a ditch, white cows observing him from the pavement.

At times he had assumed Asquith had forgotten the act, lost it in the drunkenness, blacked it out. But he could tell, at other times, that Asquith was already bidding farewell, leaving for the rest of his life, and to what was to be the dissolution of his promise. As an artifact it may or may not have been valuable. The broken cat was the end of their friendship, and it marked the end of youth for both of them, so much fragmented volcanic glass attended by cows.

Speke sat in his office, at his desk, and Holub sat before him, in his moonlight-bright suit. There was, now, just the slightest smudge of ash on one shoulder, small enough to be a cigar crumb. Holub gave a quick smile, the briefest flash of brown tooth.

This was exactly as they had sat one thousand years before, on Holub's first visit.

Speke closed his eyes for a few heartbeats. I should have listened to this man. I should have believed the truth about Asquith.

"Miss Warren has told me," Holub began.

Speke was in no shape for a verbal chess match. "I killed him."

"She told me exactly what happened."

"I strangled him."

"After he had killed your wife."

"It's all my fault."

Holub hesitated. "Why don't you have a drink or something, Mr. Speke. I can see how drained you are."

Why so much compassion? Speke eyed Holub. "I'm okay." It sounded like a lie.

Holub thought over his words. He picked them carefully. "How did you happen to kill Asquith?"

Holub had hesitated over the word "kill." Since when did detectives choose their verbs so carefully? Speke had always assumed that policeman kept to the safe side of language, both laconic and factual, but, at the same time, had no qualms about being blunt. "I used my hands."

"You strangled him?"

Speke's lungs failed to operate. A weight squeezed his chest. "That's what I said."

Holub shouldn't be sitting here by himself. This wasn't right at all, Speke thought. There should be at least one or two other detectives, or a stenographer—this wasn't going the way he had anticipated. Shouldn't there be at least a recording. He was, after all, making a confession.

"You didn't consider stabbing him?"

Speke was puzzled.

"We found a charred knife. A butcher knife."

Speke flexed his hands. He shook his head. "No, I took his life with these."

"That's doing it the hard way," said Holub drily.

Wonderful, thought Speke. A cop with a sense of humor. This sort of humor was leaden, crushing. "Maybe I should have used a weapon. I didn't think." Almost apologetically, but also dismissively: don't toy with me.

"It's hard to strangle someone, you know."

Speke said nothing.

"It takes a good deal of strength if you use your bare hands." There was the most peculiar kindness in Holub's voice. "It doesn't happen often."

"I'm not a weak man."

"Because the truth is, Mr. Speke, we have looked for quite a while now." Holub stopped. "A lot of us, for quite a while, under very bright lights. Sometimes—I hate to mention this—when a body is burning it moves around a little. So we had to be sure."

Be sure, Speke echoed to himself.

"We can't find Asquith's body anywhere." Holub paused, grasping one hand with the other and leaning forward. "We can't find him at all."

Speke made no sound.

"He's gone."

· 46 ·

I t was dawn, and the air tasted of burn.
        A sea wind, from the Pacific far beyond the Coast Range,
stirred Speke's hair. The sky was ripe with summer overcast,
and a fine drizzle hung in the air, hesitated, and drifted down.
Black paste coated shoes, and crept up pant legs, tracked across
what remained of the lawn's green.

Speke stood on the porch of the house answering the questions,
the questions he had already answered, and would, he knew, answer again, perhaps years from now. He told them how much he
owed to Asquith. I was nothing more than a man who wanted to
live. I was ambitious for that life made of light.

He knew that he was not believed, or believed and given credit
for his modesty. No one cared who inspired the plays. Did he hurt
you, they wanted to know. Had Speke felt personally threatened
"like anyone else would have under the circumstances?"

Hamilton Speke was all that mattered. And Speke knew even he
could no longer tell what the truth was. Had Asquith been able to
write a single line of dialogue? Had he really been able to understand what would make a character laugh or weep? Asquith would
never have been able to write the play about the black cat. Speke
knew that. He knew that Asquith's silence, the weight of blank
pages he was unable to fill, was what brought him forth from his
living sleep.

Perhaps, Speke thought, Asquith is listening, even now.

The thought made it true, the fine rain drifting slowly like the
breath of someone listening in the cool, curing morning air. The
mikes thrust at him, and the faces around him were both eager
and professionally sated, the eyes of airline pilots or oral surgeons
pleased with the results of their new equipment. Hamilton would
always look good on the news. He would look good on the noon
news today, giving this shadow from his past credit for his songs
and his plays. Even as he told the truth he knew that the truth
would slip away, and become another story entirely. Hamilton
Speke was being humble in his triumph.

He was telling the truth, and the truth meant nothing. Hamilton Speke was a hero yet again.

That noon he sat in his office. Sarah had just been explaining, in her capable German, that Hamilton was not available for any further interviews today.

She hung up the phone.

"I want to talk to them," said Speke, meaning it, and sounding determined. He was watching one of his many backup televisions, this one a prototype Sony had loaned him "to see if it was adequate."

The remote would not work. Speke squeezed it and shook it, but nothing happened.

The sound was off. There were ten-year-old black and white photos of Asquith on the screen, Asquith appearing both younger and overweight. And then there were shots of Speke, manly, spade over his shoulder, cheeks smudged, as though by one of Scamp's makeup artists, with a touch of ash. "My most notable creation," said Speke, gazing at his image. "The character I worked hardest to bring to life."

"You shouldn't answer any more questions," said Sarah.

"I want them to know everything."

"They won't care. They love you."

"I owe them the truth."

"You don't owe them anything more."

"You are always so sure of yourself, Sarah."

She touched his face, his lips, his eyelids, with her cool, sure fingers. "You owe something to yourself, Hamilton," she said at last.

"And to you," he began.

"No, there is something you owe to yourself, something you've long ago given up."

"I'm the most self-centered person you'll ever know."

She put a finger across his lips.

On the soundless television there was a sequence of two men and a dog climbing from the back of a pickup, and then the news flowed on to other subjects, a riot in what looked like a European city, and the faces of what appeared to be government officials speaking without sound on the screen.

Outside, men searched.

Speke watched from the window until he felt confined by the house and had to join the searchers. Dogs stretched their leashes. The paw and footprints ripped the soft, pale silt of the ash. The figures of the men were bright colors, orange nylon jackets, yellow kerchiefs, among the blackened trees.

One of the men spoke into a radio. Another took a coffee break, leaning against a green pickup. He straightened as Speke passed and wished him a good morning. Speke returned his greeting without thinking, thankful for the company of capable people. The burned grass was crisp beneath his feet. Each step was like pressing his boots into burned toast.

Sometimes a burning body will move around, one of the searchers explained. The heat of the fire will thrash a corpse one way and another. Arm here. Cranium there. All over the place. "But I've rarely known a fire to make bones disappear," said the man, a young man, all earnestness and sinew. "There's usually something left."

There were stipples of drizzle in the ash.

There is always, Speke reminded himself, something left.

He searched with them. One or two of the black knots of brush still streamed smoke. The smoke was elegant, a fine, scribbling signature in the air. The men were polite to Speke, and stepped aside for him. "Don't worry," said one of the searchers, a deputy sheriff in a denim shirt. "If he's here he's ours."

Each gnarl of oak, each bole of sage, looked like human death. Asquith, Speke thought. You're still here. Somewhere. You are too magic to let the fire burn you, but you are not so magic that you can become invisible.

He wanted them to find Asquith alive. He wanted them to find him dead. He wanted them to find some trace of his old friend, and he wanted them to find nothing. The men searched, the dogs snuffling the gray dust.

An airplane banked under the low clouds. It circled slowly. The searchers watched it, and Speke watched with them. His heart pumped hard in his chest, constricting his breath. The plane banked and circled again, a tight circle.

"He sees something," said a searcher.

The plane's flight was a spiral of ever-increasing focus. The pilot saw something. He saw, and he wanted to see more. The plane surged, its engine finding a new, higher song. The aircraft banked again, nearly standing on one wing.

Asquith, Speke found himself breathing: they found you.

No one moved. Even the dogs panted, waiting. The plane throttled-up, lifted its nose, and described a long half circle in another direction. In a few moments it was gone.

The searchers relaxed. One of them scraped a stone to one side with his workboot.

Speke patted one of the dogs, and the creature had that open, cheering smile that dogs give so often, that acknowledgement of a fellow creature's greeting.

Two nights later Speke stepped before the mirror and saw the face of scalded corpse.

His own face was blistered, broken, reddened. His entire epidermis was painful. Taking a step hurt.

He returned to bed, not as shakily as he might have expected, took three more antihistamines, yet another Darvon, and punched the pillow.

The smell of fresh paint was everywhere. The bouyant odor of newness cheered him, in a minor-key, half-distracted way. He told himself that he still had faith in the future. He told himself that Sarah would continue to love him as he found himself loving her.

Endure—wasn't that what mattered? Or is there something more important than surviving? Otherwise, Speke thought, the cockroach would be the most admired of all creatures.

What sort of creature was I on those plain, suburban evenings listening to my father's lathe or his Sears electric drill? What did I believe in, even then, but the same empty life I believed in until just a few days ago? I have been a child too long. These childish things must fall away.

Leaving me—what?

Where in me, he wondered, is that stone which is still alive, that outcropping which will be what is left of me, the mesa that is my soul? Even so, the smell in the air was not the stink of death. There was something like perfume from the charred bay trees, from the black wires of the sage.

From territory that belonged to Asquith.

AFTER

· 47 ·

They soaked in the sun of Samos, and strolled among fallen columns of marble like two people discovering a civilization that was not dead, but only in hiding, trembling in the tomato red blossoms of poppies.

He found himself taking her hand, and holding it, like a man pulling a treasure from its refuge in the darkness so he could reassure himself that it had not yet been stolen. It was a simple enough act, but in the sudden cool dark of a chapel in an olive grove, or on the sun-bleached road of a village, he found himself taking her hand as though just discovering her, and wanting to stay just as he was forever.

One evening in Istanbul, the domes of a dozen mosques before them, the sounds of geese, dogs and children rising toward their balcony from the street, Speke said, "We won't waste any more time."

"We didn't," she said, offering her hand.

He took it, and studied it as though he would read her palm.

"But we really didn't," Sarah said. "I think you are one of those people who have never wasted a single day."

This time when they made love it was the conjugation of a new human speech, the speech within the words that fill the air, and clutter the pages. It was the shadow speech flowering and filling each fingertip, each cleft and nipple with knowledge, and with faith.

It was only on their return, the drive already breaking new green along either side of the ruts, that Speke felt it rise around him, both the old enchantment of this place, like being able to descend again to childhood, and the old threat.

He stepped from the car, and the trees, in leaf that disguised the char-weathered bark, stood still like forms which had been, just moments before, in flight.

He could smell it with each breath, not an odor, certainly not the scent of death, but something sure and dry in the empty spaces between leaves.

Asquith is here somewhere.

He is still here.

· 48 ·

It was morning, and the house, and the land around the house, was hushed. There was a chill in the air, and the warmth of the stove warmed Speke's outstretched hands. The smell of baking made the light into something he wanted to eat, as though time itself were a food.

Sometimes he found himself gazing into his hands. Were these, he found himself wondering, the two hands that took the life of my old friend?

He had never believed in palmistry. It was an archaic, irrational holdover from a time of superstition and fear. And yet, he found himself these days wondering how much of human life might be fixed, fated from birth. He found himself studying the lines of his palm.

All travel, Speke knew, carries with it this text, the hash-marked plain of the palm. The strongest grasp is always part space. The palm shows a map of courses that are both beginning and end, and even when we love we cradle with this branched cartograph, this stitchery strong enough to search the world for the places that can be visited but never kept, the paths and culverts and fields all ways away.

He had been making his own muffins. It had not seemed right to hire a new housekeeper, and now, six months after Clara's death, he had finally made a muffin that did not crumble when he took it out of the baking tin. It was not as good as Clara's, Speke chided himself, but at least it had a shape, a peak, a symmetry, like a miniature cottage made of food.

What would Clara say? He could imagine her voice, her shy, and yet forthright phrasing: Not too bad, Mr. Speke.

He carried the muffins to the table. Sarah praised them. "Wonderful, Ham. Really delicious."

He leaned on the table, surprised at the pleasure he felt at her praise. "They aren't really all that delicious." He wanted to add: are they?

She was persisting in her praise when the phone rang and he

heard a familiar voice filtering through the distant answering machine.

He played back the message three times. "There's a possible lead on Asquith. Not much of one, but it's better than nothing. I'd appreciate it if you'd give me a call."

The air thinned, the colors faded to gray.

Asquith, Speke thought. They have found you at last.

"You don't have to call Holub if you don't want to," Sarah was saying.

He did not answer.

"I'll call him, if you want."

Speke took a breath. He shook his head, and gave her what he knew must be a sickly smile: No.

This is something I have to do.

He sat at the telephone for a long while before he could force himself to return Holub's call.

"Mexico," said Holub breezily, in response to his question. "Showed up on a video of passengers changing planes in Mexico City. At least, we think he did. The quality of the video isn't exactly great."

"Where was he going?"

"You have no idea how many agencies have been looking for this man."

"Where?" Speke repeated.

"East. A Mexicana flight to—I'm looking it up. Merida. On the Yucatan."

Speke said nothing, although his hands were tingling.

"What I wanted to know is this—do you have any idea where he might be going?"

From Merida across the scrub jungle, through the heat. To the ferry to Cozumel, thought Speke. Or some place like it. Someplace where the parrots make those impossible, desperate-sounding and beautiful cries.

"So he didn't just vanish," Speke was saying. "He didn't get absorbed into the air or the land or just become so much ether. He was a physical being. He had to *be* somewhere."

Holub paused briefly before asking, "Did he have a favorite place that you know of."

"In Mexico?" Speke asked, stalling.

"A favorite town, or a favorite resort. A favorite beach."

"Every day I try to find him." Try to find his skeleton, he meant, proof that he was dead. Because if he found no proof, then Asquith was alive, out there in the world somewhere.

"Any place you ever heard him talking about?" Holub was asking.

The bottom of the sea there is so pale, Speke thought, that you can watch the parrotfish just as easily as you could watch birds in the air.

Holub was silent.

Speke wanted to destroy the man who had killed Clara and Maria. And yet he felt that killing Maria was the last harm Asquith would ever do. One way or another, the killer was finished. Asquith would do no further harm.

How do I know this, he asked himself. How do I know anything about Asquith?

Because I mourn for him, he thought. Because I know that Asquith is gone, even if his body survived. The play is finished. The theater is dark.

Help me, he prayed to the souls of Clara, and the forever enigmatic Maria. Help me—tell me what to do.

Holub was waiting. Speke took a deep breath, and let it out slowly.

"No," he said. "I can't think of a place where Asquith might be."

The rain was small, not rain so much as vapor, breath, and it collected in the rough wool of his sweater. It descended through the branches, and glistened on the Indian rocks. The sky lowered itself to the earth, and trees vanished.

There was only silence, the steady murmur of the place itself, the sort of sounds that had flowed long before the first human speech.

The mist was heavy. Speke watched the land shrink to a small circle, where he sat beside the mortar holes. This is where the Indians had ground their acorns. The acorns, he reminded himself, from these trees.

The rye seed Brothers had scattered was sprouting, like a night sky of green stars. The ancient trees were already breaking into new growth. The fire, Brothers had said, was good for the trees, and woke them to life. It had seemed impossible, but the gardener was turning out to be right. To nearly die sometimes cures something in living things, a lassitude that claims even the oak.

Everyone knew the truth now. No one was much interested. His old acquaintance, Jessica Moe, whom he remembered drinking espresso on Green Street, had rushed a book into print proving that Asquith couldn't write a coherent sentence, and that Speke was the force behind the plays after all. Even that point of view was half obliterated by the rapture over what the public saw as Speke the Hero.

The press was full of stories of Speke battling the poker-wielding, drug-crazed freak from his past. Speke as Hercules. Speke as grief-enraged husband. Speke as defender of the other woman in his life, the lovely Sarah Warren. Speke as Olympian. He deserved women by the dozen. Magazines were full of hackneyed imagery: Speke as David against the fire's Goliath. Speke as Ulysses, warrior against the firestorm. Speke as Speke—bigger than life, larger than the truth.

It was all true, it was all false. He had to laugh. The fiction was all mixed in, a little manure brown to soften the blank white of the real.

He climbed to his feet again. The trail coursed its way through the dark claws of the underbrush, and at one point he gasped and knelt, thinking: bone.

And it was bone, something the fire had not stained. It was the chalky, giant shin of something not human, a cow most likely, a big club of calcium he hefted for a moment, and then let drop. He followed the path, and stopped to study the twin nicks of a deer print in the drizzle-scarred dirt. A young deer, Speke thought, on its way to the lake. He did not believe in spirits. He did not believe in ghosts at all. He did, though, have faith in animals, his fellow spirits, haunting his world, unseen.

Bell's early chapters had arrived. The book was not titled formally, yet, but its working title was *Buried Sun—the Life of Timothy Asquith*. Speke was pleased with what he had read, and he had promised to help promote the book, which offered proof that the plays and the songs were the work of one man, working alone. The early studio tapes, those late-night songwriting sessions in Crystal Studios, showed Asquith complaining, arguing, refusing to sit still. Bell's book maintained that Asquith was the inspiration, the spark, the prod, but the words and the music belonged to Speke.

Bell had also, just the day before, sent along a one-act, an early work by the pre-Speke Asquith. It was called *Noonsmith*. The play, for two actors, featured dialogue that amounted to little more than argument. The play was badly written, ragged, inept. The most sympathetic reading could only be painful.

Speke wiped the black mud from his shoes on the front step. He entered the house. The piranha flickered in its world of water, a silver flame.

That night he woke from a dream. He could not remember the dream, but the color of it stayed with him, the light of a blue sun in a white sky, a sky as blank as paper, as breath.

Sarah stirred beside him, but she did not wake. He swept on his bathrobe, and slipped out of the bedroom. He passed quietly through the house, feeling very much like a shadow, a figure of no substance.

He was shivering. He sat in his office. The computer screen was blank. He switched on the lamp, and he switched on the computer, but he still did not know his own desire.

I should get up now, and go back to bed with Sarah, where I belong.

Perhaps it was the winter, climbing with its cold and light rain over the big house, but there was a creak. There was a breath of cold, great cold, greater cold than this house had ever experienced before.

There was a sound like a step behind Speke as he sat there, his fingers poised at the keyboard. His neck was cold, as at the touch of frozen speech. He had the impression, without knowing why, that he was not alone, and yet he was not frightened.

He began to poke the keyboard with one finger. Act One. Scene One. A very safe beginning. A play, perhaps even a musical. He could hear the music. Words jiggled into place on the screen. A few more words, a few more sentences. He leaned forward and typed a paragraph, a long blast of dialogue from a nervous, defensive man, the voice of an old friend.

Speke found himself smiling.

Two young men were on a ferry from the Yucatan, the blue of

the water so transparent the fish scattered away from the shadow of the vessel, flung themselves across the white sand of the bottom.

The two men knew each other well, but they did not know the coast they approached, their future, the shaggy line of palms bent one way and another, and in some places stripped to bare poles by a recent hurricane.

Speke leaned even closer, unwilling to watch the words form on the screen. He was telling the truth, the story as it had really happened. He found himself laughing silently, alight with the greatest joy.

It was brilliant.